**Praise for #1** *New Yo...*
**Linda** ... P9-CDJ-656

"Linda Lael Miller creates vibrant characters and stories I defy you to forget."
—#1 *New York Times* bestselling author Debbie Macomber

"Miller is one of the finest American writers in the genre."
—*RT Book Reviews*

"*A Snow Country Christmas* is heaven-sent for Linda Lael Miller's multitude of fans and is sure to make a fan of those who have not yet had the pleasure of reading her books.... You might want to add *A Snow Country Christmas* to Santa's list, because this is a perfect stocking stuffer of a book!"
—*BookPage*

**Praise for** *USA TODAY* **bestselling author Caro Carson**

"A heartbreaker... The treatment of both the heroine's insecurities and the hero's malady is awesome."
—*RT Book Reviews* on *A Texas Rescue Christmas* (4.5 stars)

"The lonely hearts club is about to lose two members in Carson's amazingly heartfelt, love-at-first-sight Montana Maverick holiday story."
—*RT Book Reviews* on *The Maverick's Holiday Masquerade*

The daughter of a town marshal, **Linda Lael Miller** is a *New York Times* bestselling author of more than one hundred historical and contemporary novels. Linda's books have hit #1 on the *New York Times* bestseller list seven times. Raised in Northport, Washington, she now lives in Spokane, Washington. www.LindaLaelMiller.com

Despite a no-nonsense background as a West Point graduate and US Army officer, *USA TODAY* bestselling author **Caro Carson** has always treasured the happily-ever-after of a good romance novel. After reading romances no matter where in the world the army sent her, Caro began a career in the pharmaceutical industry. Little did she know the years she spent discussing science with physicians would provide excellent story material for her new career as a romance author. Now Caro is delighted to be living her own happily-ever-after with her husband and two children in the great state of Florida, a location that has saved the coaster-loving theme-park fanatic a fortune on plane tickets.

#1 *New York Times* Bestselling Author

# LINDA LAEL MILLER

# A STONE CREEK CHRISTMAS

WITHDRAWN

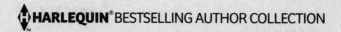

HARLEQUIN® BESTSELLING AUTHOR COLLECTION

If you purchased this book without a cover you should be aware that this book is stolen property. It was reported as "unsold and destroyed" to the publisher, and neither the author nor the publisher has received any payment for this "stripped book."

ISBN-13: 978-1-335-15072-1

A Stone Creek Christmas

Copyright © 2018 by Harlequin Books S.A.

The publisher acknowledges the copyright holders of the individual works as follows:

A Stone Creek Christmas
Copyright © 2008 by Linda Lael Miller

A Cowboy's Wish Upon a Star
Copyright © 2016 by Caro Carson

Recycling programs for this product may not exist in your area.

All rights reserved. Except for use in any review, the reproduction or utilization of this work in whole or in part in any form by any electronic, mechanical or other means, now known or hereafter invented, including xerography, photocopying and recording, or in any information storage or retrieval system, is forbidden without the written permission of the publisher, Harlequin Enterprises Limited, 22 Adelaide St. West, 40th Floor, Toronto, Ontario M5H 4E3, Canada.

This is a work of fiction. Names, characters, places and incidents are either the product of the author's imagination or are used fictitiously, and any resemblance to actual persons, living or dead, business establishments, events or locales is entirely coincidental.

This edition published by arrangement with Harlequin Books S.A.

For questions and comments about the quality of this book, please contact us at CustomerService@Harlequin.com.

® and TM are trademarks of Harlequin Enterprises Limited or its corporate affiliates. Trademarks indicated with ® are registered in the United States Patent and Trademark Office, the Canadian Intellectual Property Office and in other countries.

www.Harlequin.com

**Printed in U.S.A.**

# CONTENTS

**Also available from Linda Lael Miller**

**HQN Books**

### The Carsons
of Mustang Creek

A Snow Country Christmas
Forever a Hero
Once a Rancher
Always a Cowboy

### The Brides of Bliss County

Christmas in Mustang Creek
The Marriage Season
The Marriage Charm
The Marriage Pact

### McKettricks of Texas

An Outlaw's Christmas
A Lawman's Christmas
McKettricks of Texas: Austin
McKettricks of Texas: Garrett
McKettricks of Texas: Tate

### The Creed Cowboys

The Creed Legacy
Creed's Honor
A Creed in Stone Creek

### Stone Creek

The Bridegroom
The Rustler
A Wanted Man
The Man from Stone Creek

### The McKettricks

A McKettrick Christmas
McKettrick's Heart
McKettrick's Pride
McKettrick's Luck
McKettrick's Choice

### The Montana Creeds

A Creed Country Christmas
Montana Creeds: Tyler
Montana Creeds: Dylan
Montana Creeds: Logan

### Mojo Sheepshanks

Arizona Wild
(previously published
as Deadly Gamble)
Arizona Heat
(previously published
as Deadly Deception)

# A STONE CREEK CHRISTMAS

## Linda Lael Miller

For Sandi Howlett, dog foster mom, with love.
Thank you.

# Chapter One

Sometimes, especially in the dark of night, when pure exhaustion sank Olivia O'Ballivan, DVM, into deep and stuporous sleep, she heard them calling—the finned, the feathered, the four-legged.

Horses, wild or tame, dogs beloved and dogs lost, far from home, cats abandoned alongside country roads because they'd become a problem for someone, or left behind when an elderly owner died.

The neglected, the abused, the unwanted, the lonely.

Invariably, the message was the same: *Help me*.

Even when Olivia tried to ignore the pleas, telling herself she was only *dreaming,* she invariably sprang to full wakefulness as though she'd been catapulted from the bottom of a canyon. It didn't matter how many eighteen-hour days she'd worked, between making stops at farms and ranches all over the county, putting in her time at the veterinary clinic in Stone Creek, overseeing the plans for the new, state-of-the-art shelter her famous big brother, Brad, a country musician, was building with the proceeds from a movie he'd starred in.

Tonight it was a reindeer.

Olivia sat blinking in her tousled bed, trying to catch her breath. Shoved both hands through her short dark hair. Her current foster dog, Ginger, woke up, too, stretching, yawning.

*A reindeer?*

"O'Ballivan," she told herself, flinging off the covers to sit up on the edge of the mattress, "you've really gone around the bend this time."

But the silent cry persisted, plaintive and confused.

Olivia only sometimes heard actual words when the animals spoke, though Ginger was articulate—generally, it was more of an unformed concept made up of strong emotion and often images, somehow coalescing into an intuitive imperative. But she could see the reindeer clearly in her mind's eye, standing on a frozen roadway, bewildered.

She recognized the adjoining driveway as her own. A long way down, next to the tilted mailbox on the main road. The poor creature wasn't hurt—just lost. Hungry and thirsty, too—and terribly afraid. Easy prey for hungry wolves and coyotes.

"There are no reindeer in Arizona," Olivia told Ginger, who looked skeptical as she hauled her arthritic yellow Lab/golden retriever self up off her comfy bed in the corner of Olivia's cluttered bedroom. "Absolutely, positively, no doubt about it, there *are no reindeer in Arizona.*"

*"Whatever,"* Ginger replied with another yawn, al-

ready heading for the door as Olivia pulled sweatpants on over her boxer pajama bottoms. She tugged a hoodie, left over from one of her brother's preretirement concert tours, over her head and jammed her feet into the totally unglamorous work boots she wore to wade through pastures and barns.

Olivia lived in a small rental house in the country, though once the shelter was finished, she'd be moving into a spacious apartment upstairs, living in town. She drove an old gray Suburban that had belonged to her late grandfather, called Big John by everyone who knew him, and did not aspire to anything fancier. She had not exactly been feathering her nest since she'd graduated from veterinary school.

Her twin sisters, Ashley and Melissa, were constantly after her to "get her act together," find herself a man, have a family. Both of them were single, with no glimmer of honeymoon cottages and white picket fences on the horizon, so in Olivia's opinion, they didn't have a lot of room to talk. It was just that she was a few years older than they were, that was all.

Anyway, it wasn't as if she didn't want those things—she did—but between her practice and the "Dr. Dolittle routine," as Brad referred to her admittedly weird animal-communication skills, there simply weren't enough hours in the day to do it all.

Since the rental house was old, the garage was detached. Olivia and Ginger made their way through a deep, powdery field of snow. The Suburban was no spiffy rig—most of the time it was splattered with muddy slush and worse—but it always ran, in any kind of weather. And it would go practically anywhere.

"Try getting to a stranded reindeer in that sporty

little red number Melissa drives," Olivia told Ginger as she shoved up the garage door. "Or that silly hybrid of Ashley's."

*"I wouldn't mind taking a spin in the sports car,"* Ginger replied, plodding gamely up the special wooden steps Olivia dragged over to the passenger side of the Suburban. Ginger was getting older, after all, and her joints gave her problems, especially since her "accident." Certain concessions had to be made.

"Fat chance," Olivia said, pushing back the steps once Ginger was settled in the shotgun seat, then closing the car door. Moments later she was sliding in on the driver's side, shoving the key into the ignition, cranking up the geriatric engine. "You know how Melissa is about dog hair. You might tear a hole in her fancy leather upholstery with one of those Fu-Manchu toenails of yours."

*"She likes dogs,"* Ginger insisted with a magnanimous lift of her head. *"It's just that she thinks she's allergic."* Ginger always believed the best of everyone in particular and humanity in general, even though she'd been ditched alongside a highway, with two of her legs fractured, after her first owner's vengeful boyfriend had tossed her out of a moving car. Olivia had come along a few minutes later, homing in on the mystical distress call bouncing between her head and her heart, and rushed Ginger to the clinic, where she'd had multiple surgeries and a long, difficult recovery.

Olivia flipped on the windshield wipers, but she still squinted to see through the huge, swirling flakes. "My sister," she said, "is a hypochondriac."

*"It's just that Melissa hasn't met the right dog yet,"* Ginger maintained. *"Or the right man."*

"Don't start about men," Olivia retorted, peering out, looking for the reindeer.

*"He's out there, you know,"* Ginger remarked, panting as she gazed out at the snowy night.

"The reindeer or the man?"

*"Both,"* Ginger said with a dog smile.

"What am I going to do with a reindeer?"

*"You'll think of something,"* Ginger replied. *"It's almost Christmas. Maybe there's an APB from the North Pole. I'd check Santa's Web site if I had opposable thumbs."*

"Funny," Olivia said, not the least bit amused. "If you had opposable thumbs, you'd order things off infomercials just because you like the UPS man so much. We'd be inundated with get-rich-quick real estate courses, herbal weight loss programs and stuff to whiten our teeth." The ever-present ache between her shoulder blades knotted itself up tighter as she scanned the darkness on either side of the narrow driveway. Christmas. One more thing she didn't have the time for, let alone the requisite enthusiasm, but Brad and his new wife, Meg, would put up a big tree right after Thanksgiving, hunt her down and shanghai her if she didn't show up for the family festival at Stone Creek Ranch, especially since Mac had come along six months before, and this was Baby's First Christmas. And because Carly, Meg's teenage sister, was spending the semester in Italy, as part of a special program for gifted students, and both Brad and Meg missed her to distraction. Ashley would throw her annual open house at the bed-and-breakfast, and Melissa would probably decide she was allergic to mistletoe and holly and develop convincing symptoms.

Olivia would go, of course. To Brad and Meg's because she loved them, and *adored* Mac. To Ashley's open house because she loved her kid sister, too, and could mostly forgive her for being Martha Stewart incarnate. Damn, she'd even pick up nasal spray and chicken soup for Melissa, though she drew the line at actually cooking.

*"There's Blitzen,"* Ginger said, adding a cheerful yip.

Sure enough, the reindeer loomed in the snow-speckled cones of gold from the headlights.

Olivia put on the brakes, shifted the engine into neutral. "You stay here," she said, pushing open the door.

*"Like I'm going outside in* this *weather,"* Ginger said with a sniff.

Slowly Olivia approached the reindeer. The creature was small, definitely a miniature breed, with eyes big and dark and luminous in the light from the truck, and it stood motionless.

*"Lost,"* it told her, not having Ginger's extensive vocabulary. If she ever found a loving home for that dog, she'd miss the long conversations, even though they had very different political views.

The deer had antlers, which meant it was male.

"Hey, buddy," she said. "Where did you come from?"

*"Lost,"* the reindeer repeated. Either he was dazed or not particularly bright. Like humans, animals were unique beings, some of them Einsteins, most of them ordinary joes.

"Are you hurt?" she asked, to be certain. Her intuition was rarely wrong where such things were concerned, but there was always the off chance.

Nothing.

She approached, slowly and carefully. Ran skillful hands over pertinent parts of the animal. No blood, no obvious breaks, though sprains and hairline fractures were a possibility. No identifying tags or notched ears.

The reindeer stood still for the examination, which might have meant he was tame, though Olivia couldn't be certain of that. Nearly every animal she encountered, wild or otherwise, allowed her within touching distance. Once, with help from Brad and Jesse McKettrick, she'd treated a wounded stallion who'd never been shod, fitted with a halter, or ridden.

"You're gonna be okay now," she told the little deer. It *did* look as though it ought to be hitched to Santa's sleigh. There was a silvery cast to its coat, its antlers were delicately etched and it was petite—barely bigger than Ginger.

She cocked a thumb toward the truck. "Can you follow me to my place, or shall I put you in the back?" she asked.

The reindeer ducked its head. Shy, then. And weary.

"But you've already traveled a long way, haven't you?" Olivia went on.

She opened the back of the Suburban, pulled out the sturdy ramp she always carried for Ginger and other four-legged passengers no longer nimble enough to make the jump.

The deer hesitated, probably catching Ginger's scent.

"Not to worry," Olivia said. "Ginger's a lamb. Hop aboard there, Blitzen."

*"His name is Rodney,"* Ginger announced. She'd turned, forefeet on the console, to watch them over the backseat.

"On Dasher, on Dancer, on Prancer or—Rodney," Olivia said, gesturing, but giving the animal plenty of room.

Rodney raised his head at the sound of his name, seemed to perk up a little. Then he pranced right up the ramp, into the back of the Suburban, and lay down on a bed of old feed sacks with a heavy reindeer snort.

Olivia closed the back doors of the rig as quietly as she could, so Rodney wouldn't be startled.

"How did you know his name?" Olivia asked once she was back in the driver's seat. "All I'm getting from him is 'Lost.'"

*"He told me,"* Ginger said. *"He's not ready to go into a lot of detail about his past. There's a touch of amnesia, too. Brought on by the emotional trauma of losing his way."*

"Have you been watching soap operas again, while I'm away working? *Dr. Phil? Oprah?*"

*"Only when you forget and leave the TV on when you go out. I don't have opposable thumbs, remember?"*

Olivia shoved the recalcitrant transmission into reverse, backed into a natural turnaround and headed back up the driveway toward the house. She supposed she should have taken Rodney to the clinic for X-rays, or over to the homeplace, where there was a barn, but it was the middle of the night, after all.

If she went to the clinic, all the boarders would wake up, barking and meowing fit to wake the whole town. If she went to Stone Creek Ranch, she'd probably wake the baby, and both Brad and Meg were sleep deprived as it was.

So Rodney would have to spend what remained of the night on the enclosed porch. She'd make him a bed with some of the old blankets she kept on hand, give him water, see if he wouldn't nosh on a few of Ginger's kibbles. In the morning she'd attend to him properly.

Take him to town for those X-rays and a few blood tests, haul him to Brad's if he was well enough to travel, fix him up with a stall of his own. Get him some deer chow from the feed and grain.

Rodney drank a whole bowl of water once Olivia had coaxed him up the steps and through the outer door onto the enclosed porch. He kept a watchful eye on Ginger, though she didn't growl or make any sudden moves, the way some dogs would have done.

Instead, Ginger gazed up at Olivia, her soulful eyes glowing with practical compassion. *"I'd better sleep out here with Rodney,"* she said. *"He's still pretty scared. The washing machine has him a little spooked."*

This was a great concession on Ginger's part, for she loved her wide, fluffy bed. Ashley had made it for her, out of the softest fleece she could find, and even monogrammed the thing. Olivia smiled at the image of her blond, curvaceous sister seated at her beloved sewing machine, whirring away.

"You're a good dog," she said, her eyes burning a little as she bent to pat Ginger's head.

Ginger sighed. Another day, another noble sacrifice, the sound seemed to say.

Olivia went into her bedroom and got Ginger's bed. Put it on the floor for her. Carried the water bowl back to the kitchen for a refill.

When she returned to the porch the second time, Rodney was lying on the cherished dog bed, and Ginger was on the pile of old blankets.

"Ginger, your bed—?"

Ginger yawned yet again, rested her muzzle on her forelegs and rolled her eyes upward. *"Everybody needs a soft place to land,"* she said sleepily. *"Even reindeer."*

\* \* \*

The pony was not a happy camper.

Tanner Quinn leaned against the stall door. He'd just bought Starcross Ranch, and Butterpie, his daughter's pet, had arrived that day, trucked in by a horse-delivery outfit hired by his sister, Tessa, along with his own palomino gelding, Shiloh.

Shiloh was settling in just fine. Butterpie was having a harder time of it.

Tanner sighed, shifted his hat to the back of his head. He probably should have left Shiloh and Butterpie at his sister's place in Kentucky, where they'd had all that fabled bluegrass to run in and munch on, since the ranch wasn't going to be his permanent home, or theirs. He'd picked it up as an investment, at a fire-sale price, and would live there while he oversaw the new construction project in Stone Creek—a year at the outside.

It was the latest in a long line of houses that never had time to become homes. He came to each new place, bought a house or a condo, built something big and sleek and expensive, then moved on, leaving the property he'd temporarily occupied in the hands of some eager real estate agent.

The new project, an animal shelter, was not his usual thing—he normally designed and erected office buildings, multimillion-dollar housing compounds for movie stars and moguls, and the occasional government-sponsored school, bridge or hospital, somewhere on foreign soil—usually hostile. Before his wife, Katherine, died five years ago, she'd traveled with him, bringing Sophie along.

But then—

Tanner shook off the memory. Thinking about the

way Katherine had been killed required serious bourbon, and he'd been off the sauce for a long time. He'd
never developed a drinking problem, but the warning
signs had been there, and he'd decided to save Sophie—
and himself—the extra grief. He'd put the cork back in
the bottle and left it there for good.

It should have been him, not Kat. That was as far as
he could go, sober.

He shifted his attention back to the little cream-
colored pony standing forlornly in its fancy new stall.
He was no vet, but he didn't have to be to diagnose the
problem. The horse missed Sophie, now ensconced in
a special high-security boarding school in Connecticut.

He missed her, too. More than the horse did, for
sure. But she was *safe* in that high-walled and distant
place—safe from the factions who'd issued periodic
death threats over things he'd built. The school was like
a fortress—he'd designed it himself, and his best friend,
Jack McCall, a Special Forces veteran and big-time security consultant, had installed the systems. They were
top-of-the-line, best available. The children and grand-
children of presidents, congressmen, Oscar winners and
software inventors attended that school—it had to be
kidnap-proof, and it was.

Sophie had begged him not to leave her there.

Even as Tanner reflected on that, his cell phone rang.
Sophie had chosen the ring tone before their most re-
cent parting—the theme song from *How the Grinch
Stole Christmas*.

He, of course, was the Grinch.

"Tanner Quinn," he said, even though he knew this
wasn't a business call. The habit was ingrained.

"I *hate* this place!" Sophie blurted without preamble. "It's like a *prison!*"

"Soph," Tanner began, on another sigh. "Your roommate sings lead for your favorite rock band of all time. How bad can it be?"

"I want to come home!"

*If only we had one,* Tanner thought. The barely palatable reality was that he and Sophie had lived like Gypsies—if not actual fugitives—since Kat's death.

"Honey, you know I won't be here long. You'd make friends, get settled in and then it would be time to move on again."

"I want you," Sophie all but wailed. Tanner's heart caught on a beat. "I want Butterpie. I want to be a *regular kid!*"

Sophie would never be a "regular kid." She was only twelve and already taking college-level courses—another advantage of attending an elite school. The classes were small, the computers were powerful enough to guide satellites and the visiting lecturers were world-renowned scientists, historians, linguistics experts and mathematical superstars.

"Honey—"

"Why can't I live in Stoner Creek, with you and Butterpie?"

A smile tugged at one corner of Tanner's mouth. "*Stone* Creek," he said. "If there are any stoners around here, I haven't made their acquaintance yet."

Not that he'd really made *anybody's* acquaintance. He hadn't been in town more than a few days. He knew the real estate agent who'd sold him Starcross, and Brad O'Ballivan, because he'd built a palace for him once, outside Nashville, which was how he'd gotten talked into the animal-shelter contract.

Brad O'Ballivan. He'd thought the hotshot country-and-western music star would never settle down. Now he was over-the-top in love with his bride, Meg, and wanted all his friends married off, too. He probably figured if he could fall that hard for a woman out here in Noplace, U.S.A., Tanner might, too.

"Dad, please," Sophie said, sniffling now. Somehow his daughter's brave attempt to suck it up got to Tanner even more than the crying had. "Get me out of here. If I can't come to Stone Creek, maybe I could stay with Aunt Tessa again, like I did last summer...."

Tanner took off his hat, moved along the breezeway to the barn doorway, shut off the lights. "You know your aunt is going through a rough time right now," he said quietly. *A rough time?* Tessa and her no-account husband, Paul Barker, were getting a divorce. Among other things, Barker had gotten another woman pregnant—a real blow to Tess, who'd wanted a child ever since she'd hit puberty—and now she was fighting to hold on to her home. She'd bought that horse farm with her own money, having been a successful TV actress in her teens, and poured everything she had into it—including the contents of her investment portfolio. Against Tanner's advice, she hadn't insisted on a prenup.

*We're in* love, she'd told him, starry-eyed with happiness.

Paul Barker hadn't had the proverbial pot to piss in, of course. And within a month of the wedding he'd been a signer on every account Tess had. As the marriage deteriorated, so did Tess's wealth.

Cold rage jangled along Tanner's nerves, followed

the fault line in his soul. At Kat's suggestion, he'd set up a special trust fund for Tess, way back, and it was a damn good thing he had. To this day, she didn't know the money existed—he and Kat hadn't wanted Barker to tap in to it—and when she did find out, her fierce Quinn pride would probably force her to refuse it.

At least if she lost the horse farm to Barker and his dream team of lawyers—more like *nightmare* team— she'd have the means to start over. The question was, would she have the *heart* to make a new beginning?

"Dad?" Sophie asked. "Are you still there?"

"I'm here," Tanner said, looking around at the night-shrouded landscape surrounding him. There must have been a foot of snow on the ground already, with more coming down. Hell, November wasn't even over yet.

"Couldn't I at least come home for Christmas?"

"Soph, we don't *have* a home, remember?"

She was sniffling again. "Sure we do," she said very softly. "Home is where you and Butterpie are."

Tanner's eyes stung all of a sudden. He told himself it was the bitterly cold weather. When he'd finally agreed to take the job, he'd thought, *Arizona.* Cacti. Sweeping desert vistas. Eighty-degree winters.

But Stone Creek was in *northern* Arizona, near Flagstaff, a place of timber and red rock—and the occasional blizzard.

It wasn't like him to overlook that kind of geographical detail, but he had. He'd signed on the dotted line because the money was good and because Brad was a good friend.

"How about if I come back there? We'll spend Christmas in New York—skate at Rockefeller Center, see the Rockettes—"

Sophie loved New York. She planned to attend college there, and then medical school, and eventually set up a practice as a neurosurgeon. No small-time goals for *his* kid, but then, the doctor gene had come from Kat, not him. Kat. As beautiful as a model and as smart as they come, she'd been a surgeon, specializing in pediatric cardiology. She'd given all that up, swearing it was only temporary, to have Sophie. To travel the world with her footloose husband...

"But then I wouldn't get to see Butterpie," Sophie protested. A raw giggle escaped her. "I don't think they'd let her stay at the Waldorf with us, even if we paid a pet deposit."

Tanner pictured the pony nibbling on the ubiquitous mongo flower arrangement in the hotel's sedate lobby, with its Cole Porter piano, dropping a few road apples on the venerable old carpets. And he grinned. "Probably not."

"Don't you want me with you, Dad?" Sophie spoke in a small voice. "Is that it? My friend Cleta says her mom won't let her come home for Christmas because she's got a new boyfriend and she doesn't want a kid throwing a wet blanket on the action."

Cleta. Who named a poor, defenseless kid Cleta?

And what kind of person put "action" before their own child, especially at Christmas?

Tanner closed his eyes, walking toward the dark house he didn't know his way around in yet, since he'd spent the first couple of nights at Brad's, waiting for the power to be turned on and the phones hooked up. Guilt stabbed through his middle. "I love you more than anything or anybody else in the world," he said gruffly, and he meant it. Practically everything he did was geared to provide for Sophie, to protect her from the name-less, faceless forces who hated him. "Trust me, there's no *action* going on around here."

"I'm going to run away, then," she said resolutely.

"Good luck," Tanner replied after sucking in a deep breath. "That school is hermetically sealed, kiddo. You know that as well as I do."

"What are you so afraid of?"

*Losing you.* The kid had no way of knowing how big, and how dangerous, the world was. She'd been just seven years old when Kat was killed, and barely re-membered the long flight home from northern Africa, private bodyguards occupying the seats around them, the sealed coffin, the media blitz.

"U.S. Contractor Targeted by Insurgent Group," one headline had read. "Wife of American Businessman Killed in Possible Revenge Shooting."

"I'm not afraid of anything," Tanner lied.

"It's because of what happened to Mom," Sophie in-sisted. "That's what Aunt Tessa says."

"Aunt Tessa ought to mind her own business."

"If you don't come and get me, I'm breaking out of here. And there's no telling where I'll go."

Tanner had reached the old-fashioned wraparound porch. The place had a certain charm, though it needed a lot of fixing up. He could picture Sophie there all too easily, running back and forth to the barn, riding a yel-low bus to school, wearing jeans instead of uniforms. Tacking up posters on her bedroom walls and holding sleepovers with ordinary friends instead of junior ce-lebrities and other mini-jet-setters.

"Don't try it, Soph," he said, fumbling with the knob, shouldering open the heavy front door. "You're fine at

Briarwood, and it's a long way between Connecticut and Arizona."

"Fine?" Sophie shot back. "This place isn't in a parallel dimension, you know. Things *happen*. Marissa Worth got ptomaine from the potato salad in the cafeteria, just last week, and had to be airlifted to Walter Reed. Allison Mooreland's appendix ruptured, and—"

"Soph," Tanner said, flipping on the lights in the entryway.

Which way was the kitchen?

His room was upstairs someplace, but where?

He hung up his hat, shrugged off his leather coat, tossed it in the direction of an ornate brass peg designed for the purpose.

Sophie didn't say a word. All the way across country, Tanner could feel her holding her breath.

"How's this? School lets out in May. You can come out here then. Spend the summer. Ride Butterpie all you want."

"I might be too big to ride her by summer," Sophie pointed out. Tanner wondered, as he often did, if his daughter wouldn't make a better lawyer than a doctor. "Thanksgiving is in three days," she went on in a rush. "Let me come home for that, and if you still don't think I'm a good kid to have around, I'll come back to Briarwood for the rest of the year and pretend I love it."

"It's not that I don't think you're a good kid, Soph." In the living room by then, Tanner paused to consult a yellowed wall calendar left behind by the ranch's previous owner. Unfortunately, it was several years out of date.

Sophie didn't answer.

"Thanksgiving is in three days?" Tanner muttered,

dismayed. Living the way he did, he tended to lose track of holidays, but it figured that if Christmas was already a factor, turkey day had to be bearing down hard.

"I could still get a ticket if I flew standby," Sophie said hopefully.

Tanner closed his eyes. Let his forehead rest against the wall where a million little tack holes testified to all the calendars that had gone before this one. "That's a long way to travel for a turkey special in some greasy spoon," he said quietly. He knew the kid was probably picturing a Norman Rockwell scenario—old woman proudly presenting a golden-brown gobbler to a beaming family crowded around a table.

"Someone will invite you to Thanksgiving dinner," Sophie said, with a tone of bright, brittle bravery in her voice, "and I could just tag along."

He checked his watch, started for the kitchen. If it wasn't where he thought it was, he'd have to search until he found it, because he needed coffee. Hold the Jack Daniel's.

"You've been watching the Hallmark Channel again," he said wearily, his heart trying to scramble up his windpipe into the back of his throat. There were so many things he couldn't give Sophie—a stable home, a family, an ordinary childhood. But he *could* keep her safe, and that meant staying at Briarwood.

A long, painful pause ensued.

"You're not going to give in, are you?" Sophie asked finally, practically in a whisper.

"Are you just figuring that out, shortstop?" Tanner retorted, trying for a light tone.

She huffed out a weight-of-the-world sigh. "Okay, then," she replied, "don't say I didn't warn you."

# *Chapter Two*

It was a pity Starcross Ranch had fallen into such a state of disrepair, Olivia thought as she steered the Suburban down the driveway to the main road, Ginger beside her in the passenger seat, Rodney in the back. The place bordered her rental to the west, and although she passed the sagging rail fences and the tilting barn every day on her way to town, that morning the sight seemed even lonelier than usual.

She braked for the stop sign, looked both ways. No cars coming, but she didn't pull out right away. The vibe hit her before she could shift out of neutral and hit the gas.

"Oh, no," she said aloud.

Ginger, busy surveying the snowy countryside, offered no comment.

"Did you hear that?" Olivia persisted.

Ginger turned to look at her. Gave a little yip. Today, evidently, she was pretending to be an ordinary dog— as if *any* dog was ordinary—incapable of intelligent conversation.

The call was coming from the ancient barn on the Starcross property.

Olivia took a moment to rest her forehead on the cold steering wheel. She'd known Brad's friend the big-time contractor was moving in, of course, and she'd seen at least one moving truck, but she hadn't known there were any animals involved.

"I could ignore this," she said to Ginger.

*"Or not,"* Ginger answered.

"Oh, hell," Olivia said. Then she signaled for a left turn—Stone Creek was in the other direction—and headed for the decrepit old gate marking the entrance to Starcross Ranch.

The gate stood wide open. No sheep or cattle then, probably, Olivia reasoned. Even greenhorns knew live-stock tended to stray at every opportunity. Still, *some* kind of critter was sending out a psychic SOS from that pitiful barn.

They bumped up the rutted driveway, fishtailing a little on the slick snow and the layer of ice underneath, and Olivia tooted her horn. A spiffy new red pickup stood in front of the house, looking way too fancy for the neighborhood, but nobody appeared to see who was honking.

Muttering, Olivia brought the Suburban to a rattling stop in front of the barn, got out and shut the door hard.

"Hello?" she called.

No answer. Not from a human being, anyway.

The animal inside the barn amped up the psychic summons.

Olivia sprinted toward the barn door, glancing upward once at the sagging roof as she entered, with some trepidation. The place ought to be condemned. "Hello?" she repeated.

It took a moment for her eyes to adjust to the dimmer light, since the weather was dazzle-bright, though cold enough to crystallize her bone marrow.

*"Over here,"* said a silent voice, deep and distinctly male.

Olivia ventured deeper into the shadows. The ruins of a dozen once-sturdy stalls lined the sawdust-and-straw aisle. She found two at the very back, showing fresh-lumber signs of recent restoration efforts.

A tall palomino regarded her from the stall on the right, tossed his head as if to indicate the one opposite.

Olivia went to that stall and looked over the half gate to see a small, yellowish-white pony gazing up at her in befuddled sorrow. The horse lay forlornly in fresh wood shavings, its legs folded underneath.

Although she was technically trespassing, Olivia couldn't resist unlatching the gate and slipping inside. She crouched beside the pony, stroked its nose, patted its neck, gave its forelock an affectionate tug.

"Hey, there," she said softly. "What's all the fuss about?"

A slight shudder went through the little horse.

*"She misses Sophie,"* the palomino said, from across the aisle.

Wondering who Sophie was, Olivia examined the pony while continuing to pet her. The animal was sound, well fed and well cared for in general.

The palomino nickered loudly, and that should have been a cue, but Olivia was too focused on the pony to pay attention.

"Who are you and what the hell are you doing sneaking around in my barn?" demanded a low, no-nonsense voice.

Olivia whirled, and toppled backward into the straw. Looked up to see a dark-haired man glowering down at her from over the stall gate. His eyes matched his blue denim jacket, and his Western hat looked a little too new.

"Who's Sophie?" she asked, getting to her feet, dusting bits of straw off her jeans.

He merely folded his arms and glared. He'd asked the first question and, apparently, he intended to have the first answer. From the set of his broad shoulders, she guessed he'd wait for it until hell froze over if necessary.

Olivia relented, since she had rounds to make and a reindeer owner to track down. She summoned up her best smile and stuck out her hand. "Olivia O'Ballivan," she said. "I'm your neighbor—sort of—and..." *And I heard your pony calling out for help?* No, she couldn't say that. It was all too easy to imagine the reaction she'd get. "And since I'm a veterinarian, I always like to stop by when somebody new moves in. Offer my services."

The blue eyes sized her up, clearly found her less than statuesque. "You must deal mostly with cats and poodles," he said. "As you can see, I have horses."

Olivia felt the sexist remark like the unexpected back-snap of a rubber band, stinging and sudden. Adrenaline coursed through her, and she had to wait a few moments for it to subside. "This horse," she said when she'd regained her dignity, indicating the pony with a gesture of one hand, "is depressed."

One dark eyebrow quirked upward, and the hint of a smile played at the corner of Tanner Quinn's supple-looking mouth. That had to be who he was, since he'd said "*I* have horses," not "we" or "they." Anyhow, he didn't look like an ordinary ranch hand.

"Does she need to take happy pills?" he asked.

*"She wants Sophie,"* the palomino said, though of course Mr. Quinn didn't hear.

"Who's Sophie?" Olivia repeated calmly.

Quinn hesitated for a long moment. "My daughter," he finally said. "How do you happen to know her name?"

Olivia thought fast. "My brother must have mentioned her," she answered, heading for the stall door and hoping he'd step back so she could pass.

He didn't. Instead, he stood there like a support beam, his forearms resting on top of the door. "O'Ballivan," he mused. "You're Brad's sister? The one who'll be running the shelter when it's finished?"

"I think I just said Brad is my brother," Olivia replied, somewhat tartly. She felt strangely shaken and a little cornered, which was odd, because she wasn't claustrophobic and despite her unremarkable height of five feet three inches, she knew how to defend herself. "Now, would you mind letting me out of this stall?"

Quinn stepped back, even executed a sweeping bow.

*"You're not leaving, are you?"* the palomino fretted. *"Butterpie needs help."*

"Give me a second here," Olivia told the concerned horse. "I'll make sure Butterpie is taken care of, but it's going to take time." An awkward moment passed before she realized she'd spoken out loud, instead of using mental e-mail.

Quinn blocked her way again, planting himself in the middle of the barn aisle, and refolded his arms. "Now," he said ominously, "I *know* I've never mentioned that pony's name to anybody in Stone Creek, including Brad."

Olivia swallowed, tried for a smile but slid right down the side of it without catching hold. "Lucky guess," she said, and started around him.

He caught hold of her arm to stop her, but let go immediately.

Olivia stared up at him. The palomino was right; she couldn't leave, no matter how foolish she might seem to Tanner Quinn. Butterpie was in trouble.

"Who are you?" Tanner insisted gruffly.

"I told you. I'm Olivia O'Ballivan."

Tanner took off his hat with one hand, shoved the other through his thick, somewhat shaggy hair. The light was better in the aisle, since there were big cracks in the roof to let in the silvery sunshine, and she saw that he needed a shave.

He gave a heavy sigh. "Could we start over, here?" he asked. "If you're who you say you are, then we're going to be working together on the shelter project. That'll be a whole lot easier if we get along."

"Butterpie misses your daughter," Olivia said. "*Severely.* Where is she?"

Tanner sighed again. "Boarding school," he answered, as though the words had been pried out of him. The denim-colored eyes were still fixed on her face.

"Oh," Olivia answered, feeling sorry for the pony

*and* Sophie. "She'll be home for Thanksgiving, though, right? Your daughter, I mean?"

Tanner's jawline looked rigid, and his eyes didn't soften. "No," he said.

"No?" Olivia's spirits, already on the dip, deflated completely.

He stepped aside. Before, he'd blocked her way. Now he obviously wanted her gone, ASAP.

It was Olivia's turn with the folded arms and stubborn stance. "Then I have to explain that to the horse," she said.

Tanner blinked. "What?"

She turned, went back to Butterpie's stall, opened the door and stepped inside. *"Sophie's away at boarding school,"* she told the animal silently. *"And she can't make it home for Thanksgiving. You've got to cheer up, though. I'm sure she'll be here for Christmas."*

"What are you doing?" Tanner asked, sounding testy again.

"Telling Butterpie that Sophie will be home at Christmas and she's got to cheer up in the meantime." He'd asked the question; let him deal with the answer.

"Are you crazy?"

"Probably," Olivia said. Then, speaking aloud this time, she told Butterpie, "I have to go now. I have a lost reindeer in the back of my Suburban, and I need to do some X-rays and then get him settled in over at my brother's place until I can find his owner. But I'll be back to visit soon, I promise."

She could almost hear Tanner grinding his back teeth.

"You should stand up," Olivia told the pony. "You'll feel better on your feet."

The animal gave a snorty sigh and slowly stood.

Tanner let out a sharp breath.

Olivia patted Butterpie's neck. "Excellent," she said. "That's the spirit."

"You have a reindeer in the back of your Suburban?" Tanner queried, keeping pace with Olivia as she left the barn.

"See for yourself," she replied, waving one hand toward the rig.

Tanner approached the vehicle, and Ginger barked a cheerful greeting as he passed the passenger-side window. He responded with a distracted wave, and Olivia decided there might be a few soft spots in his steely psyche after all.

Rubbing off dirt with one gloved hand, Tanner peered through the back windows.

"I'll be damned," he said. "It *is* a reindeer."

"Sure enough," Olivia said. Ginger was all over the inside of the rig, barking her brains out. She liked good-looking men, the silly dog. Actually, she liked *any* man. "Ginger! Sit!"

Ginger sat, but she looked like the poster dog for a homeless-pets campaign.

"Where did you get a reindeer?" Tanner asked, drawing back from the window to take a whole new look at Olivia.

Ridiculously, she wished she'd worn something remotely feminine that day, instead of her usual jeans, flannel work shirt and mud-speckled down-filled vest. Not that she actually owned anything remotely feminine.

"I found him," she said, opening the driver's door. "Last night, at the bottom of my driveway."

For the first time in their acquaintance, Tanner smiled, and the effect was seismic. His teeth were white and straight, and she'd have bet that was natural enamel, not a fancy set of veneers. "Okay," he said, stretching the word out a way. "Tell me, Dr. O'Ballivan—how does a reindeer happen to turn up in Arizona?"

"When I find out," Olivia said, climbing behind the wheel, "I'll let you know."

Before she could shut the door, he stood in the gap. Pushed his hat to the back of his head and treated her to another wicked grin. "I guess there's a ground-breaking ceremony scheduled for tomorrow morning at ten," he said. "I'll see you there."

Olivia nodded, feeling unaccountably flustered.

Ginger was practically drooling.

"Nice dog," Tanner said.

*"Be still, my heart,"* Ginger said.

"Shut up," Olivia told the dog.

Tanner drew back his head, but the grin lurked in his eyes.

Olivia blushed. "I wasn't talking to you," she told Tanner.

He looked as though he wanted to ask if she'd been taking her medications regularly. Fortunately for him, he didn't. He merely tugged at the brim of his too-new hat and stepped back.

Olivia pulled the door closed, started up the engine, ground the gearshift into first and made a wide 360 in front of the barn.

*"That* certainly went well," she told Ginger. "We're going to be in each other's hip pockets while the shelter is being built, and he thinks I'm certifiable!"

Ginger didn't answer.

Half an hour later, the X-rays were done and the blood had been drawn. Rodney was good to go.

Tanner stood in the middle of the barnyard, staring after that wreck of a Suburban and wondering what the hell had just hit him. It felt like a freight train.

His cell phone rang, breaking the spell.

He pulled it from his jacket pocket and squinted at the caller ID panel. Ms. Wiggins, the executive principal at Briarwood. She'd certainly taken her time returning his call—he'd left her a message at sunrise.

"Tanner Quinn," he said automatically.

"Hello, Mr. Quinn," Ms. Wiggins said. A former CIA agent, Janet Wiggins was attractive, if you liked the armed-and-dangerous type. Tanner didn't, particularly, but the woman had a spotless service record, and a good résumé. "I'm sorry I couldn't call sooner—meetings, you know."

"I'm worried about Sophie," he said. A cold wind blew down off the mountain looming above Stone Creek, biting into his ears, but he didn't head for the house. He just stood there in the barnyard, letting the chill go right through him.

"I gathered that from your message, Mr. Quinn," Ms. Wiggins said smoothly. She was used to dealing with fretful parents, especially the guilt-plagued ones. "The fact is, Sophie is not the only student remaining at Briarwood over the holiday season. There are several others. We're taking all the stay-behinds to New York by train to watch the Thanksgiving Day parade and dine at the Four Seasons. You would know that if you read our weekly newsletters. We send them by e-mail every Friday afternoon."

*I just met a woman who talks to animals—and thinks they talk back.*

Tanner kept his tone even. "I read your newsletters faithfully, Ms. Wiggins," he said. "And I'm not sure I like having my daughter referred to as a 'stay-behind.'"

Ms. Wiggins trilled out a very un-CIA-like giggle. "Oh, we don't use that term in front of the pupils, Mr. Quinn," she assured him. "Sophie is *fine*. She just tends to be a little overdramatic, that's all. In fact, I'm encouraging her to sign up for our thespian program, beginning next term—"

"You're sure she's all right?" Tanner broke in.

"She's one of our most emotionally stable students. It's just that, well, kids get a little sentimental around the holidays."

*Don't we all?* Tanner thought. He always skipped Thanksgiving and Christmas both, if he couldn't spend them with Sophie. Up until now it had been easy enough, given that he'd been out of the country last year, and the year before that. Sophie had stayed with Tessa, and he'd ordered all her gifts online.

Remembering that gave him a hollow feeling in the middle of his gut.

"I know Sophie is stable," he said patiently. "That doesn't mean she's completely okay."

Ms. Wiggins paused eloquently before answering. "Well, if you would like Sophie to come home for Thanksgiving, we'd certainly be glad to make the arrangements."

Tanner wanted to say yes. Instantly. *Book a plane. Put her on board. I don't care what it costs.* But it would only lead to another tearful parting when it came time for Sophie to return to school, and Tanner couldn't bear another one of those. Not just yet, anyway.

"It's best if Sophie stays there," he said.

"I quite agree," Ms. Wiggins replied. "Last-minute trips home can be very disruptive to a child."

"You'll let me know if there are any problems?"

"Of course I will," Ms. Wiggins assured him. If there was just a hint of condescension in her tone, he supposed he deserved it. "We at Briarwood pride ourselves on monitoring our students' mental health as well as their academic achievement. I promise you, Sophie is not traumatized."

Tanner wished he could be half as sure of that as Ms. Wiggins sounded. A few holiday platitudes were exchanged, and the call ended. Tanner snapped his phone shut and dropped it into his coat pocket.

Then he turned back toward the barn.

Could a horse get depressed?

Nah, he decided.

But a man sure as hell could.

A snowman stood in the center of the yard at the homeplace when Olivia drove in, and there was one of those foldout turkeys taped to the front door. Brad came out of the barn, walking toward her, just as Meg, her sister-in-law, stepped onto the porch, smiling a welcome.

"How do you like our turkey?" she called. "We're really getting into the spirit this year." Her smile turned wistful. "It's strange, without Carly here, but she's having such a good time."

Grinning, Olivia gestured toward Brad. "He'll do," she teased.

Brad reached her, hooked an arm around her neck

and gave her a big-brother half hug. "She's referring to the paper one," he told her in an exaggerated whisper.

Olivia contrived to look surprised. "Oh!" she said.

Brad laughed and released her from the choke hold. "So what brings you to Stone Creek Ranch, Doc?"

Olivia glanced around, taking in the familiar surroundings. Missing her grandfather, Big John, the way she always did when she set foot on home ground. The place had changed a lot since Brad had semiretired from his career in country music—he'd refurbished the barn, replaced the worn-out fences and built a state-of-the-art recording studio out back. At least he'd given up the concert tours, but even with Meg and fourteen-year-old Carly and the baby in the picture, Olivia still wasn't entirely convinced that he'd come home to stay.

He'd skipped out before, after all, just like their mother.

"I have a problem," she said in belated answer to his question.

Meg had gone back inside, but she and Brad remained in the yard.

"What sort of problem?" he asked, his eyes serious.

"A reindeer problem," Olivia explained. *Oh, and I got off to a fine start with your friend the contractor, too.*

Brad's brow furrowed. "A what?"

*"I need to get out of this truck,"* Ginger transmitted from the passenger seat. *"Now."*

With a slight sigh Olivia opened Ginger's door so she could hop out, sniff the snow and leave a yellow splotch. That done, she trotted off toward the barn, probably looking for Brad's dog, Willie.

"I found this reindeer," Olivia said, heading for the

back of the Suburban and unveiling Rodney. "I was hoping he could stay here until we find his owner."

"What if he doesn't have an owner?" Brad asked reasonably, running a hand through his shaggy blond hair before reaching out to stroke the deer.

"He's tame," Olivia pointed out.

"Tame, but not housebroken," Brad said.

Sure enough, Rodney had dropped a few pellets on his blanket.

"I don't expect you to keep him in the house," Olivia said.

Brad laughed. Reached right in and hoisted Rodney down out of the Suburban. The deer stumbled a little, wobbly legged from riding, and looked worriedly up at Olivia.

"You'll be safe here," she told the animal. She turned back to Brad. "He can stay in the barn, can't he? I know you have some empty stalls."

"Sure," Brad said after a hesitation that would have been comical if Olivia hadn't been so concerned about Rodney. "Sure," he repeated.

Knowing he was about to ruffle her hair, the way he'd done when she was a little kid, Olivia took a step back.

"I want something in return, though," Brad continued.

"What?" Olivia asked suspiciously.

"You, at our table, on Thanksgiving," he answered. "No excuses about filling in at the clinic. Ashley and Melissa are both coming, and Meg's mother, too, along with her sister, Sierra."

The invitation didn't come as any surprise to Olivia—Meg had mentioned holding a big Thanksgiving blow-out weeks ago—but the truth was, Olivia preferred to work on holidays. That way, she didn't miss Big John so much, or wonder if their long-lost mother might come waltzing through the door, wanting to get to know the grown children she'd abandoned so many years before.

"Livie?" Brad prompted.

"Okay," she said. "I'll be here. But I'm on call over Thanksgiving, and all the other vets have families, so if there's an emergency—"

"Liv," Brad broke in, "*you* have a family, too."

"I meant wives, husbands, children," Olivia said, embarrassed.

"Two o'clock, you don't need to bring anything, and wear something you haven't delivered calves in."

She glared up at him. "Can I see my nephew now," she asked, "or is there a dress code for that, too?"

Brad laughed. "I'll get Rudolph settled in a nice, cozy stall while you go inside. Check the attitude at the door—Meg wasn't kidding when she said she was in the holiday spirit. Of course, she's working extra hard at it this year, with Carly away."

Willie and Ginger came from behind the barn, Willie rushing to greet Olivia.

"His name is Rodney," Olivia said. "Not Rudolph."

Brad gave her a look and started for the barn, and Rodney followed uncertainly, casting nary a backward glance at Olivia.

Willie, probably clued in by Ginger, was careful to give Rodney a lot of dog-free space. Olivia bent to scratch his ears.

He'd healed up nicely since being attacked by a wolf or coyote pack on the mountain rising above Stone Creek Ranch. With help from Brad and Meg, Olivia had brought him back to town for surgery and follow-up care. He'd bonded with Brad, though, and been his dog ever since.

With Ginger and Willie following, Olivia went into the house.

Mac's playpen stood empty in the living room.

Olivia stepped into the nearest bathroom to wash her hands, and when she came out, Meg was standing in the hallway, holding six-month-old Mac. He stretched his arms out to Olivia and strained toward her, and her heart melted.

She took the baby eagerly and nuzzled his neck to make him laugh. His blondish hair stood up all over his head, and his dark blue eyes were round with mischievous excitement. Giggling, he tried to bite Olivia's nose.

"He's grown!" Olivia told Meg.

"It's only been a week since you saw him last," Meg chided, but she beamed with pride.

Olivia felt a pang, looking at her. Wondered what it would be like to be that happy.

Meg, blond like her husband and son, tilted her head to one side and gave Olivia a humorously pensive once-over. "Are you okay?" she asked.

"I'm fine," Olivia said, too quickly. Mac was gravitating toward his playpen, where he had a pile of toys, and Meg took him and gently set him inside it. She turned back to Olivia.

Just then Brad blew in on a chilly November wind. Bent to pat Ginger and Willie.

"Rudolph is snug in his stall," Brad said. "Having some oats."

"Rudolph?" Meg asked, momentarily distracted.

Olivia was relieved. She and Meg were very good

friends, as well as family, but Meg was half again too perceptive. She'd figured out that something was bothering Olivia, and in another moment she'd have insisted on finding out what was up. Considering that Olivia didn't know that herself, the conversation would have been pointless.

"Liv will be here for Thanksgiving," Brad told Meg, pulling his wife against his side and planting a kiss on the top of her head.

"Of course she will," Meg said, surprised that there'd ever been any question. Her gaze lingered on Olivia, and there was concern in it.

Suddenly Olivia was anxious to go.

"I have two million things to do," she said, bending over the playpen to tickle Mac, who was kicking both feet and waving his arms, before heading to the front door and beckoning for Ginger.

"We'll see you tomorrow at the ground-breaking ceremony," Meg said, smiling and giving Brad an affectionate jab with one elbow. "We're expecting a big crowd, thanks to Mr. Country Music here."

Olivia laughed at the face Brad made, but then she recalled that Tanner Quinn would be there, too, and that unsettled feeling was back again. "The ground's pretty hard, thanks to the weather," she said, to cover the momentary lapse. "Let's hope Mr. Country Music still has the muscle to drive a shovel through six inches of snow and a layer of ice."

Brad showed off a respectable biceps, Popeye-style, and everybody laughed again.

"I'll walk you to the truck," he said, when Olivia would have ducked out without further ado.

He opened the driver's door of the Suburban, and

Ginger made the leap, scrabbling across to the passenger seat. Olivia looked at her in surprise, since she usually wasn't that agile, but Brad reclaimed her attention soon enough.

"Is everything okay with you, Livie?" he asked. He and the twins were the only people in the world, now that Big John was gone, who called her Livie. It seemed right, coming from her big brother or her sisters, but it also made her ache for her grandfather. He'd loved Thanksgiving even better than Christmas, saying he figured the O'Ballivans had a great deal to be grateful for.

"Everything's fine," Olivia said. "Why does everybody keep asking me if I'm okay? Meg did—now you."

"You just seem—I don't know—kind of sad."

Olivia didn't trust herself to speak, and suddenly her eyes burned with moisture.

Brad took her gently by the shoulders and kissed her on the forehead. "I miss Big John, too," he said. Then he waited while she climbed onto the running board and then the driver's seat. He shut the door and waved when she went to turn around, and when she glanced into the rearview mirror, he was still standing there with Willie, both of them staring after her.

# *Chapter Three*

Although Brad liked to downplay his success, especially now that he didn't go out on tour anymore, he was clearly still a very big deal. When Olivia arrived at the building site on the outskirts of Stone Creek at nine forty-five the next morning, the windswept clearing was jammed with TV news trucks and stringers from various tabloids. Of course the townspeople had turned out, too, happy that work was about to begin on the new animal shelter—and proud of their hometown boy.

Olivia's feelings about Brad's fame were mixed—he'd been away playing star when Big John needed him most, and she wasn't over that—but seeing him up there on the hastily assembled plank stage gave her a jolt of joy. She worked her way through the crowd to stand next to Meg, Ashley and Melissa, who were grouped in a little cluster up front, fussing over Mac. The baby's blue snow-suit was so bulky that he resembled the Michelin man.

Ashley turned to smile at Olivia, taking in her trim, tailored black pantsuit—a holdover from her job inter-view at the veterinary clinic right after she'd finished graduate school. She'd ferreted through boxes until she'd found it, gone over the outfit with a lint roller to get rid of the ubiquitous pet hair, and hoped for the best.

"I guess you couldn't quite manage a dress," Ash-ley said without sarcasm. She was tall and blond, clad in a long skirt, elegant boots and a colorful patchwork jacket she'd probably whipped up on her sewing ma-chine. She was also stubbornly old-fashioned—no cell phone, no Internet connection, no MP3 player—and Olivia had often thought, secretly of course, that her younger sister should have been born in the Victorian era, rather than modern times. She would have fit right into the 1890s, been completely comfortable cooking on a wood-burning stove, reading by gaslight and di-recting a contingent of maids in ruffly aprons and scal-loped white caps.

"Best I could do on short notice," Olivia chimed in, exchanging a hello grin with Meg and giving Mac's mittened hand a little squeeze. His plump little cheek felt smooth and cold as she kissed him.

"Since when is a *year* 'short notice'?" Melissa put in, grinning. She and Ashley were fraternal twins, but except for their deep blue eyes, they bore no notice-able resemblance to each other. Melissa was small, an inch shorter than Olivia, and wore her fine chestnut-colored hair in a bob. Having left the law office where she worked to attend the ceremony, she was clad in her usual getup of high heels, pencil-straight skirt, fitted blazer and prim white blouse.

Up on stage, Brad tapped lightly on the microphone.

Everybody fell silent, as though the whole gathering had taken a single, indrawn breath all at the same time. The air was charged with excitement and civic pride and the welcome prospect of construction jobs to tide over the laid-off workers from the sawmill.

Meg's eyes shone as she gazed up at her husband. "Isn't he something?" she marveled, giving Olivia a little poke with one elbow as she shifted Mac to her other hip.

Olivia smiled but didn't reply.

"Sing!" someone shouted, somewhere in the surging throng. Any moment now, Olivia thought, they'd all be holding up disposable lights in a flickering-flame salute.

Brad shook his head. "Not today," he said.

A collective groan rose from the crowd.

Brad put up both hands to silence them.

"He'll sing," Melissa said in a loud and certain whisper. She and Ashley, being the youngest, barely knew Brad. He'd been trying to remedy that ever since he'd moved back from Nashville, but it was slow going. They admired him, they were grateful to him, but it seemed to Olivia that her sisters were still in awe of their big brother, too, and therefore a strange shyness possessed them whenever he was around.

Brad asked Olivia and Tanner to join him on stage.

Even though Olivia had expected that, she wished she didn't have to go up there. She was a behind-the-scenes kind of person, uncomfortable at the center of attention. When Tanner appeared from behind her, took her arm and hustled her toward the wooden steps, she caught her breath. Stone Creekers raised an uproarious cheer, and Olivia flushed with embarrassment, but Tanner seemed untroubled.

He wore too-new, too-expensive boots, probably custom-made, to match his too-new hat, along with jeans, a black silk shirt and a denim jacket. He seemed as at home getting up in front of all those people as Brad did—his grin dazzled, and his eyes were bright with enjoyment.

*Drugstore cowboy,* Olivia thought, but she couldn't work up any rancor. Tanner Quinn might be laying on the Western bit a little thick, but he did look good. Way, way too good for Olivia's comfort.

Brad introduced them both: Tanner as the builder, and Olivia—"You all know my kid sister, the horse doctor"—as the driving force behind the project. Without her, he said, none of this would be happening.

Never having thought of herself as a driving force behind anything in particular, Olivia grew even more flustered as Brad went on about how she'd be heading up the shelter when it opened around that time next year.

More applause followed, the good-natured, home-town kind, indulgent and laced with chuckles.

*Let this be over,* Olivia thought.

"Sing!" someone yelled. The whole audience soon took up the chant.

"Here's where we make a run for it," Tanner whispered to Olivia, and the two of them left the stage. Tanner vanished, and Olivia went back to stand with her sisters and Meg.

Brad grinned, shaking his head a little as one of his buddies handed up a guitar. "One," he said firmly. After strumming a few riffs and turning the tuning keys this way and that, he eased into "Meg's Song," a ballad he'd written for his wife.

Holding Mac and looking up at Brad with an expression of rapt delight, Meg seemed to glow from the inside. A sweet, strange alchemy made it seem as though only Brad, Meg and Mac were really *there* during those magical minutes, on that blustery day, with the snow crusting hard around everybody's feet. The rest of them might have been hovering in an adjacent dimension, like actors waiting to go on.

When the song ended, the audience clamored for more, but Brad didn't give in. Photographers and reporters shoved in close as he handed off the guitar again, descended from the stage and picked up a brand-new shovel with a blue ribbon on the handle. The ribbon, Olivia knew, was Ashley's handiwork; she was an expert with bows, where Olivia always got them tangled up, fiddling with them until they were grubby.

"Are you making a comeback?" one reporter demanded.

"When will you make another movie?" someone else wanted to know.

Still another person shoved a microphone into Brad's face; he pushed it away with a practiced motion of one arm. "We're here to break ground for an animal shelter," he said, and only the set of his jaw gave away the annoyance he felt. He beckoned to Olivia, then to Tanner, after glancing around to locate him.

Then, with consummate showmanship, Brad drove the shovel hard into the partially frozen ground. Tossed the dirt dangerously close to one reporter's shoes.

Olivia thought of the finished structure, and what it would mean to so many stray and unwanted dogs, cats and other critters, and her heart soared. That was the moment the project truly became real to her.

*It was really going to happen.*

There were more pictures taken after that, and Brad gave several very brief interviews, carefully steering each one away from himself and stressing the plight of animals. When one reporter asked if it wouldn't be better to build shelters for homeless *people*, rather than dogs and cats, Brad responded that compassion ought to begin at the simplest level, with the helpless, voiceless ones, and grow from there.

Olivia would have hugged her big brother in that moment if she'd been able to get close enough.

"Hot cider and cookies at my place," Ashley told her and Melissa. She was already heading for her funny-looking hybrid car, gleaming bright yellow in the wintry sunshine. "We need to plan what we're taking to Brad and Meg's for Thanksgiving dinner."

"I have to get back to work," Melissa said crisply. "Cook something and I'll pay you back." With that, she made for her spiffy red sports car without so much as a backward glance.

Olivia had rounds to make herself, though none of them were emergencies, and she had some appointments at the clinic scheduled for that afternoon, but when she saw the expression of disappointment on Ashley's face, she stayed behind. "I'll change clothes at your house," she said, and got into the Suburban to follow her sister back through town. Ginger had elected to stay home that day, claiming her arthritis was bothering her, and it felt odd to be alone in the rig.

Ashley's home was a large white Victorian house on the opposite side of Stone Creek, near the little stream with the same name. There was a white picket fence and plenty of gingerbread woodwork on the façade, and an ornate but tasteful sign stood in the snowy yard, bearing the words "Mountain View Bed-and-Breakfast" in elegant golden script. "Ashley O'Ballivan, Proprietor."

In summer, the yard burgeoned with colorful flowers.

But winter had officially come to the high country, and the blooming lilacs, peonies and English roses were just a memory. The day after Thanksgiving, the Christmas lights would go up outside, as though by the waving of an unseen wand, and a huge wreath would grace the leaded-glass door, making the house look like a giant greeting card.

Olivia felt a little sad, looking at that grand house. It was the off-season, and guests would be few and far between. Ashley would rattle around in there alone like a bean in the bottom of a bucket.

She needed a husband and children.

Or at least a cat.

"Brad was spectacular, wasn't he?" Ashley asked, bustling around her big, fragrant kitchen to heat up the spiced cider and set out a plate of exquisitely decorated cookies.

Olivia, just coming out of the powder room, where she'd changed into her regulation jeans, flannel shirt and boots, helped herself to a paper bag from the decoupaged wooden paper-bag dispenser beside the back door and stuffed the pantsuit into it. "Brad was—Brad," she said. "He loves being in the limelight."

Ashley went still and frowned, oddly defensive. "His heart's in the right place," she replied.

Olivia went to Ashley and touched her arm. She'd

removed the patchwork jacket, hanging it neatly on a gleaming brass peg by the front door as they came in, and her loose-fitting beige cashmere turtleneck made Olivia feel like a thrift-store refugee by comparison.

"I wasn't criticizing Brad, Ash," she said quietly. "It's beyond generous of him to build the shelter. We need one, and we're lucky he's willing to help out."

Ashley relaxed a little and offered a tentative smile. Looked around at her kitchen, which would have made a great set for some show on the Food Channel. "He bought this house for me, you know," she said as the cider began to simmer in its shiny pot on the stove.

Olivia nodded. "And it looks fabulous," she replied. "Like always."

"You *are* planning to show up for Thanksgiving dinner out at the ranch, aren't you?"

"Why wouldn't I?" Olivia asked, even as her stomach knotted. Who had invented holidays, anyway? Everything came to a screeching stop whenever there was a red-letter day on the calendar—everything except the need and sorrow that seemed to fill the world.

"I know you don't like family holidays," Ashley said, pouring steaming cider into a copper serving pot and then into translucent china teacups waiting in the center of the round antique table. Olivia would have dumped it straight from the kettle, and probably spilled it all over the table and floor in the process.

She just wasn't domestic. All those genes had gone to Ashley.

Her sister's eyes went big and round and serious. "Last year you made some excuse about a cow needing an appendectomy and ducked out before I could serve the pumpkin pie."

Olivia sighed. Ashley had worked hard to prepare the previous year's Thanksgiving dinner, gathering recipes for weeks ahead of time, experimenting like a chemist in search of a cure, and looked forward to hosting a houseful of congenial relatives.

"Do cows even *have* appendixes?" Ashley asked.

Olivia laughed, drew back a chair at the table and sat down. "That cider smells fabulous," she said, in order to change the subject. "And the cookies are works of art, almost too pretty to eat. Martha Stewart would be so proud."

Ashley joined her at the table, but she still looked troubled. "Why do you hate holidays, Olivia?" she persisted.

"I don't hate holidays," Olivia said. "It's just that all that sentimentality—"

"You miss Big John and Mom," Ashley broke in quietly. "Why don't you just admit it?"

"We all miss Big John," Olivia admitted. "As for Mom—well, she's been gone a long time, Ash. A *really* long time. It's not a matter of missing her, exactly."

"Don't you ever wonder where she went after she left Stone Creek, if she's happy and healthy—if she remarried and had more children?"

"I try not to," Olivia said honestly.

"You have abandonment issues," Ashley accused.

Olivia sighed and sipped from her cup of cider. The stuff was delicious, like everything her sister cooked up.

Ashley's Botticelli face brightened; she'd made another of her mercurial shifts from pensive to hopeful. "Suppose we found her?" she asked on a breath. "Mom, I mean—"

"Found her?" Olivia echoed, oddly alarmed.

"There are all these search engines online," Ashley enthused. "I was over at the library yesterday afternoon, and I searched Google for Mom's name."

*Oh. My. God,* Olivia thought, feeling the color drain out of her face.

"*You* used a computer?"

Ashley nodded. "I'm thinking of getting one. Setting up a Web site to bring in more business for the B and B."

Things were changing, Olivia realized. And she *hated* it when things changed. Why couldn't people leave well enough alone?

"There are more Delia O'Ballivans out there than you would ever guess," Ashley rushed on. "One of them must be Mom."

"Ash, Mom could be dead by now. Or going by a different name…"

Ashley looked offended. "You sound like Brad and Melissa. Brad just clams up whenever I ask him about Mom—he remembers her better, since he's older. 'Leave it alone' is all he ever says. And Melissa thinks she's probably a crack addict or a hooker or something." She let out a long, shaky breath. "I thought *you* missed Mom as much as I do. I really did."

Although Brad had never admitted it, Olivia suspected he knew more about their mother than he was telling. If he wanted Ashley and the rest of them to let the proverbial sleeping dogs lie, he probably had a good reason. Not that the decision was only his to make.

"I miss *having* a mother, Ash," Olivia said gently. "That's different from missing Mom specifically. She left us, remember?"

Remember? How *could* Ashley remember? She'd been a toddler when their mother boarded an afternoon bus out of Stone Creek and vanished into a world of strangers. She was clinging to memories she'd merely imagined, most likely. To a fantasy mother, the woman who should have been, but probably never was.

"Well, I want to know why," Ashley insisted, her eyes full of pain. "Maybe she regretted it. Did you ever think of that? Maybe she misses us, and wants a second chance. Maybe she expects us to reject her, so she's afraid to get in touch."

"Oh, Ash," Olivia murmured, slouching against the back of her chair. "You haven't actually made contact, have you?"

"No," Ashley said, tucking a wisp of blond hair behind her right ear when it escaped from her otherwise categorically perfect French braid, "but if I find her, I'm going to invite her to Stone Creek for Christmas. If you and Brad and Melissa want to keep your distance, that's your business."

Olivia's hand shook a little as she set her cup down, causing it to rattle in its delicate saucer. "Ashley, you have a right to see Mom if you want to," she said carefully. "But Christmas—"

"What do you care about Christmas?" Ashley asked abruptly. "You don't even put up a tree most years."

"I care about you and Melissa and Brad. If you do manage to find Mom, great. But don't you think bringing her here at Christmas, the most emotional day of the year, before anybody has a chance to get used to the idea, would be like planting a live hand grenade in the turkey?"

Ashley didn't reply, and after that the conversation was stilted, to say the least. They talked about what to contribute to the Thanksgiving shindig at Brad and

Meg's place, decided on freshly baked dinner rolls for Ashley and a selection of salads from the deli for Olivia, and then Olivia left to make rounds.

Why was she so worried? she wondered, biting down hard on her lower lip as she fired up the Suburban and headed for the first farm on her list. If she was alive, Delia had done a good job of staying under the radar all these years. She'd never written, never called, never visited. Never sent a single birthday card. And if she was dead, they'd all have to drop everything and mourn, in their various ways.

Olivia didn't feel ready to take that on.

Before, the thought of Delia usually filled her with grief and a plaintive, little-girl kind of longing. The very cadence of her heartbeat said, *Come home. Come home.*

Now, today, it just made her very, very angry. How could a woman just leave four children and a husband behind and forget the way back?

Olivia knotted one hand into a fist and bonked the side of the steering wheel once. Tears stung her eyes, and her throat felt as though someone had run a line of stitches around it with a sharp needle and then pulled them tight.

Ashley was expecting some kind of fairy-tale reunion, an *Oprah* sort of deal, full of tearful confessions and apologies and cartoon birds trailing ribbons from their chirpy beaks.

For Olivia's money, it would be more like an apocalypse.

Tanner heard the rig roll in around sunset. Smiling, he closed his newspaper, stood up from the kitchen table and wandered to the window. Watched as Olivia

O'Ballivan climbed out of her Suburban, flung one defiant glance toward the house and started for the barn, the golden retriever trotting along behind her.

She'd come, he knew, to have another confab with Butterpie. The idea at once amused him and jabbed through his conscience like a spike. Sophie was on the other side of the country, homesick as hell and probably sticking pins in a daddy doll. She missed the pony, and the pony missed her, and *he* was the hard-ass who was keeping them apart.

Taking his coat and hat down from the peg next to the back door, he put them on and went outside. He was used to being alone, even liked it, but keeping company with Doc O'Ballivan, bristly though she sometimes was, would provide a welcome diversion.

He gave her time to reach Butterpie's stall, then walked into the barn.

The golden came to greet him, all wagging tail and melting brown eyes, and he bent to stroke her soft, sturdy back. "Hey, there, dog," he said.

Sure enough, Olivia was in the stall, brushing Butterpie down and talking to her in a soft, soothing voice that touched something private inside Tanner and made him want to turn on one heel and beat it back to the house.

He'd be damned if he'd do it, though.

This was *his* ranch, *his* barn. Well-intentioned as she was, *Olivia* was the trespasser here, not him.

"She's still very upset," Olivia told him without turning to look at him or slowing down with the brush.

For a second Tanner thought she was referring to Sophie, not the pony, and that got his hackles up.

Shiloh, always an easy horse to get along with, stood

contentedly in his own stall, munching away on the feed Tanner had given him earlier. Butterpie, he noted, hadn't touched her supper as far as he could tell.

"Do you know anything at all about horses, Mr. Quinn?" Olivia asked.

He leaned against the stall door, the way he had the day before, and grinned. He'd practically been raised on horseback; he and Tessa had grown up on their grandmother's farm in the Texas hill country, after their folks divorced and went their separate ways, both of them too busy to bother with a couple of kids. "A few things," he said. "And I mean to call you Olivia, so you might as well return the favor and address me by my first name."

He watched as she took that in, dealt with it, decided on an approach. He'd have to wait and see what that turned out to be, but he didn't mind. It was a pleasure just watching Olivia O'Ballivan grooming a horse.

"All right, *Tanner*," she said. "This barn is a disgrace. When are you going to have the roof fixed? If it snows again, the hay will get wet and probably mold…."

He chuckled, shifted a little. He'd have a crew out there the following Monday morning to replace the roof and shore up the walls—he'd made the arrangements over a week before—but he felt no particular compunction to explain that. He was enjoying her ire too much; it made her color rise and her hair fly when she turned her head, and the faster breathing made her perfect breasts go up and down in an enticing rhythm. "What makes you so sure I'm a greenhorn?" he asked mildly, still leaning on the gate.

At last she looked straight at him, but she didn't move from Butterpie's side. "Your hat, your boots—that fancy red truck you drive. I'll bet it's customized."

Tanner grinned. Adjusted his hat. "Are you telling me real cowboys don't drive red trucks?"

"There are lots of trucks around here," she said. "Some of them are red, and some of them are new. And *all* of them are splattered with mud or manure or both."

"Maybe I ought to put in a car wash, then," he teased. "Sounds like there's a market for one. Might be a good investment."

She softened, though not significantly, and spared him a cautious half smile, full of questions she probably wouldn't ask. "There's a good car wash in Indian Rock," she informed him. "People go there. It's only forty miles."

"Oh," he said with just a hint of mockery. "*Only* forty miles. Well, then. Guess I'd better dirty up my truck if I want to be taken seriously in these here parts. Scuff up my boots a bit, too, and maybe stomp on my hat a couple of times."

Her cheeks went a fetching shade of pink. "You are twisting what I said," she told him, brushing Butterpie again, her touch gentle but sure. "I meant…"

Tanner envied that little horse. Wished he had furry hide, so he'd need brushing, too.

"You *meant* that I'm not a real cowboy," he said. "And you could be right. I've spent a lot of time on construction sites over the last few years, or in meetings where a hat and boots wouldn't be appropriate. Instead of digging out my old gear, once I decided to take this job, I just bought new."

"I bet you don't even *have* any old gear," she challenged, but she was smiling, albeit cautiously, as though she might withdraw into a disapproving frown at any second.

He took off his hat, extended it to her. "Here," he teased. "Rub that around in the muck until it suits you."

She laughed, and the sound—well, it caused a powerful and wholly unexpected shift inside him. Scared the hell out of him and, paradoxically, made him yearn to hear it again. "That would be a little drastic," she said.

Tanner put his hat back on. "You figure me for a rhinestone cowboy," he said. "What else have you decided about me?"

She considered the question, evidently drawing up a list in her head.

Tanner was fascinated—and still pretty scared.

"Brad told me you were widowed," she said finally, after mulling for a while. "I'm sorry about that."

Tanner swallowed hard, nodded. Wondered how much detail his friend had gone into, and decided not to ask. He'd told Brad the whole grim story of Kat's death, once upon a time.

"You're probably pretty driven," Olivia went on, concentrating on the horse again. "It's obvious that you're successful—Brad wouldn't have hired you for this project if you weren't the best. And you compartmentalize."

"Compartmentalize?"

"You shut yourself off from distractions."

"Such as?"

"Your daughter," Olivia said. She didn't lack for nerve, that was for sure. "And this poor little horse. You'd like to have a dog—you like Ginger a lot—but you wouldn't adopt one because that would mean making a commitment. Not being able to drop everything and everybody and take off for the next Big Job when the mood struck you."

Tanner felt as though he'd been slapped, and it didn't

help one bit that everything she'd said was true. Which didn't mean he couldn't deny it.

"I *love* Sophie," he said grimly.

She met his gaze again. "I'm sure you do. Still, you find it easy enough to—compartmentalize where she's concerned, don't you?"

"I do not," he argued. He *did* "compartmentalize"—he had to—but he sure as hell wouldn't call it easy. Every parting from Sophie was harder on him than it was on her. He was the one who always had to suck it up and be strong.

Olivia shrugged, patted the pony affectionately on the neck and set aside the brush. "I'll be back tomorrow," she told the animal. "In the meantime, think good thoughts and talk to Shiloh if you get too lonesome."

Tanner racked his brain, trying to remember if he'd told Olivia the gelding's name. He was sure it hadn't come up in their brief but tempestuous acquaintance. "How did you...?"

"He told me," Olivia said, approaching the stall door and waiting for him to step out of her way, just like before.

"Are you seriously telling me I've got Mr. Ed in my barn?" he asked, moving aside so she could pass.

She crossed to Shiloh's stall, reached up to stroke his nose when he nuzzled her and gave a companionable nicker. "You wouldn't understand," she said, with so much smug certainty that Tanner found himself wanting to prove a whole bunch of things he'd never felt the need to prove before.

"Because I compartmentalize?" Tanner gibed.

"Something like that," Olivia answered blithely. She

turned from Shiloh, snapped her fingers to attract the dog's attention and started for the barn door.

"See you tomorrow, if you're here when I come by to look in on Butterpie."

Utterly confounded, Tanner stood in the doorway watching as Olivia lowered a ramp at the back of the Suburban for Ginger, waited for the dog to trot up it, and shut the doors.

Moments later she was driving off, tooting a merry "so long" on the horn.

That night he dreamed of Kat.

*She was alive again, standing in the barn at Butterpie's stall gate, watching as the pony nibbled hay at its feeder. Tall and slender, with long dark hair, Kat turned to him and smiled a welcome.*

He hated these dreams for *being* dreams, not reality. At the same time he couldn't bring himself to wake up, to leave her.

The settings were always different—their first house, their quarters in the American compound in some sandy, dangerous foreign place, even supermarket aisles and gas stations. He'd be standing at the pump, filling the vehicle *de jour,* and look up to see Kat with a hose in her hand, gassing up that old junker she'd been driving when they met.

He stood at a little distance from her, there in the barn aisle, well aware that after a few words, a few minutes at most, she'd vanish. And it would be like losing her all over again.

She smiled, but there was sadness in her eyes, in the set of her full mouth. "Hello, Tanner," she said very softly.

He couldn't speak. Couldn't move. Somehow he knew that this visit was very different from all the ones that had gone before.

She came to stand in front of him, soft as summer in her white cotton sundress, and touched his arm as she looked up into his face.

"It's time for me to move on," she told him.

*No.*

The word swelled up inside him, but he couldn't say it.

And Kat vanished.

# Chapter Four

Olivia awakened on the following Thursday morning feeling as though she hadn't slept at all the night before, with Ginger's cold muzzle pressed into her neck and the alarm clock buzzing insistently. She stirred, opened her eyes, slapped down the snooze button, with a muttered "Shut *up!*"

Iridescent frost embossed the window glass in intricate fans and swirls, turning it opaque, but the light got through anyway, signaling the arrival of a new day—like it or not.

*Thanksgiving,* Olivia recalled. *The official start of the holiday season.*

She groaned and yanked the covers up over her head.

Ginger let out an impatient little yip.

"I know," Olivia replied from under two quilts and a flannel sheet worn to a delectable, hard-to-leave softness. It was so warm under those covers, so cozy. Would that she could stay right there until sometime after the Second Coming. "I know you need to go outside."

Ginger yipped again, more insistently this time.

Bleary-eyed, Olivia rolled onto her side, tossed back the covers and sat up. She'd slept in gray sweats and heavy socks—less than glamorous attire, for sure, but toasty and loose.

After hitting the stop button on the clock so it wouldn't start up again in five minutes, she stumbled out of the bedroom and down the hall toward the small kitchen at the back of the house. Passing the thermostat, she cranked it up a few degrees. As she groped her way past the coffeemaker, she jabbed blindly at yet another button to start the pot she'd set up the night before. At the door she shoved her feet into an old pair of ugly galoshes and shrugged into a heavy jacket of red-and-black-plaid wool—Big John's chore coat.

It still smelled faintly of his budget aftershave and pipe tobacco.

The weather stripping stuck when she tried to open the back door, and she muttered a four-letter word as she tugged at the knob. The instant there was a crack to pass through, Ginger shot out of that kitchen like a clown dog from a circus cannon. She banged open the screen door beyond, too, without slowing down for the enclosed porch.

"Ginger!" Olivia yelled, startled, before taking one rueful glance back at the coffeemaker. It shook and gurgled like a miniature rocket trying to lift off the counter, and it would take at least ten minutes to produce enough java to get Olivia herself off the launch pad. She needed to buy a new one—item number seventy-two on her domestic to-do list. The timer had given out weeks ago, and the handle on the carafe was loose.

And where the hell was the dog headed? Ginger *never* ran.

Olivia shook the last clinging vestiges of sleep out of her head and tromped through the porch and down the outside steps, taking care not to slip on the ice and either land on her tailbone or take a flyer into the snow-bank beside the walk.

"Ginger!" she called a second time as the dog streaked halfway down the driveway, shinnied under the rail fence between Olivia's place and Tanner's and bounded out into the snowy field.

Goose-stepping it to the fence, Olivia climbed onto the lowest rail and shaded her eyes from the bright, cold sun. What was Ginger chasing? Coyotes? Wolves? Either way, that was a fight an aging golden retriever couldn't possibly win.

Olivia was about to scramble over the fence and run after the dog when she saw the palomino in the distance, and the man sitting tall in the saddle.

Tanner.

The horse moved at a smooth trot while Ginger ca-vorted alongside, flinging up snow, like a pup in a su-perchow commercial.

Olivia sighed, partly out of relief that Ginger wasn't about to tangle with the resident wildlife and partly be-cause Tanner was clearly headed her way.

She looked down at her rumpled sweats; they were clean, but the pants had worn threadbare at the knees and there was a big bleach stain on the front of the shirt. She pulled the front of Big John's coat closed with one hand and ran the other through her uncombed hair.

Tanner's grin flashed as white as the landscape around him when he rode up close to the fence. Despite the grin, he looked pale under his tan, and there was a hollow look in his eyes. The word *haunted* came to mind.

"Mornin', ma'am," he drawled, tugging at the brim of his hat. "Just thought I'd mosey on over and say howdy."

"How very Western of you," Olivia replied with a reluctant chuckle.

Ginger, winded by the unscheduled run, was panting hard.

"What in the world got into you?" Olivia scolded the dog. "Don't you ever do that again!"

Ginger crossed the fence line and slunk toward the house.

When Olivia turned back to Tanner, she caught him looking her over.

Wise guy.

"It would be mighty neighborly of you to offer a poor wayfaring cowboy a hot cup of coffee," he said. He sat that horse as if he was part of it—a point in his favor. He might dress like a dandy, but he was no stranger to a saddle.

"Glad to oblige, mister," Olivia joked, playing along. "Unless you insist on talking like a B-movie wrangler for much longer. That could get old."

He laughed at that, rode to the rickety gate a few yards down the way, leaned to work the latch easily and joined Olivia on her side. Taking in the ramshackle shed and detached garage, he swung down out of the saddle to walk beside her, leading Shiloh by a slack rein.

"Looks to me like you don't have a whole lot of room to talk about the state of my barn," he said. His eyes were twinkling now under the brim of his hat, though he still looked wan.

It was harder going for Olivia—her legs were shorter, the galoshes didn't fit so they stuck at every step, and the snow came to her shins. "I rent this place," she said, feeling defensive. "The owner lives out of state and doesn't like to spend a nickel on repairs if he can help it. In fact, he's been threatening to sell it for years."

"Ah," Tanner said with a sage nod. "Are you just passing through Stone Creek, Doc? I had the impression you were a lifelong resident, but maybe I was wrong."

"Except for college and veterinary school," Olivia answered, "I've lived here all my life." She looked around at the dismal rental property. "Well, not right here—"

"Hey," Tanner said, quietly gruff. "I was kidding."

She nodded, embarrassed because she'd been caught caring what he thought, and led the way through the yard toward the back door.

Tanner left Shiloh loosely tethered to the hand rail next to the porch steps.

Inside the kitchen, Olivia fed a remorseful Ginger, washed her hands at the sink and got two mugs down out of the cupboard. The coffeemaker was just flailing in for a landing, mission accomplished.

"Excuse me for a second, will you?" Olivia asked after filling mugs for herself and Tanner and giving him his. She slipped into the bedroom, closed the door, put down her coffee cup and quickly switched out the chore coat and her sweats for her best pair of jeans and the blue sweater Ashley had knitted for her as a Christmas gift. She even went so far as to splash her face with water in the tiny bathroom, give her teeth a quick brushing and run a comb through her hair.

When she returned to the kitchen, Tanner was sitting in a chair at the table, looking as if he belonged there, and Ginger stood with her head resting on his thigh while he stroked her back.

Something sparked in Tanner's weary eyes when he looked up—maybe amusement, maybe appreciation. Maybe something more complicated.

Olivia felt a wicked little thrill course through her system.

"Thanksgiving," she said without planning to, almost sighing out the word.

"You don't sound all that thankful," Tanner observed.

"Oh, I am," Olivia insisted, taking a sip from her mug.

"Me, too," Tanner said. "Mostly."

She bit her lower lip, stole a glance at the clock above the sink. It was early—two hours before she needed to check in at the clinic. So much for excusing herself to go to work.

"Mostly?" she echoed, keeping her distance.

"There are things I'd change about my life," Tanner told her. "If I could."

She drew nearer then, interested in spite of herself, and sat down, though she kept the width of the table between them. "What would you do differently?"

He sighed, and a bleak expression darkened his eyes. "I'd have kept the business smaller, for one thing," he said. The briefest flicker of pain contorted his face. "Not gone international. How about you?"

"I'd have spent more time with my grandfather," she

replied after giving the question some thought. "I guess I figured he was going to be around forever."

"That was his coat you were wearing before."

"How did you guess that?"

"My grandmother had one just like it. I think they must have sold those at every farm supply store in America, back in the day."

Olivia relaxed a little. "How's Butterpie?"

Tanner sighed, met Olivia's gaze. Held it. "She's not eating," he said.

"I was afraid of that," Olivia murmured, distracted.

"I thought my grandmother was going to live forever, too," Tanner told her.

It took Olivia a moment to catch up. "She's gone, then?"

Tanner nodded. "Died on her seventy-eighth birthday, hoeing the vegetable garden. Just the way she'd have wanted to go—quick, and doing something she loved to do. Your grandfather?"

"Heart attack," Olivia said, running her palms along the thighs of her jeans. Why were they suddenly moist?

Tanner was silent for what seemed like a long time, though it was an easy silence. Then he finished his coffee and stood. "Guess I'd better not keep you," he said, crossing the room to set his cup in the sink.

Ginger's liquid eyes followed him adoringly.

"I'd like to look in on Butterpie on my way into town, if that's okay with you?" Olivia said.

One side of Tanner's fine mouth slanted slightly upward. "Would it stop you if it *wasn't* okay with me?"

She grinned. "Nope."

He chuckled at that. "I've got some things to do in town," he said. "Gotta pick up some wine for Thanksgiving dinner. So if I don't see you in my barn, we'll meet up at Brad and Meg's place later on."

Of *course* her brother and sister-in-law would have invited Tanner to join them for Thanksgiving dinner. He was a friend, and he lived alone. Still, Olivia felt blindsided. Holidays were hard enough without stirring virtual strangers into the mix. Especially *attractive* ones.

"See you then," she said, hoping her smile didn't look forced.

He nodded and left, closing the kitchen door quietly behind him. Olivia immediately went to the window to watch him mount Shiloh and ride off.

When he was out of sight, and only then, Olivia turned from the window and zeroed in on Ginger.

"What were you *thinking,* running off like that? You're not a young dog, you know."

*"I just got a little carried away, that's all,"* Ginger said without lifting her muzzle off her forelegs. Her eyes looked soulful. *"Are you wearing that getup to Thanksgiving dinner?"*

Olivia looked down at her jeans and sweater. "What's wrong with my outfit?" she asked.

*"Touchy, touchy. I was just asking a simple question."*

"These jeans are almost new, and Ashley made the sweater. I look perfectly fine."

*"Whatever you say."*

"Well, what do *you* think I should wear, O fashionista dog?"

*"The sweater's fine,"* Ginger observed. *"But I'd switch out the jeans for a skirt. You* do *have a skirt, don't you?"*

"Yes, I have a skirt. I also have rounds to make before dinner, so I'm changing into my work clothes right now."

Ginger sighed an it's-no-use kind of sigh. *"Paris Hilton you ain't,"* she said, and drifted off to sleep.

Olivia returned to her bedroom, put on her normal grubbies, suitable for barns and pastures, then located her tan faux-suede skirt, rolled it up like a towel and stuffed it into a gym bag. Knee boots and the blue sweater went in next, along with the one pair of panty hose she owned. They had runs in them, but the skirt was long and the boots were high, so it wouldn't matter.

When she got back to the kitchen, Ginger was stretching herself.

"You're coming with me today, aren't you?" Olivia asked.

Ginger eyed the gym bag and sighed again. *"As far as next door, anyway,"* she answered. *"I think Butterpie could use some company."*

"What about Thanksgiving?"

*"Bring me a plate,"* Ginger replied.

Oddly disappointed that Ginger didn't want to spend the holiday with her, Olivia went outside to fire up the Suburban and scrape off the windshield. After she'd lowered the ramp in the back of the rig, she went back to the house for Ginger.

"You're all right, aren't you?" Olivia asked as Ginger walked slowly up the ramp.

*"I'm not used to running through snow up to my chest,"* the dog told her. *"That's all."*

Still troubled, Olivia stowed the ramp and shut the doors on the Suburban. Ginger curled up on Rodney's blanket and closed her eyes.

When they arrived at Tanner's place, his truck was parked in the driveway, but he didn't come out of the house, and Olivia didn't knock on the front door. She repeated the ramp routine, and then she and Ginger headed into the barn.

Shiloh was back in his stall, brushed down and munching on hay.

Olivia paused to greet him, then opened the door to Butterpie's stall so she and Ginger could go in.

Butterpie stood with her head hanging low, but perked up slightly when she saw the dog.

"You've got to eat," Olivia told the pony.

Butterpie tossed her head from side to side, as though in refusal.

Ginger settled herself in a corner of the roomy stall, on a pile of fresh wood shavings, and gave another big sigh. *"Just go make your rounds,"* she said to Olivia. *"I'll get her to take a few bites after you're gone."*

Olivia felt bereft at the prospect of leaving Ginger and the pony. She found an old pan, filled it with water at the spigot outside, returned to set it down on the stall floor. "This is weird," she said to Ginger. "What's Tanner going to think if he finds you in Butterpie's stall?"

*"That you're crazy,"* Ginger answered. *"No real change in his opinion."*

"Very funny," Olivia said, not laughing. Or even smiling. "You're sure you'll be all right? I could come back and pick you up before I head for Stone Creek Ranch."

Ginger shut her eyes and gave an eloquent snore.

After that, there was no point in talking to her.

Olivia gave Butterpie a quick but thorough examination and left.

Tanner bought a half case of the best wine he could find—Stone Creek had only one supermarket, and the liquor store was closed. He should have lied, he thought as he stood at the checkout counter, paying for his purchases. Told Brad he had plans for Thanksgiving.

He was going to feel like an outsider, passing a whole afternoon and part of an evening with somebody else's family.

Better that, though, he supposed, than eating alone in the town's single sit-down restaurant, remembering Thanksgivings of old and missing Kat and Sophie.

Kat.

"Is that good?" the clerk asked.

Distracted, Tanner didn't know what the woman was talking about at first. Then she pointed to the wine. She was very young and very pretty, and she didn't seem to mind working on Thanksgiving when practically everybody else in the western hemisphere was bellying up to a turkey feast someplace.

"I don't know," Tanner said in belated answer to her cordial question. He'd been something of a wine aficionado once, but since he didn't indulge anymore, he'd sort of lost the knack. "I go by the labels, and the price."

The clerk nodded as if what he'd said made a lick of sense, and wished him a happy Thanksgiving.

He wished her the same, picked up the wine box, the six bottles rattling a little inside it, and made for the door.

The dream came back to him, full force, as he was setting the wine on the passenger seat of his truck.

Kat, standing in the aisle of the barn, in that white summer dress, telling him she wouldn't be back.

It was no good telling himself he'd only been dreaming in the first place. He'd held on to those night visits—they'd gotten him through a lot of emotional white water. It had been Kat who'd said he ought to watch his drinking. Kat who'd advised him to accept the Stone

Creek job and oversee it himself instead of sending in somebody else.

Kat who'd insisted the newspapers were wrong; she hadn't been a target—she'd been caught in the cross fire of somebody else's fight. Sophie, she'd sworn, was in no danger.

She'd faded before his eyes like so much thin smoke a couple of nights before. The wrench in his gut had been powerful enough to wake up him up. The dream had stayed with him, though, which was the same as having it over and over again. Last night he'd been unable to sleep at all. He'd paced the dark empty house for a while, then, unable to bear it any longer, he'd gone out to the barn, saddled Shiloh and taken a moonlight ride.

For a while he'd tried to outride what he was feeling—not loss, not sorrow, but a sense of letting go. Of somehow being set free.

He'd *loved* Kat, more than his own life. Why should her going on to wherever dead people went have given him a sense of liberation, even exaltation, rather than sorrow?

The guilt was almost overwhelming. As long as he'd mourned her, she'd seemed closer somehow. Now the worst was over. There had been some kind of profound shift, and he hadn't regained his footing.

They'd been out for hours, he and Shiloh, when he was crossing the field between his place and Olivia's and that dog of hers came racing toward him. He'd have gone home, put Shiloh up with some extra grain for his trouble, taken a shower and fallen into bed if it hadn't been for Ginger and the sight of Olivia standing on the bottom rail of the fence.

She'd been wearing sweats and silly rubber boots and an old man's coat, and for all that, she'd managed to look sexy. He'd finagled an invitation for coffee—hell, he'd flat out invited *himself*—and thought about taking her to bed the whole time he was there.

Not that he would have made a move on Doc. It was way too soon, and she'd probably have conked him over the head with the nearest heavy object, but he'd been tempted, just the same.

Tempted as he'd never been, since Kat.

At home he left the wine in the truck and headed for the barn.

Shiloh was asleep, standing up, the way horses do. When Tanner looked over the stall door at Butterpie, though, his eyes started to sting. Butterpie was lying in the wood shavings, and Olivia's dog was cuddled up right alongside her, as though keeping some kind of a vigil.

"I'll be damned," Tanner muttered. He'd grown up in the country, and he'd known horses to have nonequine companions—cows, cats, dogs and even pygmy goats. But he'd never seen anything quite like this.

He figured he probably should take Ginger home— Olivia might be looking for her—but he couldn't quite bring himself to part the two animals.

"You hungry, girl?" he asked Ginger, thinking what a fine thing it would be to have a dog. The problem was, he moved around too much—job to job, country to country. If he couldn't raise his own daughter, how could he hope to take good care of a mutt?

Ginger made a low sound in her throat and looked up at him with those melty eyes of hers. He made a quick trip into the house for a hunk of cube steak and a bowl of water, and set them both down where she could reach them.

She drank thirstily of the water, nibbled at the steak.

Tanner patted her head. He'd seen her jump into Olivia's Suburban the day before, so she still had some zip in her, despite the gray hairs around her muzzle, but she hadn't gotten over that stall door by herself. Olivia must have left her here, to look after the pony.

When he spotted an old grain pan in the corner, overturned, he knew that was what had happened. She must have found the pan in the junk around the barn, filled it with water and left it so the dog could drink. Then one of the animals, most likely Butterpie, had stepped on the thing and spilled the contents.

He was pondering that sequence of events when his cell phone rang.

Sophie.

"This parade bites," she said without any preamble. "It's cold, and Mary Susan Parker keeps sneezing on me and we're not allowed to get into the minibar in our hotel suite! Ms. Wiggins took the keys away."

Tanner chuckled. "Hello and happy Thanksgiving to you, too, sweetheart," he said, so glad to hear her voice that his eyes started stinging again.

"It's not like we want to drink *booze* or anything," Sophie complained. "But we can't even help ourselves to a soda or a candy bar!"

"Horrible," Tanner commiserated.

An annoyed silence crackled from Sophie's end.

"Butterpie has a new friend," Tanner said, to get the conversation going again. In a way, talking to Sophie made him miss her more, but at the same time he wanted to keep her on the line as long as possible. "A dog named Ginger."

He'd caught Sophie's interest that time. "Really? Is it your dog?"

It was telling, Tanner thought, that Sophie had said "your dog" instead of "our dog." "No. Ginger lives next door. She's just here for a visit."

"I'm lonely, Dad," Sophie said, sounding much younger than her twelve years. She was almost shouting to be heard over a brass band belting out "Santa Claus Is Coming to Town." "Are you lonely, too?"

"Yes," he replied. "But there are worse things than being lonely, Soph."

"Right now I can't think of any. Are you going to be all alone all day?"

Crouching now, Tanner busied himself scratching Ginger's ears. "No. A friend invited me to dinner."

Sophie sighed with apparent relief. "Good. I was afraid you'd nuke one of those frozen TV dinners or something and eat it while you watched some football game. And that would be *pathetic*."

"Far be it from me to be pathetic," Tanner said, but a lump had formed in his throat and his voice came out sounding hoarse. "Anything but that."

"What friend?" Sophie persisted. "What friend are you having dinner with, I mean?"

"Nobody you know."

"A woman?" Was that *hope* he heard in his daughter's voice? "Have you met someone, Dad?"

Damn. It *was* hope. The kid probably fantasized that he'd remarry one day, and she could come home from boarding school for good, and they'd all live happily ever after, with a dog and two cars parked in the same garage every night, like a normal family.

That was never going to happen.

Ginger looked up at him in adoring sympathy when he rubbed his eyes, tired to the bone. His sleepless night was finally catching up with him—or that was what he told himself.

"No," he said. "I haven't met anybody, Soph." Olivia's face filled his mind. "Well, I've met somebody, but I haven't *met* them, if you know what I mean."

Sophie, being Sophie, *did* know what he meant. Exactly.

"But you're dating!"

"No," Tanner said quickly. Bumming a cup of coffee in a woman's kitchen didn't constitute a date, and neither did sitting at the same table with her on Thanksgiving Day. "No. We're just—just friends."

"Oh." Major disappointment. "This whole thing bites!"

"So you said," Tanner replied gently, wanting to soothe his daughter but not having the first clue how to go about it. "Maybe it's your mind-set. Since today's Thanksgiving, why not give gratitude a shot?"

She hung up on him.

He thought about calling her right back, but decided to do it later, after she'd had a little time to calm down, regain her perspective. She was a lucky kid, spending the holiday in New York, watching the famous parade in person, staying in a fancy hotel suite with her friends from school.

"Women," he told Ginger.

She gave a low whine and laid her muzzle on his arm.

He stayed in the barn a while, then went into the house, took a shower, shaved and crashed, asleep before his head hit the pillow.

And Kat did not come to him.

Olivia had stopped by Tanner's barn on the way to Stone Creek Ranch, hoping to persuade Ginger to take a break from horsesitting, but she wouldn't budge.

Arriving at the homeplace, she checked on Rodney,

who seemed content in his stall, then, gym bag in hand, she slipped inside the small bath off the tack room and grabbed a quick, chilly shower. She shimmied into those wretched panty hose, donned the skirt and the blue sweater and the boots, and even applied a little mascara and lip gloss for good measure.

Never let it be said that she'd come to a family dinner looking like a—*veterinarian.*

And the fact that Tanner Quinn was going to be at this shindig had absolutely *nothing* to do with her decision to spruce up.

Starting up the front steps, she had a sudden, poignant memory of Big John standing on that porch, waiting for her to come home from a high school date with Jesse McKettrick. After the dance all the kids had gone to the swimming hole on the Triple M, and splashed and partied until nearly dawn.

Big John had been furious, his face like a thundercloud, his voice dangerously quiet.

He'd given Jesse what-for for keeping his granddaughter out all night, and grounded Olivia for a month.

She'd been outraged, she recalled, smiling sadly. Tearfully informed her angry grandfather that *nothing had happened* between her and Jesse, which was true, if you didn't count necking. Now, of course, she'd have given almost anything to see that temperamental old man again, even if he *was* shaking his finger at her and telling her that in his day, young ladies knew how to behave themselves.

Lord, how she missed him, missed his rants. *Especially* the rants, because they'd been proof positive that he cared what happened to her.

The door opened just then, and Brad stepped out

onto the porch, causing the paper turkey to flutter on its hook behind him.

"Ashley's going to kill me," Olivia said. "I forgot to pick up salads at the deli."

Brad laughed. "There's so much food in there, she'll never know the difference. Now, come on in before we both freeze to death."

Olivia hesitated. Swallowed. Watched as Brad's smile faded.

"What is it?" he asked, coming down the steps.

"Ashley's looking for Mom," she said. She hadn't planned to bring that up that day. It just popped out.

*"What?"*

"She's probably going to announce it at dinner or something," Olivia rushed on. "Is it just me, or do you think this is a bad idea, too?"

"It's a very bad idea," Brad said.

"You know something about Mom, don't you? Something you're keeping from the rest of us." It was a shot in the dark, a wild guess, but it struck the bull's-eye, dead center. She knew that by the grim expression on Brad's famous face.

"I know enough," he replied.

"I shouldn't have brought it up, but I was thinking about Big John, and that led to thinking about Mom, and I remembered what Ashley told me, so—"

"It's okay," Brad said, trying to smile. "Maybe she won't bring it up."

Olivia doubted they could be that lucky. Ashley was an O'Ballivan through and through, and when she got on a kick about something, she had to ride it out to the bitter end. "I could talk to her..."

Brad shook his head, pulled her inside the house. It

was too hot and too crowded and too loud, but Olivia was determined to make the best of the situation, for her family's sake, if not her own.

Big John would have wanted it that way.

She hunted until she found Mac, sitting up in his playpen, and lifted him into her arms. "It smells pretty good in here, big guy," she told him. There was a fragrant fire crackling on the hearth, and Meg had lit some scented candles, and delicious aromas wafted from the direction of the kitchen.

Out of the corner of her eye Olivia spotted Tanner Quinn standing near Brad's baby grand piano, dressed up in a black suit, holding a bottle of water in one hand and trying hard to look as though he was enjoying himself.

Seeing his discomfort took Olivia's mind off her own. Still carrying Mac, she started toward him.

A cell phone went off before she could speak to him—*How the Grinch Stole Christmas*—and Tanner immediately reached into his pocket. Flipped open the phone.

As Olivia watched, she saw the color drain out of his face.

The water bottle slipped, and he caught it before it fell, though barely.

"What's wrong?" Olivia asked.

Mac, perfectly happy a moment before that, threw back his head and wailed for all he was worth.

"My daughter," Tanner said, standing stock-still. "She's gone."

# *Chapter Five*

This was the call Tanner had feared since the day Kat died. Sophie, gone missing—or worse. Now that it had actually happened, he seemed to be frozen where he stood, fighting a crazy compulsion to run in all directions at once.

Olivia handed off the baby to Brad, who'd appeared at her side instantly, and touched Tanner's arm. "What do you mean, she's gone?"

Before he could answer, the cell ran through its little ditty again.

He didn't bother checking the caller ID panel. "Sophie?"

"Jack McCall," his old friend said. "We found Sophie, buddy. She's okay, if a little—make that a lot—disgruntled."

Relief washed over Tanner like a tidal wave, making

him sway on his feet. "She's really all right?" Jack had been there for Tanner when Kat was killed, and if there was a blow coming, he might try to soften it.

Olivia stood looking up at him, waiting, her hand still resting lightly on his arm, fingers squeezing gently.

"She's *fine*," Jack said easily. "Like I said, she's not real happy about being nabbed, though."

"Where was she?" Tanner had to feel around inside his muddled brain for the question, thrust it out with force.

"Grand Central," Jack answered. "She sneaked away from the school group while they were making their way through the crowds after the parade. Fortunately, one of my guys spotted her right away, and tailed her to the station. She was buying a train ticket west."

Coming home. Sophie had been trying to come home.

Brad pulled out the piano bench, and Tanner sat down heavily, tossing his friend a grateful glance.

"Question of the hour," Jack went on. "What do we do now? She swears she'll run away again if we take her back to school, and I believe her. The kid is serious, Tanner."

Tanner let out a long sigh. He felt sick, light-headed, imagining all the things that could have happened to Sophie. And very, very glad when Olivia sat down on the bench beside him, her shoulder touching his. "Can you bring her here?" he asked. "To Stone Creek?"

"I'll come with her as far as Phoenix," Jack said. "I'll have my people there bring her the rest of the way by helicopter. The jet's due in L.A. by six o'clock Pacific time, and it's a government job, high-security south-of-the-border stuff, so I can't get out of the gig."

Tanner glanced sidelong at Olivia. She took his hand and clasped it. "I appreciate this, Jack," he said into the phone, his voice hoarse with emotion. "Send Sophie home."

Olivia smiled at that. Brad let out a sigh, grinned and went back to playing host at a family Thanksgiving dinner, taking his son with him. Folks started milling toward the food, laid out buffet-style in the dining room.

"Ten-four, old buddy," Jack said. "Maybe I'll stop in out there and say hello on my way back from Señorita-ville. Book me a room somewhere, will you? I could do with a few months of R & R."

A few minutes before, Tanner couldn't have imagined laughing, ever again. But he did then. "That would be good," he said, choking up again. "Your being here, I mean. I'll ask around, find you a place to stay."

"Adios, amigo," Jack told him, and rang off.

"Sophie's okay?" Olivia asked softly.

"Until I get my hands on her, she is," Tanner answered.

"Stay right here," Olivia said, rising and taking off for the dining room beyond.

A short time later she was back, carrying two plates. "You need to eat," she informed Tanner.

And that was how they shared Thanksgiving dinner, sitting on Brad O'Ballivan's piano bench, with the living room all to themselves and blessedly quiet. Tanner was surprised to discover that he wasn't just hungry, he was ravenous.

"Feeling better?" Olivia asked when he was finished.

"Yeah," he answered. "But I don't think I'm up to socializing all afternoon."

"Me, either," Olivia confessed. She'd only picked at her food.

"Is there a sick cow somewhere?" Tanner asked, indulging in a slight grin. After the shock Sophie had given him, he was still pretty shaken up. "That would probably serve as an excuse for getting the heck out of here."

"They're all ridiculously healthy today," Olivia said.

Tanner chuckled. "Sorry to hear that," he teased.

She laughed, but the amusement didn't quite get as far as her eyes. Tanner wondered why the holiday made her so uncomfortable, but he didn't figure he knew her well enough to ask. He knew why *he* didn't like them— because the loss of his wife and grandmother stood out in sharp relief against all that merriment. And maybe that was Olivia's reason, too.

"I *am* pretty concerned about Butterpie," she said, as if inspired. "What do you say we steal one of the fifty-eight pumpkin pies lining Meg's kitchen counter and head back to your barn?"

Maybe it was the release of tension. Maybe it was because Olivia looked and smelled so damn good—almost as good as she had that morning, out by the fence and then later on, in her kitchen. Either way, the place he wanted to take her wasn't his barn.

"Okay," he said. "But if you're caught pie-napping, I'll deny being in cahoots with you."

Again that laugh, soft and musical and utterly feminine. It rang in Tanner's brain, then lodged itself square in the center of his heart. "Fair enough," she said.

She took their plates and left again, making for the kitchen.

Tanner found Brad standing by the sideboard in the

big dining room, affably directing traffic between the food and the long table, where there was a lot of happy talk and dish clattering going on.

"Everything okay, buddy?" Brad asked, watching Tanner's face.

"I got a little scare," Tanner answered, shoving a hand through his hair. He knew a number of famous people, and not one of them was as down-home and levelheaded as Brad O'Ballivan. He was a man who had more than enough of everything, and knew it, and lived a comparatively simple life. "Just the same, I need a little alone time."

Brad nodded. Caught sight of Olivia coming out of the kitchen with the purloined pie and small plastic container, stopping to speak to Meg as she passed the crowded table. His gaze swung right back to Tanner. "Alone time, huh?" he asked.

"It's not what you think," Tanner felt compelled to say, feeling some heat rise in his neck.

Brad arched an eyebrow. Regarded him thoughtfully. "You're a good friend," he said. "But I love my sister. Keep that in mind, all right?"

Tanner nodded, liking Brad even more than before. Look out for the womenfolk—it was the cowboy way. "I'll keep it in mind," he replied.

He and Olivia left Stone Creek Ranch at the same time, he in his too-clean red truck, she in that scruffy old Suburban. The drive to Starcross took about fifteen minutes, and Olivia was out of her rig and headed into the barn before he'd parked his pickup.

Butterpie was on her feet, Ginger rising from a stretch when Tanner caught up to Olivia in front of the stall door. Olivia opened the plastic container, revealing leftover turkey.

"Tell Butterpie Sophie's coming home," he said, without intending to say any such thing.

Olivia smiled, inside the stall now, letting Ginger scarf up cold turkey from the container. "I already did," she replied. "That's why Butterpie is up. She could use a little exercise, so let's turn her out in the corral for a while."

Tanner nodded, found a halter and slipped it over Butterpie's head. Led her outside and over to the corral gate, and turned her loose.

Olivia and Ginger stood beside him, watching as the pony looked around, as if baffled to find herself outside in the last blaze of afternoon sunlight and the heretofore pristine snow. The dog barked a couple of times, as if to encourage Butterpie.

Tanner shook his head. Ridiculous, he thought. Dogs didn't *encourage* horses.

He recalled finding Ginger huddled close to Butterpie in the stall earlier in the day. Or *did* they?

Butterpie just stood there for a while, then nuzzled through the snow for some grass.

Whether the little horse had cheered up or not, *he* certainly had. Butterpie hadn't eaten anything since she'd arrived at Starcross Ranch, and now she was ready to graze. He went back into the barn and came out with a flake of hay, tossed it into the corral.

Butterpie nosed it around a bit and began to nibble.

Olivia watched for a few moments, then turned to Tanner and took smug note of the hay stuck to the front of his best suit. "You might be a real cowboy after all," she mused, and that simple statement, much to Tanner's amazement, pleased him almost as much as knowing Sophie was safe with his best friend, Jack McCall.

"Thanks," he said, resting his arms on the top rail of the corral fence and watching Butterpie eat.

When the pony came to the gate, clearly ready to return to the barn, Tanner led her back to her stall and got her settled in. Olivia and Ginger followed, waiting nearby.

"So what happened with Sophie?" Olivia asked when Tanner came out of the stall.

"I'll explain it over coffee and pie," he said, holding his figurative breath for her answer. If Olivia decided to go home, or make rounds or something, he was going to be seriously disappointed.

"This place used to be wonderful," Olivia said, minutes later, when they were in his kitchen, with the coffee brewing and the pie sitting on the table between them.

Tanner wished he'd taken down the old calendar, spackled the holes in the wall from the tacks that had held up its predecessors. Replaced the flooring and all the appliances, and maybe the cupboards, too. The house still looked abandoned, he realized, even with him living in it.

What did *that* mean?

"I'll fix it up," he said. "Sell it before I move on." It was what he always did. Buy a house, keep a careful emotional distance from it, refurbish it and put it on the market, always at a profit.

Something flickered in Olivia's eyes. Seeing that *he'd* seen, she looked away, though not quickly enough.

"Did you know the previous owner well?" he asked, to get her talking again. The sound of her voice soothed him, and right then he needed soothing.

"Of course," she said, turning the little tub of whipped cream, stolen along with the pie and the leftovers for Ginger, in an idle circle on the tabletop. "Clarence was one of Big John's best friends. He was widowed sometime in the mid-nineties—Clarence, I mean—and after that he just lost interest in Starcross." She paused, sighed, a small frown creasing the skin between her eyebrows. "He got rid of the livestock, cow by cow, horse by horse. He stopped doing just about everything." Another break came then. "It's the name, I think."

"The name?"

"Of the ranch," Olivia clarified. "Starcross. It's— sad."

Tanner found himself grinning a little. "What would you call it, Doc?" he asked. The coffee was finished, and he got up to find some cups and pour a dose for both of them.

She considered his question as if there were really a name change in the offing. "Something, well, *happier*," she said as he set the coffee down in front of her, realized they'd need plates and forks for the pie and went back to the cupboards to rustle some up. "More positive and cheerful, I guess, like The Lucky Horseshoe, or The Diamond Spur. Something like that."

Tanner had no intention of giving the ranch a new name—why go to all the trouble when he'd be leaving in a year at the longest?—but he enjoyed listening to Olivia, watching each new expression cross her face. The effect was fascinating.

And oh, that face.

The body under it was pretty spectacular, too.

Tanner shifted uncomfortably in his chair.

"Don't you think those names are a little preten-tious?" he asked, cutting into the pie.

"Corny, maybe," Olivia admitted, smiling softly. "But not pretentious."

He served her a piece of pie, then cut one for himself. Watched with amusement and a strange new tenderness as she spooned on the prepackaged whipped cream. She looked pink around the neck, perhaps a little discomforted because he was staring.

He averted his eyes, but a moment later he was looking again. He couldn't seem to help it.

"You took the first chance you could get to bolt out of that Thanksgiving shindig at your brother's place," he said carefully. "Why is that, Doc?"

"Why do you keep calling me 'Doc'?" She *was* nervous, then. Maybe she sensed that Tanner wanted to kiss her senseless and then take her upstairs to his bed.

"Because you're a doctor?"

"I have a name."

"A very beautiful name."

She grinned, and some of the tension eased, which might or might not have been a good thing. "Get a shovel," she said. "It's getting deep in here."

He laughed, pushed away his pie.

"I should go now," she said, but she looked and sounded uncertain.

*Hallelujah,* Tanner thought. She was tempted, at least.

"Or you could stay," he suggested casually.

She gnawed at her lower lip. "Is it just me?" she asked bluntly. "Or are there sexual vibes bouncing off the walls?"

"There are definitely vibes," he confirmed.

"We haven't even kissed."

"That would be easy to remedy."

"And we've only known each other a few days."

"We're both adults, Olivia."

"I can't just—just go to bed with you, just because I—"

"Just because you want to?"

Challenge flared in her eyes, and she straightened her shoulders. "Who says I want to?"

"Do you?"

"Yes," she said, after a very long time. Then, quickly, "But that doesn't mean I will."

"Of course it doesn't."

"People ought to say no to themselves once in a while," she went on, apparently grasping at moral straws. "This society is way too into instant gratification."

"I promise you," Tanner said drily, "it won't be instant."

Color flooded her face, and he could see her pulse beating hard at the base of her throat.

"When was the last time you made love?" he asked when she didn't say anything. Nor, to his satisfaction, did she jump to her feet and bolt for the door.

Tanner's hopes were rising, and so was something else.

"That's a pretty personal question," she said, sounding miffed. She even went so far as to glance over at the dog, sleeping the sleep of the innocent on the rug in front of the stove.

"I'll tell if you will."

"It's been a while," she admitted loftily. "And maybe I don't *want* to know who you've had sex with and how recently. Did that ever occur to you?"

"A while as in six months to a year, or never?"

"I'm not a virgin, if that's what you're trying to find out."

"Good," he said.

"I'm leaving," she said. But she didn't get up from her chair. She didn't call the dog, or even put down her fork, though she wasn't taking in much pie.

"You're free to do that."

"Of course I am."

"*Or* we could go upstairs, right now."

She swallowed visibly, and her wonderful eyes widened.

Hot damn, she was actually considering it.

Letting herself go. Doing something totally irresponsible, just for the hell of it. Tanner went hard, and he was glad she couldn't see through the tabletop.

"No strings attached?" she asked.

"No strings," Tanner promised, though he felt a little catch inside, saying the words. He wondered at his reaction, but not for long.

He was a man, after all, sitting across a table from one of the loveliest, most confusing women he'd ever met.

"I suppose we're just going to obsess until we do it," Olivia said. Damn, but she was full of surprises. He'd expected her to be talking herself *out* of going to bed with him, not *into* it.

"Probably," Tanner said, very seriously.

"Get it out of the way."

"Out of our systems," Tanner agreed, wanting to keep the ball rolling. Watching for the right time to make his move and all the time asking himself what the hell he was doing.

He stood up.

She stood up. And probably noticed his erection.

Would she run for it after all?

Tanner waited.

She waited.

"Can I kiss you?" he asked finally. "We could decide after that."

"Good idea," Olivia said, but her pulse was still fluttering visibly, at her temple now as well as her throat, and her breathing was quick and shallow, raising and lowering her breasts under that soft blue sweater.

She didn't move, so it fell to Tanner to step in close, take her face in his hands and kiss her, very gently at first, then with tongue.

What was she *doing?* Olivia fretted, even as she stood on tiptoe so Tanner could kiss her more deeply. Sure, it had been a while since she'd had sex—ten months, to be exact, with the last man she'd dated—but it wasn't as if she were *hot to trot* or anything like that.

This...*this* was like storm chasing—venturing too close to a tornado and getting sucked in by the whirlwind. She felt both helpless and all-powerful, standing there in Tanner Quinn's dreary kitchen—helpless because she'd known even before they left Stone Creek Ranch that this would happen, and all-powerful because *damn it,* she wanted it, too.

She wanted hot, sticky, wet *sex.* And she knew Tanner could give it to her.

They kissed until her knees felt weak, and she sagged against Tanner.

Then he lifted her into his arms. "You're sure about this, Doc?"

She swallowed, nodded. "I'm sure."

Ginger raised her head, lowered it again and went back to sleep.

His room was spacious and relatively clean, though he probably hadn't made the bed since he'd moved in. Olivia noted these things with a detached part of her brain, but her elemental, primitive side wanted to rip off her clothes as if they were on fire.

Tanner undressed her slowly, kissing her bare shoulder when he unveiled it, then her upper breast. When he tongued her right nipple, then her left, she gasped and arched her back, wanting more.

He stopped long enough to shed his suit coat and toss aside his tie.

Olivia handled the buttons and buckle and finally the zipper.

And they were both naked.

He kissed her again, eased her down on the side of the bed, knelt on the floor to kiss her belly and her thighs. "Where's the whipped cream when you need it?" he teased, his voice a low rumble against her flesh.

"Oh, God," Olivia said, because she knew what he was going to do, and because she wanted so much for him to do it.

He burrowed through the nest of curls at the apex of her thighs, found her with his mouth, suckled, gently at first, then greedily.

He made a low sound to let her know he was enjoying her, but she barely heard it over the pounding of her heart and the creaking of the bed springs as her hips rose and fell in the ancient dance.

He slid his hands under her, raised her high off the bed and feasted on her in earnest. The first orgasm broke soon after that, shattering and sudden, and so long that Olivia felt as though she were being tossed about on the head of a fiery geyser.

Just when she thought she couldn't bear the pleasure for another moment—or live without it—he allowed her to descend. She marveled at his skill even as she bounced between one smaller, softer climax after another.

At last she landed, sated and dazed, and let out a croony sigh.

She heard the drawer on the bedside stand open and close.

"Still sure?" Tanner asked, shifting his body to reach for what he needed.

She nodded. Gave another sigh. "Oh, very sure," she said.

He turned her on the bed, slipped a pillow under her head and kissed her lightly. She clasped her hands behind his head and pulled him closer, kissed him back.

This part was for him, she thought magnanimously. She'd had her multiclimax—now it was time to be generous, let Tanner enjoy the satisfaction he'd earned.

Oh, God, had he earned it.

Except that when he eased inside her, she was instantly aroused, every cell in her body screaming with need. She couldn't do it; she couldn't come like that a second time without disintegrating—could she?

She was well into the climb, though, and there was no going back.

They shared the next orgasm, and the one after that.

And then they slept.

It was dark in the room when Olivia awakened, panic-stricken, to a strange whuff-whuff-whuff sound permeating the roof of that old house. Tanner was nowhere to be seen.

She flew out of bed, scrambled into her clothes, except for the panty hose, which she tossed into the trash—what *was* that deafening noise?—and dashed down the back stairs into the kitchen. Ginger, on her feet and barking, paused to give her a knowing glance.

"Shut up," Olivia said, hurrying to the window.

Tanner was out there, standing in what appeared to be a floodlight, looking up. Then the helicopter landed, right there in the yard.

Olivia rubbed her eyes hard, but when she looked again, the copter was still there, black and ominous against the snow. The blades slowed and then a young girl got out of the bird, stood still. Tanner stooped as he went toward the child, put an arm around her shoulders and steered her away, toward the house.

He paused when the copter lifted off again, waved.

Sophie had arrived, Olivia realized. And in grand style, too.

"Do I look like I've just had sex?" she asked Ginger in a frantic whisper.

*"I wouldn't know what you look like when you've just had sex,"* Ginger answered. *"I'm a dog, remember?"*

"Before you start yelling at me," Sophie said, looking up at Tanner with Kat's eyes, "can I just say hello to Butterpie?"

Tanner, torn between wishing he believed in spanking kids and a need to hold his daughter safe and close and tight, shoved his hands into the pockets of his leather jacket. "The barn's this way," he said, though it was plainly visible, and started walking.

Sophie shivered as she hurried along beside him. "We could," she said breathlessly, "just dispense with the yelling entirely and go on from there."

"Fat chance," Tanner told her.

"I'm in trouble, huh?"

"What do you think?" Tanner retorted, trying to sound stern. In truth, he was so glad to see Sophie, he hardly trusted himself to talk.

He should have woken Olivia when he got the call from Jack's pilot, he thought. Warned her of Sophie's impending arrival.

As if she could have missed hearing that helicopter.

"I think," Sophie said with the certainty of youth, "I'm really happy to be here, and if you yell at me, I can take it."

Tanner suppressed a chuckle. This was no time to be a pal. "You could have been kidnapped," he said. "The list of things that might have happened to you—"

"*Might* have," Sophie pointed out sagely. "That's the key phrase, Dad. Nothing *did* happen, except one of Uncle Jack's guys collared me at Grand Central. *That* was a tense moment, not to mention embarrassing."

Having made that statement, Sophie dashed ahead of him and into the barn, calling Butterpie's name.

By the time he flipped on the overhead lights, she was already in the stall, hugging the pony's neck.

Butterpie whinnied with what sounded like joy.

And Olivia appeared at Tanner's elbow. "We'll be going now," she said quietly, watching the reunion with a sweet smile. "Ginger and I."

"Wait," Tanner said when she would have turned away. "I want you to meet Sophie."

"This is your time, and Sophie's," Olivia said, standing on tiptoe to kiss his cheek. "Tomorrow, maybe."

It was a simple kiss, nothing compared to the ones they'd shared upstairs in his bedroom. Just the same,

Tanner felt as though he'd stepped on a live wire. His skeleton was probably showing, like in a cartoon.

"Maybe you feel like explaining what I'm doing here at this hour," she reasoned, with a touch of humor lingering on her mouth, "but I don't."

Reluctantly Tanner nodded.

Ginger and Olivia left, without Sophie ever noticing them.

At home, Olivia showered, donned a ragged chenille bathrobe and listened to her voice mail, just in case there was an emergency somewhere. She'd already checked her cell phone, but you never knew.

The only message was from Ashley. "Where *were* you?" her younger sister demanded. "Today was *Thanksgiving!*"

Olivia sighed, waited out the diatribe, then hit the bullet and pressed the eight key twice to connect with Ashley.

"Mountain View Bed-and-Breakfast," Ashley answered tersely. She already knew who was calling, then. Hence the tone.

"Any openings?" Olivia asked, hoping to introduce a light note.

Ashley wasn't biting. She repeated her voice mail message, almost verbatim, ending with another "Where were you?"

"There was an emergency," Olivia said. What else could she say? *I was in bed with Tanner Quinn and I had myself a hell of a fine time, thank you very much.*

Suspicion, tempered by the knowledge that emergencies were a way of life with Olivia. "What kind of emergency?"

Olivia sighed. "You don't want to know," she said. It was true, after all. Ashley was a normal, healthy woman, but that didn't mean she'd want a blow-by-blow description—so to speak—of what she and Tanner had done in his bed.

"Another cow appendectomy?" Ashley asked, half sarcastic, half uncertain.

"A clandestine operation," she said, remembering the black helicopter. *That* would give the local conspiracy theorists something to chew on for a while, if they'd seen it.

"Really? There was an operation?"

Tanner was certainly an operator, Olivia thought, so she said yes.

"And here I thought you were probably having sex with that contractor Brad hired to build the shelter," Ashley said with an exasperated little sigh.

Olivia swallowed a giggle. Spoke seriously. "Ashley O'Ballivan, why would you think a thing like that?"

"Because I saw you leave with him," Ashley answered. Her tone turned huffy again. "I wanted to tell Brad and Melissa that I've decided to look for Mom," she complained. "And I couldn't do it without you there."

Olivia sobered. "Pretty heavy stuff, when Brad and Meg had a houseful of guests, wouldn't you say?"

Ashley went quiet again.

"Ash?" Olivia prompted. "Are you still there?"

"I'm here."

"So why the sudden silence?"

Another pause. A long one that gave Olivia plenty of time to worry. Then, finally, the bomb dropped. "I think I've already found her."

## *Chapter Six*

"This place," Sophie said, looking around at the ranch-house kitchen the next morning, "needs a woman's touch. Or maybe a crack decorating crew from HGTV or DIY."

Tanner, still half-asleep, stood at the counter pouring badly needed coffee. Between Sophie's great adventure and all that sex with Olivia, he felt disoriented, out of step with his normal world. "You watch HGTV and DIY?" he asked after taking a sip of java to steady himself.

"Doesn't everybody?" Sophie countered. "I've been thinking of flipping houses when I grow up." She looked so much like her mother, with her long, shiny hair and expressive eyes. Right now those eyes held a mixture of trepidation, exuberance and sturdy common sense.

"Trust me," Tanner said, treading carefully, finding

his way over uncertain ground, because they weren't really talking about real estate and he knew it. "Flipping houses is harder than a thirty-minute TV show makes it seem."

"You should know," Sophie agreed airily, taking in the pitiful kitchen again. "You'll manage to turn this one over for a big profit, though, just like all the others."

Tanner dragged a chair back from the table and sort of fell into it. "Sit down, Soph," he said. "We've got more important things to discuss than the lineup on your favorite TV channels."

Sophie crossed the room dramatically and dropped into a chair of her own. She'd had the pajamas she was wearing now stashed in her backpack, which showed she'd been planning to ditch the school group in New York, probably before she left Briarwood. Now she was playing it cool.

Tanner thought of Ms. Wiggins's plans to steer her into the thespian program at school, and stifled a grimace. His sister, Tessa, had been a show-business kid, discovered when she did some catalog modeling in Dallas at the age of eight. She'd done commercials, guest roles and finally joined a long-running hit TV series. As far as he was concerned, that had been the wrong road. It was as though Tessa—wonderful, smart, beautiful Tessa—had peaked at twenty-one, and been on a downhill slide ever since.

"You're mad because I ran away," Sophie said, sitting up very straight, like a witness taking the stand. She seemed to think good posture might sway the judge to decide in her favor. In any case, she was still acting.

"Mad as hell," Tanner agreed. "That was a stupid,

dangerous thing to do, and don't think you're going to get away with it just because I'm so glad to see you."

The small face brightened. "*Are* you glad to see me, Dad?"

"Sophie, of course I am. I'm your father. I miss you a lot when we're apart."

She sighed and shut off the drama switch. Or at least dimmed it a little. "Most of the time," she said, "I feel like one of those cardboard statues."

Tanner frowned, confused. "Run that by me again?"

"You know, those life-size depictions you see in the video store sometimes? Johnny Depp, dressed up like Captain Jack, or Kevin Costner like Wyatt Earp, or something like that?"

Tanner nodded, but he was still pretty confounded. There was nothing two-dimensional about Sophie—she was 3-D all the way.

But did she know that?

"It's as if I'm made of cardboard as far as you're concerned," she went on thoughtfully. "When I'm around, great. When I'm not, you just tuck me away in a closet to gather dust until you want to get me out again."

Tanner's gut clenched, hard. And his throat went tight. "Soph—"

"I know you don't really think of me that way, Dad," his daughter broke in, imparting her woman-child wisdom. "But it *feels* as if you do. That's all I'm saying."

"And I'm saying I don't want you to feel that way, Soph. Ever. All I'm doing is trying to keep you safe."

"I'd rather be happy."

Another whammy. Tanner got up, emptied his cup at the sink and nonsensically filled it up again. Stood with his back to the counter, leaning a little, watching his daughter and wondering if all twelve-year-olds were as complicated as she was.

"You'll understand when you're older," he ventured.

"I understand *now*," Sophie pressed, and she looked completely convinced. "You're the bravest man I know—you were Special Forces in the military, with Uncle Jack—but you're scared, too. You're scared I'll get hurt because of what happened to Mom."

"You can't possibly remember that very well."

Benevolent contempt. "I was *seven*, Dad. Not two." She paused, and her eyes darkened with pain. "It was awful. I kept thinking, *This can't be real, my mom can't be gone,* but she was."

Tanner went to his daughter, laid a hand on top of her head, too choked up to speak.

Sophie twisted slightly in the chair, so she could look up at him. "Here's the thing, Dad. Bad things happen to people. Good people, like you and me and Mom. You have to cry a lot, and feel really bad, because you can't help it, it hurts so much. But then you've got to go on. Mom wouldn't want us living apart like we do. I *know* she wouldn't."

He thought of the last dream-visit from Kat, and once again felt a cautious sense of peace rather than the grief he kept expecting to hit him. He also recalled the way he'd abandoned himself in Olivia's arms the day before, in his bed, and a stab of guilt pricked his conscience, small and needle sharp.

"Your mother," he said firmly, "would want what's best for you. And that's getting a first-rate education in a place where you can't be hurt."

"Get real, Dad," Sophie scoffed. "I could get hurt *anywhere,* including Briarwood."

Regrettably, that was true, but it was a whole lot less likely in a place he'd designed himself. The school was a fortress.

Or was it, as Sophie had said more than once, a prison?

You had to take the good with the bad, he decided.

"You're going back to Briarwood, kiddo," he said.

Sophie's face fell. "I could be a big help around here," she told him.

The desperation in her voice bruised him on the inside, but he had to stand firm. The stakes were too high.

"Can't I just stay until New Year's?" she pleaded.

Tanner sighed. "Okay," he said. "New Year's. Then you *have to go back.*"

"What about Butterpie?" Sophie asked, always one to press an advantage, however small. "Admit it. She hasn't been doing very well without me."

"She can go with you," Tanner said, deciding the matter as the words came out of his mouth. "It's time Briarwood had a stable, anyway. Ms. Wiggins has been hinting for donations for the last year."

"I guess that's better than a kick in the pants," Sophie said philosophically. Where did she *get* this stuff?

In spite of himself, Tanner laughed. "It's my best offer, shorty," he said. "Take it or leave it."

"I'll take it," Sophie said, being nobody's fool. "But that doesn't mean I won't try to change your mind in the meantime."

Tanner opened the refrigerator door, ferreted around for the makings of a simple breakfast. If he hadn't been so busy rolling around in the sack with Olivia yesterday afternoon, he thought, he'd have gone to the grocery store. Stocked up on kid food.

Whatever that was.

"Try all you want," he said. "My mind is made up. Go get dressed while I throw together an omelet."

"Yes, sir!" Sophie teased, standing and executing a pretty passable salute. She raced up the back stairs, presumably to rummage through her backpack, the one piece of luggage she'd brought along, for clothes. Tanner simultaneously cracked eggs and juggled the cordless phone to call Tessa.

His sister answered on the third ring, and she sounded disconsolate but game. "Hello, Tanner," she said.

No matter how she felt, Tessa always tried to be a good sport and carry on. It was a trait they shared, actually, a direct dispensation from their unsinkable grandmother, Lottie Quinn.

"Hey," he responded, whipping the eggs with a fork, since he hadn't bothered to ship his kitchen gear to Stone Creek and there was no whisk. He was going to have to go shopping, he realized, for groceries, for household stuff and for all the things Sophie would need.

*Shopping,* on the busiest day of the retail year.

The thought did not appeal.

"How's Sophie?" Tessa asked, with such immediacy that for a moment Tanner thought she knew about the Great Escape. Then he realized that Tessa worried about the kid as much as he did. She disapproved of Briarwood, referring to him as an "absentee father," which never failed to get under his hide and nettle like a thorn. But she worried.

"She's here for Christmas," he said, as though he'd planned things to turn out that way. They'd need a tree, too, and lights, he reflected with half his mind, and all sorts of those hangy gewgaws to festoon the branches. Things were getting out of hand, fast, now that Hurricane Sophie had made landfall. "Why don't you join us?"

"Nobody to watch the horses," Tessa replied.

"You okay?" Tanner asked, knowing she wasn't and wishing there was one damned thing he could do about it besides wait and hope she'd tell him if she needed help. There were probably plenty of people to look after Tessa's beloved horses—most of her friends were equine fanatics, after all—but she didn't like to ask for a hand.

Another joint inheritance from Lottie Quinn.

"Getting divorced is a bummer any time of year," she said. "Over the holidays it's a *mega*bummer. Everywhere I turn, I hear "Have Yourself a Merry Little Christmas," or something equally depressing."

Tanner turned on the gas under a skillet and dobbed in some butter, recalling the first Christmas after Kat's death. He'd left Sophie with Tessa, checked in to a hotel and gone on a bourbon binge.

Not one of his finer moments.

When he'd sobered up, he'd sworn off the bottle and stuck to it.

"Look, Tess," he said gruffly. "Call one of those horse transport outfits and send the hay-burners out here. I've got a barn." Yeah, one that was falling down around his ears, he thought, but he owned a construction company. He could call in the crew early, the one he'd scheduled for Monday, pay them overtime for working the holiday weekend. "This is a big house, so there's plenty of room. And Sophie says the place needs a woman's touch."

Tess was quiet. "Feeling sorry for your kid sister, huh?"

"A little," Tanner said. "You're going through a tough time, and I hate that. But maybe getting away for a while would do you some good. Besides, I could use the help."

She laughed, and though it was a mere echo of the old, rich sound, it was still better than the brave resignation he'd heard in Tessa's voice up till then. "Sophie's still a handful, then."

"Sophie," Tanner said, "is a typhoon, followed by a tidal wave, followed by—"

"You haven't met anybody yet?"

Tanner wasn't going anywhere near that one—not yet, anyway. Sure, he'd gone to bed with one very pretty veterinarian, but they'd both agreed on the no-strings rule. "You never know what might happen," he said, too heartily, hedging.

Another pause, this one thoughtful. "I can't really afford to travel right now, Tanner. Especially not with six horses."

The eggs sizzled in the pan. Since he'd forgotten to put in chopped onions—did he even *have* an onion?— he decided he and Sophie would be having scrambled eggs for breakfast, instead of an omelet. "I can make a transfer from my account to yours, on my laptop," he said. "And I'm going to do that, Tess, whether you agree to come out to Arizona or not."

"It's hard being here," Tessa confessed bleakly. That was when he knew she was wavering. "The fight is wearing me out. Lawyers are coming out of the woodwork. I'm not even sure I want this place anymore." A short silence. Tanner knew Tess was grappling with that formidable pride of hers. "I could really bring the horses?"

"Sure," he said. "I'll make the arrangements."

"I'd rather handle that myself," Tessa said. He could tell she was trying not to cry. Once they were off the phone, she'd let the tears come. All by herself in that big Kentucky farmhouse that wasn't a home anymore. "Thanks, Tanner. As brothers go, you're not half-bad."

He chuckled. "Thanks." He was about to offer to line up one of Jack McCall's jets to bring her west, but he decided that would be pushing it. Tessa was nothing if not self-reliant, and she might balk at coming to Stone Creek at all if he didn't let her make at least some of the decisions.

Sophie clattered into the kitchen, wearing yesterday's jeans, funky boots with fake fur around the tops and a heavy cable-knit sweater. Her face shone from scrubbing, and she'd pulled her hair back in a ponytail.

"Talk to Hurricane Sophie for a minute, will you?" he asked, to give his sister a chance to collect herself. "I'm about to burn the eggs."

"Aunt Tessa?" Sophie crowed into the phone. "I'm at Dad's new place, and it's way awesome, even if it is a wreck. The wallpaper's peeling in my room, and my ceiling sags…"

Tanner rolled his eyes and set about rescuing breakfast.

"*Serious* shopping is required," Sophie went on, after listening to Tess for a few seconds. Or, more properly, waiting for her aunt to shut up so she could talk again. "But first I want to ride Butterpie. Dad's going to let me take her back to school—"

Tanner tuned out the conversation, making toast and a mental grocery list at the same time.

"When will you get here?" Sophie asked excitedly.

Tanner tuned back in. He'd forgotten to ask that question while he was on the phone with Tessa.

"You'll get here when you get here," Sophie repeated after a few beats, smiling. "Before Christmas, though, right?" Catching Tanner's eye, Sophie nodded. "Keep us updated... I love you, too... I'll tell him—bye."

Tanner lobbed partially cold eggs onto plates. "No ETA for Aunt Tessa?" he asked. He set the food on the table and then went to the counter to boot up his laptop. As soon as he'd eaten, he'd pipe some cash into his sister's depleted bank account.

"She loves you." Sophie's eyes danced with anticipation. "She said she's got some stuff to do before she comes to Arizona, but she'll definitely be here before Christmas."

Tanner sat down and ate, but his brain was so busy, he barely tasted the eggs and toast. Which was probably good, since he wasn't the best cook in this or any other solar system. Then again, he wasn't the worst, either.

"You know what I want for Christmas?" Sophie asked, half an hour later as she washed dishes at the old-fashioned sink and Tanner sat at the table, tapping at the keyboard on his laptop. "And don't say, 'Your two front teeth,' either, because that would be a *really* lame joke."

Tanner grinned. "Okay, I won't," he said with mock resignation. "What do you want for Christmas?"

"I want you and me and Aunt Tessa to live here forever," she said. "Like a family. An aunt isn't the same as a mom, but we're all blood, the three of us. It could work."

Tanner's fingers froze in midtap. "Honey," he said quietly, "Aunt Tessa's young. She'll get married again eventually, and have a family of her own, just like you will when you grow up."

"I want to have a family *now*," Sophie said stubbornly. "I've been waiting long enough." With that, she turned back to the sink, rattling the dishes around, and her spine was rigid.

Tanner closed his eyes for a long moment, then forced himself to concentrate on the task at hand—transferring a chunk of money to Tessa's bank account.

He'd think about the mess he was in later.

Olivia might have driven right past Starcross Ranch on her way to town if Ginger hadn't insisted that they stop and look in on Butterpie. In the cold light of a new day, Olivia wasn't eager to face Tanner Quinn.

Last night's wanton hussy had given way to *today's* embarrassed Goody Two-shoes.

And there were other things on her mind, too, most notably Ashley's statement on the phone the night before, that she thought she'd found their mother. No matter how Olivia had prodded, her sister had refused to give up any more information.

Olivia had already called the clinic, and she had a light caseload for the day, since another vet was on call. Normally that would have been a relief—she could buy groceries, get her hair trimmed, do some laundry. But she needed to check on Rodney, and Butterpie wasn't out of the woods yet, either. Yes, Sophie was home, so the pony would be ecstatic.

For as long as Tanner allowed his daughter to stay, that is.

For all Olivia knew, he was already making plans to shuttle the poor kid back to boarding school in a black helicopter.

And that thought led full circle back to her mother.

Had Ashley actually found Delia O'Ballivan—the *real* Delia O'Ballivan, not some ringer hoping to cash in on Brad's fame and fortune?

Olivia's feelings on that score were decidedly mixed. She'd dreamed of a reunion with her lost mother, just as Ashley and Melissa had, and Brad, too, at least when he was younger. They'd all been bereft when Delia left, especially since their father had died so soon afterward.

If she hadn't been driving, Olivia would have closed her eyes against that memory. She'd been there, the tomboy child, always on horseback, riding with her dad after some stray cattle, when the lightning struck, killing both him and his horse instantly.

She'd jumped off her own panicked mount and run to her dad, kneeling beside him in the dirt while a warm rain pelted down on all of them. She'd screamed—and screamed—and screamed.

Screamed until her throat was raw, until Big John came racing out into the field in his old truck.

For a long time she'd thought he'd heard her cries all the way from the house, the better part of a mile away. Later, weeks after the funeral, when the numbness was just beginning to subside, she'd realized he'd been passing on the road, and had seen that bolt of lightning jag down out of the sky. Seen his own son killed, come running and stumbling to kneel in the pounding rain, just as Olivia had, gathering his grown boy into his strong rancher's arms, and rocking him.

*No,* Big John had wailed, over and over again, his craggy face awash with tears and rain. *No!*

All these years later Olivia could still hear those cries, and they still tore holes in her heart.

Tears washed her own cheeks.

Ginger, seated on the passenger side of the Suburban as usual, leaned over to nudge Olivia's shoulder.

Olivia sniffled, straightened her shoulders and dashed her face dry with the back of one hand. Her father's death had made the local and regional news, and for a while Olivia had hoped her mother would see the reports, on television or in a newspaper, realize how badly her family needed her and come home.

But Delia *hadn't* come home. Either she'd never learned that her ex-husband, the man to whom she'd borne four children, was dead, or she simply hadn't cared enough to spring for a bus ticket.

Fantasizing about her return had been one thing, though, and knowing it might *actually happen* was another.

She sucked in a deep breath and blew it out hard, making her bangs dance against her forehead.

Maybe Delia, if she *was* Delia, still wouldn't want to come home. That would be a blow to Ashley, starry-eyed optimist that she was. Ashley lived in a Thomas Kinkade sort of world, full of lighted stone cottages and bridges over untroubled waters.

The snow was melting, but the ground was frozen hard, and the Suburban bumped and jostled as Olivia drove up Tanner's driveway. She stopped the rig, intending to stay only a few minutes, and got out. Ginger jumped after her without waiting to use the ramp.

The barn, alas, was empty. Shiloh's and Butterpie's stall doors stood open. Tanner and Sophie must have gone out riding, which should have been a relief—now she would have a little more time before she had to face him—but wasn't. For some reason she didn't want to examine too closely, nervous as she was, she'd been looking forward to seeing Tanner.

She came out of the barn, scanned the fields, saw them far off in the distance, two small figures on horseback. She hesitated only a few moments, then summoned Ginger and headed for the Suburban. She was about to climb behind the wheel when she noticed that the dog had stayed behind.

"You coming?" she called, her voice a little shaky.

*"I'll stay here for a while,"* Ginger answered without turning around. She was gazing off toward Sophie and Tanner.

Olivia swallowed an achy, inexplicable lump. "Don't go chasing after them, okay? Wait on the porch or something."

Ginger didn't offer a reply, or turn around. But she didn't streak off across the field as she had the morning before, either. Short of forcing the animal into the truck, Olivia didn't know what else to do besides leave.

Her first stop was Stone Creek Ranch. As she had at Starcross, she avoided the house and made for the barn. With luck, she wouldn't run into Brad, and have to go into all her concerns about Ashley's mother search.

Luck wasn't with her. Brad O'Ballivan, the world-famous, multi-Grammy-winning singer, was mucking out stalls, the reindeer tagging at his heels like a faithful hound as he worked.

He stopped, leaned on his pitchfork and offered a lopsided grin as Olivia approached, though his eyes were troubled.

"I see Rodney's getting along all right," Olivia said, her voice swelling, strangely thick, in her throat, and nearly cutting off her breath.

Brad gave a solemn nod. Tried for another grin and missed. "I'll have a blue Christmas if Santa comes to reclaim this little guy," he said. "I've gotten attached."

Olivia managed a smile, tried to catch it when it slipped off her mouth by biting her lower lip, and failed. "Why the sad face, cowboy?"

"I was about to ask you the same question—sans the cowboy part."

"Ashley thinks she found Mom," Olivia said.

Brad nodded glumly, set the pitchfork aside, leaning it against the stable wall. Crouched to pet Rodney for a while before steering him back into his stall and shutting the door.

"I guess the time has come to talk about this," Brad said. "Pull up a bale of hay and sit down."

Olivia sat, but it felt more like sinking. Bits of hay poked her through the thighs of her jeans. All the starch, as Big John used to say, had gone out of her knees.

Brad sat across from her, studied her face and said—nothing.

"Where are Meg and Mac?" Olivia asked.

"Mac's with his grandma McKettrick," Brad answered. "Meg's shopping with Sierra and some of the others."

Olivia nodded. Knotted her hands together in her

lap. "Brad, talk to me. Tell me what you know about Mom—because you know *something*. I can tell."

"She's alive," Brad said.

Olivia stared at him, astonished, and angry, too. "And you didn't think the rest of us might be interested in that little tidbit of information?"

"She's a drunk, Livie," Brad told her, holding her gaze steadily. He looked as miserable as Olivia felt. "I tried to help her—she wouldn't be helped. When she calls, I still cut her a check—against my better judgment."

Olivia actually felt the barn sway around her. She had to lean forward and put her head between her knees and tell herself to breathe slowly.

Brad's hand came to rest on her shoulder.

She shook it off. *"Don't!"*

"Liv, our mother is not a person you'd want to know," Brad said quietly. "This isn't going to turn out like one of those TV movies, where everybody talks things through and figures out that it's all been one big, tragic misunderstanding. Mom left because she didn't want to be married, and she sure as hell didn't want to raise four kids. And there's no evidence that she's changed, except for the worse."

Olivia lifted her head. The barn stopped spinning like the globe Big John used to keep in his study. What had happened to that globe?

"What's she like?"

"I told you, Liv—she's a drunk."

"She's got to be more than that. The worst drunk in the world is more than just a drunk...."

Brad sighed, intertwined his fingers, let his hands fall between his knees. The look in his eyes made Olivia ache. "She's pretty, in a faded-rose sort of way. Too thin, because she doesn't eat. Her hair's blond, but not shiny and thick like it was when we knew her before. She's—hard, Olivia."

"How long have you been in touch with her?"

"I'm not 'in touch' with her," Brad answered gently, though his tone was gruff. "She called my manager a few years ago, told him she was my mother, and when Phil passed the word on to me, I went to see her. She didn't ask about Dad, or Big John, or any of you. She wanted to—" He stopped, looked away, his head slightly bowed under whatever he was remembering about that pilgrimage.

"Cash in on being Brad O'Ballivan's mother?" Olivia supplied.

"Something like that," Brad replied, meeting Olivia's eyes again, though it obviously wasn't easy. "She's bad news, Liv. But she won't come back to Stone Creek—not even if it means having a ticket to ride the gravy train. She flat out doesn't want anything to do with this place, or with us."

"Why?"

"Damn, Liv. Do you think I know the answer to that any better than you do? This has been harder on you and the twins—I realize that. Girls need a mother. But there were plenty of times when I could have used one, too."

Olivia reached out, touched her brother's arm. He'd had a hard time, especially after their dad was killed. He and Big John had butted heads constantly, mostly because they were so much alike—strong, stubborn, proud to a fault. And they'd been estranged after Brad ran off to Nashville and stayed there.

Oh, Brad had visited a few times over the years. But

he'd always left again, over Big John's protests, and then the heart attack came, and it was too late.

"Are you thinking about Big John?" he asked.

It was uncanny, the way he could see into her head sometimes. "Yeah," she said. "His opinion of Delia was even lower than yours. He'd probably have stood at the door with a shotgun if she'd showed her face in Stone Creek."

"The door? He'd have been up at the gate, standing on the cattle guard," Brad answered with a slight shake of his head. "Liv, what are we going to do about Ashley? I think Melissa's levelheaded enough to deal with this. But Ash is in for a shock here. A pretty bad one."

"Is there something else you aren't telling me?"

Brad held up his right hand, as if to give an oath. "I've told you the whole ugly truth, insofar as I know it."

"I'll talk to Ashley," she said.

"Good luck," Brad said.

Olivia started to stand, planning to leave, but Brad stopped her by laying a hand on her shoulder.

"Hold on a second," he told her. "There *is* one more thing I need to say."

Olivia waited, wide-eyed and a little alarmed.

He drew a deep breath, let it out as a reluctant sigh. "About Tanner Quinn," he began.

Olivia stiffened. Brad could not possibly know what had happened between her and Tanner—could he? He wasn't *that* perceptive.

"What about him?"

"He's a decent guy, Liv," Brad told her. "But—"

"But?"

"Did he tell you about his wife? How she died?"

Olivia shook her head, wondering if Brad was about

to say the circumstances had been suspicious, like in one of those reality crime shows on cable TV.

"Her name was Katherine," Brad said. "He called her Kat. He won the bid on a construction job in a place where, let's just say, Americans aren't exactly welcome. It was a dangerous project, but there were millions at stake, so he agreed. One day the two of them went to one of those open-air markets—a souk I think they call it. Tanner stopped to look at something, and Kat either didn't notice or didn't wait for him. When she reached the street..." Brad paused, his eyes as haunted as if he'd been there himself. "Somebody strafed the market with some kind of automatic weapon. Kat was hit I don't know how many times, and she died in Tanner's arms, on the sidewalk."

Olivia put a hand over her mouth. Squeezed her eyes shut.

"I know," Brad muttered. "It's awful even to imagine it. I met him a couple of years after it happened." He stopped. Sighed again. "The only reason I told you was, well, I've seen Tanner go through a lot of women, Liv. He can't—or won't—commit. Not to a woman, not to his daughter. He never stays in one place any longer than absolutely necessary. It's as if he thinks he's a target."

Olivia knew Brad was right. She had only to look at Sophie, forced to take drastic measures just to visit her father over the holidays, to see the truth.

"Why the warning?" she asked.

Brad leaned forward, clunked his forehead briefly against hers. "I know the signs, little sister," he answered. "I know the signs."

# Chapter Seven

After leaving Stone Creek Ranch, the conversation with Brad draping her mind and heart like a lead net, Olivia stopped off at the clinic in town, just in case she might be needed.

She wasn't, actually, and that was kind of deflating. As the on-call vet for the current twenty-four-hour time slot, she could be sent anywhere in the county, at any moment. But today all was quiet on the Western front, so to speak.

She headed for Ashley's, fully intending to bite the mother bullet, but her sister's silly yellow car, usually parked in the driveway at that time of morning after a routine run to the post office, was gone. Crews of local college kids, home on vacation, swarmed the snowy front yard, though, bedecking every shrub and window and eave with holiday lights.

Olivia was momentarily reminded of Snoopy and his

decorated doghouse in the cartoon Christmas special she'd watched faithfully since she was three years old. The image cheered her a little.

"Commercial dog," she muttered, though Ashley didn't qualify for the term species-wise, waving to the light crew before pulling away from the curb again.

She ought to see if she could swing a haircut, she thought, cruising the slush-crusty main street of Stone Creek. Every street lamp and every store window was decorated, colored bulbs blinking the requisite bright red and green.

The Christmas-tree man had set up for business down by the supermarket—a new guy this year, she'd heard—and a plump Santa was already holding court in a spiffy-looking black sleigh with holly leaves and berries decorating its graceful lines. Its brass runners gleamed authentically, and eight life-size plastic reindeer had been hitched to the thing with a jingle-bell harness.

Olivia pulled into the lot—before she saw Tanner's red truck parked among other vehicles. She should have noticed it, she thought—it was the only clean one. She shifted into reverse, but it was too late.

Tanner, delectable in jeans and a black leather jacket, caught sight of her and waved. His young daughter, she of the dramatic helicopter arrival, stood beside him, clapping mittened hands together to keep warm as she inspected a tall, lush tree.

Annoyed by her own reticence, Olivia sighed, pulled into one of the few remaining parking spots and shut off the Suburban.

"Hey," Tanner said as she approached, working hard to smile.

Sophie was a very beautiful child—a Christmas angel in ordinary clothes. She probably looked just like her mother, the woman who had died so tragically, in Tanner's arms, no less. The one he'd loved too much to ever forget, according to Brad.

While they were making love the day before, had Tanner been pretending Olivia was Katherine?

Olivia blushed. Amped up her smile.

"Olivia O'Ballivan," Tanner said quietly, his eyes watchful, even a little pensive as he studied her face, "meet my daughter, Sophie."

Sophie turned, smiled and put out a hand. "Hello," she said. "Dad says you're a veterinarian, and you took care of Butterpie. Thank you."

Something melted, in a far and usually inaccessible corner of Olivia's heart. "You're welcome," she answered brightly. "And so is Butterpie."

"What do you think of this tree?" Sophie asked next, turning to the massive, fragrant blue spruce she'd been examining when Olivia drove in.

Olivia's gaze slid to Tanner's face, sprang away again. "It's—it's lovely," she said.

"Ho! Ho! Ho!" bellowed the hired Santa Claus. Apparently the guy hadn't heard that the line was now considered offensive to women.

"Would you believe this place is run by a man named Kris Kringle?" Sophie said to Olivia, drawing her in somehow, making her feel included, as though they couldn't buy the tree unless she approved of it.

Tanner nudged Sophie's shoulder with a light motion of one elbow. "It's an alias, kid," he said out of the side of his mouth in a pretty respectable imitation of an old-time gangster.

"Duh," Sophie said, but she beamed up at her father, her face aglow with adoration. "And I thought he was *really* Santa Claus."

"Go get Mr. Kringle, so we can wrap this deal up," Tanner told her.

Did he see, Olivia wondered, how much the child loved him? How much she needed him?

Sophie hurried off to find the proprietor.

"I take it Sophie will be around for Christmas," Olivia ventured.

"Until New Year's," Tanner said with a nod. "Then she goes straight back to Connecticut. Butterpie's going along—he'll board in a stable near the school until Briarwood's is built—so you won't have to worry about a depressed horse."

Olivia's throat thickened. All her emotions were close to the surface, she supposed because of the holidays and the situation with her mother, which might well morph into a Situation, and the knowledge that all good things seemed to be temporary.

"I'll miss Butterpie," she managed, shoving her cold hands into the pockets of her old down vest. It was silly to draw comparisons between her own issues and Sophie's, but she couldn't seem to help it. She was entangled.

"I'll miss Sophie," Tanner said.

Olivia wanted to beat at his chest with her fists, which just went to prove she needed therapy. *She needs you!* she wanted to scream. *Don't you see that you're all she has?*

Patently none of her business. She pretended an interest in a small potted tree nearby, a Charlie Brown-ish one that suited her mood. Right then and there she decided to buy it, take it home and toss some lights onto it.

It was an act of mercy.

"Olivia—" Tanner began, and his tone boded something serious, but before he could get the rest of the sentence out of his mouth, Sophie was back with Kris Kringle.

Olivia very nearly didn't believe what she was seeing. The man wore ordinary clothes—quilted snow pants, a heavy plaid flannel shirt, a blue down vest and a Fargo hat with earflaps. But he had a full white beard and kind—okay, *twinkly*—blue eyes. Round red cheeks, and a bow of a mouth.

"A fine choice indeed," he told Olivia, noting her proximity to the pathetic little tree no one else was likely to buy. Only the thought of it, sitting forgotten on the lot when Christmas arrived, amid a carpet of dried-out pine needles, kept her from changing her mind. "I could tie on some branches for you with twine. Thicken it up a little."

Olivia shook her head, rummaged in her pocket for money, being very careful not to look at Tanner and wondering why she felt the need to do that. "It's fine the way it is. How much?"

Kringle named a figure, and Olivia forked over the funds. She felt stupid, being so protective of a tree, and she didn't even own any decorations, but Charlie Brown was going home with her anyway. They'd just have to make the best of things.

"Dad told me you found a real reindeer," Sophie said to Olivia when she would have grabbed her tree, said goodbye and made a hasty retreat.

This drew Kris Kringle's attention, Olivia noted out of the corner of her eye. He perked right up, listening intently. Zeroing in. If he thought he was going to use

that poor little reindeer to attract customers, he had another think coming.

Sure enough, he said, "I just happen to be missing
a reindeer."

Olivia didn't believe him, and even though she knew
that was because she didn't *want* to believe him, her
radar was up and her antennae were beeping. "Is that
so?" she asked somewhat stiffly, while Tanner and Sophie looked on with heightened interest. "How did you
happen to misplace this reindeer, Mr.—?"

"Kringle," the old man insisted with a smile in his
eyes. "We did a personal appearance at a birthday party,
and he just wandered off."

"I see," Olivia said. "Didn't you look for him?"

"Oh, yes," Kringle replied, looking like a right jolly
old elf and all that. "No tracks to be found. We hunted
and hunted. Is Rodney all right?"

Olivia's mouth fell open. Kringle *must* be the reindeer's rightful owner if he knew his name. It would
be too much of a coincidence otherwise. "He's—he's
fine," she said.

Kringle smiled warmly. "The other seven have been
*very* worried, and so have I, although I've had an idea
all along that Rodney was on a mission of some kind."

Olivia swallowed. She'd wanted to find Rodney's
rightful owner so he could go home. So why did she
feel so dejected?

"The other seven what?" Tanner asked with a dry
note in his voice.

"Why, the other seven reindeer, of course," Kringle
answered merrily after tossing a conspiratorial glance
Sophie's way. "If Rodney is safe and well taken care of,

though, we won't fret about him. Not until Christmas Eve, anyway. We'll need him back by then for sure."

If Olivia had had a trowel handy, she would have handed it to the guy, so he could lay it on thicker. He really knew how to tap in to Christmas, that was for sure.

"I thought Santa's reindeer had names like Prancer and Dancer," Sophie said, sounding serious.

Tanner, meanwhile, got out his wallet to pay for the big spruce.

"Well, they do," Kringle said, still in Santa mode. "But they're getting older, and Donner's developed a touch of arthritis. So I brought Rodney up out of the ranks, since he showed so much promise, especially at flying. He's only been on trial runs so far, but this Christmas Eve he's on the flight manifest for the whole western region."

Tanner and Olivia exchanged looks.

"You don't need Rodney back until Christmas Eve?" Olivia asked. An owner was an owner, crazy or not. She took one of her dog-eared business cards out of her vest pocket, wrote Brad's private number on the back with a pen Tanner provided and handed it to Kringle. "He's at Stone Creek Ranch."

"I'll pick him up after I close the lot on the twenty-fourth," Kringle said, still twinkling, and even going so far as to tap a finger to the side of his nose. If there had been a chimney handy, he probably would have rocketed right up it. He examined the card, nodded to himself and tucked it away. "Around six o'clock," he added. "Even the last-minute Louies will have cleared out by then."

"Right," Olivia murmured, wondering if she'd made a mistake telling him where to find Rodney.

"Let me load up that tree for you," Tanner said, hoisting Charlie Brown by his skinny, crooked trunk before Olivia could get a hold on it. Brown needles rained to the pavement.

Sophie tagged along with Tanner and Olivia while Kringle carried the big spruce to Tanner's pickup truck. Branches of the lush tree rustled, and the evergreen scent intensified.

A few fat flakes of snow wafted down.

Olivia felt like a figure in a festive snow globe. Man, woman and child, with Christmas tree. Which was silly.

"My tree weighs all of three pounds," she pointed out to Tanner under her breath. "Aren't you supposed to be working on the new shelter?"

"More like thirty, with this pot." Tanner grinned and held the little tree out of her reach. "Nothing much gets done on a holiday weekend," he added, as if it was some big news flash or something. "Shouldn't you be helping a cow give birth?"

"Cows don't commonly give birth at this time of year," Olivia pointed out. "It's a springtime sort of thing."

"Yeah, Dad," Sophie interjected, rolling her eyes. "Yeesh."

Olivia had to laugh. "Yeah," she said, opening the rear doors of the Suburban to receive Charlie Brown. *"Yeesh."*

"How about joining Sophie and me for supper tonight?" Tanner asked, blocking the way when she would have closed the doors again.

"We live in a dump," Sophie said philosophically. "But it's home."

Olivia felt another pang at the word *home.* The rental

she lived in definitely didn't qualify, and though she had a history at Stone Creek Ranch, it belonged to Brad and Meg and Mac now, which was as it should be. "Well…"

"Please?" Sophie asked, suddenly earnest.

Tanner grinned, waited. The kid was virtually irresistible, and nobody knew that better than he did.

"Okay," Olivia said. For Sophie's sake and not—not *at all*—because she wanted to get in any deeper with Tanner Quinn than she already was.

"Six o'clock?" Tanner asked.

"Six o'clock," Olivia confirmed, casting another glance at Kris Kringle, now busy instructing the hired Santa Claus on how to hold the sleigh reins. She'd call Wyatt Terp, the marshal over in Indian Rock, the county seat, she decided, and get him to run a background check on this dude, just in case he had a rap sheet or the men in white coats were looking for him.

Tanner and Sophie said their goodbyes and left, and Olivia sat in the driver's seat of her Suburban for a few moments, working up the courage to call Wyatt. The only name she could give him was Kris Kringle, and *that* was bound to liven up an otherwise dull day in the cop shop.

"You mean there really *is* a Kris Kringle?" she asked ten minutes later, her cell phone pressed to one ear as she pulled into the lot at the hardware store to buy lights and tinsel for Charlie Brown.

"You'd be surprised how many there are," Wyatt said drolly.

"So you have something on him, then? You're sure it's the same guy?"

"Kristopher Kringle, it says here. Christmas-tree farmer with a place up near Flagstaff. Only one traffic violation—he was caught driving a horse-drawn sleigh on the freeway two winters ago."

Olivia shut off the Suburban, eyes popping. The painted sign on the weathered brick side of the hardware store read, in time-faded letters, "Smoke Caliber Cigarettes. They're Good for You!"

"Nothing like, say, animal cruelty?"

"Nope," Wyatt said. Olivia could hear some yukking going on in the background. Either the cops were celebrating early or the marshal had the phone on "speaker." "Santa's clean, Doc."

Olivia sighed. She was relieved, of course, to learn that Kringle was neither an escaped maniac nor a criminal, but on some level, she realized, she'd been hoping *not* to find Rodney's owner.

How crazy was that?

She got out of the car, after promising Charlie Brown she'd be back soon, and went inside to shop for a tree wardrobe. She bought two strands of old-fashioned bubbling lights, a box of shiny glass balls in a mixture of red, gold and silver, and some tinsel.

*Ho, ho, ho,* she thought, stashing her purchases in the back of the rig, next to Charlie. *Deck the halls.*

Even though they had a million things to do, Sophie insisted on stopping at Stone Creek Middle School when they drove past it. It was a small brick building, and the reader board in front read "Closed for Thanksgiving Vacation! See You Monday!"

The whole town, Tanner thought, feeling grumbly, was relentlessly cheerful. And what was up with that Kris Kringle yahoo, back at the tree lot, claiming he had seven reindeer at home, waiting to lift off on Christmas Eve?

Sophie cupped her hands and peered through the plate-glass door at the front of the school, her breath fogging it up. "Wow," she said. "The computer room at Briarwood is bigger than this whole place."

"Can we go now, Soph? We still need to pick up lights and ornaments and some things for you to wear, not to mention groceries."

Sophie turned and made a face at him. "Bah-humbug," she said. "Why are you so crabby all of a sudden?" She paused to waggle her eyebrows. "You looked real happy when Olivia was around."

"That guy at the tree lot…"

"What?" Sophie said, skipping back down the snowy steps to the walk. "You think he's a serial killer or something, just because he claims to be Santa?"

"Where do you get these things?" Tanner asked.

"He's delusional, that's all," said the doctor's daughter. "And probably harmless."

"Probably," Tanner agreed. He knew then what was troubling him—Olivia clearly didn't want to surrender custody of the reindeer until she knew "Kris Kringle" was all right. And he cared, more than he liked, what Olivia wanted and didn't want.

"Danger lurks everywhere!" Sophie teased, making mitten claws with her hands in an attempt to look scary. "You just can't be *too careful!*"

"Cut it out, goofball," Tanner said, chuckling in spite of himself as they both got back in the truck. "You don't know anything about the world. If you did, you wouldn't have run away from the field trip and tried to board an iron horse headed west."

"Are we going to talk about *that* again?" Sophie fastened her seat belt with exaggerated care. "I'm a proactive person, Dad. Don't you want me to be *proactive?*"

Tanner didn't answer. Whatever he said would be wrong.

"That Santa shouldn't be saying 'ho, ho, ho,'" Sophie informed him as they pulled away from the curb. Next stop, the ranch, to drop off the tree, then on to a mall he'd checked on MapQuest, outside Flagstaff. "It isn't politically correct."

"Ask me what I think of political correctness," Tanner retorted.

"Why would I do that when I already know?" Sophie responded cheerfully. "At Briarwood we call Valentine's Day 'Special Relationship Day' now."

"What's next? 'Significant Parental Figure Day' for Father's and Mother's Day?"

Sophie laughed, her cheeks bright with cold and excitement. "It does sound kind of silly, doesn't it?"

"Big-time," Tanner said. He couldn't even tell a woman on his executive staff that her hair looked nice without risking a sexual-harassment suit. Where would it all end?

At home, Tanner unloaded the tree and set it on the front porch so the branches could settle, while Sophie went out to the barn to eyeball the horses. In looks she resembled Kat, but she sure took after Tessa when it came to hay-burners.

"That dog is still here," she reported when she came back. "The one that was waiting on the porch when we got back from riding this morning. Shouldn't we take her home or something?"

"Ginger lives next door, with Olivia," Tanner reminded Sophie. "If she wants to go home, she can get there on her own."

"I hope she isn't depressed, like Butterpie was," Sophie fretted.

Tanner grinned, gave her ponytail a light tug. "She and Butterpie are buddies," he said, recalling finding the dog in the pony's stall. "Olivia will take her home after supper tonight, most likely."

"You like Olivia, don't you?" Sophie asked, with a touch of slyness, as she climbed back into the truck.

Tanner got behind the wheel, started the engine. Olivia was right. The rig was too clean—it had stood out like the proverbial sore thumb back in town, at the tree lot. Maybe he could find a creek to run it through or something. With the ground frozen hard, it wouldn't be easy to come up with mud.

So where were the other guys getting all that macho dirt streaking their rigs and clogging their grilles?

"Of course I like her," he said. "She's a friend."

"She's pretty."

"I'll grant you that one, shorty. She's very pretty."

"You could marry her."

Tanner, in the process of turning the truck around, stopped it instead. "Don't go there, Soph. Olivia's a hometown girl, with a family and a veterinary practice. I'll be moving on to a new place after Stone Creek. And neither one of us is looking for a serious relationship."

Sophie sighed, and her shoulders sloped as though the weight of the world had just been laid on them. "I almost wish that Kris Kringle guy really was Santa Claus," she said. "Then I could tell him I want a mom for Christmas."

Tanner knew he was being played, but his eyes

burned and his throat tightened just the same. No accounting for visceral reactions. "That was pretty underhanded, Soph," he said. "It was blatant manipulation. And guilt isn't going to work with me. You should know that by now."

Sophie folded her arms and sulked. Only twelve and already she'd mastered the you're-too-stupid-to-live look teenage girls were so good at. Tessa had been world champ, but clearly the torch had been passed. "What*ever*."

"I know you'd like to have a mother, Sophie."

"You know, but you don't care."

"I *do* care."

A tear slid down Sophie's left cheek, and Tanner knew it wasn't orchestrated to win his sympathy, because she turned her head quickly, so he wouldn't see.

"I do care, Sophie," he repeated.

She merely nodded. Gave a sniffle that tore at his insides.

Maybe someday she'd understand that he was only trying to protect her. Maybe she wouldn't.

He wondered if he could deal with the latter possibility. Suppose, even as a grown woman, Sophie still resented him?

Well, he thought grimly, this wasn't *about* him. It was about keeping Sophie safe, whether she liked it or not.

He took the turnoff for Flagstaff, bypassing Stone Creek completely. Sophie was female. Shopping would make her feel better, and if that didn't work, there was still the Christmas tree to set up, and Olivia coming over for supper.

They'd get through this, he and Sophie.

"The time's going to go by really fast," Sophie lamented, breaking the difficult silence and still not looking at him. "Before I know it, I'll be right back at Briarwood. Square one."

Tanner waited a beat to answer, so he wouldn't snap at the kid. God knew, being twelve years old in this day and age couldn't be easy, what with all the drugs and the underground Web sites and the movement to rename *Valentine's Day,* for God's sake. No, it would be difficult with two ordinary parents and a mortgaged house, and Sophie didn't have two parents.

She didn't even have *one,* really.

"Everything's going to be all right, Soph," he said. Was he trying to convince her, or himself? Both, probably.

"I could live with Aunt Tessa on Starcross—couldn't I? And go to Stone Creek Middle School, like a regular kid?"

Tanner nearly had to pull over to the side of the road. Instead, he clamped his jaw down tight and concentrated harder on navigating the slick high-country road curving ever upward into the timbered area around Flagstaff.

He should have seen this coming, after the way Sophie had made him stop at the school in town so she could look in the windows, but the kid had a gift for blindsiding him.

"Aunt Tessa," he said evenly, "is only visiting for the holidays."

"She's bringing her horses."

"Okay, a few months at most. Can we not talk about this for a little while, Soph? Because it's a fast track to nowhere."

That was when she brought out the big guns. "They have drugs at Briarwood, you know," she said with a combination of defiance and bravado. "It's not an ivory tower, no matter *how* good the security is."

That time he *did* pull over, with a screech of tires and a lot of flying slush. *"What?"* he rasped.

"Meth," Sophie said. "Ice. That's—"

"I *know* what ice is," Tanner snapped. "So help me God, Sophie, if you're messing with me—"

"It's true, Dad."

He believed her. That was the worst thing of all. His stomach rolled, and for a moment he thought he might have to shove open the door and get sick, right then and there.

"It's a pervasive problem," Sophie said, sounding like a venerable news commentator instead of a pre-adolescent girl.

"Has anyone offered you drugs? Have you taken any?" He kept his hand on the door handle, just in case.

"I'm not stupid, Dad," she answered. "Drugs are for losers, people who can't cope unless their brains have been chemically altered."

"Would you talk like a twelve-year-old for a few minutes? Just to humor me?"

"I don't take drugs, Dad," Sophie reiterated quietly.

"How are they getting in? The drugs, I mean?"

"Kids bring them from home. I think they mostly steal them from their parents."

Tanner laid his forehead on the steering wheel and drew slow, deep breaths. *From their parents.* In his mind, he started drawing up blueprints for an ivory tower. Not that he'd use ivory, even if he could get it from a legitimate supplier.

Sophie touched his arm. "Dad, I'm trying to make a point here. Are you okay? Because you look kind of…gray. You're not having a heart attack or anything, are you?"

"Not the kind you're thinking of," Tanner said, straightening. Pulling himself together. He was a father. He needed to act like one.

When he was sure he wasn't a menace to Sophie, himself and the general driving public, he pulled back out onto the highway. Sophie fiddled with the radio until she found a station she liked, and a rap beat filled the truck cab.

Tanner adjusted the dial. Brad O'Ballivan's voice poured out of the speakers. "Have Yourself a Merry Little Christmas."

It figured. Tessa was practically being stalked by the song, according to her, and now he probably would be, too.

"Is that the guy who hired you to build the animal shelter?" Sophie asked.

Beyond relieved at the change of subject, Tanner said, "Yes."

"He has a nice voice."

"That's the word on the street."

"Even if the song *is* kind of hokey."

Tanner laughed. "I'll tell him you said so."

After that they talked about ordinary things—not drugs at Briarwood, not Sophie's longing for a mother, destined to be unrequited, not weird Kris Kringle, the reindeer man. No, they discussed a new saddle for Butterpie, and what to get Tessa for Christmas, and the pros and cons of nuking a package of frozen lasagna for supper.

Reaching the mall, Tanner parked the truck and the two of them waded in. They bought ornaments and lights and tinsel. They cleaned out the "young juniors" department in an upscale store, and chose a yellow cashmere sweater for Tessa's gift. They had a late lunch in the food court, watching as the early shoppers rushed by with their treasures.

On the way out of town they stopped at a Western supply store for the new saddle, and after that, a supermarket, where they filled two carts. When they left the store, Tanner almost tripped over a kid in ragged jeans, a T-shirt and a thin jacket, trying to give away squirmy puppies from a big box. The words "Good Xmas Presents" had been scrawled on the side in black marker.

Tanner lengthened his stride, making the shopping cart wheels rattle.

Sophie stopped her cart.

"Oh, they're so cute," she said.

"Only two left," the kid pointed out unnecessarily. There were holes in the toes of his sneakers. Had he dressed for the part?

"Sophie," Tanner said in warning.

But she'd picked up one of the puppies—a little golden-brown one of indeterminate breed, with floppy ears and big, hopeful eyes. Then the other, a black-and-white version of the dog Tanner remembered from his first-grade reader.

"Dad," she whispered, drawing up close to his side, the full cart she'd been pushing left behind by the boy and the box, to show him the puppies. "Look at that kid. He probably needs the money, and who knows what might happen to these poor little things if they don't get sold?"

Tanner couldn't bring himself to say the obvious—that Sophie would be leaving for a new school in a few weeks, since Briarwood was definitely out of the question now that he knew about the drugs. He'd just have to buy the dogs and hope that Olivia would be able to find them good homes when the time came.

At the moment, turning Sophie down wasn't an option, even if it was the right thing to do. He'd had to say no to one too many things already.

So Tanner gave the boy a ridiculous amount of money for the puppies, and Sophie scared them half to death with a squeal of delight, and they loaded up the grub and the dogs and headed back to Starcross Ranch.

# *Chapter Eight*

Olivia hadn't been able to track Ashley down, even after hunting all over town, and no emergency veterinary calls came in, either. She had her hair cut at the Curly-Q, bought some groceries and cleaning supplies at the supermarket, then she and Charlie Brown went home.

Ginger was waiting on the back porch when she arrived, balls of snow clinging to her legs and haunches from the walk across the very white field between Olivia's place and Tanner's.

*"It's about time you got here,"* the dog said, rising off her nest of blankets next to the drier.

Freezing, Olivia hustled through the kitchen door and set Charlie Brown on the table, root-bound in his bulky plastic pot. "You're the one who insisted on staying at Starcross," she said before going back out for the bags from the hardware store and supermarket.

A pool of melted snow surrounded Ginger when Olivia finished carrying everything inside. After setting the last of the bags on the counter, she threw an old towel into the drier to warm it up and adjusted the thermostat for the temperamental old furnace. She started a pot of coffee—darn, she should have picked up a new brewing apparatus at the hardware store—and filled Ginger's kibble bowl.

While the dog ate and the coffee brewed, Olivia fished the towel out of the drier and knelt on the scuffed and peeling linoleum floor to give Ginger a rubdown.

*"Were they out of good Christmas trees?"* Ginger asked, eyeing Charlie Brown, whose sparse branches seemed to droop a little at the insult.

"Be nice," Olivia whispered. "You'll hurt his feelings."

*"I suppose I should be happy that you're decorating this year,"* Ginger answered, giving Olivia's face an affectionate lick as thanks for the warm towel. *"Since you're so Christmas-challenged and all."*

Olivia stood, chuckling. "I saw these stick-on reindeer antlers for dogs at the hardware store," she said. "They have jingle bells and they light up. Treat me right or I'll buy you a pair, take your picture and post it on the Internet."

Ginger sighed. She hated costumes.

A glance at the clock told Olivia she had an hour before she was due at Starcross for supper. After her shower, she decided, she'd dig through her closet and bureau drawers again, and find something presentable to wear, so Sophie wouldn't think she was a rube.

Ginger padded after her, jumped up onto her unmade bed and curled up in the middle. Olivia laid out clean underwear, her second-best pair of jeans and a red sweatshirt from two years ago, when Ashley had been on a fabric-painting kick. It had a cutesy snowman on the front, with light-up eyes, though the battery was long dead.

Toweling off after her shower and pulling on her clothes quickly, since even with the thermostat up, the house was drafty, Olivia told Ginger about the invitation to Starcross.

*"I'll stay here,"* Ginger said. *"Reinforcements have arrived."*

"What kind of reinforcements?" Olivia asked, peering at Ginger through the neck hole as she tugged the sweatshirt on over her head.

*"You'll see,"* Ginger answered, her eyes already at half-mast as she drifted toward sleep. *"Take your kit with you."*

"Is Butterpie sick?" Olivia asked, alarmed.

*"No,"* came the canine reply. *"I would have told you right away if she was. But you'll need the kit."*

"Okay," Olivia said.

Ginger's snore covered an octave, somewhere in the alto range.

Olivia wasn't musical.

At six o'clock, straight up, she drove up in front of the ranch house at Starcross. Colored lights glowed through the big picture window, a cheering sight in the snow-flecked twilight.

Bringing her medical kit as far as the porch, Olivia set it down and knocked.

Sophie opened the door, her small face as bright as

the tree lights. The scents of piney sap and something savory cooking or cooling added to the ambience.

"Wait till you *see* what we got at the supermarket!" Sophie whooped, half dragging Olivia over the threshold.

Tanner stood framed in the entrance to the living room, one shoulder braced against the woodwork. He wore a blue Henley shirt, with a band around the neck instead of a collar, open at the throat, and jeans that looked as though they'd seen some decent wear. "Yeah," he drawled with an almost imperceptible roll of his eyes, "wait till you see."

A puppy bark sounded from behind him.

"You didn't," Olivia said, secretly thrilled.

"There are *two* of them!" Sophie exulted as the pair gamboled around Tanner to squirm and yip at Olivia's feet.

She crouched immediately, laughing and ruffling small, warm ears. So *this* was the reason Ginger had wanted her to bring the kit. These were mongrels, not purebreds, up to date on their vaccinations before they left the kennel, and they'd need their shots.

"I named them Snidely and Whiplash," Sophie said. "After the villain in *The Dudley Do-Right Show*."

"I suggested Going and Gone," Tanner interjected humorously, "but the kid wouldn't go for it."

"Which is which?" Olivia asked Sophie, ignoring Tanner's remark. Her heart was beating fast—did this mean he was thinking of staying on at Starcross after the shelter was finished?

"That's Snidely," Sophie said, pointing to the puppy with gold fur. They looked like some kind of collie-shepherd-retriever mix. "The spotted one is Whiplash."

"Let's just have a quick look at them," Olivia suggested. "My kit is on the porch. Would you get it for me, please?"

Sophie rushed to comply.

"Going and Gone?" Olivia asked very softly, watching Tanner. Now that she'd shifted, she could see the blue spruce behind him, in front of the snow-laced picture window.

But Sophie was back before he could answer.

"Later," he mouthed, and his eyes looked so serious that some of the spontaneous Christmas magic drifted to the floor like tired fairy dust.

Olivia examined the puppies, pronounced them healthy and gave them each their first round of shots. They were "box" puppies, giveaways, and that invariably meant they'd had no veterinary care at all.

"Does that hurt them?" Sophie asked, her blue eyes wide as she watched Olivia inject serum into the bunched-up scruffs of their necks with a very small needle. They'd all gathered in the living room, near the fragrant tree and the fire dancing on the hearth, Olivia employing the couch as an examining table.

"No," she said gently, putting away her doctor gear. "The injections will prevent distemper and parvo, among other things. The diseases *would* hurt, and these girls will need to be spayed as soon as they're a little older."

Sophie nodded solemnly. "They wet on the floor," she said, "but I promised Dad I'd clean up after them myself."

"Good girl," Olivia said. "If you take them outside every couple of hours, they'll get the idea." Her gaze was drawn to Tanner, but she resisted. *Going and Gone?*

The names didn't bode well. Had he actually brought these puppies home intending to get rid of them as soon as Sophie went back to school?

*No,* she thought. *He couldn't have. He couldn't be that cold.*

There was lasagna for supper, and salad. Sophie talked the whole time they were eating, fairly bouncing in her chair while the puppies tumbled and played under the table, convinced they had a home.

Even though she was hungry, Olivia couldn't eat much.

When the meal was over, Sophie and Olivia put on coats and went out to the barn to see Butterpie and Shiloh while Tanner, strangely quiet, stayed behind to clean up the kitchen.

"We bought a new saddle for Butterpie," Sophie said excitedly as they entered the hay-scented warmth of the barn. "And Dad's having all the stalls fixed up so Aunt Tessa's horses will be comfortable here."

"Aunt Tessa?" Olivia asked, admiring the saddle. She'd had one much like it as a young girl; Big John had bought it for her thirteenth birthday, probably second-hand and at considerable sacrifice to the budget.

Now, she thought sadly, she didn't even own a horse.

"Tessa's my dad's sister. She has a whole bunch of horses, and she's getting a divorce, so Dad sent her money to come out here to Arizona." Sophie drew a breath and rushed on. "Maybe you saw her on TV. She starred in *California Women* for years—and a whole bunch of shows before that."

Olivia remembered the series, though she didn't watch much television. Curiously, her viewing was mostly limited to the holidays—she always tried to catch *It's a Wonderful Life, The Bishop's Wife* and, of course, *A Charlie Brown Christmas.*

"I think I've seen it once or twice," she said, but she couldn't place Tessa's character.

Sophie sagged a little as she opened Butterpie's stall. "I think Dad's going to ask Aunt Tessa to stay here and look after Starcross Ranch and Shiloh and the puppies after he leaves," she said.

"Oh," Olivia said, deflated but keeping up a game face for Sophie's sake.

Butterpie looked fit, and she was eating again.

"I'm still hoping he'll change his mind and let me stay here," Sophie confided quietly. "My education shouldn't be interrupted—at least we agree on that much—so I get to go to Stone Creek Middle School, starting Monday, until they let out for Christmas vacation."

Olivia didn't know what to say. She had opinions about boarding schools and adopting puppies he didn't intend to raise, that was for sure, but sharing them with Sophie would be over the line. Satisfied that Butterpie was doing well, she let herself into Shiloh's stall to stroke his long side.

He nuzzled her affectionately.

And her cell phone rang.

Here it was. The sick-cow call Olivia had been expecting all day.

But the number on the caller ID panel was Melissa's private line at the law office. What was she doing working this late, and on a holiday weekend, too?

"Mel? What's up?"

"It's Ashley," Melissa said quietly. "She just called me from some Podunk town in Tennessee. She caught the shuttle to the airport early this morning, evidently, and flew out of Phoenix without telling any of us."

"Tennessee?" Olivia echoed, momentarily confused. Or was she simply trying to deny what she already knew, deep down?

"I guess Mom's living there now," Melissa said.

Sophie stepped out of Butterpie's stall just as Olivia stepped out of Shiloh's, her face full of concern. They turned their backs on each other to work the latches, securing both horses for the night.

"Oh, my God," Olivia said.

"She's a wreck," Melissa went on, sounding as numb as Olivia felt. "Ashley, I mean. Things turned out badly—so badly that Brad's chartering a jet to go back there and pick up the pieces."

Sophie caught hold of Olivia's arm, steered her to a bale of hay and urged her to sit down.

She sat, gratefully. Standing up any longer would have been impossible, with her knees shaking the way they were.

"Should I go get my dad?" Sophie asked.

Olivia shook her head, then closed her eyes. "What happened, Mel? What did Ashley say on the phone?"

"She just said she should have listened to you and Brad. She was crying so hard, I could hardly understand her. She told me where she was staying and I called Brad as soon as we hung up."

Ashley. The innocent one, the one who believed in happy endings. She'd just run up against an ugly reality, and Olivia was miles away, unable to help her. "I'm going to call Brad and tell him I want to go, too," she said, about to hang up.

"I tried that," Melissa answered immediately. "He

said he wanted to handle this alone. My guess is he's already on his way to Flagstaff to board the jet."

Olivia fought back tears of frustration, fury and resignation. "When did Ashley call?" she asked, fighting for composure. Sophie was already plenty worried—the look on her face proved that—and it wouldn't do to fall apart in front of a child.

"About half an hour ago. I called Brad right away, and we were on the phone for a long time. As soon as we hung up, I called you."

"Thanks," Olivia said woodenly.

"Are you all right?" Melissa asked.

"No," Olivia replied. "Are you?"

"No," Melissa admitted. "And I won't be until the twin-unit is back home in Stone Creek, where she belongs. I know you want to call Brad and beat your head against a brick wall trying to get him to let you go to Tennessee with him, so I'll let you go."

"Go home," Olivia told her kid sister. "It's a holiday weekend and you shouldn't be working."

Melissa's chuckle sounded more like a sob. Olivia was terrified, so Melissa, what with the twin bond and all, had to be ready to dissolve. "Like *you* have any room to talk," she said. "Can I come out to your place, Liv, and spend the night with you and Ginger?"

"Meet you there," Olivia said, following up with a goodbye. She speed-dialed Brad in the next moment.

"No," he said instead of the customary hello.

"Where are you?"

"Almost to Flagstaff. The jet's waiting. When I know anything, I'll call you."

Clearly, asking him to come back for her, or wait till she could get to the airport, would, as her sister had predicted, be a waste of breath. Besides, Melissa needed her, or she wouldn't have asked to spend the night.

"Okay," Olivia said. A few moments later she shut her cell phone.

Sophie stood watching her. "Did something bad happen?"

Olivia stood. Her knees were back in working order, then. That was something. "It's a family thing," she said. "Nothing you need to worry about. I have to go home right away, though."

Sophie nodded sagely. "Shall I go get your doctor bag?" she asked. "I'll explain to Dad and everything."

"Thanks," Olivia said, heading for the Suburban.

Sophie raced for the house, but it was Tanner who brought the medical kit out to her.

"Anything I can do?" he asked, handing it through the open window of the Suburban.

Olivia shook her head, not trusting herself to speak.

To her utter surprise, Tanner leaned in, cupped his hand at the back of her head and planted a gentle but electrifying kiss on her mouth. Then he stepped away, and she put the Suburban into gear and drove out.

Tanner stood in the cold, watching Olivia's taillights disappear in the thickening snowfall.

The shimmering colors on the Christmas tree in the front room seemed to mock him through the steam-fogged glass. Whatever Olivia's problem was, he probably couldn't make it right. It was a "family thing," according to Sophie's breathless report, and he wasn't family.

He shoved his hands into his hip pockets—he hadn't bothered with a coat—and thought about, of all things, the puppies. There was no way he could ask Olivia to find them homes after he moved on. Tessa might or might not be willing to stay on at Stone Creek and look after Snidely and Whiplash.

He'd dug himself a big hole, with Sophie *and* with Olivia, and getting out was going to take some doing. Fast-talking wouldn't pack it.

Inside the house, Sophie was making a bed for the puppies in a cardboard box fluffed up with an old blanket.

"Did somebody die?" she asked when Tanner entered the living room.

The question poleaxed him. Sophie had lost her mother when she was seven years old. Did every crisis prompt her to expect a funeral?

"I don't think so, honey," he said gruffly. He should have hugged her, but he couldn't move. He just stood there, like a fool, in the middle of the living room.

Sophie looked at the Christmas tree. "Maybe we could finish decorating tomorrow," she said. "I don't feel much like it now."

"Me, either," Tanner admitted. "Let's take the puppies outside before you bed them down."

Sophie nodded, and they put on their coats and each took a puppy.

The dogs squatted obediently in the thickening snow.

"I like Olivia," Sophie said.

"I do, too," Tanner replied. *Maybe a little too much.*

"It was fun having her here to eat supper with us."

Tanner nodded, draped an arm around Sophie's small shoulders. She felt so little, so insubstantial, inside her bulky nylon jacket.

"I showed her my new saddle."

"It's a nice piece of gear."

The puppies were finished. Tanner scooped one up, and Sophie collected the other. They plodded toward the house, with its half-decorated Christmas tree, peeling wallpaper and outdated plumbing fixtures.

Flipping *this* house, Tanner thought ruefully, was going to be a job.

Once Sophie and the dogs were settled upstairs, in the room she'd declared to be hers, Tanner unplugged the tree lights and wandered into the kitchen to log on at his laptop. He had some supply invoices to look over, fortunately, and that would keep his mind occupied. Keep him from worrying about what had happened in Olivia's family to knock her off balance like that.

He could call Brad and ask, of course, but he wasn't going to do that. It would be an intrusion.

So he poured himself a cup of lukewarm coffee, drew up a chair at the table and opened his laptop.

The invoices were there, all right. But they might as well have been written in Sanskrit, for all the sense he could make of them.

After half an hour he gave up.

It was too early to go to sleep, so he snapped on the one TV set in the house, a little portable in the living room, and flipped through channels until he found a weather report.

Snow, snow and more snow.

He sighed and changed channels again, settled on a holiday rerun of *Everybody Loves Raymond*. Here, at least, was a family even more dysfunctional than his own.

In a perverse sort of way, it cheered him up.

Melissa arrived with an overnight case only twenty minutes after Olivia got home. Her blue eyes were red rimmed from crying.

Of all the O'Ballivan siblings, Melissa was the least emotional. But she stood in Olivia's kitchen, her shoulders stooped and dusted with snowflakes, and choked up when she tried to speak.

Olivia immediately took her younger sister into her arms. "It's okay," she said. "Everything will work out, you'll see."

Melissa nodded, sniffled and pulled away. "God," she said, trying to make a joke, "this place is *such* a dive."

"It'll do until I can move in above the new shelter," Olivia said, pointing toward the nearby hall. "The guest room is ready. Put your stuff away and we'll talk."

Melissa had spotted Charlie Brown, still standing in his nondescript pot in the center of the kitchen table. "You bought a Christmas tree?" she marveled.

Olivia set her hands on her hips. "Why is that such a surprise to everybody?" she asked, realizing only when the words were out of her mouth that *Ginger* had offered the only other comment on the purchase.

Melissa sighed and shook her head. Ginger escorted her to the spare room, and back. Melissa had shed her coat, and she was pushing up the sleeves of her white sweater as she reentered the kitchen.

"Let's get the poor thing decorated," she said.

"Good idea," Olivia agreed.

The tree was fairly heavy, between the root system and the pot, and Melissa helped her lug it into the living room.

Olivia pushed an end table in front of the window, after moving a lamp, and Charlie was hoisted to eye level.

"This is sort of—cheerful," Melissa said, probably

being kind, though whether she felt sorry for Olivia or the tree was anybody's guess.

Olivia pulled the bubble lights and ornaments from the hardware-store bags. "Maybe I should make popcorn or something."

"That," Melissa teased after another sniffle, "would constitute *cooking*. And you promised you wouldn't try that at home."

Olivia laughed. "I'm glad you're here, Mel."

"Me, too," Melissa said. "We should get together more often. We're always working."

"You work more than I do," Olivia told her good-naturedly. "You need to get a life, Melissa O'Ballivan."

"I *have* a life, thank you very much," Melissa retorted, heading for Olivia's CD player and putting on some Christmas music. "Anyway, if anybody's going to preach to me about overdoing it at work and getting a life, it isn't going to be you, Big Sister."

"Are you dating anybody?" Olivia asked, opening one of the cartons of bubble lights. When they were younger, Big John had hung lights exactly like them on the family tree every year. Then they'd become a fire hazard, and he'd thrown them out.

"The last one ended badly," Melissa confessed, busy opening the ornament boxes and putting hangers through the little loops. So busy that she wouldn't meet Olivia's gaze.

"How so?"

"He was married," Melissa said. "Had me fooled, until the wife sent me a photo Christmas card showing them on a trip to the Grand Canyon last summer. Four kids and a dog."

"Yikes," Olivia said, wanting to hug Melissa, or at

least lay a hand on her shoulder, but holding back. Her sister seemed uncharacteristically brittle, as though she might fall apart if anyone touched her just then. "You really cared about him, huh?"

"I cared," Melissa said. "What else is new? If there's a jerk within a hundred miles, I'll find him, rope him in and hand him my heart."

"Aren't you being a little hard on yourself?"

Melissa shrugged offhandedly. "The one before that wanted to meet Brad and present him with a demo so he could make it big in showbiz." She paused. "But at least *he* didn't have children."

"Mel, it happens. Cut yourself a little slack."

"You didn't see those kids. Freckles. Braces. They all looked so happy. And why not? How could they know their dad is a class-A, card-carrying schmuck?"

Once again Olivia found herself at a loss for words. She concentrated on clipping the lights to Charlie Brown's branches.

"Par-ump-pah-pum..." Bing Crosby sang from the CD player.

"I might as well tell you it's the talk of the family," Melissa said, picking up the conversational ball with cheerful determination, "that you skipped out of Thanksgiving to sneak off with Tanner Quinn."

Olivia stiffened. "I didn't 'sneak off' with him," she said. *Not much,* said her conscience.

"Don't be so defensive," Melissa replied, widening her eyes. "He's a hunk. I'd have left with him, too."

"It wasn't—"

"It wasn't what I think?" Melissa challenged, smiling now. "Of course it was. Are you in love with him?"

Olivia opened her mouth, closed it again.

Bing Crosby sang wistfully of orange groves and sunshine. He was dreaming of a white Christmas.

He could have hers.

"Are you?" Melissa pressed.

"No," Olivia said.

"Too bad," Melissa answered.

Olivia looked at her watch, pretending she hadn't heard that last remark. By now Brad was probably in the air, jetting toward Tennessee.

*Hold on, Ashley,* she thought. *Hold on.*

The call didn't come until almost midnight, and when it did, both Melissa and Olivia, snacking on leathery egg rolls snatched from the freezer and thawed in the oven, dived for the kitchen phone.

Olivia got there first. Home-court advantage.

"She's okay," Brad said. "We'll be back sometime tomorrow."

"Put her on," Olivia replied anxiously.

"I don't think she's up to that right now," Brad answered.

"Tell her Melissa's here with me, and we'll be waiting when she gets home."

Brad agreed, and the call ended.

"She's all right, then?" Melissa asked carefully.

Olivia nodded, but she wasn't entirely convinced it was the truth. The only thing to do now was get some sleep—Melissa needed a night's rest, and so did she.

In her room, with Ginger sharing the bed, Olivia stared up at the ceiling and worried. Across the hall, in the tiny spare room, Melissa was probably doing the same thing.

Tanner, watching from his bedroom window, saw the lights go out across the field, in Olivia's house. He went to look in on Sophie and the puppies one more time, then showered, brushed his teeth, pulled on sweats and stretched out for the night.

Sleep proved elusive, and when it came, it was shallow, a partial unconsciousness ripe for lucid dreams. And not necessarily good ones.

He found himself in what looked like a hospital corridor, near the nurses' desk, and when a tall, dark-haired woman came out of a room, wearing scrubs and carrying a chart, he thought it was Kat.

She was back, then. The last dream hadn't been a goodbye after all.

He tried to speak to her, but it was no use. He was no more articulate than the droopy Christmas garlands and greeting cards taped haphazardly to the walls and trimming the desk.

The general effect was forlorn, rather than festive.

The woman in scrubs slapped the chart down on the counter and sighed.

There were shadows under her eyes, and she was too thin. No wedding ring on her left hand, either.

"Nurse?" she called.

A heavy woman appeared from a back room. "Do you need something, Dr. Quinn?"

Dr. Quinn, medicine woman. It was a joke he and Sophie shared when they talked about her career plans.

Sophie. This was *Sophie*—some kind of ghost of Christmas future.

Tanner tried hard to wake up, but it didn't happen for him. During the effort, he missed whatever Sophie said in reply to the nurse's question.

"I thought you'd go home for Christmas this year,"

the nurse said chattily. "I'd swear I saw your name on the vacation list."

Sophie studied the chart, a little frown forming between her eyebrows. "I swapped with Dr. Severn," she answered distractedly. "He has a family."

Tanner felt his heart break. *You* have a family, Sophie, he cried silently.

"Anyway, my dad's overseas, building something," Sophie went on. "We don't make a big deal about Christmas."

*Sophie,* Tanner pleaded.

But she didn't hear him. She snapped the chart shut and marched off down the hospital corridor again, disappearing into a mist.

*My dad's overseas, building something. We don't make a big deal about Christmas.*

Sophie's words lingered in Tanner's head when he opened his eyes. He ran the back of his arm across his wet face, alone in the darkness.

So much for sleep.

## Chapter Nine

Over what was left of the weekend, the snow melted and the roads were lined with muddy slush. It made the decorations on Main Street look as though they were trying just a shade too hard, by Olivia's calculations.

Brad and Ashley didn't get back to Stone Creek until Monday afternoon. Melissa and Olivia were waiting at Ashley's, along with Ginger, when Brad's truck pulled up outside. They'd considered turning on the outside lights to welcome Ashley home, but in the end it hadn't seemed like a good idea.

Olivia had brewed fresh coffee, though.

Melissa had brought a box of Ashley's favorite doughnuts from the bakery.

As they peered out the front window, watching as Brad helped Ashley out of the truck and held on to her arm as they approached the gate, both Olivia and Melissa knew coffee and doughnuts weren't going to be enough.

Ashley looked thinner—was that possible after only a couple of days?—and even from a distance, Olivia could see that there were deep shadows under her eyes.

Melissa rushed for the door and opened it as Brad brought Ashley up the steps. He shot a look of bruised warning at Melissa, then Olivia.

"I don't want to talk about it," Ashley said.

"You don't have to," Olivia told her softly, reaching for Ashley and drawing back when her sister flinched, huddled closer to Brad, as though she felt threatened. She wouldn't look at either Olivia or Melissa, but she did stoop to pat Ginger's head. "I just want to sleep."

Once Ashley was inside the house, Melissa urged her toward the stairs. The railing was buried under an evergreen garland.

"That must have been a very bad scene," Olivia said to Brad when the twins were on their way upstairs, followed by Ginger.

He nodded, his expression glum. Now that Olivia looked at him, she realized that he looked almost as bad as Ashley did.

"What happened?" Olivia prompted when her brother didn't say anything.

"She wouldn't tell me any more than she just told you." There was more, though. Olivia knew that, by Brad's face, even before he went on. "A desk clerk at Ashley's hotel told me she checked in, all excited, and a woman came to see her—the two of them met in the hotel restaurant for lunch. The woman was Mom, of course. She swilled a lot of wine, and things went sour, fast. According to this clerk, Mom started screaming that if she'd wanted 'a bunch of snot-nosed brats hanging off her,' she'd have stayed in Stone Creek and rotted."

The words, and the image, which she could picture only too well, struck Olivia like blows. It didn't help that she would have expected something similar out of any meeting with her mother.

"My God," she whispered. "Poor Ashley."

"It gets worse," Brad said. "Mom raised such hell in the restaurant that the police were called. Turns out she'd violated probation by getting drunk, and now she's in jail. Ashley's furious with me because I wouldn't bail her out."

A sudden headache slammed at Olivia's temples with such ferocity that she wondered if she was blowing a blood vessel in her brain. She nodded to let Brad know she'd heard, but her eyes were squeezed shut.

"I tried to get Ashley to stop at the doctor's office on the way into town a little while ago—maybe get some tranquilizers or something—but she said she just wanted to go home." He paused. "Liv, are you okay?"

"I've been better," she answered, opening her eyes. "Right now I'm not worried about myself. I should have known Ashley would have done something like this—tried to stop her—"

"It isn't your fault," Brad said.

Olivia nodded, but she probably wasn't very convincing, to Brad or herself.

"I've got to get home to Meg and the baby," Brad told her. "Can you and Melissa take it from here?"

Again Olivia nodded.

"You'll call if she seems to be losing ground?"

Olivia stood on tiptoe and kissed her brother's un-shaven, wind-chilled cheek. "I'll call," she promised.

After casting a rueful glance toward the stairs, Brad turned and left.

Olivia was halfway up those same stairs when Melissa appeared at the top, a finger to her lips.

"She's resting," she whispered. Apparently Ginger had elected to stay in Ashley's room.

Together, Olivia and Melissa retreated to the kitchen.

"Did she say anything?" Olivia prodded.

"Just that it was terrible," Melissa replied, "and that she still doesn't want to talk about it."

Olivia's cell phone chirped. Great. After the slowest weekend on record, professionally speaking anyway, she was suddenly in demand.

"Dr. O'Ballivan," she answered, having seen the clinic's number on the ID panel.

"There's a horse colicking at the Wildes' farm," the receptionist, Becky, told her. "It's bad and Dr. Elliott is on call, but he's busy...."

Colic. The ailment could be deadly for a horse. "I'm on my way," Olivia said.

"Go," Melissa said when she'd hung up. "I'll look after Ashley. Ginger, too."

Having no real choice, Olivia hurried out to the Sub-urban and headed for the Wildes'.

The next few hours were harrowing, with teenaged Sherry Wilde, the owner of the sick horse, on the verge of hysteria the whole time. Olivia managed to save the bay mare, but it was a fight.

She was so drained afterward that she pulled over and sat in the Suburban with her head resting on the steering wheel, once she'd driven out of sight of the house and barn, and cried.

Presently she heard another rig pull up behind her and, since she was about halfway between Stone Creek and Indian Rock, she figured it was Wyatt Terp or one of his deputies, out on patrol, stopping to make sure she was okay. Olivia sniffled inelegantly and lifted her head.

But the face on the other side of the window was Tanner's, not Wyatt's.

She hadn't seen him since supper at his place a few nights before.

He gestured for her to roll down the window.

She did.

"Engine trouble?" he asked.

Olivia shook her head. She must look a sight, she thought, with her eyes all puffy and her nose red enough to fly lead for Kris Kringle. She was a professional, good under pressure, and it was completely unlike her to sit sniveling beside the road.

"Move over," he said after locking his own vehicle by pressing a button on the key fob. "I'm driving."

"I'm all right—really…"

He already had the door open, and he was standing on the running board.

Olivia scrambled over the console to the passenger side once she realized he wasn't going to give in.

"Where to?" he asked.

"Home, I guess," Olivia said. She'd called the bed-and-breakfast before leaving the Wildes' farm, and Melissa had told her Ashley still wanted to be left alone. The family doctor had dropped by, at Brad's request, and given Ash a mild sedative.

Melissa planned to stay overnight.

"When you're ready to talk," Tanner said, checking the rearview mirror before pulling onto the road, "I'll be ready to listen."

"It might be a while," Olivia said, after a few moments spent struggling to get a grip. "Where's Sophie?"

Tanner grinned. "She stayed after school to watch the drama department rehearse for the winter play," he said. "We'll pick her up on our way if you don't mind."

It went without saying that Olivia didn't mind, but she said it anyway.

Sophie was waiting with friends when they pulled up in front of the middle school. She looked puzzled for a moment, then rushed, smiling, toward the Suburban.

"We really should go back and get your truck," Olivia fretted, glancing at Tanner as Sophie climbed into the rear seat.

"Maybe it will get dirty," Tanner said cheerfully. Then, when Olivia didn't smile, he added, "I'll send somebody from the construction crew to pick it up."

"Can we get pizza?" Sophie wanted to know.

"We have horses to feed," Tanner told her. "Not to mention Snidely and Whiplash. We'll order pizza after the chores are done."

"Our tree is all decorated," Sophie told Olivia. "You should come and see it."

"I will," Olivia said.

"Are you coming down with a cold?" Sophie wanted to know. "You sound funny."

"I'm all right," Olivia answered, touched.

They were about a mile out of town, on the far side of Stone Creek, when they spotted Ginger trudging alongside the road. Olivia's mouth fell open—she'd thought the dog was still at Ashley's.

"What's Ginger doing out here all alone?" Sophie demanded.

"I don't know," Olivia said, struggling in vain to open the passenger-side door even as Tanner stopped the Suburban, got out and lifted the weary dog off the ground. Carried her in his arms to the back of the rig and settled her on the blankets.

"I don't think she's hurt," Tanner said once he was behind the wheel again. "Just tired and pretty footsore."

A tear slipped down Olivia's cheek, and she wiped it away, but not quickly enough.

"Hey," he said, his voice husky. "It can't be that bad."

Olivia didn't answer.

Ashley would be all right.

Ginger would be, too.

But she wasn't so sure about herself.

At some point, without even realizing it, she'd fallen in love with Tanner Quinn. Talk about a dismal revelation.

Reaching her place, Tanner let Sophie stay behind with Olivia and Ginger while he went on to Starcross to feed Butterpie and Shiloh and see to the puppies, as well.

Holding off tears with everything she had, Olivia peeled off her vest, turned up the heat and gave Ginger a quick but thorough exam. Tanner's diagnosis had been correct—she was worn out, and she'd need some salve on the pads of her feet, but otherwise she was fine. "Why didn't you stay at Ashley's?" she asked. "I would have come back for you."

Ginger just looked up at her, eyes full of exhaustion and devoted trust.

"Can I order pizza?" Sophie asked, hovering by the phone.

Olivia smiled a fragile smile, nodded. *Keep busy,* she thought. *Keep busy.* She filled Ginger's water and kibble bowls and dragged her fluffy Ashley-made bed into the kitchen. Ginger turned a few circles and collapsed, obviously spent and blissfully happy to be home.

Sophie placed the pizza order and sat down cross-legged on the floor to pet Ginger, who slumbered on.

"Did Ginger run away?" she asked.

Olivia was making coffee. Maybe Santa would bring her a new percolator. Was it too late to write to him? Did he have an e-mail address?

Was she losing her ever-loving *mind?*

Yes, if she'd fallen for Tanner. He was as unavailable as Melissa's last guy.

"She and I were visiting my sister in town earlier," Olivia explained, amazed at how normal she sounded. "Ginger must have decided to come home on her own."

"I ran away once," Sophie confessed.

"So I heard," Olivia answered, listening more intently now. Watching the girl out of the corner of her eye.

"It was a stupid thing to do," Sophie elaborated.

"And dangerous," Olivia agreed.

"I just wanted to come home," Sophie said. "Like Ginger."

Olivia's throat thickened again. "How do you like Stone Creek Middle School?" she asked, forging bravely on. *Oh, and by the way, I'm hopelessly in love with your father.*

"They're doing *Our Town,* the week between Christmas and New Year's," Sophie said. "I would have tried out for the part of Emily if I lived here."

"They do *Our Town* every year," Olivia answered. "It's a tradition."

"Were you in it when you were in middle school?"

"No. I had stage fright. So I worked sets and costumes. But my older brother, Brad, had a leading role one year, and both my sisters, Ashley and Melissa, had parts when their turn came."

"You have stage fright?"

"I didn't get the show-business gene. That went to Brad."

"Dad has some of his CDs. I kind of like the way he sings."

"Me, too," Olivia said.

"Did you always want to be a veterinarian?"

Olivia left the coffeepot and sat down at the table, near Sophie and the sweetly slumbering Ginger. "For as long as I can remember," she said.

"I want to be a people doctor," Sophie said. "Like my mom was."

"I'm sure you'll be a good one."

Sophie looked very solemn, and she might have been about to say something more about her mother, but the Suburban rolled noisily up alongside the house just then. A door slammed.

Tanner was back from feeding horses and puppies, and the pizza would be arriving soon, no doubt.

*Maybe I'm over him,* Olivia thought. *Maybe fighting for a horse's life made me overemotional.*

He knocked and came inside, shivering. Flecks of hay decorated his clothes. "It's cold out there," he said.

Nope, she wasn't over him.

Olivia's hand shook a little as she gestured toward the coffeepot. "Help yourself," she told him. She was ridiculously glad he was there, he and Sophie both.

Sophie got up from the floor while Tanner poured coffee, and wandered into the living room.

"Hey," she called right away. "Your little tree looks pretty good."

"Thanks," Olivia called back as she and Tanner exchanged low-wattage smiles.

*I love you,* Olivia said silently. *How's that for foolish?*

"How come there aren't any presents under it?"

"Soph," Tanner objected.

Sophie appeared in the doorway between the kitchen and living room.

"There are a lot of guys at our house, fixing up the barn," she told Olivia. "It's a good thing, too, because Aunt Tessa's horses will be tired when they get here."

"Are they on their way?" Olivia asked Tanner.

He nodded. "Tessa's bringing them herself," he said. "I wanted her to fly and let a transport company bring them, but she has a head as hard as Arizona bedrock."

"I think I'm going to like her," Olivia said.

Sophie beamed, nodding in agreement. "Once she's out here with us, she'll get over her break-up in no time!"

Olivia looked at Tanner. "Break-up?"

"Divorce," he said. "None of them are easy, but this one's a meat grinder."

"I'm sorry," Olivia told him, and she meant it. She remembered how broken up her dad had been after Delia skipped out. Knew only too well how *she* would feel when Tanner left Stone Creek for good.

"Can I plug in your Christmas tree?" Sophie asked.

"Sure," Olivia said.

Sophie disappeared again.

Tanner and Olivia looked at each other in silence.

Mercifully, the pizza delivery guy broke the spell by honking his car horn from the driveway.

Tanner grinned and started for the door.

"My turn to provide supper," Olivia said, easing past him.

When she came back with the goods, snow-speckled and wishing she'd taken the time to put on her coat, Tanner was setting the table.

Ginger roused herself long enough to sniff the air. Pizza was one of her favorites, although Olivia never gave her more than a few bites.

Supper was almost magical—they might have been a family, Tanner and Olivia and Sophie, talking around the table as they ate in the warm, cozy kitchen.

Sophie snuck a few morsels to Ginger, and Olivia pretended not to see.

Because Tanner's truck had been picked up and driven to Starcross, Olivia gave her neighbors a ride home when the time came. She waited until they'd both gone inside, after waving from the porch, and watched as the tree lights sprang to life in the front window.

Sophie's doing, she supposed.

On the way back to her place, because she still wanted to cry, Olivia called Ashley's house again.

"She's fine, mother hen," Melissa told her. "I talked her into having some soup a little while ago, and a cup of tea, too. She says she'll be her old self again after a bubble bath."

Olivia's relief was so great that she didn't ask if anybody had noticed Ginger's escape. Nor, of course, did she announce that she was in love.

"I can't seem to find the dog, though," Melissa said. "It's a big house. She must be here somewhere."

"She's home," Olivia said.

"You picked her up?"

"She walked."

"Oh, God, Livie, I'm sorry—she must have slipped out through Ashley's pet door in the laundry room—"

"Ginger's fine," Olivia assured her worried sister.

"Thank God," Melissa replied. "Why do you suppose she put in a pet door—Ashley, I mean—when she doesn't have a *pet?*"

"Maybe she wants one."

"I could stop by the shelter and adopt a kitten for her or something."

"Don't you dare," Olivia said. "Adopting an animal is a commitment, and Ashley has to make that decision on her own."

"Okay, Dr. Dolittle," Melissa teased. "*Okay.* Spare me the responsible pet owner lecture, all right? I was just thinking out loud."

"Why don't *you* adopt a dog or a cat?"

"I'm allergic, remember?" Melissa answered, giving a sneeze right on cue. It was the first sign of Melissa's hypochondria that Olivia had seen in recent days.

"Right," Olivia replied.

By then the snow was coming down so thick and fast, she could barely see her driveway. *Please God,* she prayed silently, *no emergencies tonight.*

She and Melissa swapped goodbyes, and she ended the call.

A nice hot bubble bath didn't sound half-bad, she

thought when the cold air hit her as she got out of the Suburban. Maybe she'd light a few candles, put on her snuggly robe after the bath, make cocoa and watch something Christmasy and sentimental on TV.

Talk herself out of loving a no-strings-attached kind of man.

Ginger got up when she came in, ate a few kibbles and immediately headed for the back door.

So much for getting warm.

Olivia went outside with the dog.

*"It's not as if I plan to run away, you know,"* Ginger remarked.

Through the storm, Olivia could just make out the lights over at Starcross. The sight comforted her and, at the same time, made her feel oddly isolated.

"I wouldn't have thought you'd try to walk all the way home from Stone Creek," Olivia scolded. "Ginger, it's at least five miles."

*"I made it, didn't I?"* Having completed her outside enterprise, Ginger headed for the back porch, stopping to shake off the snow before going on into the kitchen.

Olivia tromped in after her, hugging herself. Shut the door and locked it.

"I'm taking a bubble bath," she said. "Don't bother me unless you're bleeding or the place catches fire."

Ginger took hold of her dog bed with her teeth and hauled it into the living room, in front of the tree. In the softer light, Charlie Brown looked almost—well— *bushy.* Downright festive, even.

She'd unplugged the bubble lights before leaving to take Tanner and Sophie home. Now she bent to plug them in again, waited until the colorful liquid in the little glass vials began to bubble cheerfully.

She immediately thought of Big John, but tonight the memory of her grandfather didn't hurt. She smiled, remembering what a big deal he'd always made over Christmas, spending money he probably didn't have, taking them all up into the timber country to look for just the right tree, sitting proud and straight backed in the audience at each new production of *Our Town*. In retrospect, she knew he'd been trying to make up for the losses in their lives—hers, Brad's, Ashley's and Melissa's.

The year Brad was in the play, Ashley had cried all the way home to the ranch. Big John had carried her into the house and demanded to know what the "waterworks" were all about.

"All those dead people sitting in folding chairs!" Ashley had wailed. "Is Daddy someplace like that, all in shadow, sitting in a folding chair?"

Big John's face had been a study in manfully controlled emotion. "No, honey," he'd said gruffly, there in the kitchen at Stone Creek Ranch, while Brad and Olivia and Melissa peeled out of their coats. "*Our Town* is just a story. Your daddy isn't sitting around in a folding chair, and you can take that to the bank. He's too busy riding horses, I figure. The way I figure it, they've got some mighty good trails up there in heaven, and there aren't any shadows to speak of, either."

Ashley's eyes had widened almost to saucer size, but she'd stopped crying. "How do you know, Big John?" she'd asked, gazing up at him. "Is it in the Bible?"

Brad, a pretty typical teenager, had given a snort at that.

Big John had quelled him with a look. "No," he told Ashley, resting a hand on her shoulder. "It probably isn't in the Bible. But there are some things that just make sense. How many cowboys would want to go to heaven if there weren't any horses to ride?"

Ashley had brightened at the question. In her child's mind, the argument made sense.

Blinking, Olivia returned to the present moment.

"Time for that hot bath I promised myself," she told Ginger.

*"I wouldn't mind one either,"* Ginger said.

And so it was that Olivia bathed the dog first, toweled her off and then scrubbed out the tub for her own turn.

When she finished, she put on flannel pajamas and her favorite bathrobe and padded out to the living room.

Ginger had the TV on, watching *Animal Planet*.

"How did you do that?" Olivia asked. There were some things that strained even an animal communicator's credulity.

*"If you step on the remote just right, it happens,"* Ginger replied.

"Oh, good grief," Olivia said, glancing in Charlie Brown's direction.

*"I wouldn't have thought he could look that good,"* Ginger observed, following Olivia's gaze.

She reclaimed the remote. Checked the channel guide.

"We're watching *The Bishop's Wife*," she told Ginger.

Ginger didn't protest. She liked Cary Grant, too.

*"After it's over,"* the dog said, *"we can talk about how you're in love with Tanner."*

"I don't want to talk about it," Ashley said, for the fourth or fifth time, the next morning when Olivia stopped by her house on the way to the clinic, Ginger in tow. Melissa had already gone to work.

Olivia was still in love, but she was adjusting.

"Fair enough," she replied. Ashley looked almost like her old self, and she was expecting paying guests later in the day. Rolling out piecrusts in preparation for some serious baking.

Some people drank when they were upset. Others chain-smoked.

Ashley baked.

"Tell me about the guests," Olivia said, trying to snitch a piece of pie dough and getting her hand slapped for her trouble.

"They're long-term," Ashley answered, rolling harder, so the flour flew. Some of it was in her hair, and a lot more decorated her holly-sprigged chef's apron. "Tanner Quinn called and booked the rooms. He said he needed space for four people, and he'd vouch for their character because they all work for him."

Olivia raised an eyebrow. "I see," she said, considering another attempt at the pie dough and doing a pretty good job of hiding the fact that Tanner's name made the floor tremble under her feet.

"Don't even think about it," Ashley said, sounding like her old self. *Almost* her old self, anyway. She was still pretty ragged around the edges, but if she didn't want to talk about their mother just yet, Olivia would respect that.

Even if it killed her.

"Nice of him," she said. "Tanner, I mean. He could have put the crew up at the Sundowner Motel, or over in Indian Rock."

Ashley pounded at the pie dough and rolled vigor-

ously again. It looked like a good upper-arm workout.
"All I know is they're paying top dollar, and they'll be
here until next spring. Merry Christmas to me. For a
few months, anyway, I won't need any more 'loans'
from Brad to keep the business going."

Olivia didn't miss the slight edge in her sister's voice.
"Ash," she said. "This will get easier. I promise it will."

"I should have listened to you."

"But you didn't, and that's okay. You're a grown
woman, with a perfect right to make your own decisions."

"She's *horrible,* Liv."

"Let it go, Ash."

"Do you know why she was on probation? For shop-
lifting, and writing bad checks, and—and God knows
what else."

"Brad said you were miffed because he wouldn't
bail her out."

Ashley set down the rolling pin, backed away from
the counter. Flour drifted down onto Ginger's head like
finely sifted snow. "He was right," Ashley said. "He was
right not to bail that—that *woman* out!"

"I can stay if you want me to," Olivia said.

Ashley shook her head, hard. "No," she insisted.
"But I wouldn't mind if Ginger were here to keep me
company."

Olivia looked at Ginger. Knew instantly that she
wanted to stay.

"Don't you dare try to walk home again," she told
the dog. "I'll pick you up after I finish my last call."

"Oh, for Pete's sake," Ashley said. Like Brad and
Melissa, she had always taken the Dr. Dolittle thing
with a grain of salt. Make that a barrel. Only Big John

had really understood—he'd said his grandmother could talk to animals, too.

"Later," Olivia said, and dashed out through the back, though she did stop briefly to secure the latch on the pet door, in case Ginger got another case of wanderlust.

Now that he had crews working, the shelter project took off. The barn at Starcross was coming along nicely, too. Tanner was pleased.

Or he *should* have been.

Sophie loved school—specifically Stone Creek Middle School. She'd already found some friends, and she was making good progress at house-training the puppies, too. She did her chores without being asked, exercising Butterpie every day.

That morning, when he came back inside from feeding the horses, she was already making breakfast.

"I used your laptop," she'd confessed immediately.

"Is that why you're trying to make points?"

Sophie had laughed. "Nope. I had to check my e-mail. All hell's breaking loose at Briarwood."

He hadn't been surprised to hear that, since he'd called both Jack McCall and Ms. Wiggins soon after the drug conversation with Sophie that day in the truck, and read them every line of the riot act, twice over.

Ms. Wiggins had promised a thorough and immediate investigation.

Jack had asked if he was sure Sophie wasn't playing him, so she could stay with him in Stone Creek.

"I *really* can't go back there now, Dad," Sophie had told him, turning serious again. "Everybody knows I'm the one who blew the whistle, and that won't win me the Miss Popularity pin."

He'd ruffled her hair. "Don't worry about it. You'll be going to a new school, anyway." He'd found a good one in Phoenix, just over two hours away by car, but he was saving the details for a surprise. He wanted Tessa to be there when he broke the good news, and Olivia, too, if possible.

Olivia.

Now, there was a gift he'd like to unwrap again.

As soon as Tessa got there and he had somebody to hold down the fort with Sophie, he was going to ask Olivia O'Ballivan, DVM, out on a real date. Take her to dinner somewhere fancy, up in Flagstaff, or in nearby Sedona.

In the meantime, he'd have to tough it out. Work hard. Take a lot of cold showers.

A worker went by, whistling "Have Yourself a Merry Little Christmas."

Tanner almost told him to shut the hell up.

# *Chapter Ten*

There was no slowing down Christmas. It was bearing down on Stone Creek at full throttle, hell-bent-for-election, as Big John used to say. Watering Charlie Brown in her living room before braving snowy roads to get to the clinic for a full day of appointments, Olivia hummed a carol under her breath.

The week since Ashley had come home from Tennessee had been a busy one, rushing by. Olivia had had supper with Sophie and Tanner twice, once at her place, once at theirs.

And she hadn't been able to shake off loving him.

It was for real.

The big tree in the center of town would be lighted as soon as the sun went down that night, to the noisy delight of the whole community, and after that, over at the high school gymnasium, the chamber of commerce was throwing their annual Christmas carnival, with a dance to follow.

In the kitchen Ginger began to bark.

Olivia frowned and went to investigate. They'd already been outside, and she hadn't heard anybody drive in.

Passing the kitchen window, she saw a late-model truck pulling in at Starcross, pulling a long, mud-splashed horse trailer behind it.

Sophie's much-anticipated aunt Tessa, Tanner's sister, had finally arrived. That would be a relief to Tanner—more than once over the past week he'd admitted he was on the verge of heading out to look for Tessa. Even though Tessa called every night, according to Sophie, to report her progress, Tanner had been jumpy.

"He worries a lot about what *could happen,*" Sophie had told Olivia, on the q.t., while the two of them were frying chicken in the kitchen at Starcross. Then, as if concerned that Olivia might be turned off by the admission, she'd added, "But he's *really* brave. He saved Uncle Jack's life *twice* in the Gulf War."

"And modest, too," Olivia had teased.

But Sophie's expression was serious. "Uncle Jack told me about it," she'd said. "Not Dad."

Now, with Ginger barking fit to deafen her, Olivia made an executive decision. She'd stop by Starcross on the way to town and offer a brief welcome to Tessa. It was the neighborly thing to do, after all.

And if she was more than a little curious about the soon-to-be-divorced former TV star, well, nothing wrong with that. Brad would have to share his local-celebrity status, at least temporarily.

Showing up would be an intrusion of sorts, though,

Olivia reasoned as she and Ginger slipped and slid down the icy driveway to the main road. Who knew what kind of shape Tessa Quinn Whoever might be in after driving practically across country with a load of horses and a broken heart?

All the more reason to offer a friendly greeting, Olivia decided.

Tanner had probably already left for the construction site in town, and Sophie was surely in school, secretly lusting after the role of Emily in next year's production of *Our Town*. Stone Creek never got tired of that play—perhaps because it reminded them to be grateful for ordinary blessings.

It bothered Olivia to think Tessa might have no one to welcome her, help her unload her prized horses and settle them into stalls. Since all her morning appointments were things a veterinary assistant could handle, Olivia decided she'd offer whatever assistance she could.

Only, Tanner was there when Olivia arrived, and so was Sophie.

She and Tessa—a tall, dark-haired woman who resembled Tanner—were just breaking up a hug. Tanner was pulling out the ramp on the horse trailer, but he stopped and smiled as Olivia drove up.

Her heart beat double time.

Sophie was obviously filling Tessa in on the new arrival as Olivia got out of the Suburban, leaving Ginger behind in the passenger seat. Tessa's wide-set gray eyes, friendly but reserved, too, took Olivia's measure as she approached, hands in the pockets of her down vest.

What, if anything, Olivia wondered, had Tanner told his sister about the veterinarian-next-door?

Nothing, Olivia hoped. And everything.

Except for a few stolen kisses when Sophie happened to be out of range, nothing had happened between Olivia and Tanner since Thanksgiving.

For all that she was playing with fire and she knew it, Olivia was past ready for another round of hot sex with the first man she'd ever loved—and probably the last.

Tanner made introductions; Tessa wiped her palms down the slim thighs of her gray corduroy pants before offering Olivia a handshake. The caution lingered in her eyes, though, and she slipped an arm around Sophie's shoulders after the hellos had been said, and pulled her against her side.

"I'm trying to talk Tessa into going to the tree-lighting and the Christmas carnival and dance tonight," Tanner said, watching his sister with an expression of fond, worried relief. "So far, it's no-go."

"It's been a long drive," Tessa said, smiling somewhat feebly. "I'd rather stay here. Maybe I'll stop feeling as if the road is still rolling under me."

"I'll stay with you," Sophie told her aunt, clinging with both arms and looking up with a delight that made Olivia feel an unbecoming rush of envy. "We can order pizza."

"You don't want to miss the tree-lighting," Tessa said to Sophie, squeezing her once and kissing the top of her head. "Or the carnival. *That* sounds like a lot of fun." The woman looked almost shell-shocked, the way Ashley had when Brad brought her home from Tennessee, and it wasn't because of the endless highways and roadside hotels.

*Will I look like that when Tanner's gone?* Olivia asked herself, even though she already knew the answer.

"Dad could bring me back after," Sophie insisted. "Couldn't you, Dad?"

Tanner looked at Olivia.

Tessa's glance bounced between the two of them.

"Are you up for a Christmas dance, Doc?" Tanner asked. It was a simple question, but it sounded grave under the watchful eyes of Tessa and Sophie.

"I guess so," Olivia said, because jumping up and down and shouting "Yes, yes, yes!" would have given her away.

"Note the wild enthusiasm," Tanner said, grinning.

"I *think* she said yes," Tessa remarked, her smile warming noticeably.

"Do you have a dress?" Sophie inquired, her brow furrowed. Clearly she was worried that Olivia would skip off to the Christmas festivities in her customary cow-doctor getup.

"Maybe I'll buy one," Olivia said, after chuckling. She still felt as if she'd swallowed a handful of jumping beans, though.

Buying a dress she'd probably never wear again?

*What I did for love.*

When she was a creaky old spinster veterinarian, she'd show the dress to her brother's and sisters' kids and tell them the story. The G-rated part, anyway.

She checked her watch, which was a perfectly normal thing to do. She even smiled. "I guess I'd better get to the clinic," she said. Then, achingly aware of Tanner standing at the edge of her vision, she added, "Unless you need some help unloading those horses?"

"I think I can handle it, Doc," he said good-naturedly. "But if you're in a favor-doing mood, you can drop Sophie off at school."

"Sure," Olivia said, pleased.

"I thought I'd take today off," Sophie piped up.

"You're in or you're out, kiddo," Tanner told her. "You were dead set on continuing your education, remember?"

"Go," Tessa told her niece. "I'll probably be asleep all day anyway."

Sophie nodded, very reluctantly, but in that quicksilver way of children, she had a warm smile going by the time she climbed into the front seat of the Suburban. Ginger, always accommodating, when it came to Sophie, anyway, had already moved to the back, her big furry head blocking the rearview mirror.

"Where are you going to plant Charlie Brown when Christmas is over?" Sophie asked, snapping her seat belt into place and settling in.

"I hadn't thought about it," Olivia admitted. "Maybe in town, on the grounds of the new shelter. I'll be living upstairs when it's finished."

"I wish all Christmas trees came in pots, so they could be planted afterward," Sophie said. "That way, they wouldn't die."

"Me, too," Olivia said.

"Do you think trees have feelings?"

Ginger had shifted just enough to allow Olivia a glance in the rearview. Olivia caught a glimpse of Tanner, leading the first horse down the ramp and toward the newly refurbished barn.

"I don't know," Olivia answered belatedly, "but they're living things, and they deserve good treatment."

Mercifully, the conversation took a different track after that, though the subject of trees lingered in Olivia's mind, leading to Kris Kringle at the lot in town, and finally to Rodney, who was living the high life in Brad's barn at Stone Creek Ranch. For that little stretch of time, she didn't think about Tanner.

Much.

"Aunt Tessa is pretty, don't you think?" Sophie asked as ramshackle country fences whizzed by on both sides of the Suburban.

"She certainly is," Olivia agreed, feeling unusually self-conscious about her clothes and her bobbed hair. Tessa's locks flowed, wavy and almost as dark as Tanner's, past her shoulders. "I don't recall seeing her on TV, though."

"We got you the season one DVD of *California Women* for Christmas," Sophie said with a spark of mischief in her eyes. "It was supposed to be a surprise, though."

Sophie and Tanner had bought her a Christmas present?

Lord, what was she going to give them in return? She hadn't even shopped for Mac yet, let alone Brad and Meg, Ashley and Melissa, and the office staff and the other vets she worked with at the clinic.

"It's no big deal," Sophie assured her, evidently reading her expression.

Fruitcake? Olivia wondered, distracted. One of those things that came in a colorful tin and had a postapocalyptic sell-by date? If they didn't eat it, it could double as a doorstop.

"How come you're frowning like that?" Sophie pressed.

"I'm just thinking," Olivia said as they reached the outskirts of town. The hardware store had fruitcake;

she'd seen a display when she bought the lights and ornaments for Charlie Brown.

And what kind of loser bought bakery goods in a hardware store?

This was a job for super-Ashley, she of the wildly wielded rolling pin and the flour-specked hair. Olivia would drop in on her on her lunch break, she decided, to (a) borrow a dress for the dance, thereby saving posterity from the tale, and (b) persuade her sister to whip up something impressive for the Quinns' Christmas present.

"This is cool," Sophie said a few minutes later when Olivia pulled up to the curb in front of Stone Creek Middle School. "Almost like having a mom." Having dropped that one, she turned to say a quick goodbye to Ginger, and then she disappeared into the gaggle of kids milling on the lawn.

Olivia's hands trembled on the steering wheel as she eased out of a tangle of leaving and arriving traffic.

*"We still have half an hour before you're due at the clinic,"* Ginger said, brushing Olivia's face with her plumy tail as she returned to the front seat. *"Let's go by the tree lot and have a word with Kris Kringle. For Rodney's sake, we need to know he's on the level."*

"Not going to happen," Olivia said firmly. "I've got some paperwork to catch up on before I start seeing patients and, besides, Kringle checked out with Indian Rock PD. Plus, Rodney's doing okay at the homeplace. I get daily reports from either Meg or Brad, and we've been to visit our reindeer buddy twice in the last three days."

Ginger was determined to be helpful, apparently. Or just to butt in. *"How's your mother?"*

"I do not want to talk about my mother."

*"Denial,"* Ginger accused. *"Sooner or later, you're going to have to see her, just to get closure."*

"You need to stop watching talk-TV while I'm at work," Olivia said. "Besides, Mommy dearest is in the clink right now."

*"No, she isn't. Brad got her a lawyer and had her moved to a swanky 'recovery center' in Flagstaff."*

Olivia almost ran the one red light in Stone Creek. "How do you know these things?"

*"Rodney told me the last time we visited. He heard Brad and Meg talking about it in the barn."*

"And you're just getting around to mentioning this now?"

*"I knew you wouldn't take it well. And there's the being in love with Tanner thing."*

Olivia grabbed her cell phone and speed-dialed her sneaky brother. Mr. Tough, refusing to bail their mom out of the hoosegow back in Tennessee. He hadn't said a single word to her about bringing Delia to Arizona, or to the twins, either. They'd have told her if he had.

"Is Mom in a treatment center in Flagstaff?" she demanded the moment Brad said hello.

"How did you know that?" Brad asked, sounding both baffled and guilty.

"Never mind how I know. I just do."

Brad heaved a major sigh. "Okay. Yes. Mom's in Flagstaff. I was going to tell you and the twins after Christmas."

"Why the change of heart, Brad?" Olivia snapped, annoyed for the obvious reason and, also, because Ginger was right. If she wanted any closure, she'd have to visit her mother, and after what had happened to Ashley, the prospect had all the appeal of locking herself in a cage with a crazed grizzly bear.

"She's our mother," Brad said after a long silence. "I wanted to turn my back on her, the way she turned hers on us, but in the end I couldn't do it."

Olivia's eyes stung. Good thing she was pulling into the clinic lot, because she couldn't see well enough to drive at the moment. "I know you did the right thing," she said as Ginger nudged her shoulder sympathetically. "But I'll be a while getting used to the idea of Mom living right up the road, after all these years."

"Tell me about it," Brad said. "It's a long-term thing, Liv. Basically, the prognosis for her recovery isn't good."

Olivia sat very still in the Suburban, nosed up to the wall of the clinic, clutching the phone so tightly in her right hand that her knuckles ached. "Are you telling me she's dying?"

"We're all dying," Brad answered. "I'm telling you that, in this case, 'treatment center' is a euphemism for one of the best mental hospitals in the world. She could live to be a hundred, but she'll probably never leave Palm Haven."

"She's crazy?"

"She's fried her brain, between the booze and snorting a line of coke whenever she could scrape the money together. So, yeah. *She's crazy.*"

"Oh, God."

"They're adjusting her medication, and she'll eat regularly, anyway. I'm not planning to pay her a visit until sometime after the first, and I'd suggest you wait, too. This is Mac's first Christmas, and I plan to enjoy it."

Becky, the receptionist, beckoned from the side door of the clinic.

"I've got to go," Olivia said, nodding to Becky that she'd be right in. "Will you and Meg be at the tree-lighting and all that?"

"Definitely the tree-lighting. Probably the carnival, too. But maybe not the dance. Mac's getting a tooth, so he's not his usual sunny self."

Olivia laughed, blinked away tears.

This was life, she supposed. Their mother's tragedy on the one hand, a baby having his first Christmas and sprouting teeth on the other.

Falling in love with the wrong man at the wrong time.

What could you do but tough it out?

The Sophie-of-Christmas-future haunted Tanner—she still came to him almost every night in his dreams, and of course he mulled them over during the days. In one memorable visit he'd found her living alone in an expensive but sparsely furnished apartment, with only a little ceramic tree to mark the presence of a holiday. He'd counted two Christmas cards tacked to her wall. In another, she tried to get through to him by phone, wanting to wish him a Merry Christmas. He'd been unreachable. And in a third installment he'd seen her standing wistfully at the edge of a city playground, watching a flock of young mothers and their children skating on a frozen pond.

Was this really a glimpse of the future, Ebenezer Scrooge–style, or was he just torturing himself with parental guilt?

Either way, he'd come to dread closing his eyes at night.

"Sophie looks happy," Tessa remarked from her

seat at the kitchen table. Now that she'd finally arrived safely at Starcross at least, Tanner had one fewer thing to worry about. "And I like Olivia. Something special going on between the two of you?"

"What makes you think that?" he asked, hedging.

Tessa smiled at him over the rim of her coffee cup. "Oh, maybe the way you sort of held your breath when you asked her to the dance, until she said yes, and the way she blushed—"

"If I remember correctly," Tanner broke in, "she said 'I guess so.'"

"Could it be you're finally thinking of settling down, Big Brother?"

Tanner dragged back a chair and sat. "A week ago, even a *day* ago, I probably would have said no. Emphatically. But I'm getting pretty worried about Sophie."

Tessa arched an eyebrow, waited in silence.

"I've been having these crazy dreams," he confessed, after a few moments spent trying to convince himself that Tessa would think he was nuts if he told her about them.

"What kind of crazy dreams?" Tessa asked gently, pushing her coffee cup aside, folding her arms and resting them on the table's edge.

Tanner shoved a hand through his hair. "It's as if I travel through time," he admitted, every word torn out of him like a strip of hide. "Sophie's in her thirties, and she's a doctor, but she's alone in the world."

"Hmmm," Tessa said. "The doctor is in. Advice, five cents."

Tanner gave a raw chuckle. "Put it on my bill," he said.

"How do you fit into these dreams?"

"I'm off building something, in some other part of the world. At the same time, I'm there somehow, watching Sophie. And who knows where you are. I don't want to scare you or anything, but you haven't been a guest star."

"Go on," Tessa said.

"I love my daughter, Tessa," Tanner said. "I don't want her to end up—well, alone like that."

Tessa's gray eyes widened, and a smile flicked at the corner of her mouth. She was still beautiful, and she still got acting offers, but she always turned them down because it would mean leaving her horses. "Sophie's been miserable at boarding school," she said. "Last fall, when it was time for her to go back, she begged me to let her stay on with me at the farm. I wanted so much to say yes, and damn *your* opinion in the matter, but things were going downhill fast between Paul and me even then. She'd heard us fighting all summer, and I knew it wasn't good for her."

"I thought she was *safe* at school."

"'Thought'? Past tense? What's happened, Tanner?"

Briefly Tanner explained what Sophie had told him about the easy availability of meth and ice at Briarwood. "It's not like Stone Creek is Brigadoon or anything." He sighed. "A kid can probably score any kind of drug right here in rural America. But I really thought I had all the bases covered."

"Give Sophie a little credit," Tessa said, and though her tone was firm, she reached across the table to touch Tanner's hand. "She's way too smart to do drugs."

"I know," Tanner answered. "But I've always thought she'd be happy when she grew up—that she'd come to understand that I had her best interests at heart, sending her away to school...."

"And the dreams made you question that?"

Tanner nodded. "They're so—so *real,* Tess. I can't shake the feeling that Sophie's going to have no life outside her work—all because she doesn't know how to be part of a family."

"Heavy stuff," Tessa said. "Are you in love with Olivia?"

"I don't know what I feel," Tanner answered, after a long silence. "And I don't necessarily have to get married to give Sophie a home, do I? I could sell off the overseas part of the business, or just close it down. I'd still have to do some traveling, but if you were here—"

"Hold it," Tessa broke in. "I can't promise I'm going to stay, Tanner. And one way or the other, I don't intend to live off your generosity like some poor relation."

"You won't have to," Tanner said. "There's money, Tess. Kat and I set it aside for you a long time ago."

Tessa's cheeks colored up. Her pride was kicking in, just as Tanner had known it would. *"What?"*

"You put me through college on what you earned when you were acting, Tessa," he reminded her. "You took care of Gram while I was in the service and then getting the business started. You're *entitled* to all the help I can give you."

Tessa went from pink to pale. Her eyes narrowed. "I can provide for myself," she said.

"Can you?" Tanner countered. "Good for you. Because that's more than I could do when I was in college and for a long time after that, and it's more than Gram could have managed, too, with just her Social Security and the take from that roadside vegetable stand of hers."

"How *much* money, Tanner?"

"Enough," Tanner said. He got up, walked to the small desk in the corner of the kitchen and jerked a bound folder out of the drawer. Returning to the table, he tossed it down in front of her.

Tessa opened the portfolio and stared at the figures, her eyes rounding at all those zeroes.

"The magic of compound interest," Tanner said.

"This money should be Sophie's," Tessa whispered, her voice thin and very soft. "My God, Tanner, this is a *fortune*."

"Sophie has a trust fund. I started it with Kat's life insurance check, and the last time I looked, it was around twice that much."

Tessa swallowed, looked up at him in shock, momentarily speechless.

"You can draw on it, or let it grow. My accountant has the tax angle all figured out, and it's in my name until the divorce is final, so Paul can't touch it." Still standing, Tanner folded his arms. "It's up to you, Tess. You're real good at giving. How are you at *receiving?*"

Tessa huffed out a stunned breath. "I could buy out Paul's half of the horse farm—"

"*Or* you could start over, right here, with a place of your own. No bad memories attached. Times are hard, and there are a lot of good people looking to sell all or part of their land."

"I can't think. Tanner, this is—this is unbelievable! I knew you were doing well, but I had no idea…"

"I'm late," he said.

On his way out, he checked on the puppies, found them sleeping in their box by the stove, curled up together as if they were still in the womb. They were so small, so helpless, so wholly trusting.

His throat tightened as he took his coat off the peg on the wall by the back door. He couldn't help drawing a parallel between the pups and Sophie.

"I'll be at the job site in town," he said. "You have my cell number if you need anything."

Tessa was still hunched over the portfolio. Her shoulders were shaking a little, so Tanner figured she was crying, though he couldn't be sure, with her back to him and all.

"Will you be okay here alone?" he asked gruffly.

She nodded vigorously, but didn't turn around to meet his gaze.

That damnable pride again.

Grabbing up his truck keys from the counter, he left the house. It was snowing so hard by then, he figured he'd probably let the construction crew off an hour or two early.

And Olivia had agreed to go to the dance with him that night.

It wasn't quite the date he'd had in mind, but she was planning to wear a dress, and Tessa would be on hand to keep an eye on Sophie after the tree-lighting and the carnival.

This was shaping up to be a half-decent Christmas.

Climbing behind the wheel of the truck, Tanner started the engine, whistling "Jingle Bells" under his breath, and headed for town.

Ashley, with the help of a few very tall elves in college sweatshirts, was on a high ladder decorating her annual mongo Christmas tree when Olivia and Ginger showed up at noon.

"I need to borrow a dress for the dance," Olivia said.

"Hello to you, too," Ashley replied. She still looked a little feeble, but she was obviously into the holiday spirit, or she wouldn't have been decking the halls. And if she had a clue that Delia was in Flagstaff, luxuriously hospitalized, it didn't show. "I'm taller than you are. Anything I loaned you would have to be hemmed. I don't have time for that, and you can't sew."

"I sew all the time. It's called surgery. Ashley, this is an emergency. Can I raid your closet? Please? The hardware store doesn't sell dresses, and I don't have time to drive up to Flagstaff and shop."

Ashley waved her toward the stairs. "Anything but the blue velvet number with the little beads. I'm wearing that myself."

Olivia wiggled her eyebrows. Ginger snugged herself up on the hooked rug in front of the crackling blaze in the fireplace and relaxed into a power nap. That dog was at home anywhere. And everywhere.

"You have a date?" Olivia asked.

"As a matter of fact, I do," Ashley replied, carefully draping a single strand of tinsel over a branch. She'd do that two jillion times, to make the tree look perfect. "It's a blind date, if you must know. A friend of Tanner Quinn's—he's going to be staying here. The friend, not Tanner."

Olivia paused at the base of the stairway. "I hope it goes well," she said. "It could be awkward living under the same roof with a bad date until next spring."

"Thanks a heap, Liv. Now I'm *twice* as nervous."

Olivia hurried up the stairs. She still had to broach

the subject of Ashley whipping up something spectacular for her to give Tanner, Sophie and Tessa for Christmas. An ice castle, made of sugar, she thought. Failing that, fancy cookies would work—the kind with colored frosting and sugar sparkles.

But the outfit had to come first.

Ashley's room was almost painfully tidy—the bed made, all the furniture matching, the prints tastefully arranged on the pale pink walls. Everywhere she looked, there was lace, or ruffles, or both.

It was almost impossible to imagine a man in that room.

Olivia sighed, thinking of her own jumbled bed, liberally sprinkled with dog hair. Her clothes were all over the floor, and she hadn't seen the surface of the dresser in weeks.

Yikes. If the date with Tanner went the way she hoped it would, she'd wish she'd spruced the place up a little—but at least he wouldn't have to contend with lace and ruffles.

She would cut out of the clinic an hour early that afternoon, assuming there were no disasters in the interim. Run the vacuum cleaner, dust a little, change the sheets.

She turned her mind back to the task at hand. Ashley's closet was jammed, but organized. Even color coded, for heaven's sake. Olivia swiped a pair of black velvet palazzo pants—probably gaucho pants on Ashley—and tried them on. If she rolled them up at the waist and wore her high-heeled boots, she probably wouldn't catch a toe in a hem and fall on her face.

A red silk tank top and a glittering silver shawl completed the ensemble.

Piece of cake, Olivia thought smugly, heading out of the room and back down the stairs with the garments draped over one arm.

At the bottom of the steps, just opening her mouth to pitch the sugar-ice-castle idea to Ashley, she stopped in her tracks.

A guy stood just inside the front door, and what a guy he was. Military haircut, hard body, straight back and shoulders. Wearing black from head to foot. Only the twinkle in his hazel eyes as he looked up at Ashley saved him from looking like a CIA agent trying to infiltrate a terrorist cell.

Ashley, staring back at him, seemed in imminent danger of toppling right off the ladder.

The air sizzled.

"Jack McCall," Ashley marveled. "You son of a bitch!"

## Chapter Eleven

Jack McCall grinned and saluted. "Good to see you again, Ash," he said, admiring her with a sweep of his eyes. "Are we still going to the dance together tonight?"

Ashley shinnied down the ladder, which was no mean trick in a floor-length Laura Ashley jumper. "I wouldn't go *anywhere* with you, you jerk," she cried. "Get out of my house!"

Olivia's mouth fell open. Ashley was the consummate bed-and-breakfast owner. She *never* screamed at guests—and Mr. McCall was clearly a guest, since he had a suitcase—much less called them sons of bitches.

"Sorry," McCall said, crossing his eyes a little at the finger Ashley was about to shake under his nose. "The deal's made, the lease is signed and I'm here until spring. On and off."

The college-student elves had long since fled, but Olivia and Ginger remained, both of them fascinated.

*"She's crazy about him,"* Ginger said.

"Look, Ash," McCall went on smoothly, "I know we had that little misunderstanding over the cocktail waitress, but don't you think we ought to let bygones be bygones?"

This man worked for Tanner? Olivia thought, trying to catch up with the conversation. He didn't look like the type to work for anyone but himself—or maybe the president.

Where had Ashley met him?

And what was the story with the cocktail waitress?

"I was young and stupid," Ashley spouted, putting her hands on her hips.

"But very beautiful." Jack McCall sighed. "And you still are, Ash. It's good to see you again."

"I bet you said the same thing to the cocktail waitress!" Ashley cried.

Jack looked, Olivia thought, like a young, modern version of Cary Grant. Impishly chagrined and way too handsome. And where had she heard his name before?

"She meant nothing to me," Jack said.

Olivia rolled her eyes. What a charmer he was. But he and Ashley looked perfect together, even if Ashley *was* trembling with fury.

It was time to step in, before things escalated.

Olivia hurried over and took her sister by the arm, tugging her toward the kitchen and, at the same time, chiming rapid-fire at McCall, over one shoulder, "Hi. I'm Olivia O'Ballivan, Ashley's sister. Glad to meet you. Make yourself at home while I talk her into building an ice castle out of sugar, will you? Thanks."

"An *ice castle?*" Ashley demanded once they were in the kitchen.

"With turrets, and lights inside. I'll pay you big bucks. Who *is* that guy, Ash?"

Ashley's shoulders sagged. She blew out a breath, and her bangs fluttered in midair. "He's nobody," she said.

"Get real. I know passion when I see it."

"I knew him in college," Ashley admitted.

"You never mentioned dating the reincarnation of Cary Grant."

"He dropped me for a cocktail waitress. Why would I want to mention that? I felt like an idiot."

"That was a while ago, Ash."

"Don't you have to get back to work or something?"

Ginger meandered in. *"There'll be a hot time in the old town tonight,"* she said.

"Hush," Olivia said.

"I will *not* hush," Ashley said. "And what's this about a sugar ice castle with lights inside?"

"I need something special to give the Quinns for Christmas, and you're the only one I know with that kind of—"

"Time on her hands?" Ashley finished ominously.

"Talent," Olivia said sweetly. "The only one with that kind of *talent.*"

"You are *so* full of it."

Olivia batted her eyelashes. "But I'm your big sister, and you love me. I'm always there for you, and if you ever had a pet, I'd give it free veterinary care. For life."

"No sugar castle," Ashley said. "I have a million things to do, with all these guests checking in." She paused. "If I murdered Jack McCall, would you testify that I was with you and give me an alibi?"

"Only if you made me a few batches of your stupendous Christmas cookies so I could give them to Sophie and Tanner."

Ashley smiled in spite of her earlier ire, but pain lingered in her eyes, old and deep. Jack McCall *had* hurt her, and suddenly he seemed a whole lot less charming than before. "I'll bake the cookies," she said. "God knows where I'll find the time, but I'll do it."

Olivia kissed her sister's cheek. "I'm beyond grateful. Are you really going to refuse to rent McCall a room?"

"It's Christmas," Ashley said musingly. "And anyway, if he's here, under my roof, I can find lots of ways to get back at him. By New Year's, he'll be *begging* to break the lease."

Olivia laughed, held up the armload of clothes. "Thanks, Ash," she said. "In this getup, I'll be a regular Cinderella."

*"Shall I stay here and spy, or go back to the clinic with you?"* Ginger inquired, looking from Ashley to Olivia.

"You're going with me," Olivia said on the way back to the living room. She'd have gone out the back way, as the fleeing elves probably had, but she wanted one more look at Jack McCall.

"I'm not going anywhere," Ashley argued, following. "I've still got to tie at least a hundred bows on the branches of the Christmas tree."

"I was talking to Ginger," Olivia explained breezily.

"And I suppose she talked back?" Ashley asked.

"Skeptic," Olivia said.

Jack McCall had taken off his coat, and his bag sat at the base of the stairs. Evidently he was planning to stay on. The poor guy probably had no idea how many passive-aggressive ways there were for a crafty bed-and-breakfast owner to make an unwanted guest hit the road.

Too much starch in the sheets.

Too much salt in the stew.

The possibilities were endless.

Olivia was smiling broadly as she and Ginger descended Ashley's front steps, headed for the Suburban.

Fat flakes of snow drifted down from a heavy sky as the entire population of Stone Creek and half of Indian Rock gathered in the town's tiny park for the annual tree-lighting ceremony.

Sophie stood at Olivia's left side, Tanner at her right.

Brad had been roped into being the MC, but it was an informal gig, and he didn't have to sing. He announced that the high school gym was all decked out for the carnival and the dance afterward, and reminded the crowd that all the proceeds would go to worthy causes.

An enormous live spruce awaited splendor, its branches dark and fragrant, strings of extension cord running from beneath it. Roots enclosed in burlap, it would be planted when the ground thawed, like all the other Stone Creek Christmas trees before it.

"Are we ready?" Brad asked, holding the switch.

"YES!" roared the townspeople in one happy voice.

Brad flipped the plastic lever, and what seemed like millions of tiny colored lights shimmered in the cold winter night, like stars trapped in the branches.

The applause sounded like a herd of cattle stampeding.

The din had barely subsided when sleigh bells jingled, right on cue.

Tanner grinned down at Olivia and took her hand. She felt a little trill, though she was a bit nervous because she'd already had to surreptitiously roll up her borrowed palazzo pants a couple of times.

"Could it be?" Brad said into the mic. "Could *Santa Claus* be right here in Stone Creek?"

The smaller children in the crowd waited in breathless silence, their eyes huge with wonder and anticipation.

It happened every year. Santa arrived on a tractor from the heavy-equipment rental place, bells jingling an accompaniment through a scratchy PA system, the man in the red suit waving and tossing candy and shouting, "Ho! Ho! *Ho!*"

This year was a little different, it turned out.

Kris Kringle himself drove the fancy tree-lot sleigh, the one with the brass runners, into the center of the park—pulled by seven real live reindeer and a donkey. He wore hands down the best Santa suit Olivia had ever seen, and instead of candy, he had a huge, bulky green velvet bag in the back of the sleigh.

"Very authentic," Tanner told Olivia, his eyes sparkling.

There were actual wrapped presents in the bag, they soon saw, and Kris Kringle distributed them, making sure every child received one.

Even Sophie, too old at twelve to believe in Santa, got a small red-and-white striped package.

Brad must have been behind the gifts, Olivia thought. Times were hard, and a lot of Stone Creek families had been out of work since late summer. It would be just like her brother to see that they got something for Christmas in a pride-sparing way like this.

"Wow," Sophie said, staring at the package, then casting a sidelong glance at Tanner. "Can I open it?"

"Why not?" Tanner asked, looking mystified. Olivia knew he was throwing a turkey-and-trimmings feast for the whole community on Christmas Day, down at the senior citizens' center—Sophie had spilled the beans about that—but he didn't seem to be in on the presents-for-every-kid-in-town thing.

Sophie ripped into the package, drew in a breath when she saw what it was—an exquisite miniature snow globe with horses inside, one like Shiloh, the other the spitting image of Butterpie.

"Is this from you, Dad?" she asked after swallowing hard.

Tanner was staring curiously at Kris Kringle, who glanced his way and smiled before turning his attention back to the children clamoring to pet the lone donkey and the seven reindeer.

"Gently, now," Kringle called, a right jolly old elf. "They have a long trip to make on Christmas Eve and they're not used to crowds."

"Can they fly?" one child asked. Olivia spotted the questioner, a little boy in outgrown clothes, clutching an unopened package in both hands. She'd gone to high school with his parents, both of whom had been drawing unemployment since the sawmill closed down for the winter. It was rumored that the husband had just been hired as a laborer at Tanner's construction site, but of course that didn't mean their Christmas would be plush. The family would have bills to catch up on.

"Why, of course they can fly, Billy Johnson," Kringle replied jovially.

"Oh, brother," Tanner sighed.

Mr. Kringle had gotten to know everybody in town, Olivia thought, just since the day after Thanksgiving. Otherwise he wouldn't have known Billy's name.

"What about the donkey?" a little girl inquired. Like Billy's, her clothes showed some wear, and she had a package, too, also unopened. Olivia didn't recognize her, figuring she and her family must be new in town. "There wasn't any *donkey* in the St. Nicholas story."

"I've had to improvise, Sandra," Kringle explained kindly. "One of my reindeer—" here he paused, sought and unerringly found Olivia's face in the gathering, and winked "—has been on vacation."

"Oh," said the little girl.

Brad, having left the stage after lighting up the tree, had made his way through the crowd, carrying a snow-suited, gurgling Mac on one hip. Like every other kid, Mac had a present, and he was bonking Brad on the head with it as they approached.

"The packages were a nice touch," Olivia said, drawing her brother aside.

"I was expecting Fred Stevens, stuffed into the chamber of commerce's ratty old corduroy suit and driving a tractor," Brad said, looking puzzled. Even when *they* were kids, Mr. Stevens, a retired high school principal and the grand poo-bah at the lodge, had done the honors. "And I don't know anything about the presents."

No one else in Stone Creek, besides Tanner, had the financial resources to buy and wrap so many gifts. Olivia narrowed her eyes. "You can level with me," she whispered. "I know you and Meg arranged for this, just like when you made a lot of toys and food baskets magically appear on certain people's porches last Christmas Eve. You put one over on poor Fred somehow and paid Kringle to fill in."

Brad frowned. Took the present from Mac's hand, putting an end to the conking. "No, I didn't," he said. "Fred loves this job. I wouldn't have talked him out of it."

"Okay, but you must have bought the presents. I *know* the town council, the chamber of commerce, both churches *and* the lodge couldn't have pulled this off."

"I haven't got a clue where these packages came from," Brad insisted, and his gaze strayed to Kris Kringle, who was preparing to drive away in his sleigh. "Unless…"

"Don't be silly," Olivia said. "The man runs a Christmas-tree lot and makes personal appearances at birthday parties. Wyatt ran a background check on him, and there's no way he could afford a giveaway on this scale. Nor, my dear brother, is he Santa Claus."

Brad shoved a hand through his hair, scanning the crowd, probably looking for his wife. "Look, I admit Meg and I are planning to scatter a few presents around town this year," he told her earnestly. "But if I was in on this one, believe me, I'd tell you."

Sophie stood nearby, shaking her snow globe for Mac's benefit. The baby strained over Brad's shoulder, trying to grab it.

Olivia turned to Tanner. "Then you must have done it."

"I wish I had," Tanner said thoughtfully. "The turkey dinner on Christmas Day seemed more practical to me." He grinned, putting one arm around Sophie and one around Olivia. "Let's go check out that carnival."

A look passed between Brad and Tanner.

"Have fun," Brad said, with a note of irony and perhaps warning in his voice.

"We will," Tanner replied lightly, slugging Brad in the Mac-free arm.

Brad gave him an answering slug.

*Men,* Olivia thought.

The carnival, like the tree-lighting ceremony, was crowded. The gym had been decorated with red and green streamers and giant gold Christmas balls, and there were booths set up on all four walls—fudge for sale in this one, baked goods in that one. Adults settled in for a rousing evening of bingo, the prizes all donated by local merchants, and there were games for the children—the "fishing hole" being the most popular.

For a modest fee, a child could dangle a long wooden stick with a string on the end of it over a shaky blue crepe-paper wall. After a tug, they'd pull in their line and find an inexpensive toy attached.

Sophie was soon bored, though good-naturedly so. She kept taking the snow globe out of her purse and shaking it to watch the snow swirl around Shiloh and Butterpie.

Tanner bought her a chili dog and a Coke and asked if she was ready to go home. She said she was.

"Ride along?" Tanner asked Olivia.

"I think I'll sit in on a round of bingo," she answered. The ladies from her church were running the game, and they'd been beckoning her to join in from the beginning.

Tanner nodded. "Save the first dance for me," he

whispered into her ear. "And the last. And all the ones in between."

Feeling like a teenager at her first prom, Olivia nodded.

"It's weird that that guy knows about Butterpie and Shiloh," Sophie commented, munching on the chili dog as she and Tanner headed for Starcross in the truck. The snow was coming down so thick and fast that Tanner had the windshield wipers on. "A *nice* kind of weird, though."

"It must have been a coincidence, Soph."

"Heaven forbid," Sophie said loftily, "that I might want to believe in one teeny, tiny Christmas *miracle.*"

He thought of the dreams. Sophie as a lonely adult, working too hard, with no life outside her medical practice. A chill rippled down his spine, even though the truck's heater was going full blast. "Believe, Sophie," he said quietly. "Go ahead and believe."

He felt her glance, quick and curious. "What?"

"Maybe I *have* been too serious about things."

"Ya think?" Sophie quipped, but there was a taut thread of hope strung through her words, and it sliced deep into Tanner's heart.

"Look, I've been thinking—how would you like to go to school in Phoenix? There's a good one there, with an equestrian program and excellent security. I was going to wait until Christmas to bring it up, but—"

"I'd rather go to Stone Creek Middle School."

What had he expected her to say? The place was still a boarding school, even if it did have horse facilities. "I know that, Sophie. But I travel a lot and—"

"And Aunt Tessa will be here, so I'd be fine if you

were away." Sophie was watching him closely. "What are you so afraid of, Dad?"

He thrust out a sigh. "That you'll be hurt. Your mom—"

"Dad, this is Stone Creek. There aren't any terrorists here. There's nobody to be mad and want to shoot at us because you built some bridge for the U.S. government where the local bomb-brewers didn't *want* a bridge."

Tanner's hands tightened on the steering wheel. He'd had no idea Sophie knew that much. Did she know about the periodic death threats, too? The ones that had prompted him to hire Jack McCall's men-in-black to guard Briarwood? Hell, he'd even had a detail looking out for Sophie when she was on the horse farm every summer, with Tessa.

"I feel safe here, Dad," Sophie went on gently. "I want you to feel safe, too. But you don't, because Uncle Jack wouldn't be in town if you did."

"How did you know Jack was here? He didn't get in until today."

"I saw him at the carnival with a pretty blond lady who didn't seem to like him," Sophie answered matter-of-factly. "Some kids play 'Where's Waldo?' Thanks to you, *I* play 'Where's Jack?' And I'm *real* good at spotting him."

"He's here on personal business," Tanner said. "Not to trail you."

"What kind of personal business?"

"How would I know? Jack doesn't tell me everything—he's got a private side." A "private side"? The man rappelled down walls of compounds behind enemy lines. He rescued kidnap victims and God knew what else. Tanner didn't have a lot of information about Jack's operation, beyond services rendered on Sophie's behalf at very high fees, and he didn't want to.

He slept better that way, and Jack, the secretive bastard, wouldn't have told him anyhow.

Oh, yeah. He was *way* happier. Except when he dreamed about Dr. Sophie Quinn, ghost of Christmas future, or thought about leaving Stone Creek and probably never seeing Olivia again.

"Soph," he said, skidding a little on the turnoff to Starcross, "when you grow up, are you going to hate me for making you go to boarding school?"

"I could never hate you, Dad." She said the words with such gentle equanimity that Tanner's throat constricted. "I know you're doing the best you can."

Sigh.

"I thought you'd be happy about Phoenix," he said after a pause. "It's only two hours from here, you know."

"What will that matter, if you're in some country where they want to put your head on a pike because you build things?"

It was a good thing they'd reached the driveway at Starcross; if they'd still been on the highway, Tanner might have run the truck into the ditch. "Is that what you think is going to happen?"

"I worry about it all the time. I'm human, you know."

"You're way too smart to be human. You're an alien from the Planet Practical."

She laughed, but there wasn't much humor in the sound. "I watch CNN all the time when you're out of the country," she confessed. "Sometimes really bad things happen to contractors working overseas."

Tanner pulled the truck up close to the house. He was anxious to get back to Olivia, but not so anxious that he'd leave Sophie in the middle of a conversation like this one. "What if I promised not to work outside the U.S.A., Soph? Ever again?"

The look of reluctant hope on the face Sophie turned to Tanner nearly broke him down. "You'd do that?"

"I'd do that, shorty."

She flung herself across the console, after springing the seat belt, and threw both arms around his neck, hugging him hard. He felt her tears against his cheek, where their faces touched. "Can I tell Aunt Tessa?" she sniffled.

"Yes," he said gruffly, holding on to her. Wishing she'd always be twelve, safe with him and Tessa at Starcross Ranch, and never become a relationship-challenged adult working eighteen-hour days out of loneliness as much as ambition.

It would be his fault if Sophie's life turned out that way. He'd been the one to set the bad example.

"I love you, Soph," he said.

She gave him a smacking kiss on the cheek and pulled away. "Love you, too, Dad," she replied, turning to get out of the truck.

He walked her inside the house, torn between wanting to stay home and wanting to be with Olivia.

Tessa had the tree lights on, and she and the puppies were cozied up together on the couch, watching a Christmas movie on TV.

"Dad is never going to work outside the country again!" Sophie shouted gleefully, bounding into the room like a storm trooper.

"Is that so?" Tessa asked, smiling, her gaze pensive as she studied Tanner. Was that skepticism he saw in her eyes?

"Dad's going back to dance the night away with Olivia," Sophie announced happily. "How about some hot chocolate, Aunt Tessa? I know how to make it."

"Good idea," Tessa said.

Sophie said a quick goodbye to Tanner as she passed him on her way to the kitchen.

"I hope you're going to keep your word," Tessa told him when Sophie was safely out of earshot.

"Why wouldn't I?"

"It's tempting, all that money. All those adrenaline rushes."

"I can resist temptation."

Tessa grinned. "Except where Olivia O'Ballivan is concerned, I suspect. Go ahead and 'dance the night away.' I'll take good care of Sophie, and if the place is overrun by revenge-seeking foreign extremists, I'll be sure and give you a call."

Tanner chuckled. Something inside him let go suddenly, something that had held on for dear life ever since that awful day on a street thousands of miles away, when Kat had died in his arms. "I *have* been a little paranoid, haven't I?" he asked.

"A little?" Tessa teased.

"There's a lady waiting at the bingo table," he told his sister. "Gotta go."

"See you tomorrow," Tessa said knowingly.

He let that one pass, waggling his fingers in farewell. "Later, Soph!" he called.

And then he left the house, sprinting for his truck.

"I need to get out of these pants before I kill myself," Olivia confided several hours later, when they'd both worn out the soles of their shoes dancing to the lodge orchestra's Christmas retrospective.

Tanner laughed. "Far be it from me to interfere," he said. Then he tilted his head back and looked up. "Is that mistletoe?"

"No," Olivia said. "It's three plastic Christmas balls hanging from a ribbon."

"Have you no imagination? No vision?"

"I can imagine myself in something a lot more comfortable than my sister's clothes," she told him. "I really hate to face it, but I'm going to have to *shop*."

"A woman who hates shopping," Tanner commented. "Will you marry me, Olivia O'Ballivan?"

It was a joke, and Olivia knew that as well as he did, but an odd, shivery little silence fell between them just the same. She seemed to draw away from him a little, even though he was holding her close as they swayed to the music.

"Let's get out of here," he said. Not exactly a mood enhancer, he reflected ruefully, but it was an honest sentiment.

She nodded. The pulse was beating at the base of her throat again.

The snow hadn't let up—it was worse, if anything— and Tanner drove slowly back over the same course he'd followed with Sophie earlier that evening.

"Seriously," he began, picking up the conversation they'd had on the dance floor as though there had been no interval between then and now, "do you plan on getting married? Someday, I mean? Having kids and everything?"

Olivia gnawed on her lower lip for a long moment. "Someday, maybe," she said at last.

"What kind of guy would you be looking for?"

She smiled, until she saw that he was serious. The realization, like the pulse, was visible. "Well, he'd have to love animals, and be okay with my getting called out on veterinary emergencies at all hours of the day and night. It would be nice if he could cook, since I'm in the remedial culinary group." She paused, watching him. "And the sex would have to be very, very good."

He laughed again. "Is there an audition?"

"As a matter of fact, there is," she said. "Tonight."

Heat rushed through Tanner. If she kept talking like that, the windshield would fog up, making visibility even worse.

When they arrived at Olivia's place Ginger greeted them at the door, wanting to go outside.

*He'd have to love animals...*

Tanner took Ginger out and waited in the freezing cold until she'd done what she had to do.

Olivia was waiting when he got back inside. "Hungry?" she asked.

*It would be nice if he could cook...*

Was she testing him?

"I could whip up an omelet," he offered.

She crossed to him, put her arms around his neck. "Later," she said.

*And the sex would have to be very, very good.*

Five minutes later, after some heavy kissing, he was helping her out of the palazzo pants. And everything *else* she was wearing.

## Chapter Twelve

He'd gone and fallen in love, Tanner realized, staring up at the ceiling as the first light of dawn crept across it. Olivia, sleeping in the curve of his arm, naked and soft, snuggled closer.

*He loved her.*

When had it happened? The first time they met, in his barn? Thanksgiving afternoon, before, during or after the kind of sex he'd never expected to have again? Or last night, at the dance?

Did it matter?

It was irrevocable. A no-going-back kind of thing.

He stirred to look at the clock on the bedside stand. Almost eight—Sophie would be up and on her way to school on the bus, well aware that dear old Dad hadn't come home last night.

What had Tessa told her?

He spoke Olivia's name.

She sighed and cuddled up closer.

"Doc," he said, more forcefully. "It's morning."

She bolted upright, looked at the clock. Shot out of bed. Realizing she was naked, she pulled on a pink robe. Her cheeks were the same color. "What are you doing here?" she demanded.

"You *know* what I'm doing here," he pointed out, in no hurry to get out of the warm bed.

"That was last night," she said, shoving a hand through her hair.

"Was I supposed to sneak out before sunrise? If I was, you didn't mention it."

Her color heightened. "What will Sophie think?"

"She's probably praying we'll get married, so she'll have a mom. She wants to grow up in Stone Creek."

To his surprise, Olivia's eyes filled with tears.

"Hey," he said, flinging back the covers and going to her, and the cold be damned. "What's the matter, Doc?" he asked, taking her into his arms.

"I love you," she sobbed into his bare shoulder. "That's what's wrong!"

He held her away, just far enough to look into her up-turned face. "No, Doc," he murmured. "That's what's *right*."

"What?"

"I love you, too," he said. "And it's cold out here. Can I share that bathrobe?"

She laughed and tried to stretch the sides of it around him. Her face felt wet against his chest. "This all happened so fast," she said. Then she tilted her head back and looked up at him again. "Are you sure? It wasn't just—just the sex?"

"The sex was world-class," he replied, kissing the top of her head. "But it's a lot more than that. The way you tried to cheer Butterpie up. That goofy reindeer you rescued, and the fact that you ran a background check on his owner. The old Suburban, and your grandfather's jacket, and that pitiful-looking little Christmas tree."

"What happens now?"

"We have sex again?"

She punched him, but she was grinning, all wet faced and happy. And his butt was freezing, since the robe didn't cover it. "Not that. Tomorrow. Next week. Next month…"

"We date. We sleep together, whenever we get the chance." He caught his hand under her chin and gently lifted. "We rename the ranch and renovate the house."

"Rename the ranch?"

"You said it once. 'Starcross' isn't a happy name. What do you want to call it, Doc?"

She wriggled against him. "How about 'Star*fire* Ranch'?" she asked.

"Works for me," he said, about to kiss her. Steer her back to bed. Hell, they were both late—might as well make it count.

"Wait," she said, pulling back. Her eyes were huge and blue and if he fell into them, he'd drown. And count himself lucky for it. "What about Sophie? Does she get to stay in Stone Creek?"

"She stays," Tanner said, after heaving a sigh.

"We'll keep her safe, Tanner," Olivia said. "Together."

He nodded.

And they went back to bed, though the lovemaking came a long time later.

Tanner told Olivia all about Kat, and how she'd died, and how he'd blamed himself and feared for Sophie.

And Olivia told him about her mother, and how she'd left the family. How her father had died, and her grandfather had carried on after that as best he could. How it was when animals talked to her.

When the deepest, most private things had been said, and only then, they made love.

On the morning of Christmas Eve, Olivia stood in a hospital corridor, peering through a little window at the main reason she'd been afraid to get married, long before she met Tanner Quinn.

He waited downstairs, in the lobby. She had to do this alone, but it was better than nice to know he was there.

Olivia closed her eyes for a moment, rested her forehead against the glass.

Restless, unhappy, Delia had left a husband and four children behind one blue-skyed summer day. Just gotten on a bus and boogied.

Olivia's worst fear, one she'd successfully sublimated for as long as she could remember, was that the same heartless streak might be buried somewhere in *her,* as well. That it might surface suddenly, causing her to abandon people and animals who loved and trusted her.

It was a crazy idea—she knew that. She was the steady type, brave, thrifty, loyal and true.

But then, Delia had seemed that way, too. She'd read Ashley and Melissa bedtime stories and listened to their prayers, played hide-and-seek with them while she was hanging freshly laundered sheets in the backyard, let Olivia wear clear nail polish even over her dad's protests. She'd taken all four of them to afternoon movies, sometimes even on school days, where they shared a big bucket of popcorn. She'd helped Brad with his homework practically every night.

And then she'd left.

Without a word of warning she'd simply vanished. Why?

Olivia opened her eyes.

The woman visible through that window didn't look as though she could answer that question or any other. She'd retreated inside herself, according to her doctors, and she might not come out again.

It happened with people who had abused alcohol and drugs over a long period of time, the doctors had said.

Olivia drew a deep breath, pushed open the door and went in.

Everyone had a dragon to fight. This was hers.

Delia looked too small to have caused so much trouble and heartache, and too broken. Huddled in a chair next to a tabletop Christmas tree decorated with paper chains and nothing else, she looked at Olivia with mild interest, then looked away again.

Olivia crossed to her, touched her thin shoulder.

She flinched away. Though she didn't speak, the look in her eyes said, *Leave me alone.*

"It's me, Mom," she said. "Olivia."

Delia simply stared, giving no sign of recognition.

Olivia dropped to a crouch beside her mother's chair. "I guess I'll never know why you left us," she said moderately, "and maybe it doesn't matter now. We turned out well, all of us."

Delia's vacant eyes were a soft, faded blue, like worn denim, or a fragile spring sky. Slowly, almost imperceptibly, she nodded.

Tears burned Olivia's eyes. "I'm in love, Mom," she said. "His name is Tanner. Tanner Quinn, and he has a twelve-year-old daughter, Sophie. I—I want to be a good stepmother to Sophie, and I guess, in some strange way, I needed to see you to know I could do this. That I could really be a wife and a mother—"

Delia didn't speak. She didn't cry or embrace her daughter or ask for a second chance. In short, there was no miracle.

And yet Olivia felt strangely light inside, as though there had been.

"Anyway, I'm planning to come back and see you as often as I can." She stood up straight again, opened her purse. Took out a small wrapped package. It was a bulb in a prepared planter, guaranteed to bloom even in the dead of winter. She'd wanted to bring perfume—one of her memories of Delia was that she'd loved smelling good—but that was on the hospital's forbidden gift list, because of the alcohol content. "Merry Christmas, Mom."

*I'm not you.*

She laid the parcel in Delia's lap, bent to kiss the top of her head and left.

Downstairs, Tanner drew her into a hug. Kissed her temple. "You gonna be okay, Doc?" he asked.

"Better than okay," she answered, smiling up at him. "Oh, much, much better than okay."

At six o'clock straight up, Kris Kringle officially closed the tree lot. He'd sold every one—nothing left now but needles and twine. The plastic reindeer and the hired Santa were gone, but the sleigh was still there.

He looked up and down the street.

Folks were inside their warm lighted houses and their churches now, as they should be on Christmas Eve. When he was sure nobody was looking, he gave a soft whistle.

The reindeer came—all except Rodney, that is. Took their usual places in front of the sleigh, waiting to be hitched up.

He frowned. Where was that deer?

The clippity-clop of small hooves sounded behind him on the pavement. He turned, and there was Rodney, coming toward him out of that snowy darkness, ready to take his first flight. The donkey had filled in willingly at the tree-lighting, but this was the real deal—and everybody knew donkeys couldn't fly.

"Ready?" he asked, bending over Rodney and stroking his silvery back.

He fitted the harnesses gently, having had years of practice. Climbed into the sleigh and took up the reins. They'd have to stop off at home, so he could change into his traveling clothes and, of course, fetch the first bag of gifts.

First stop, he decided: Olivia O'Ballivan's house. She'd been so kind to that little tree—next year at this time, he knew, it would be growing tall and strong on the grounds of the new shelter, glowing with colored lights.

Yes, sir. He'd deliver her present first.

That woman needed a new coffeepot.

Christmas Eve, the weather was crisp and clear with the promise of snow, and Olivia felt renewed as she watched Tanner's respectably muddy extended-cab truck coming up the driveway. They were all invited to Stone Creek Ranch for the evening—she and Tanner, Tessa and Sophie—and she knew it would be like old times, when Big John was alive. He'd always roped in half the countryside to share in the celebration.

Her heart soared a little when she heard Tanner's footsteps on the back porch, followed by his knock.

She opened the door, looked up at him with shining eyes.

He took in her red velvet skirt and matching crepe sweater with an appreciative grin, looking pretty darn handsome himself in jeans, a white shirt and his black leather jacket.

"Olivia O'Ballivan," he said with a twinkling grin. "You *shopped*."

"I sure did," she replied happily. "That big box of presents you passed on the porch is further proof. How about loading it up for me, cowboy?"

Tanner bent to greet Ginger, who could barely contain her glee at his arrival. "Anything for you, ma'am," Tanner drawled, still admiring Olivia's Christmas getup. "Tessa and Sophie went on ahead in Tessa's rig," he added, to explain their absence. "I told them we'd be right behind them."

He straightened, and Ginger went back to her bed.

"She's not going with us?" Tanner asked, referring, of course, to the dog.

"She claims she's expecting a visitor," Olivia said.

Tanner's grin quirked one corner of his kissable mouth. "Well, then," he said, making no move to leave the kitchen *or* load up the box of presents.

"What?" Olivia asked, shrugging into her good coat.

"I have something for you," Tanner said, and for all

his worldliness, he looked and sounded shy. "But I'm wondering if it's too soon."

Olivia's heartbeat quickened. She waited, watching him, hardly daring to breathe.

It couldn't be. They'd only just agreed that they loved each other....

Finally Tanner gave a decisive, almost rueful sigh, crossed to her, laid his hands on her shoulders and gently pressed her into one of the chairs at the kitchen table. Then, just like in an old movie, or a romantic story, he dropped to one knee.

"Will you marry me, Olivia O'Ballivan?" he asked. "When you're darn good and ready and the time is right?"

*"Say yes,"* Ginger said from the dog bed.

As if Olivia needed any canine input. "Yes," she said with soft certainty. "When we're *both* darn good and ready, and we *agree* that the time is right."

Eyes shining with love, and what looked like relief—had he really thought she might refuse?—Tanner reached into his jacket pocket and brought out a small white velvet box. An engagement ring glittered inside, as dazzling as a captured star.

"I love you," Tanner said. "But if you don't want to wear this right away, I'll understand."

Because she couldn't speak, Olivia simply extended her left hand. Tears of joy blurred her vision, making the diamond in her engagement ring seem even bigger and brighter than it was.

Tanner slid it gently onto her finger, and it fit perfectly, gleaming there.

Olivia laughed, sniffled. "To think I got you a bathrobe!" she blubbered.

Tanner laughed, too, and stood, pulling Olivia to her feet, drawing her into his arms and sealing the bargain with a long, slow kiss.

"We'd better get going," he said with throaty reluctance when it was over.

Olivia nodded.

Tanner went to lug the box of gifts to the truck, while Olivia lingered to unplug Charlie Brown's bubbling lights.

"You're sure you won't come along?" she asked Ginger, pausing in the kitchen.

*"I'll just settle my brains for a long winter's nap,"* Ginger said, muzzle on forepaws, gazing up at Olivia with luminous brown eyes. *"Don't be surprised if Rodney's gone when you get to the ranch. It's Christmas Eve, and he has work to do."*

"I'll miss him," Olivia said, reaching for her purse.

But Ginger was already asleep, perhaps with visions of rawhide sugarplums dancing in her head.

Stone Creek Ranch was lit up when Olivia and Tanner arrived, and the yard was crowded with cars and trucks.

"There's something I need to do in the barn," Olivia told Tanner as he wedged the rig into one of the few available parking spaces. "Meet you inside?"

He smiled, leaned across the console and kissed her lightly. "Meet you inside," he said.

Rodney's stall was empty, and Olivia felt a pang at that.

She stood there for a while, marveling at the mysteries of life in general and Christmas in particular, and was not surprised when Brad joined her.

"When I came out to feed the horses," he told Olivia,

"there was no sign of Rodney the reindeer. I figured he got out somehow and wandered off, but there were no tracks in the snow. It's as if he vanished."

Olivia dried her eyes. "It's Christmas Eve," she said, repeating Ginger's words. "He has work to do." She turned, looked up at her brother. "He's all right, Brad. Trust me on that."

Brad chuckled and wrapped an arm around her shoulders. "If you say so, Doc, I believe you, but I'm going to miss the little guy, just the same."

"Me, too," Olivia said.

Brad took her hand, examined the ring. "That's quite the sparkler," he said gravely. "Are you sure about this, Liv?"

"Very sure," she said.

He kissed her forehead. "That's good enough for me," he told her.

Together they went into the house, where there was music and laughter and a tall tree, all alight. Olivia spotted Ashley and Melissa right away, and some of Meg's family, the McKettricks, were there, too.

Sophie rushed to greet Olivia. "I get to stay in Stone Creek!" she confided, her face aglow with happiness. "Dad said so!"

Olivia laughed and hugged the child. "That's wonderful news, Sophie," she said.

"I've been thinking I might want to be a veterinarian when I grow up, like you," Sophie said seriously.

"Plenty of time to decide," Olivia replied gently. Just as she'd fallen in love with Tanner, hard, fast and forever, she'd fallen in love with Sophie, too. She'd never try to replace Kat, of course, but she'd be the best possible stepmother.

"Dad told me he was going to ask you to marry him,"

Sophie added, her voice soft now as she took Olivia's hand and smiled to see her father's engagement ring shining on the appropriate finger. "He wanted to know if it was okay with me, and I said yes." A mischievous smile curved the girl's lips. "I see you did, too."

"I've never been a stepmother before, Sophie," Olivia said, her eyes burning again. "Will you be patient with me until I get the hang of it?"

"I'm almost a teenager," Sophie reminded her sagely. "I suppose you'll have to be patient with me, too."

"I can manage," Olivia assured her.

Sophie's gaze strayed, came to rest on Tessa, who was off by herself, sipping punch and watching the hectic proceedings with some trepidation, like a swimmer working up the courage to jump into the water. "I'm a little worried about Aunt Tessa, though," the child admitted. "She's been hurt a lot worse than she's letting on."

"This crowd can be a little overwhelming," Olivia replied. "Let's help her get to know some of her new neighbors."

Sophie nodded, relieved and happy.

Arm in arm, she and Olivia went to join Tessa.

"You're coming to my open house tomorrow, right?" Ashley asked hopefully, sometime later, when they'd all had supper and opened piles of gifts, and the two sisters had managed a private moment over near the fireplace.

"Of course," Olivia said, pleased that Ashley looked and sounded like her old self. "Did you manage to get rid of Jack McCall yet?"

Ashley's blue eyes shone like sapphires. "The man is impossible to get rid of," she said, nodding toward the Christmas tree, where Jack stood talking quietly with Keegan McKettrick. As if sensing Ashley's gaze, he lifted his punch cup to her in a saucy toast and nodded. "But I'm having fun trying."

Olivia laughed. "Maybe you shouldn't try *too* hard," she said.

Soon after that, with little Mac nodding off, exhausted by all the excitement, people started leaving for their own homes.

Merry Christmases were exchanged all around.

Olivia left with Tanner, delighted to see a soft snow falling as they drove toward home.

"I meant to congratulate you on how dirty this truck is," Olivia teased.

"I finally found a mud puddle," Tanner admitted with a grin.

It felt good to laugh with him.

They parted reluctantly, on Olivia's back porch. She'd be going to Ashley's tomorrow, while Tanner spent Christmas Day with Tessa and Sophie, at *Starfire* Ranch.

He kissed her thoroughly and murmured a Merry Christmas, and finally took his leave.

Olivia went inside, found Ginger waiting just on the other side of the kitchen door.

"Did your visitor show up?" Olivia asked as Ginger went past her for a necessary pit stop in the back yard.

*"See for yourself,"* Ginger said as she climbed the porch steps again, to go inside with Olivia.

Puzzled, Olivia looked around. Nothing seemed different—and yet something was. But what?

Ginger waited patiently, until Olivia finally noticed. A brand-new coffeemaker gleamed on the countertop, topped with a fluffy red bow.

Tanner couldn't have brought it, she thought, mystified. Perhaps Tessa and Sophie had dropped it off? But that wasn't possible, either—they'd already been at Stone Creek Ranch when Tanner and Olivia arrived.

"Ginger, who—?"

Ginger didn't say anything at all. She just turned and padded into the living room.

Olivia followed, musing. Brad? Ashley or Melissa?

No. Brad and Meg had given her a dainty gold bracelet for Christmas, and the twins had gone together on a spa day at a fancy resort up in Flagstaff.

The living room was dark, and Christmas Eve was almost over, so Olivia decided to light the tree and sit quietly for a while with Ginger, reliving all the wonderful moments of the day, tucking them away, one by one, within the soft folds of her heart.

Tanner, proposing marriage on one knee, in her plain kitchen.

Sophie, thrilled that she'd be a permanent resident of Stone Creek from now on. She could ride Butterpie every day, and she was already boning up on Emily's lines in *Our Town,* determined to be ready for the auditions next fall.

Ashley, so recently broken, now happily bedeviling a certain handsome boarder.

Olivia cherished these moments, and many others besides.

She leaned over to plug in Charlie Brown's lights, and that was when she saw the card tucked in among the branches.

Her fingers trembled a little as she opened the envelope.

The card showed Santa and his reindeer flying high

over snowy rooftops, and the handwriting inside was exquisitely old-fashioned and completely unfamiliar.

Happy Christmas, Olivia. Think of us on cold winter mornings, when you're enjoying your coffee. With appreciation for your kindness, Kris Kringle and Rodney.

"No way," Olivia marveled, turning to Ginger.
*"Way,"* Ginger said. *"I told you I was expecting company."*
And just then, high overhead, sleigh bells jingled.

"You look mighty handsome in that apron, cowboy," Olivia said, joining Tanner, Tessa and Sophie behind the cafeteria counter at Stone Creek High School on Christmas Day. It was almost two o'clock—time for the community Christmas dinner—and there was a crowd waiting outside. "You're understaffed, though."

Tanner's blue-denim eyes lit at the sight of Olivia taking her place beside him and tying on an apron she'd brought from home. Tessa and Sophie exchanged pleased looks, but neither spoke.

A fancy catering outfit out of Flagstaff had decorated the tables and prepared the food—turkey and prime rib and ham, and every imaginable kind of trimming and salad and holiday dessert—and they'd be clearing tables and cleaning up afterward. But Olivia knew, via Sophie, that Tanner had insisted on doing more than paying the bill.

A side door opened, and Brad and Meg came in, followed by Ashley and Melissa, fresh from Ashley's open house at the bed-and-breakfast. They were all pushing up their sleeves as they approached, ready to lend a hand. Meg was especially cheerful, since Carly had shared in the festivities, via speaker-phone. She'd be back in Stone Creek soon after New Year's, eager to take Sophie under her wing and 'show her the ropes.'

Of course, having spent the morning at Ashley's herself, Olivia had been expecting them.

Tanner swallowed, visibly moved. "I never thought— I mean, it's Christmas, and…"

Olivia gave him a light nudge with her elbow. "It's what country people do, Tanner," she told him. "They help. Especially if they're family."

"Shall I let them in before they break down the doors?" Brad called, grinning. He didn't seem to mind that he looked a little silly in the bright red sweater Ashley had knitted for his Christmas gift. On the front, she'd stitched in a cowboy Santa Claus, strumming a guitar.

Tanner nodded, after swallowing again. "Let them in," he said. Then he turned to Olivia, Tessa and Sophie. "Ready, troops?"

They had serving spoons in hand. Sophie even sported a chef's hat, strung with battery-operated lights.

"Ready!" chorused the three women who loved Tanner Quinn.

Brad opened the cafeteria doors and in they came, the ones who were down on their luck, or elderly, or simply lonely. The children were spruced up in their Sunday best, wide-eyed and shy. Some carried toys they'd received from Brad and Meg in last night's secret-Santa front-porch blitz, others wore new clothes and a few of the older ones were rocking to MP3 players.

Ashley, Melissa and Meg ushered the elderly ladies and gentlemen to tables, took their orders and brought them plates.

Everyone else went through the line—proud, hard-working men who might have been ashamed to partake of free food, even on a holiday, if the whole town hadn't been invited to join in, tired-looking women who'd had one too many disappointments but were daring to hope things could be better, teenagers doing their best to be cool.

As she filled plate after plate, Olivia felt her throat constrict with love for these townspeople—*her* people, the home folks—and for Tanner Quinn. After all, this dinner had been his idea, and he'd spent a fortune to make it happen.

She was most touched, though, when the mayor showed up, and a dozen of the town's more prosperous families. They had fine dinners waiting at home, and Christmas trees surrounded by gifts—but they'd come to show that this was no charity event.

It was for everybody, and their presence made that plain.

When the last straggler had been served, when plates had been wrapped in foil for delivery to shut-ins, and the caterers had loaded the copious leftovers in their van for delivery to the nursing home, the people of Stone Creek lingered, swapping stories and jokes and greetings.

*This,* Olivia thought, watching them, seeing the new hope in their eyes, *is Christmas.*

Inevitably, Brad's guitar appeared.

He sat on the edge of one of the tables, tuned it carefully and cleared his throat.

A silence fell, fairly buzzing with anticipation.

"I'm not doing this alone," Brad said, grinning as he addressed the gathering. All these people were his friends and, by extension, his family. To Olivia, it was a measure of his manhood that he could wear that sweater in public. He knew how hard Ashley had worked to prepare her gift, and because he loved his kid sister, he didn't mind the amused whispers.

A few chuckles rose from the tables. It was partly because of his words, Olivia supposed, and partly because of the sweater.

He strummed a few notes, and then he began to sing.

"Silent night, holy night..."

And voice by voice, cautious and confident, old and young, warbling alto and clear tenor, the carol grew, until all of Stone Creek was singing.

Olivia looked up into Tanner's eyes, and something passed between them, something silent and fundamental and infinitely precious.

"Do I qualify?" he asked her when the song faded away.

"As what?"

"A real cowboy," Tanner said with a grin teetering at the corners of his mouth.

Olivia stood on tiptoe and kissed him lightly. "Yes," she told him happily. "You're the real deal, Tanner Quinn."

"Was it the muddy truck?" he teased.

She laughed. "No," she answered, laying a hand to his chest and spreading her fingers wide. "It's that big, wide-open-spaces heart of yours."

He looked up, frowned ruefully. "No mistletoe," he said.

Olivia slipped her arms around his neck, right there in the cafeteria at Stone Creek High School, with half the town looking on. "Who needs mistletoe?"

* * * * *

**Also available from Caro Carson**

**Harlequin Special Edition**

*American Heroes*

*The Lieutenants' Online Love*
*The Captains' Vegas Vows*

*Texas Rescue*

*A Cowboy's Wish Upon a Star*
*Her Texas Rescue Doctor*
*Following Doctor's Orders*
*A Texas Rescue Christmas*
*Not Just a Cowboy*
*How to Train a Cowboy*

*Montana Mavericks:*
*What Happened at the Wedding?*

*The Maverick's Holiday Masquerade*

*The Doctors MacDowell*

*The Bachelor Doctor's Bride*
*The Doctor's Former Fiancée*
*Doctor, Soldier, Daddy*

Don't miss *The Majors' Holiday Hideaway*
from Harlequin Special Edition in stores now!

Visit the Author Profile page
at Harlequin.com for more titles.

# A COWBOY'S WISH
# UPON A STAR

Caro Carson

This book is dedicated to You, the reader
who spent time to meet me at the book signing,
or spent time to send me the note to say you love
the love stories that I spent time to write.
Thank you.

# Chapter One

It was the end of the world.

Sophia Jackson strained to see something, anything that looked like civilization, but the desolate landscape was no more than brown dirt and scrubby bits of green plants that stretched all the way to the horizon.

She might have been in one of her own movies.

The one that had garnered an Academy Award nomination for her role as a dying frontier woman had been filmed in Mexico, but this part of Texas looked close enough. The one that had made her an overnight success as a Golden Globe winner for her portrayal of a doomed woman in a faraway galaxy had been filmed in Italy, but again, this landscape was eerily similar.

Doomed. Dying. Isolated.

She'd channeled those emotions before. This time,

however, no one was going to yell *cut*. No one was going to hand her a gold statue.

"Are we there yet?" She sounded demanding, just like the junior officer thrust into a leadership role on a space colony.

Well, not really. She had the ear of an actor; she could catch nuance in tone and delivery, even in—or especially in—her own voice. She didn't sound like a commander. She sounded like a diva.

*I have the right to be a diva. I've got the gold statue to prove it.*

She tossed her hair back with a jingle of her chandelier earrings, queen of the backseat of the car.

In the front bucket seats, her sister's fiancé continued to drive down the endless road in silence, but Sophia caught the quick glance he shared with her sister. The two of them didn't think she was a young military officer. They didn't even think of her as a diva.

She was an annoying, spoiled brat who was going to be dropped off in the middle of abso-freaking-lutely nowhere.

Her sister, Grace, reached back between the seats to pat her on the knee. "I haven't been here before, either, but it can't be too much farther. Isn't it perfect, though? The paparazzi will never find you out here. This is just what we were hoping for."

Sophia looked at Grace's hand as it patted the black leather which covered her knee. Grace's engagement ring was impossible to miss. Her sister had been her rock, her constant companion, until very recently. Now, wearing a different kind of rock on her left hand, Grace was giddy at the prospect of marrying the man who'd encouraged her to dump her own sister.

Sophia mentally stuck out her tongue at the back of the man's head. Her future brother-in-law was a stupid doctor named Alex, and he'd never once been impressed with Sophia Jackson, movie star. Since the day Sophia and Grace had arrived in Texas, he'd only paid attention to Grace.

Grace's hand moved from Sophia's knee to Alex's shoulder. Then to the back of his neck. The diamond played peek-a-boo as her sister slid her hand through her fiancé's dark hair.

Sophia looked away, out the side window to the desolate horizon. The nausea was rising, so she chomped on her chewing gum. Loudly. With no class. No elegance. None of the grace that the world had once expected of the talented Sophia Jackson.

*Pun intended. I have no Grace, not anymore.*

Grace didn't correct her gum-smacking. Grace no longer cared enough to correct her.

Sophia was on her own. She'd have to survive the rest of her nine-month sentence all by herself, hiding from the world. In the end, all she'd have to show for it would be a flabby stomach and stretch marks. Like a teenager in the last century, she was pregnant and ashamed, terrified of being exposed. She had to be sent to the country to hide until she could have the baby, give it up for adoption, and then return to the world and spend the rest of her life pretending nothing had ever happened.

*If* she had a world to return to. That was a very big *if*.

No one in Hollywood would work with her. It had nothing to do with the pregnancy. No one knew about that, and she wasn't far enough along to even begin to show. No, the world of movie stardom was boxing her out solely because of her reputation.

A box office giant, an actor whom Sophia had always dreamed of working with, had recently informed a major studio he would not do the picture if she were cast opposite him. Her reputation had sunk that low. They said there was no such thing as bad publicity, but the publicity she'd been generating had hurt her. Her publicist and her agent had each informed her that she was unmarketable as is.

*Ex-publicist. Ex-agent. They both left me.*

Panic crawled up the back of her throat. They were all leaving her. Publicist, agent, that louse of a slimy boyfriend she'd been stupid enough to run away with. And worst of all, within the next few minutes, her sister. She was losing the best personal assistant in the world, right when she needed a personal assistant the most.

There was no such thing as loyalty in Hollywood. Not even her closest blood relative was standing by her side. Nausea turned to knots.

"Oh, my goodness," her sister laughed. The tone was one of happy, happy surprise.

Alex's laugh was masculine, amused. "Just in case you needed a reminder that you're in the middle of a genuine Texas cattle ranch…"

He brought their car to a stop—as if he had a choice. The view through the windshield was now the bulky brown back of a giant steer. A thousand pounds of animal blocked their way, just standing there on the road they needed to use, the road that would lead them to an empty ranch house where Sophia would be abandoned, alone, left behind.

Knots turned to panic. She needed to get this over with. Her world was going to end, and she couldn't drag this out one second longer.

*Let's rip this bandage off.*

"Move, you stupid cow!" she hollered from the backseat.

"Sophia, that's not going to help."

But Sophia had already half vaulted over Alex's shoulder and slammed her palm on the car horn. "Get out of the road."

The cow stared at her through the glass, unmoving. God above, she was tired of being stared at. Everyone was always waiting for her to do something, to be crazy or brilliant, to act out every emotion while they watched passively. Grace was staring at her now, shaking her head.

"Move!" Sophia laid on the horn again.

"Stop it." Alex firmly took her arm and pushed her toward the backseat. His stare was more of a glare.

He and Grace both turned back toward the front. Sophia had spoiled their little delight at a cow in the road, at this unexpected interlude in their sweet, shared day.

*I can't stand it, I can't stand myself, I can't stand this one more minute.*

She yanked on the door handle and shoved the door open.

"Sophia! Stay in the car." Grace sounded equal parts exasperated and fearful.

Sophia was beyond fear. Panic, nausea, knots—a terrible need to get this over with. Once the ax fell, once she was cut off from the last remnants of her life, she could fall apart. She wanted nothing more than to fall apart, and this stupid cow was preventing it.

She slammed the car door and waved her arms over her head, advancing on the cow. Or maybe it was a bull. It had short horns. Whatever it was, it flinched.

Emboldened—or just plain crazy, like they all said—Sophia waved her arms over her head some more and advanced toward the stupid, stationary cow. The May weather was warm on the bare skin of her midriff as her crop top rose higher with each wave of her arms. On her second step, she nearly went down as her ankle twisted, the spike heel of her over-the-knee boot threatening to sink into the brown Texas dirt.

"Move, do you hear me? Move." She gestured wide to the vast land all around them. "Anywhere. Anywhere but right here."

The cow snorted at her. Chewed something. Didn't care about her, didn't care about her at all.

Tears were spilling over her cheeks, Sophia realized suddenly. Her ankle hurt, her heart hurt, her stomach hurt. The cow looked away, not interested in the least. Being ignored was worse than being stared at. The beast was massive, far stockier than the horses she'd worked with on the set as a dying frontier woman. She shoved at the beast's shoulder anyway.

"Just *move!*" Its hide was coarse and dusty. She shoved harder, accomplishing nothing, feeling her own insignificance. She might as well not exist. No career, no sister, no friends, no life.

She collapsed on the thick, warm neck of the uncaring cow, and let the tears flow.

Someone on the ranch was in trouble.

Travis Chalmers tossed his pliers into the leather saddlebag and gave the barb wire one last tug. Fixed.

He scooped up his horse's trailing reins in one hand, smashed his cowboy hat more firmly over his brow, and swung into the saddle. That car horn meant something else needed fixing, and now. He only hoped one of his men hadn't been injured.

The car horn sounded again. Travis kicked the horse into a gallop, heading in the direction of the sound. It didn't sound like one of the ranch trucks' horns. A visitor, then, who could be lost, out of gas, stranded by a flat tire—simple fixes.

He kept his seat easily and let the horse have her head. Whatever the situation was, he'd handle it. He was young for a foreman, just past thirty, but he'd been ranching since the day he was born, seemed like. Nothing that happened on a cattle operation came as a surprise to him.

He rode up the low rise toward the road, and the cause of the commotion came into view. A heifer was standing in the road, blocking the path of a sports car that clearly wouldn't be able to handle any off-road terrain, so it couldn't go around the animal. That the animal was on the road wasn't a surprise; Travis had just repaired a gap in the barb wire fence. But leaning on the heifer, her back to him, was a woman.

What a woman, with long hair flowing perfectly down her back, her body lean and toned, her backside curvy—all easy to see because any skin that wasn't bared to the sun and sky was encased in tight black clothing. But it was her long legs in thigh-high boots that made him slow his horse in a moment of stunned confusion.

She had to be a mirage. No woman actually wore thigh-high leather boots with heels that high. Those boots sent sexual signals that triggered every adolescent memory of a comic book heroine. Half-naked, high-heeled—a character drawn to appeal to the most primal part of a man's mind.

Not much on a cattle ranch could surprise him, except seeing *that* in the middle of the road.

The horse continued toward the heifer, its focus absolute. So was Travis's. He couldn't take his eyes off the woman as he rode toward her.

She lifted her head and turned his way. With a dash of her cheek against her black-clad shoulder, she turned all the way around and leaned against the animal, stretching her arms along its back like it was her sofa. As the wind blew her hair back from her face, silver and gold shining in the sun, she held her pose and watched him come for her.

Boots, bare skin, black leather—they messed with his brain, until the car door opened and the driver began to get out, a man. Then the passenger door opened, too, and the heifer swung her head, catching the smell of horse and humans on the wind. The rancher in him pushed aside the adolescent male, and he returned his horse to a quicker lope with a *tch* and a press of his thigh.

That heifer wasn't harmless. Let her get nervous, and a half ton of beef on the hoof could do real harm to the humans crowding her, including the sex goddess in boots.

"Afternoon, folks." Travis took in the other two at a glance. Worried woman, irritated man. He didn't look at the goddess as he stopped near the strange little grouping. His heart had kicked into a higher gear at the sight of her, something the sound of the horn and the short gallop had not done. It was damned disconcerting. Everything about her was disconcerting. "Stay behind those doors, if you don't mind."

"Sophia, it's time to get back in the car now," the man said, exaggeratedly patient and concerned, as if he were talking a jumper off a ledge.

"No."

"Oh, Sophie." The woman gave the smallest shake of her head, her eyes sad. Apparently, this Sophie had disappointed her before.

Sophie. Sophia. He looked at her again. Sophia Jackson, of course. Unmistakable. A movie star on his ranch, resting against his heifer, a scenario so bizarre his brain had to work to believe his eyes.

She hadn't taken her blue eyes off him, but she'd raised her chin in challenge. The *no* was meant for him, was it?

"Walk away," he said mildly, keeping his voice even for the heifer's benefit—and hers. "I'll get this heifer on her way so you can get on yours."

"No. She likes me." Sophia's long, elegant fingers stroked the roan hide of the cattle.

"Is that right?" He reached back to grab his lasso and held the loops in one hand.

"My cow doesn't want to leave me. She's loyal and true."

It was an absurd thing to say. Travis didn't have time for absurd.

"Watch your toes." He rode forward, crowding the heifer, crowding Sophia Jackson, and slapped the heifer on the hindquarters with the coiled rope. She briskly left the road.

Sophia Jackson looked a little smaller and a lot sillier, standing in the road by herself. He looked down at her famous face as she watched the heifer leave. She actually looked sad, like she didn't want the heifer to go, which was as absurd as everything else about the situation.

Travis wheeled his horse away from Sophia in order to talk to the driver.

"Where are you heading?"

"Thanks for moving that animal. I'm Alex Gregory. This is my fiancée, Grace."

Travis waited, but the man didn't introduce the woman in boots. He guessed he was supposed to recognize her. He did. Still, it seemed rude to leave her out.

"Travis Chalmers." He touched the brim of his hat and nodded at the worried woman, then twisted halfway around in his saddle to touch his hat and nod again at the movie star in their midst.

"Chalmers, the foreman?" asked the man, Alex. "Good to meet you. The MacDowells told me they'd explained the situation to you."

*Not exactly.*

Travis hooked his lasso onto the saddle horn. "You're the one who's gonna live in Marion MacDowell's house for a few months?"

"No, not us. Her. Sophia is my fiancée's sister. She needs a place to hide."

He raised a brow at the word. "Hide from what?"

"Paparazzi," Grace answered. "It's been a real issue after the whole debacle with the—well, it's always an issue. But Sophie needs some time to…to…" She smiled with kindness and pity at her sister. "She needs some time."

Sophie stalked around the car on spiked heels, looking like a warrior queen who could kick some serious butt, but instead she got in the backseat and slammed the door.

"Time and privacy," Alex added. "The MacDowells assured us your discretion wouldn't be an issue."

His mare shifted under him and blew an impatient breath through her nose.

"Should we go to the house and have this discussion there?" Grace asked.

Travis kept an eye on the heifer that was ambling away. "I'm gonna have to round up that heifer and put her back on the right side of the fence. Got to check on the branding after that, but I'll be back at sundown. I go past the main house on the way to my place. I'll stop in."

"We weren't planning to stay all day." The woman threw a look of dismay to her fiancé.

They couldn't expect him to quit working in the middle of the day and go sit in a house to chat. He ran the River Mack ranch, and that meant he worked even longer hours than he expected from his ranch hands.

Heifers that wandered through broken fences couldn't be put off until tomorrow. May was one of the busiest months of the year, between the last of the calving and the bulk of the branding. Travis hadn't planned on spending any time whatsoever talking to whomever the MacDowells were loaning their house, but obviously, there was more to the situation than the average houseguest.

"All right, then. Let's talk." He swung himself off the horse, a concession to let them know they had his time and attention. Besides, if he stayed on horseback, he couldn't see Sophia in the car. It felt like he needed to keep an eye on her, the same as he needed to do with the wandering heifer.

On the ground, he still couldn't see much through the windshield. He caught a glimpse of black leather, her hands resting on her knees. Her hands were clenched into fists.

Travis shook his head. She was a woman on edge.

"Sophia just needs to be left alone," her sister said.

"I can do that." He had no intention of staying in the vicinity of someone as disturbing to his peace of mind as that woman.

"If men with cameras start snooping around, please, tell them nothing. Don't even deny she's here."

"Ma'am, if men with cameras come snooping around this ranch, I will be escorting them off the property."

"Oh, really? You can do that?" She seemed relieved—amazed and relieved.

What did these people expect? He took his hat off and ran his hand through his hair before shoving the hat right back on again. His hair was getting too long, but no cowboy had time in May to go into town and see a barber.

"We don't tolerate trespassers," he explained to the people who clearly lived in town. "I'm not in the business of distinguishing between cameramen and cattle thieves. If you don't belong here, you will be escorted off the land."

"The paparazzi will offer you money, though. Thousands."

Before Travis could set her straight on this insinuation that he could be bribed to betray a guest of the MacDowells, Alex cut in. "That's only if they find her. We've gone to great lengths to arrange this location. We took away her cell phone so that she wouldn't accidentally store a photo in the cloud with a location stamp.

Hackers get paid to look for things like that. That's how extreme the hunting for her can be."

"She's got a burner phone for emergencies," Grace said. "But if you could check on her...?"

Travis was aware that the front doors to the car were wide open, man and woman each standing beside one. Surely, the subject of this conversation could hear every word. It seemed rude to talk about her as if she weren't there.

"If she wants me to check on her, I will. If she wants me to leave her alone, I will."

He looked through the windshield again. The fists had disappeared. One leather-clad knee was being bounced, jittery, impatient.

"How many other people work on this ranch?" the man asked.

"Will they leave my sister alone?" the woman asked.

Travis was feeling impatient himself. This whole conversation was moving as far from his realm of normal as the woman hiding in the car was.

That was what she was doing in there. Rather than being part of a conversation about herself, she was hiding. This was all a lot of nonsense in the middle of branding season, but from long habit developed by working with animals, Travis forced himself to stand calmly, keep the reins loose in his hands, and not show his irritation. These people were strangers in the middle of the road, and Travis owed them nothing.

"I'm not in the habit of discussing the ranch's staffing requirements with strangers."

The man nodded once. He got it. The woman bit her lip, and Travis understood she was worried about more than herself.

"But since this is your sister, I'll tell you the amount of ranch hands living in the bunkhouse varies depending on the season. None of us are in the habit of going to the main house to introduce ourselves to Mrs. Mac-Dowell's houseguests." Travis spoke clearly, to be sure the woman in the car heard him. "If your sister doesn't want to be seen, then I suggest she stop standing in the middle of an open pasture and hugging my livestock."

The black boot stopped bouncing.

Grace dipped her chin to hide her smile, looking as pretty as her movie star sister—minus the blatant sexuality.

"Now if you folks would like to head on to the house, I've got to be going."

"Thank you," Grace said, but the worry returned to her expression. "If you could check on her, though, yourself? She's more fragile than she looks. She's got a lot of decisions weighing her down. This is a very delicate situa—"

The car horn ripped through the air. Travis nearly lost the reins as his mare instinctively made to bolt without him. *Goddammit.*

No sooner had he gotten his horse's head under control than the horn blasted again. He whipped his own head around toward the car, glaring at the two adults who were still standing there. For God's sake, did they have to be told to shut her up?

"Tell her to stop."

"Like that'll do any good." But the man bent to look into the car. "Enough, Sophie."

"Sophie, please…"

One more short honk. Thank God his horse trusted him, because the mare barely flinched this time, but it was the last straw for Travis. Reins in hand, he stalked past the man and yanked open the rear door.

Since she'd been leaning forward to reach the car horn, Sophia's black-clad backside was the first thing he saw, but she quickly turned toward him, keeping her arm stretched toward the steering wheel.

"Don't do that again."

"Quit standing around talking about me. This is a waste of time. I want to get to the house. Now." She honked the horn again, staring right at him as she did it.

"What the hell is wrong with you? I just said don't do that."

"Or else what?"

She glared at him like a warrior, but she had the attitude of a kindergartner.

"Every time you honk that horn, another cowboy on this ranch drops what he's doing to come and see if you need help. It's not a game. It's a call for help."

She blinked. Clearly, she hadn't thought of that, but then she narrowed her eyes and reached once more for the steering wheel.

"You honk that horn again, and you will very shortly find the road blocked by men on horses, and we will not move until you turn the car around and take yourself right back to wherever it is you came from."

Her hand hovered over the steering wheel.

"Do it," he said. "Frighten my horse one more time. You will never set foot on this ranch again."

Her hand hovered. He stared her down, waiting, almost willing her to test him. He would welcome a chance to remove her from the ranch, and he wasn't a man to make empty threats.

"I don't want to be here, anyway," she said.

He jerked his head toward the steering wheel. "You know how to drive, don't you? Turn the car around then, instead of honking that damned horn."

The silence stretched between them.

Her sister had leaned into the car, so she spoke very softly. "Sophie, you've got nowhere else to go. You cannot live with me and Alex."

Travis saw it then. Saw the way the light in Sophia's eyes died a little, saw the way her breath left her lips. He saw her pain, and he was sorry for it.

She sagged back into her seat, burying her backside along with the rest of her body in the corner. She crossed her arms over her middle, not looking at her sister, not looking at him. "Well, God forbid I should piss off a horse."

Travis stood and shut the door. He scanned the pasture, spotted the heifer twice as far away as she'd been a minute ago. Those young ones had a sixth sense about getting rounded up, sometimes. If they didn't want to be penned in, they were twice as hard to catch.

Didn't matter. Travis hadn't met one yet that could outsmart or outrun him.

He had a heifer to catch, branding to oversee, a ranch to run. By the time the sun went down, he'd want nothing more than a hot shower and a flat surface to sleep on.

But tonight, he'd stop by the main house and check on a movie star—a sad, angry movie star who had nowhere else to go, no other family to take her in. Nowhere except his ranch.

With a nod at the sister and her fiancé, Travis swung himself back into the saddle. The heifer had given up all pretense at grazing and was determinedly trotting toward the horizon, putting distance between herself and the humans.

Travis would have sighed, if cowboys sighed. Instead, he spoke to his horse under his breath. "You ready for this?"

He pointed the mare toward the heifer and sent her into motion with a squeeze of his thigh. They had a long, hard ride ahead.

# Chapter Two

She was alone.

She was alone, and she was going to die, because Grace and Alex had left her, and even though Alex had flipped a bunch of fuses and turned on the electricity, and even though Grace had carried in two bags of groceries from the car and set them on the blue-tiled kitchen counter, Sophia's only family had abandoned her before anyone realized the refrigerator was broken, and now the food was going to spoil and they wouldn't be back to check on her for a week and by then she'd be dead from starvation, her body on the kitchen floor, her eyes staring sightlessly at the wallpaper border with its white geese repeated ad nauseam on a dull blue background.

Last year, she'd worn Givenchy as she made her acceptance speech.

*I hate my life.*

Sophia sat at the kitchen table in a hard chair and cried. No one yelled *cut*, so she continued the scene, putting her elbows on the table and dropping her head in her hands.

*I hate myself for letting this become my life.*

Was that what Grace and Alex wanted her to come to grips with? That she'd messed up her own life?

*Well, duh, I'm not a moron. I know exactly why my career is circling the drain in a slow death spiral.*

Because no one wanted to work with her. And no one wanted to work with her because no one liked her ex, DJ Deezee Kalm.

Kalm was something of an ironic name for the jerk. Deezee had brought nothing but chaos into her life since she'd met him…wow, only five months ago?

Five months ago, Sophia Jackson had been the Next Big Thing. No longer had she needed to beg for a chance to audition for secondary characters. Scripts from the biggest and the best were being delivered to her door by courier, with affectionate little notes suggesting the main character would fit her perfectly.

Sophia and her sister—her loyal, faithful assistant—had deserved a chance to celebrate. After ten long years of hard work, Sophia's dreams were coming true, but if she was being honest with herself—*and isn't that what this time alone is supposed to be about? Being honest with myself?*—well, to be honest, she might have acted elated, but she'd been exhausted.

A week in Telluride, a tiny mining town that was now a millionaires' playground in the Rocky Mountains, had seemed like a great escape. For one little week, she wouldn't worry about the future impact of her every decision. Sophia would be seen, but maybe she wouldn't be stared at among the rich and famous.

But DJ Deezee Kalm had noticed her. Sophia had been a sucker for his lies, and now she couldn't be seen by anyone at all for the next nine months. Here she was, alone with her thoughts and some rapidly thawing organic frozen meals, the kind decorated with chia seeds and labeled with exotic names from India.

*There you go. I fell for a jerk, and now I hate my life. Reflection complete.*

She couldn't dwell on Deezee, not without wanting to throw something. If she chucked the goose-shaped salt shaker against the wall, she'd probably never be able to replace the 1980s ceramic. That was the last thing she needed: the guilt of destroying some widow's hideous salt shaker.

She stood with the vague idea that she ought to do something about the paper bags lined up on the counter, but her painful ankle made fresh tears sting her eyes. She'd twisted it pretty hard in the dirt road when she'd confronted that cow, although she'd told Alex the Stupid Doctor that she hadn't. She sat down again and began unzipping the boots to free her toes from their spike-heeled torture.

That cow in the road…she hoped it had given that cowboy a run for his money. She hoped it was still outrunning him right this second, Mr. Don't-Honk-That-Horn-or-Else. Now that she thought about it, he'd had perfect control of his horse as he'd galloped away from them like friggin' Indiana Jones in a Spielberg film, so he'd lied to her about the horn upsetting his horse. Liar, liar. Typical man.

*Don't trust men. Lesson learned. Can I go back to LA now?*

But no. She couldn't. She was stuck here in Texas, where Grace had dragged her to make an appearance on behalf of the Texas Rescue and Relief organization. Her sister had hoped charity work and good deeds could repair the damage Sophia had done to her reputation. Instead, in the middle of just such a big charity event, Deezee had shown up and publicly begged Sophia to take him back. Sophia had been a sucker again. With cameras dogging their every move, she'd run away to a Caribbean island with him, an elopement that had turned out to be a big joke.

Ha, ha, ha.

*Here's something funny, Deezee. When I peed on a plastic stick, a little plus sign showed up.*

Sophia had returned from St. Barth to find her sister engaged to a doctor with Texas Rescue, a man who, un-like Deezee, seemed to take that engagement seriously. Now her sister never wanted to go back to LA with her, because Alex had her totally believing in fairy tale love. Grace believed Texas would be good for Sophia, too. Living here would give her a chance to rest and *relax*.

Right. Because of that little plus sign, Grace thought Sophia needed some stress-free *alone time* to decide what she wanted to do with her future, as if Sophia had done anything except worry about both of their futures for the past ten years. Didn't Grace know Sophia was sick of worrying about the future?

Barefooted, Sophia went to the paper bags and pulled out all the cold and wet items and stuck them in the sink. They'd already started sweating on the tiled countertop. She dried her cheek on her shoulder and faced the fridge.

It had been deliberately turned off by the owner, a woman who didn't want to stay in Texas and *relax* in her own home now that her kids were grown and married. Before abandoning her house to spend a year volunteering for a medical mission in Africa, Mrs. MacDowell had inserted little plastic wedges to keep the doors open so the refrigerator wouldn't get moldy and funky while it was unused.

Sophia was going to be moldy and funky by the time they found her starved body next week. She had a phone for emergencies; she used it.

"Grace? It's me. Alex didn't turn the refrigerator on." Sophia felt betrayed. Her voice only sounded bitchy.

"Sophie, sweetie, that's not an emergency." Grace spoke gently, like someone chiding a child and trying to encourage her at the same time. "You can handle that. You know how to flip a switch in a fuse box."

"I don't even know where the fuse box is."

Grace sighed, and Sophia heard her exchange a few words with Alex. "It's in the hall closet. I've gotta run now. Bye."

"Wait! Just hang on the line with me while I find the fuse box. What if the fuse doesn't fix it?"

"I don't know. Then you'll have to call a repairman, I guess."

"Call a repairman?" Sophia was aghast. "Where would I even find a repairman?"

"There's a phone on the wall in the kitchen. Mrs. MacDowell has a phone book sitting on the little stand underneath it."

Sophia looked around the 1980s time capsule of a

kitchen. Sure enough, mounted on the wall was a phone, one with a handset and a curly cord hanging down. It was not decorated with a goose, but it was white, to fit in the decor.

"Ohmigod, that's an antique."

"I made sure it works. It's a lot harder for paparazzi to tap an actual phone line than it would be for them to use a scanner to listen in to this phone call. You can call a repairman."

Sophia clenched her jaw against that lecturing tone. From the day her little sister had graduated from high school, Sophia had paid her to take care of details like this, treating her like a star's personal assistant long before Sophia had been a star. Now Grace had decided to dump her.

"And how am I supposed to pay for a repairman?"

"You have a credit card. We put it in my name, but it's yours." Grace sounded almost sad. Pitying her, actually, with just a touch of impatience in her tone.

Sophia felt her sister slipping away. "I can say my name is Grace, but I can't change my face. How am I supposed to stay anonymous if a repairman shows up at the door?"

"I don't know, Sophie. Throw a dish towel over your head or something."

"You don't care about me anymore." Her voice should have broken in the middle of that sentence, because her heart was breaking, but the actor inside knew the line had been delivered in a continuous whine.

"I love you, Sophie. You'll figure something out. You're super smart. You took care of me for years. This will be a piece of cake for you."

*A piece of cake.* That tone of voice…

Oh, God, her sister sounded just like their mother. Ten years ago, Mom and Dad had been yanked away from them forever, killed in a pointless car accident. At nineteen, Sophia had become the legal guardian of Grace, who'd still had two years of high school left to go.

Nothing had been a piece of cake. Sophia had quit college and moved back home so that Grace could finish high school in their hometown. Sophia had needed to make the life insurance last, paying the mortgage with it during Grace's junior and senior years. She'd tried to supplement it with modeling jobs, but anything local only paid a pittance. For fifty dollars, she'd spent six hours gesturing toward a mattress with a smile on her face.

It had really been her first acting job, because during the entire photo shoot, she'd had to act like she wasn't mourning the theater scholarship at UCLA that she'd sacrificed. With a little sister to raise, making a mattress look desirable was as close as Sophia could come to show business.

That first modeling job had been a success, eventually used nationwide, but Sophia hadn't been paid one penny more. Her flat fifty-dollar fee had been spent on gas and groceries that same day. Grace had to be driven to school. Grace had to eat lunch in the cafeteria.

Now Grace was embarking on her own happy life and leaving Sophia behind. It just seemed extra cruel that Grace would sound like Mom at this point.

"I have to run," her mother's voice said. "I love you, Sophie. You can do this. Bye."

*Don't leave me. Don't ever leave me. I miss you.*

The phone was silent.

This afternoon, Sophia had only wanted to hide away and fall apart in private. Now, she was terrified to. If she started crying again, she would never, ever stop.

She nearly ran to the hall closet and pushed aside the old coats and jackets to find the fuse box. They were all on, a neat row of black switches all pointing to the left. She flicked a few to the right, then left again. Then a few more. If she reset every one, then she would have to hit the one that worked the refrigerator.

It made no difference. The refrigerator was still dead when she returned to the kitchen. The food was still thawing in the sink. Her life still sucked, only worse now, because now she missed her mother all over again. Grace sounded like Mom, and she'd left her like Mom. At least when Mom had died, she'd left the refrigerator running.

What a terrible thing to think. Dear God, she hated herself.

Then she laughed at the incredible low her self-pity could reach.

Then she cried.

Just as she'd known it would, once the crying started, it did not stop.

*I'm pregnant and I'm scared and I want my mother.*

Sophia sank to the kitchen floor, hugged her knees to her chest, and gave up.

Would he or wouldn't he?

Travis rode slowly, letting his mare cool down on her way to the barn while he debated with himself whether or not he'd told the sister he would check on the movie star tonight, specifically, or just check on her in general. He was bone-tired and hungry, but he had almost another mile to go before he could rest. Half a mile to the barn, quarter of a mile past that to his house. A movie star with an attitude was the last thing he wanted to deal with. Tomorrow would be soon enough to be neighborly and ask how she was settling in.

The MacDowell house, or just *the house*, as everyone on a ranch traditionally called the owner's residence, was closer to the barn than his own. As the mare walked on, the house's white porch pillars came into view, always a pretty sight. The sunset tinted the sky pink and orange behind it. Mesquite trees were spaced evenly around it. The lights were on; Sophia Jackson was home.

Then the lights went out.

On again.

What the hell?

Lights started turning off and on, in an orderly manner, left to right across the building. Travis had been in the house often enough that he knew which window was the living room. Off, on. The dining room. The foyer.

The mare chomped at her bit impatiently, picking up on his change in mood.

"Yeah, girl. Go on." He let the horse pick up her pace. Normally, he'd never let a horse hurry back to the barn; that was just sure to start a bad habit. But everything on the River Mack was his responsibility, including the house with its blinking lights, and its new resident.

The lights came on and stayed on as he rode steadily toward the movie star that he was going to check on tonight, after all.

# Chapter Three

Travis couldn't ride his horse up to the front door and leave her on the porch. There was a hitching post on the side that faced the barn, so he rode around the house toward the back. The kitchen door was the one everyone used, anyway.

The first year he'd landed a job here as a ranch hand, he'd learned real quick to leave the barn through the door that faced the house. Mrs. MacDowell was as likely as not to open her kitchen door and call over passing ranch hands to see if they'd help her finish off something she'd baked. She was forever baking Bundt cakes and what not, then insisting she couldn't eat them before they went stale. Since her sons had all gone off to medical school to become doctors, Travis suspected she just didn't know how to stop feeding young men. As a twenty-five-year-old living in the bunkhouse on canned pork-n-beans, he'd been happy to help her not let anything get stale.

Travis grinned at the memory. From the vantage point of his horse's back, he looked down into the kitchen as he passed its window and saw another woman there. Blond hair, black clothes...curled up on the floor. Weeping.

"Whoa," he said softly, and the mare stopped.

He could tell in a glance Sophia Jackson wasn't hurt, the same way he could tell in a glance if a cowboy who'd been thrown from a horse was hurt. She could obviously breathe if she could cry. She was hugging her knees to her chest in a way that proved she didn't have any broken bones. As he watched, she shook that silver and gold hair back and got to her feet, her back to him. She could move just fine. There was nothing he needed to fix.

She was emotional, but Travis couldn't fix that. There wasn't a lot of weeping on a cattle ranch. If a youngster got homesick out on a roundup or a heartbroken cowboy shed a tear over a Dear John letter after a mail call, Travis generally kept an eye on them from a distance. Once they'd regained their composure, he'd find some reason to check in with them, asking about their saddle or if they'd noticed the creek was low. If they cared to talk, they were welcome to bring it up. Some did. Most didn't.

He'd give Sophia Jackson her space, then. Whatever was making her sad, it was hers to cry over. Tomorrow night would be soon enough to check in with her.

Just as he nudged his horse back into a walk, he caught a movement out of the corner of his eye, Sophia dashing her cheek on her shoulder. He tried to put it out of his mind once he was in the barn, but it nagged at him as he haltered his mare and washed off her bit. Sophia had touched her cheek to her shoulder just like that when he'd first approached her on the road this afternoon. Had she been crying when she'd hung on to that heifer?

He rubbed his jaw. In the car, she'd been all clenched fists and anxiously bouncing knee. A woman on the edge, that was what he'd thought. Looked like she'd gone over that edge this evening.

People did. Not his problem. There were limits to what a foreman was expected to handle, damn it.

But the way she'd been turning the lights off and on was odd. What did that have to do with being sad?

His mare nudged him in the shoulder, unhappy with the way he was standing still.

"I know, I know. I have to go check on her." He turned the mare into the paddock so she could enjoy the last of the twilight without a saddle on her back, then turned himself toward the house. It was only about a hundred yards from barn to kitchen door, an easy walk over hard-packed earth to a wide flagstone patio that held a couple of wooden picnic tables. The kitchen door was protected by its original small back porch and an awning.

A hundred yards was far enough to give Travis time to think about how long he'd been in the saddle today, how long he'd be in the saddle tomorrow, and how he was hungry enough to eat his hat.

He took his hat off and knocked at the back door.

No answer.

He knocked again. His stomach growled.

"Go away." The movie star didn't sound particularly sad.

He leaned his hand on the door jamb. "You got the lights fixed in there, ma'am?"

"Yes. Go away."

Fine by him. Just hearing her voice made his heart speed up a tick, and he didn't like it. He'd turned away and put his hat back on when he heard the door open.

"Wait. Do you know anything about refrigerators?"

He glanced back and did a double take. She was standing there with a dish towel on her head, its blue and white cotton covering her face. "What in the Sam Hill are you—"

"I don't want you to see me. Can you fix a refrigerator?"

"Probably." He took his hat off as he stepped back under the awning, but she didn't back up to let him in. "Can you see through that thing?"

She held up a hand to stop him, but her palm wasn't quite directed his way. "Wait. Do you have a camera?"

"No."

"How about a cell phone?"

"Of course."

"Set it on the ground, right here." She pointed at her feet. "No pictures."

He fought for patience. This woman was out of her mind with her dish towel and her demands. He had a horse to stable for the night and eight more to feed before he could go home and scarf down something himself. "Do you want me to look at your fridge or not?"

"No one sets foot in this house with a cell phone. No one gets photos of me for free. If you don't like it, too bad. You'll just have to leave."

Travis put his hat back on his head and left. He didn't take to being told what to do with his personal property. He'd crossed the flagstone and stepped onto the hard-packed dirt path to the barn when she called after him.

"That's it? You're really leaving?"

He took his time turning around. She'd come out to the edge of the porch, and was holding up the towel just far enough to peek out from under it. He clenched his jaw against the sight of her bare stomach framed by that tight black clothing. She hadn't gotten that outfit at any Western-wear-and-feed store. The thigh-high boots were gone. Instead, she was all legs. Long, bare legs.

Damn it. He was already hungry for food. He didn't need to be hungry for anything else.

"That's it," he said, and turned back to the barn.

"Wait. Okay, I'll make an exception, but just this one time. You have to keep your phone in your pocket when you're around me."

He kept walking.

"Don't leave me. Just…don't leave. Please."

He shouldn't have looked back, but he did. There was something a little bit lost about her stance, something just unsure enough in the way she lifted that towel off one eye that made him pause. The way she was tracking him reminded him of a fox that had gotten tangled in a fence and wasn't sure if she should bite him or let him free her.

Cursing himself every step of the way, he returned to the porch and slammed the heel of his boot in the cast iron boot jack that had a permanent place by the door.

"What are you doing?" Her head was bowed under the towel as she watched him step out of one boot, then the other.

"You're worried about the wrong thing. The cell phone isn't a problem. A man coming from a barn into your house with his boots on? That could be a problem. Mrs. MacDowell wouldn't allow it." And then, because he remembered the sister's distress over the extremes to which the paparazzi had apparently gone in the past, he dropped his cell phone in one boot. "There. Now take that towel off your head."

He brushed past her and walked into the kitchen, hanging his hat on one of the hooks by the door. He opened the fridge, but the appliance clearly was dead. "You already checked the fuse, I take it."

"Yes."

Of course she had. That had been why the lights had gone on and off.

She walked up to him with her hands full of plastic triangles. "These wedges were in the doors. I took them out because I thought maybe you had to shut the door all the way to make it run. I don't see any kind of on-off switch."

The towel was gone. She was, quite simply, the most beautiful woman he'd ever seen. Her hair was messed up from the towel and her famously blue eyes were puffy from crying, but by God, she was absolutely beautiful. His heart must have stopped for a moment, because he felt the hard thud in his chest when it kick-started back to life.

She suddenly threw the plastic onto the tile floor, making a great clatter. "Don't stare at me. So, I've been crying. Big deal. Tell all your friends. 'Hey, you should see Sophia Jackson when she cries. She looks like hell.' Go get your phone and take a picture. I swear, I don't care. All I want is for that refrigerator to work. If you're just going to stand there and stare at me, then get the hell out of my house."

If Travis had learned anything from a lifetime around animals, it was that only one creature at a time had better be riled up. If his horse got spooked, he had to be calm. If a cow got protective of her calf, then it was up to him not to give her a reason to lower her head and charge. He figured if a movie star was freaked out about her appearance, then he had to not give a damn about it.

He didn't, not really. She looked like what she looked like, which was beautiful, red nose and tear stains and all. There were a lot of beautiful things in his world, like horses. Sunsets. He appreciated Sophia's beauty, but he hadn't intended to make a fuss over it. If he'd been staring at her, it had been no different than taking an extra moment to look at the sky on a particularly colorful evening.

He crossed his arms over his chest and leaned against the counter. "Is the fridge plugged into the wall?"

She'd clearly expected him to say something else. It took her a beat to snap her mouth shut. "I thought of that, but I can't see behind it, and the stupid thing is too big for me to move. I'm stuck. I've just been stuck here all day, watching all my food melt." Her upper lip quivered a little, vulnerable.

He thought about kissing just her upper lip, one precise placement of his lips on hers, to steady her. He pushed the thought away. "Did you try to move it?"

"What?"

"Did you try to move it? Or did you just look at it and decide you couldn't?" He nodded his head toward the fridge, a mammoth side-by-side for a family that had consisted almost entirely of hungry men. "Give it a shot."

"Is this how you get your jollies? You want to see if I'm stupid enough to try to move something that's ten times heavier than I am? Blondes are dumb, right? This is your test to see if I'm a real blonde. Men always want to know if I'm a real blonde. Well, guess what? I am." She grabbed the handles of the open doors and gave them a dramatic yank, heaving all her weight backward in the effort.

The fridge rolled toward her at least a foot, making her yelp in surprise. The shock on her face was priceless. Travis rubbed his jaw to keep from laughing.

She pressed her lips together and lifted her chin, and Travis had the distinct impression she was trying to keep herself from not going over the edge again.

That sobered him up. He recrossed his arms. "You can't see them, but a fridge this size has to have built-in casters. No one could move it otherwise. Not you. Not me. Not both of us together."

"I didn't know."

"Now you do."

She seemed rooted to her spot, facing the fridge. With her puffy eyes and tear-streaked face, she had definitely had a bad day. Her problems might seem trivial to him—who cared if someone snapped a photo of a famous person?—but they weighed on her.

He shoved himself to his tired feet. "Come on, I'll help you plug it in."

"No, I'll do it." She started tugging, and once she'd pulled the behemoth out another foot, she boosted herself onto the counter, gracefully athletic. Kneeling on Mrs. MacDowell's blue-tiled counter, she bent down to reach behind the fridge and grope for the cord. Travis knew he shouldn't stare, but hell, her head was behind the fridge. The dip of her lower back and the curve of her thigh didn't know they were being fully appreciated.

When she got the fridge plugged in, it obediently and immediately hummed to life. She jumped down from the countertop, landing silently, as sure of her balance as a cat. He caught a flash of her determination along with a flash of her bare skin.

Hunger ate at him, made him impatient. He picked his hat up from its hook by the door. "Good night, then."

"Where are you going?"

"Back to work." He shut the door behind himself. Stomped into the first boot, but his own balance felt off. He had to hop a bit to catch himself. He needed to get some food and some sleep, then he'd be fine.

The door swung open, but he caught it before it knocked him over. "What now?"

"I need groceries."

There was a beat of silence. Did she expect him to magically produce groceries?

"Everything melted." She looked mournfully over her shoulder at the sink, then back at him, and just... waited.

It amazed him how city folk sometimes needed to be told how the world ran. "Guess you'll be headed into town tomorrow, then."

"Me? I can't go to a grocery store."

"You need a truck? The white pickup is for general use. The keys are in the barn, on the hook by the tack room. Help yourself."

"To a truck?" She literally recoiled a half step back into the house.

"I don't know how else you intend to get to the grocery store. Just head toward Austin. Closest store is about twenty miles in, on your right."

"You have to get the groceries for me."

"Nope. It's May." He stuck his hat on, so his hands were free to pick up his second boot and shake the cell phone out of it.

"It's May? What kind of answer is that? Do you fast in May or do a colon cleanse or something?"

He looked up at her joke, but his grin died before it started. Judging by the look on her face, she wasn't joking. "The River Mack rounds up in May."

She looked at him, waiting. He realized a woman from Hollywood probably had no idea what that meant.

"We're busy. We're branding. We have to keep an eye on the late calving, the bulls—"

He stopped himself. He wasn't going to explain the rest. Managing a herd was a constant, complex operation. Bulls had to be separated from cows. The cow-calf pairs had to be moved to the richest pastures so the mamas could keep their weight up while they nursed their calves. Cows who had failed to get pregnant were culled from the herd and replaced with better, more fertile cattle.

Sophia flapped one hand toward the kitchen behind her. "I have nothing to eat. You have to help me."

He stomped into his second boot. "Not unless you're a pregnant cow."

At her gasp, he did chuckle. "Or a horse. Or a dog. You could be a chicken, and I would have to help you. I keep every beast on this ranch fed, but you, ma'am, are not a beast. You're a grown woman who can take care of herself, and you're not my problem."

She looked absolutely stricken. Had he been so harsh?

"Listen, if I'm going toward town, I don't mind picking you up a gallon of milk. That's just common courtesy. I expect you to do the same for me."

"But I can't leave the ranch."

"Neither can I." He touched the brim of his hat in farewell. "Now if you'll excuse me, I've got horses to feed before I can feed myself."

## Chapter Four

A pregnant cow.

It was fair to say women pretty much spent their lives trying not to look like pregnant cows. Yet if Sophia Jackson, Golden Globe winner and Academy Award nominee, wanted help on this ranch, she needed to look like that cow she'd hugged in the middle of the road.

She didn't look like that. She looked like a movie star, and that meant she would get no help. No sympathy.

That was nothing new. Movie stars were expected to be rolling in dough and to have an easy life. Everyone assumed movie stars were millionaires, but she was more of a hundred-thousandaire. Certainly comfortable and a far cry from her days pointing at mattresses with a smile, but the money went out at an alarming rate between jobs. Even when she was not being paid, Sophia paid everyone else: publicists, managers, agents, fitness trainers, fashion stylists…and her personal assistant, Grace.

Sophia had to pay them to do their jobs, so that she could land another job and get another burst of money. An actor only felt secure if the next job got lined up before the current job stopped paying. Then, of course, the next job after that needed to be won, a contract signed, and more money dished out.

There would be no new jobs, not for nine months. Sophia slid her palm over her perfectly flat, perfectly toned abs. The whole pregnancy concept didn't seem real. It was a plus sign on a plastic stick and nothing more. She didn't feel different. She didn't look different.

Alex the Stupid Doctor had explained that she was only weeks along, and that for a first-time mother, especially one who stayed in the kind of physical shape the world expected Sophia to be in, the pregnancy might not show until the fourth or fifth month. Maybe longer.

She could have filmed another movie in that time…

But nobody in Hollywood wanted to work with her…

Because she'd fallen for a loser who'd killed her hard-working reputation.

*Round and round we go.*

Always the same thoughts, always turning in that same vicious cycle.

If only she hadn't met DJ Deezee, that jerk…

She picked up the goose salt shaker and clenched it tightly in her fist. For the next nine months, instead of paying her entourage's salaries, Sophia would be paying rent on this house. The rent was cheaper than the stable of people it took to sustain fame, which was fortunate, because the money coming in was going to slow considerably. Her only income would be residuals from DVD sales of movies that had already sold most of what they would ever sell—and her old manager and her old agent would still take their cut from that, even though they'd abandoned her.

She was going to hide on this ranch and watch her money dwindle as she sank into obscurity. Then she'd have to start over, scrambling for any scrap Hollywood would throw to her, auditioning for any female role. Her life would be an endless circle of checking in with grouchy temps, setting her head shot on their rickety card tables, taking her place in line with the other actors, praying this audition would be the one. She wasn't sure she could withstand years of rejection for a second time.

She shouldn't have to. She'd paid her dues.

The ceramic goose in her hand should have crumbled from the force of her grip, the way it would have if she'd been in a movie. But no—for that to happen, a prop master had to construct the shaker out of glazed sugar, something a real person could actually break. Movies had to be faked.

This was all too real. She couldn't crush porcelain. She could throw it, though. Deezee regularly trashed hotel rooms, and she had to admit that it had felt therapeutic for a moment when he'd dared her to throw a vase in a presidential suite. Afterward, though…the broken shards had stayed stuck in the carpet while management tallied up the bill.

She stared for a moment longer at the goose in her hand, its blank stare unchanging as it awaited its fate. "There's nothing we can do about any of this, is there?"

The kitchen was suddenly too small, too close. Sophia walked quickly into the living room. It was bigger, more modern. Wood floors, nice upholstery, a flat-screen TV. A vase. The ceilings were high, white with dark beams. She felt suddenly small, standing in this great room in a house built to hold a big family. She was one little person dwarfed by thousands of square feet of ranch house.

She heard her sister's voice. Her mother's voice. *You've got nowhere else to go. You cannot live with me.*

She couldn't, could she? Her sister was in love, planning a wedding, giddy about living with her new husband. There was no room for a third wheel that would spin notoriety and paparazzi into their normal lives.

And her mother… Sophia could not move back home to live with her. Never again. Not in this life. Other twenty-nine-year-olds might have their parents as a safety net, but Sophia's safety net had been cut away on a highway ten years ago.

The ceilings were too high. The nausea was rising to fill the empty space, and it had nothing to do with pregnancy, nothing at all. Sophia squeezed her eyes shut and buried her face in her clenched fists. The little beak of the salt shaker goose pressed into her forehead, into her hard skull.

The house was too big. She got out, jerking open the front door and escaping onto the wide front porch. In the daylight, the white columns had framed unending stretch of brown and green earth. At night, the blackness was overwhelming, like being on a spaceship, surrounded by nothing but night sky. There were too many stars. No city lights drowned them out. She was too far from Hollywood, the only place she needed to be. *All alone, all alone…*

This was not what she wanted, not what she'd ever wanted. She'd worked so hard, but it was all coming to nothing. Life as she'd known it would end here, on a porch in the middle of nowhere, a slow, nine-month death. Already, she'd ceased to exist.

She hurled the salt shaker into the night, aiming at the stars, the too-plentiful stars.

The salt shaker disappeared in the dark. Sophia's gesture of defiance had no effect on the world at all.

*I do exist. I'm Sophia Jackson, damn it.*

If she didn't want to be on this ranch, then she didn't have to be.

*You know how to drive, don't you? Turn the car around, then, instead of blowing that damned horn.*

There was a truck, the cowboy had said. A white truck. Keys in the barn. She ran down the steps, but they ended on a gravel path, and her feet were bare. She was forced off the path, forced to slow down as she skirted the house, crossing dirt and grass toward the barn.

*I don't want to slow down. If I get off the roller coaster of Hollywood, I'll never be able to speed back up again. I refuse to slow down.*

She stepped on a rock and hissed at the pain, but she would not be denied. Instead of being more careful, she broke into a sprint—and stepped on an even sharper rock. She gasped, she hopped on one foot, she cursed.

*I'm being a drama queen.*

She was. Oh, God, she really was a drama queen—and it was going to get her nowhere. The truck would be sitting there whether she got to the barn in five seconds or five minutes. And then what? She'd drive the truck barefoot into Austin and do what, exactly?

*I'm so stupid.*

No one had witnessed her stupidity, but that hardly eased her sense of embarrassment as she made her way more carefully toward the barn. It was hard to shake that feeling of being watched after years of conditioning. Ten years, to be precise, beginning with her little sister watching her with big eyes once it was only the two of them, alone in their dead parents' house. *But Sophie, do you know how to make Mom's recipe?*

*Don't you worry. It will be a piece of cake.*

Sophia knew Grace had been counting on her last remaining family member not to crack under the pressure of becoming a single parent to her younger sister. Later, managers and directors had counted on Sophia, too, judging whether or not she would crack before offering her money for her next role. She'd had them all convinced she was a safe bet, but for the past five months, the paparazzi had been watching her with Deezee, counting on her to crack into a million pieces before their cameras, so they could sell the photos.

The paparazzi had guessed right. She'd finally cracked. The photos were all over the internet. Now no one was counting on her. Grace didn't need her anymore. Alex had stuck Sophia in this ranch house, supposedly so she'd have a place where no one would watch her. Out of habit, though, she looked over her shoulder as she reached the barn, keeping her chin up and looking unconcerned in the flattering light of the last rays of sunset. There was no one around, only the white pickup parked to the side. The cowboy must have gone to get his dinner.

Well, that made one of them. Sophia realized the nausea had subsided and hunger pangs had taken its place. Maybe inside the barn there would be some pregnant-cow food she could eat. She slid open the barn door and walked inside.

Not cows. Horses.

Sophia paused at the end of the long center aisle. One by one, horses hung their heads over their stall doors and stared at her.

"You can quit staring at me," she said, but the horses took their time checking her out with their big brown eyes, twitching their ears here and there. The palette of their warm colors as they hung their heads over their iron and wood stalls would have made a lovely setting for a rustic movie.

There were no cameras here, no press, no producers. Sophia stopped holding her breath and let herself sag against the stall to her right. Her shoulders slumped under the full weight of her fatigue.

The horse swung its head a little closer to her, and gave her slumped shoulder a nudge.

"Oh, hello." Sophia had only known one horse in her life, the one that the stunt team had assigned her to sit upon during a few scenes before her pioneer character's dramatic death. She'd liked that horse, though, and had enjoyed its company more than that of the insulting, unstable director.

"Aren't you pretty?" Sophia tentatively ran the backs of her knuckles over the horse's neck, feeling the strength of its awesome muscles under the soft coat. She walked to the next stall, grateful for the cool concrete on the battered soles of her feet.

The next horse didn't back away from her, either. Sophia petted it carefully, then more confidently when the horse didn't seem to mind. She smoothed her hand over the massive cheek. "Yes, you're very pretty. You really are."

She worked her way down the aisle, petting each one, brown and spotted, black and white. They were all so peaceful, interested in her and yet not excited by her. Except, perhaps, the last one with the dark brown face and jet-black mane. That horse was excited to snuffle her soft nose right into Sophia's hair, making Sophia smile at the tickle.

"It's my shampoo. Ridiculously expensive, but Jean Paul gives it to me for free as long as I tell everyone that I use it. So if he asks, do a girl a favor and tell him you heard I use his shampoo."

How was that going to work, now that she was out of the public eye? She rested her forehead against the horse's solid neck. "At least, he used to give it to me for free."

The horse chuffed into her hair.

"I'd share it with you, but I might not get any more, actually. Sorry about that, pretty girl. Before this is all over, I may have to borrow your shampoo. I hear horse shampoo can be great for people's hair. Would you mind?"

"Did you need something else?"

Sophia whirled around. Mr. Don't-or-Else stood there, all denim and boots and loose stance, but his brown eyes were narrowed on her like she was some kind of rattlesnake who'd slithered in to his domain.

"I thought you were gone," she said. She adjusted her posture. She was being watched after all. She should have known better than to drop her guard.

"You are not allowed in the barn without boots on."

The horse snuffled some more of her hair, clearly

approving of her even if her owner didn't. "What's this horse's name?"

"No bare feet in the barn." The cowboy indicated the door with a jerk of his strong chin—his very strong chin, which fit his square jaw. A lighting director couldn't ask for better angles to illuminate. The camera would love him.

*Travis Chalmers.* He'd tipped his hat to her this afternoon as he'd sat on his horse. Her heart had tripped a little then. It tripped a little now.

She'd already brought her ankles together and bent one knee, so very casually, she set one hand on her hip. It made her body look its best. The public always checked out her body, her clothing, her makeup, her hair. God forbid anything failed to meet their movie star expectations. They'd rip her apart on every social media platform.

Travis had already seen her looking her worst, but if he hoped she'd crack into more pieces, he was in for a disappointment.

Sophia shook her hair back, knowing it would shine even in the low light of the barn. "What's the horse's name? She and I have the same taste in shampoo."

"He's a gelding, not a girl. You can't come into the barn without boots or shoes. It's not safe. Is that clear?"

Sophia rolled her eyes in a playful way, as if she were lighthearted tonight. "If it's a boy horse, then what's *his* name? He likes me."

The cowboy scoffed at that. "You seem to think all of my stock like you."

"They do. All of them except you."

Travis's expression didn't change, not one bit, even though she'd tossed off her line with the perfect combination of sassy confidence and pretty pout. He simply wasn't impressed.

It hurt. He was the only person out here, her only possible defense against being swallowed by the loneliness, and yet he was the one person on earth who didn't seem thrilled to meet a celebrity.

Supposedly. He was still watching her.

The audition wasn't over. She could still win him over.

The anxiety to do so was familiar. Survival in Hollywood depended on winning people over. She'd had to win over every casting director who'd judged her, who'd watched her as impassively as this cowboy did while she tried to be enchanting. Indifference had to be overcome, or she wouldn't get the job and she couldn't pay the bills.

With the anxiety came the adrenaline that had helped her survive. She needed to win over Travis Chalmers, or she'd have no one to talk to at all. Ever.

So she smiled, and she took a step closer.

His eyes narrowed a fraction as his gaze dropped down her bare legs. She felt another little thrill of adrenaline. This would be easy.

"You're bleeding," he said.

"I'm—" She tilted her head but kept her smile in place. "What?"

But he was impatient, walking past her to glare at the floor behind her. "What did you cut yourself on?"

She turned around to see little round, red smears where she'd stopped to greet each horse. "It must have been a rock outside. I stepped on a couple of rocks pretty hard."

"Good."

"Good?"

He glanced at her and had the grace to look the tiniest bit embarrassed. "Good that it wasn't anything sharp in the barn. If it had been a nail or something that had cut you, then it could cut a horse, too."

"Thanks for your concern." She said it with a smile and a little shake of her chandelier earrings. "Nice to know the horses are more valuable than I am."

"Like I said earlier, it's my job to take care of every beast on this ranch. You're not a beast. You should know to wear shoes."

She wasn't sure how to answer that. She couldn't exactly insist she *was* a valuable beast that needed taken care of, and she certainly wasn't going to admit she'd run outside in a panic. Actors who panicked didn't get hired.

"Come on. I'll get you something for the bleeding."

He walked away. Just turned his back on her and walked away. Again.

After a moment, she followed, but she hadn't taken two steps when he told her to stop. "Don't keep bleeding on the floor."

"What do you want me to do?" She put both hands on her hips and faced him squarely. Who cared if it didn't show off her figure? She'd lost this audition already.

"Can't you hop on one foot?"

This had to be a test, another trick to see if she was a dumb blonde. But Travis turned into a side room that was the size of another stall, one fitted out with a deep utility sink and kitchen-style cabinets.

He wasn't watching her to see what she'd do, so maybe it wasn't a joke. After a moment of indecision, she started hopping on her good foot. The cut one hurt, anyway, and it was only a few hops to reach the sink.

Travis opened one of the cabinets. It looked like a pharmacy inside, stocked with extra-large pill bottles. He got out a box of bandages, the adhesive kind that came in individual paper wrappers. The kind her mother had put on her scrapes and cuts when she was little.

*I am not going to cry in front of this man. Not ever again.*

He tapped the counter by the sink. "Hop up. Wash your foot off in the sink."

"Why don't you come here and give me a little boost?"

He stilled, with good reason. She'd said it with a purr, an unmistakably sexual invitation for him to put his hands on her.

She hadn't meant to. It had just popped out that way, her way to distance herself from the nostalgia. Maybe a way to gain some control over him. He was giving her commands, but she could get him to obey a sexual command of her own if she really turned on the charm.

Whatever had made her say that, she had to brave it out now. Sultry was better than sad. Anything was better than sad.

She tossed her hair back, her earrings jingling like a belly dancer's costume. She turned so that she was slightly sideways to him, her bustline a curvy contrast to her flat stomach.

"The counter's too high for me. Give me a hand… or two."

*Come and touch me.* Her invitation sounded welcoming. She realized it was. He was nothing like the sleek actors or the crazy DJs she'd known, but apparently, *rugged outdoorsman* appealed to her in a big way. *You've got a big green light here, Mr. Cowboy.*

"Too high for you," he repeated, without a flicker of sexual awareness in his voice. Instead, he sounded impatient as he cut through her helpless-damsel act. "I already watched you hop up on Mrs. MacDowell's counter tonight."

Of course the counter height had been a flimsy excuse; it had been an invitation. She refused to blush at having it rejected. Instead, she backed up to the counter and braced her hands behind herself, letting her crop top ride high. With the kind of slow control that would have made her personal yoga instructor beam with approval, she used biceps and triceps and abs, and lifted herself slowly onto the counter with a smooth flex of her toned body. People would pay money to see a certain junior officer do that in a faraway galaxy.

Travis Chalmers made a lousy audience. He only turned on the water and handed her a bar of soap.

She worked the bar into a lather as she pouted. Even Deezee wouldn't have passed up the chance to touch her. Actually, that was all Deezee had ever wanted to do: touch her. If it wasn't going to end in sex, he wasn't into it. She'd texted him ten times more often than he'd texted her between dates. His idea of a date had meant they'd go somewhere to party in the public eye or drink among VIPs for a couple of hours before they went to bed together. There'd been no hanging out for the sake of spending time together.

Sophia held her foot still as the water rinsed off the suds. She'd mistaken sex for friendship, hadn't she?

"It's not a deep cut. You should heal pretty quickly." Travis dabbed the sole of her foot dry with a wad of clean paper towels, which he then handed to her. Before she could ask what she was supposed to do with damp paper towels, he'd torn the paper wrapper off a bandage and placed it over the cut. He pressed the adhesive firmly into her skin with his thumb. There was nothing sexual in his touch, but it wasn't unkind. It was almost…paternal.

"Do you have kids?" she asked.

For once, he paused at something she'd said. "No."

*You ought to.* There was something about his unruffled, unhurried manner…

Dear God, she wasn't going to start missing her father, too. She couldn't think about parents and sister any longer. Not tonight.

She snatched her foot away and jumped lightly off the counter, landing on the foot that hadn't been cut. She held up the wad of damp towels. "Where's the trash?"

"You need those paper towels to wipe up the blood on your way out. I'll get you something to wear on your feet."

On her way out. She was dismissed, and she had to go back to the empty house in the middle of nowhere. She didn't want Travis to fetch her boots; she wanted him to carry her. He was a man who rode horseback all day. A cowboy who stood tall, with broad shoulders and strong hands. He could carry her weight, and God knew Sophia was tired of carrying everything herself.

She wanted his arms around her.

But she'd failed this audition. He wasn't interested in her when she was either bossy or cute. He wasn't fazed by her sultry tone, and he didn't care about her hard-earned, perfect body. He wasn't impressed with her in any way.

She gingerly stepped into the center aisle to see where he'd gone. Across from the medical room was another stall-sized space where it seemed saddles got parked on wooden sawhorses. The next room was enclosed with proper walls and a door, with a big glass window in the wall that looked into the rest of the barn. She could see a desk and bookcase and all the usual stuff for an office inside. She felt so dumb; she hadn't known barns had offices and medical clinics inside.

Travis came in from the door at the far end of the aisle from the door she'd used. He dropped a pair of utilitarian rubber rain boots at her feet. "These will get you back to the house. Return them tomorrow, before sundown."

"So specific. Bossy much?" She could hear the snotty teenager in her voice. Whatever. She hated feeling dumb.

"Whoever brings the horses in tomorrow might want to wear them when they hose down a horse, so have them back by then."

It was a patient explanation, but she hated that he could tell she didn't know squat about how a ranch was run. "Someone else is coming? You're not going to be here tomorrow night?"

"We take turns during roundup. One of the other hands will have a chance to come in and shower and sleep in a bed. Someone's usually here before sundown."

"But I can't let anyone else see me."

He shrugged. "Then don't come into the barn at sundown."

*Then turn the car around. Then go to the grocery store.* As if life were that simple.

"If you do come into the barn, wear boots. Dish towels are optional. Good night." He walked back into the medical stall, closing cabinet doors and shutting off the light.

*Dish towels are optional.* The man thought she was a big joke. With as much dignity as she'd once been forced to muster each time a casting director had said *Don't call us, we'll call you,* Sophia stepped into the galoshes and headed for the door, bending over to wipe up little red circles as she went.

Travis returned to the center aisle in time to watch the most beautiful woman in the world stomp out of his barn like a goddess in galoshes. She slid the barn door closed behind herself with what he was certain was a deliberate bang.

Samson, his favorite gelding and apparent lover of women's shampoo, kept his head toward the door, ears pointed toward the spot where the woman had disappeared. Travis realized he and the horse were both motionless for a moment too long.

"You can stop staring at the door. She's not coming back."

The horse shifted, stamping his foot.

"All right, damn it, you're right. Her hair smelled amazing. Don't get used to it. We've got work tomorrow. It'd take more than a pretty woman to change our ways."

# Chapter Five

Three days, he stayed away.

The days were easy, filled with dirt and lassos as the animals were rounded up, counted, doctored. Calves bawled for their mamas until the cowboys released them and let them run back to the waiting herd. Travis had to change his mount every few hours to give the horses a rest, so the additional challenge of controlling different mounts with their unique personalities kept his attention focused where it ought to be.

But for three nights...

He'd stretch out on his bedroll and stare at the stars while thinking of one in particular, the star that had fallen onto his ranch. Insomnia wasn't a problem after a day of physical work, but when his tired body forced his mind to shut down, he continued thinking about Sophia Jackson in his sleep. Sophia got flirty, she got angry, she was strong and she was weak, but she was always, always tempting in every dream version of her that his brain could concoct. For three nights, he dreamed of nothing else.

It was damned annoying.

In the afternoon of the fourth day, he rode in with Clay Cooper, the hand who was next up for a night off. As foreman, Travis had to get to his office to keep up with the never-ending paperwork that went with running any business. That was reason enough for him to leave camp for the night. Not one cowboy was surprised when he left with Clay and the string of horses that were due for a day's rest and extra oats in the barn.

But Travis knew the real reason he was going in was to check on the famous Sophia Jackson. He was tired of fighting that nagging feeling that he needed to keep an eye on her, a feeling that hadn't gone away since the moment he'd met her in the road.

The house came into view. Travis's horse perked up. Travis had worked with horses too long for him not to understand what drove their behavior. The horse had perked up with anticipation because the rider had perked up with anticipation.

Travis rolled his shoulders. Took off his hat and smacked the dust off his thigh. Relaxed into the saddle.

There was nothing to anticipate. He was going to see Sophia Jackson soon. No big deal. Sophia was a movie star, but he wasn't starstruck.

The horse walked on while Travis turned that thought over once or twice. It felt true. Sure, he'd seen her in *Space Maze*. It would be hard to find someone who hadn't seen that movie. But from the tantrum she'd thrown about being stared at, and from her sister's fear of the paparazzi, he didn't think the Hollywood life-style was very attractive. It would have been better if she hadn't been a movie star.

*Better for what?*

Just easier all around. He put his hat on his head and turned back to check the string of horses following Clay. All was well.

As the foreman, he was riding in to check on the new person renting the MacDowells' house, same as he'd check on any new cowboy who came to the ranch. Hell, he'd check on any new filly or fence post. Once he was sure the MacDowells' guest had gotten her groceries and her fridge was still running, he'd mentally cross her off his to-do list and move on to the next item: he needed to order more barb wire before they got down to the last spool.

He and Clay rode past the house. Travis had planned to help Clay put up the horses first at the bunkhouse's stable before checking on Sophia, but he noticed that Clay didn't even toss a glance toward the house. It hit Travis that none of the hands who'd come and gone from camp seemed to be aware anyone was living in Mrs. MacDowell's house. Travis would've told them there was a guest staying there. No big deal. But no one had mentioned seeing any signs of life for the past three nights.

There were no signs of life now. No lights on. No curtains open to take in the evening sunset. No rocking chair on the porch out of place. Sophia was keeping herself hidden pretty well, then. Or…

Or Sophia Jackson had left the River Mack ranch.

*I don't want to be here, anyway*, she'd said, hand poised over the car's steering wheel.

It was the most likely explanation. He'd wanted her to leave when he'd first met her, so he ought to be relieved. Instead, that nagging need to see her intensified. He had to know if she was still on his land or not.

"I'll see you tomorrow," he said to Clay. He let his horse feel his hurry to reach Mrs. MacDowell's kitchen door until he stopped her at the edge of the flagstone patio. There, stretched out on one of the wooden picnic tables, was Sophia. She was laid out like she was the meal, her clothing white like a tablecloth, her body delectable, but her eyes were closed and her hand was open and relaxed as she slept.

He dismounted and looped the horse's reins loosely around the old hitching post. His horse tossed her head with a jangle of tack and the heels of Travis's boots made a hard noise with each step as he crossed the flagstone, but Sophia remained fast asleep.

He ought to be thinking of Sleeping Beauty, he supposed. Sophia was as beautiful as a princess in her innocent white clothing, if a princess wore shorts and a shirt.

Instead, he couldn't get the idea of a feast out of his head. Here was a woman who'd be a banquet for the senses. Old college memories came back, Humanities 101 and its dry textbook descriptions of Roman emperors who'd held feasts where the sex was part of the meal. The image of a fairy tale princess battled briefly with the Roman feast, but Travis's body clearly clamored for Rome.

He stopped at her side. Looked down at her, but didn't touch. "Sophia."

She didn't stir. He said her name again and waited, wondering how a shirt and shorts could look so sexy. Finally, he shook her arm. "Sophia, wake up. It's Travis."

She jerked awake, then jerked away from him, like an animal instinctively afraid of attack.

Fanciful notions from college studies evaporated in an instant. "Whoa. It's just me."

She rolled off the table, off the far side, so that she stood with the table between them. It was a seriously skittish move.

"What are you doing here?" she asked.

"This is my ranch."

"Ha. You don't spend a lot of time on it." She pushed her hair back with both hands, pausing to squeeze her temples with her palms as she looked around the horizon. "Crap. Is it already sunset?"

"Clay's already taken the horses to the stable."

She looked toward the barn, alarmed. "Did this Clay guy see me?"

Travis didn't envy her Hollywood life at all. She seemed to be on edge all the time.

She wasn't wearing a shirt and shorts, after all. It was all one piece, almost like a child's pajamas. Maybe she was embarrassed to be caught outside in her pajamas. "Don't worry. You're looking at the barn, not what we call the stables around here. The stables are on the far side of the horse pasture. You can't see it from the house."

He paused. He didn't have a reason to tell her more, except that it might buy her some time to ease into being awake. "The stables are close to the bunkhouse. Cowboys living there keep their horses in the stables."

But judging by the way she rubbed the sleep from her eyes, she'd tuned him out after *Clay can't see you*. "I have to go inside. It's sunset."

"No one else is due in tonight." His words fell on deaf

ears. Sophia stepped up on the little porch and disappeared into the house.

Travis caught himself staring at the closed door like Samson had the other night. He cursed under his breath and went to untie his horse. He had his answer: Sophia Jackson was still here. She looked fine, better than fine. She looked healthy as all get-out. It was time to move on and order that barb wire.

He led his horse to the barn. Caring for the mare was a familiar routine, one that should have let him unwind, but he had to work to ignore a lingering uneasiness. He unsaddled the mare, stored the tack, then took her outside to rinse the sweat marks from her coat with a garden hose.

The galoshes were sitting neatly by the hose, pushing his thoughts right back to Sophia.

Her presence in the barn that night had been unsettling in general. So had been one of her questions in particular: *Do you have kids?*

For just for a second, he'd thought he'd like to be able to answer *yes*. He was thirty-one and settled. He'd stood there with Sophia Jackson's perfectly arched foot in his hand and pictured himself married with a couple of little ones that he'd have to keep out of trouble. *It would be good to be a dad*, he'd thought for that flash of a second.

In reality, he didn't see himself getting married, and in his world, having children meant being married. He had nothing against the institution; he could understand why men did marry. Many a rancher's wife provided dinner every evening and clothes mended with love. They baked cakes and grew tomatoes in the garden, like Mrs. MacDowell.

Or there were wives who were partners in handling

cattle. Travis hired the same husband and wife team every fall when it came time to move the cattle to auction. The two of them seemed happy roping and riding together, and they worked smoothly in sync.

But Travis was fine as a bachelor. He liked his own cooking well enough. Working alone never bothered him. He was where he wanted to be, doing what he wanted to do. In order to even consider upending a perfectly good life, he'd have to meet a woman who was damned near irresistible.

*Like Sophia Jackson.*

Not anything like her. He'd need to find a woman who was irresistible but not crazy enough to wear a dish towel on her head and spike-heeled boots on a dirt road.

*Unless that's what makes her irresistible.*

He turned the hose back on and stuck his head in the stream of water.

*Listen to yourself. A rancher's wife and a movie star are two different creatures. Too different.*

This woman slept on top of a picnic table in the middle of the day. Crazy. A man did not marry *crazy*. A man didn't want *crazy* to be the mother of his children. Irresistible had nothing to do with it.

He shook the water out of his too-long hair as he unbuttoned his sweat-soaked plaid shirt and peeled it off. He had to lean over pretty far to keep the water off his jeans and boots, but the hose was good for taking off the first layer of trail dirt from his arms and chest.

Feeling a hundred times more clearheaded, he shut off the water and turned the mare loose in the paddock. His office was inside the barn. He kept a stack of clean T-shirts there. While he was at his desk, he'd order a dozen spools of quality barb wire, so he wouldn't have to give it a second thought for the rest of the year. Barb wire would be ordered—check. The MacDowells' houseguest was doing fine—check. He'd move on to the next item on his list.

He shoved the galoshes aside with the edge of his boot and left the darkening sky before the stars could come out and taunt his resolve.

It was useless. As he strode into the barn, he heard a distinctively feminine gasp. In the twilight of the barn's interior, Sophia practically glowed, all silver-blond hair and short, white pajamas. A star, right here in his barn. There was no list; there was nothing else to think about.

She dropped her gaze first.

Slowly.

She took him in deliberately, her gaze roaming over his wet skin, from his left shoulder to his right. To his bare chest. Lower.

*I'm not the only one around here who's hungry, then.*

The knowledge blinded him for a moment. To hell with the kind of woman he ought to want. Sophia was the woman he *did* want. Full stop. And he wanted her badly.

She came a step closer.

As water drops rolled down his skin, blood pounded through his veins, his desire for her ferocious in a way that was unfamiliar, as if he'd never really wanted a woman before.

She was about to say something, but as her lips parted, her gaze flicked from his chest back up to his eyes. Whatever she saw in his expression made her own eyes open wider. Whatever she'd been about to say turned into a little whoosh of "oh."

He couldn't remember feeling this power before, not

for any of the women who'd been so likely to be right for him. After dating for weeks or months or, once, a whole year, none had turned out to be right after all. Yet Sophia had only to exhale an *oh*, and the years of friends and lovers blurred into nothing. This woman was the one he'd been starving for.

Hunger caused problems on a ranch. Stallions kicked out stalls. Bulls destroyed fences.

"Why are you here?" he demanded. *Why you? Why now?*

She took a step closer, and a part of him—too much of him—didn't give a damn about the answers to his own questions. He just wanted her to keep coming.

She hesitated.

Then she took that next step closer, but it was too late. Her split-second pause, the widening of her eyes by a fraction of an inch, had betrayed the tiniest little bit of…fear? Perhaps fear of this power between them. Perhaps fear of him, personally. He was the bigger one, the stronger one, the one with an admittedly fresh surge of testosterone coursing through his body.

But he was no animal, no common beast, just as he'd told her she wasn't. He knew what was in his heart and mind and soul, and she didn't need to fear him.

She couldn't know that yet, not for certain. They barely knew one another. Travis didn't have any kind of minimum time limit in mind for how long he ought to know a woman before taking her to bed, but he did know this: she had to be one-hundred-percent certain of what she wanted. Sophia Jackson did not know what she wanted.

Travis stepped back.

Her frown of confusion was fleeting, replaced by a

new look of determination. She sauntered up to him, nice and close. Then she looked down his body again, her feminine eyelashes shading her blue eyes, turning him on as she ran one fingertip over his damp forearm.

"I came out here because it's lonely in that house. Very lonely."

God, that purr of hers…

It was an act. She was a good actress, but he'd seen that moment of fear or uncertainty or whatever it had been. Hunger couldn't be ignored forever, but it wouldn't kill a man to wait. Travis didn't intend to act on it or even talk about it in his barn just because he'd been caught out half-naked by a woman in skimpy pajamas.

He balled up his plaid shirt and used it to wipe the water off one arm, then the other. He pitched it through his open office door to land on his chair. *No feast today, Princess.*

"Did you need something before I go home?" he asked.

Her sexy act flipped to a more authentic anger pretty quickly. Apparently, she didn't take rejection well. "I don't need anything from you. I didn't even want you to be here. I came to see the horses."

"Is that so? In your pajamas and bare feet?" He turned his back on her and went into his office. He grabbed a T-shirt off the stack he kept on a bookcase. When he turned back, he nearly plowed her over; she'd followed him into his office, all indignation.

"I'm wearing sandals, and these aren't pajamas. You wish you could see me in my pajamas. You wish."

Her attempt at a set down was so childish, it sounded almost cute. Travis had to hide his smile by pulling his

T-shirt over his head. No harm in letting her think she'd scored a point against him.

"This is a *romper*," she huffed. "Straight from the runway. By a designer in Milan whom I wouldn't expect you to know. My stylist snatched it right out from under Kim K's nose. She probably died when I wore it first."

He stood with his hands on his hips, looking down at her, wondering what a guy like him was supposed to do with a girl like her. "I don't know Kim, but it looks real nice on you."

"Yeah. Sure." Apparently, she didn't believe his compliment. She turned her back on him and left the office, her designer clothes all in a white flutter.

Travis scrubbed his face with both hands. Then he shut off the lights and left the office, closing the door firmly. The barb wire could wait until tomorrow.

Sophia was nuzzling the spotted nose of a nice Appaloosa Travis had borrowed from the neighboring ranch for roundup. Travis watched her for a minute. The horse was loving the attention. *You're getting more action than I am, buddy.*

Still, Travis had to appreciate a person who had a natural affinity for horses. Her talent had to be natural and not learned, because he didn't think Sophia had ever set foot in a barn in her life before this week. She was wearing flip-flops, for crying out loud.

"Where's my horse?" she asked, keeping her eyes on the Appaloosa.

"Your horse?" He didn't like her wording. She had no idea what it meant to own a horse. To train, to groom, to feed, to care for without fail, to rely on when there was nobody for miles around.

"The boy horse whose name you won't tell me. You

left, and you took him with you. You took all of them. I came out here to say hello to the horses, and they were gone. Every single one."

Damn if she didn't sound like she was going to burst into tears.

"They aren't pets. They work."

"I returned the galoshes, just like you wanted, but you took the horses away. Without those horses, I've got no one to talk to. You're not interested in talking to me...or doing anything else with me."

Travis was good at picking up on animal behavior, not a woman's, but he could read her well enough. She felt betrayed. Lonely. Hell, she'd curled up into a ball and cried on a kitchen floor just days ago.

He'd have no peace of mind until he figured her out.

"Okay. You want to talk? Let's talk."

## Chapter Six

The cowboy wanted to talk.

Sophia wasn't sure if he was kidding. She combed her fingers through the spotted horse's mane and peeked at big, bad Travis Chalmers. He looked pretty serious. Then again, that was his default expression. He grinned a little now and then, but otherwise, he was a serious guy.

Not a guy. A man.

A serious man who walked around here like he ran the place. Which she supposed he did, but still…

Travis took some kind of rope-and-leather thing that was hanging over an empty stall door and coiled it up. Tied it off. Tossed it into the room where the saddles were. It landed in a crate. It seemed that being in charge meant keeping everything in order.

Deezee would have dumped the crate out, flipped

it upside down, and stood on it like it was his stage, whooping and hollering and making sure no one else could talk while he was around.

Travis glanced down the row of stalls to the neat stack of perfectly square hay bales, then leaned back against a support post and gave her his full attention. Apparently nothing else was out of place—except her. "What did you want to talk about?"

She wasn't about to unburden herself to this man. She could pour out her regrets to the horses tomorrow morning. She didn't want Travis to know what an idiot she'd been. What an idiot she'd thrown away her career for.

Yet she'd just complained that she didn't have anyone to talk to, and Travis had called her on it. She had to come up with something to say. "What's this horse's name?"

Travis dipped his chin toward the horse, as matter-of-fact as if her question wasn't childish. "That's Arizona. He was named for the state. Texas isn't really known for Appaloosas. He was bought in Arizona as a wedding gift."

*Oh, no. Please don't be married.*

Dumb reaction. The man looked hot when he was shirtless. So what? That didn't mean she wanted to have a relationship with him. It didn't matter if he was married or not. Still…

"Not a gift for your wedding?" She tried to sound unconcerned.

"Trey Waterson's wedding. His brother gave him the horse. They own the ranch just west of us."

But Travis had that little bit of a grin about his mouth; he knew exactly why she'd asked. Her acting skills must be getting rusty already. She wished she hadn't run her finger down that muscled forearm, chasing a water droplet. She wished she hadn't made that stupid comment about being lonely.

She wished he hadn't rejected her.

"I'm not married," he said, making things perfectly clear. "Never been."

The horse, Arizona, shook his mane like Sophia wanted to. *That's right, horse. We don't care, do we?*

"So you don't own these horses, then. You're just the babysitter." She sneered the word *babysitter*.

She wished it back as soon as she said it. It was so rude. When had she started responding to everything as if she needed to insult someone before they could insult her?

But the answer was easy: when she'd spent too much time with Deezee and his buddies. Their ribbing and one-upmanship had been constant. At first, it had been a novelty to be treated like one of the guys instead of a flawless movie star, but she'd soon figured out that if she gave them an inch, they took a mile.

*So maybe I've thrown up a few walls to protect myself. That's normal.*

"Some horses are mine. Some are the ranch's." Travis patted Arizona's spotted neck. "Some I borrow."

His voice was so even. He couldn't care less about her nasty little dig. Did nothing irritate him? Or did he just not show it?

Judging by Travis Chalmers, it seemed the great actors in the movie industry, legends like Clint Eastwood and John Wayne, had acted their cowboy roles with more accuracy than Sophia had realized. They delivered their dialogue in an almost monotone way—never too excited, never shouting. Like Travis. Nothing like Deezee.

It was hard to imagine Travis jumping from a church pew to a communion railing and yelling *Yo, where's the ho?*

Deezee had meant her. Sophia had been standing in the vestibule of the Caribbean chapel, trying not to sweat through her white dress, waiting for the church music to start so she could walk down the center aisle to promise her life to him. He'd meant it as a joke, just another outrageous zinger for his posse's amusement. He hadn't bothered to change into a clean T-shirt. It was just a spontaneous elopement. No need to go to any trouble.

*No crying in front of the cowboy.*

"What's my horse's name?" she demanded. "And where is he?"

"Samson. He's still at camp. And he's my horse, not yours."

"Why did you ride that other horse today, then, if Samson belongs to you?"

"Because that other horse is mine, too. I own four right now, but you could say I babysit the rest."

Thank goodness the man's only facial expressions were somber and barely-a-grin. She'd insinuated that he owned nothing. If he laughed at her for how far she'd missed the mark, she might go all crazy diva on him. She couldn't stand to be laughed at.

"Four? For one man?" But her sarcasm was stupid, and she knew it.

"You can't ride just one horse all day, every day during roundup. That's why Arizona comes to work with me during roundup, see? So I have more horses to rotate. But Samson, he's a real special cow horse. I save him for when I'm actually cutting cattle out of the herd. It's a waste of talent to use him just to ride in from camp."

"You sound like a coach with a sports team."

"I hadn't thought of it that way. It's like setting up your batting order in baseball, now that you mention it. Samson's my star player. Don't tell Arizona that, though. He's been doing a great job pinch-hitting all week." Travis winked at Sophia, and he smiled. Not a grin, but a real smile that reached all the way to his eyes, a smile like she was in on the joke and part of his team.

Good Lord. The man was beautiful. She'd thought he looked hot the moment she'd spotted him riding toward her that first day on the road. Kind of stern and remote, but so masculine on horseback that he'd cut through her haze of misery. Today, shirtless and dripping wet, he'd looked like an athlete, a man in his prime, serious and strong. But when he smiled—oh, why would the women of Texas keep a man like this out here in the middle of nowhere?

For once in her life, she was the one doing the staring.

"B-baseball?" she repeated. Then, because she'd stuttered, she sneered a little, just to let him know she didn't care. "What would a cowboy know about baseball? There aren't enough humans around here to get a game going."

She caught the slightest shake of his head as he crossed his arms over his chest—a move that did lovely things to stretch that T-shirt tight around his biceps. His smile lingered. He found her amusing. Damn him.

"True enough. This cowboy played shortstop in college. Was there anything else you wanted to talk about besides horse names and baseball?"

She wondered how much of her thoughts he could guess. Could he see how much she wished she hadn't ruined her chances with a guy like him by making a huge mistake with a guy like Deezee?

*You're an actor, Sophia. Don't let him see anything.*

It was easier just to alienate people so they'd leave her alone. Her bridges were already burned. To hell with it.

"College? For a cowboy? What do they teach you, not to step in horse manure?"

Finally, *finally*, she'd pricked through his infuriatingly calm exterior. His eyes narrowed as she held his gaze defiantly.

*That's right, I am a rattlesnake. You don't want to mess with me.* She didn't want any man to mess with her, ever again.

His voice remained even. "My degree is in animal sciences from Texas A&M. They expect students to be smart enough to avoid horse manure before they enroll." He looked at her flip-flops, pointedly, and she fought the urge to curl her toes out of sight. "But I guess some people never do figure out what boots are for."

"Are you going to kick me out of your barn again?"

*Please. Put me out of my misery. I'm screwing everything up here. Send me back to that awful, empty house and let me fall apart.*

"I'm not your babysitter. You do what you want. If you don't have the common sense to stay out of trouble, well, some folks have to learn the hard way."

"I think I can avoid cow patties, thank you very much. I have eyes."

Travis pushed away from the post. "Then you might want to get going. It's getting dark real quick. It'll be harder to see those cow patties, and critters that like to bite toes will start coming out, too. Those flip-flops aren't going to protect you from a snake or a rat."

A rat. She glanced around the aisle. This place was too neat and organized for rats.

"We keep a barn cat," Travis said, reading the skepticism she hadn't bothered to hide. "She's a good mouser, but she does earn her keep."

He wasn't going to kick her out. She was going to have to force herself back to the lonely house. She acted like it didn't freak her out. "I'm leaving, anyway."

"I'll walk you to the door."

She jerked her arm out of his reach and stepped sideways, the side of her foot hitting a square hay bale. It felt like hitting a porcupine, except for her toes. Her toes made contact with something furry.

"A rat!" She nearly knocked Travis over, jumping away from the hay bale.

He caught her with a hand on her arm, but he was already frowning at the floor, bending down and reaching—

"Don't touch it." She tried to yank him away from the rat. He stood up with something brown in his hand and she let go of his arm. "Ew."

"It's not 'ew.' It's a kitten."

It wasn't moving. For the first time since Travis had woken Sophia from her nap, she felt the nausea rising. "Did I—do you think I... I didn't hurt it, did I?"

She felt him looking at her, but she had eyes only for the kitten, the tiniest one she'd ever seen. Travis pressed its baby paws with his thumb, wiggling each limb as he did. "Nothing seems to be broken or bent. You didn't hurt it."

Thank goodness. She sank weakly onto the hay bale, then leaped up as the hay poked her rear right through her designer romper from Milan.

Travis didn't seem to notice. His attention was on the kitten. He pulled at the collar of his T-shirt and tucked the brown fluff in, keeping it in place with one hand.

"Shouldn't we put it back so the mother cat will be able to find it?"

"He's cold. The mother cat must have abandoned him a while ago. If I can get him warmed up, we might be able to slip him back in with his brothers, but this is the second time the mother has moved him out of her nest."

"Why would she do that?"

Travis shrugged, the kitten completely hidden by his hand. "She might sense that there's something wrong with it."

"But you said it's not hurt."

"As far as I can see. The mother might know something I don't. Or the mother might have decided two kittens are all she can handle, so the third one gets abandoned."

"She leaves it out to die? That's awful. Can't you do something about that?" Anxiety tinged her voice, but she didn't care. Her anxiety to *not* see a kitten die felt pretty intense.

"I am doing something about that," he said drily. "I've got a kitten stuck down my shirt."

"You're going to keep it?" That sounded good. Really good.

He sat on the hay bale, the heavy denim of his jeans so much more practical than her white silk. "This kitten is really young. His eyes aren't open yet. His best bet for survival is with his mother."

Her anxiety spiked right back up. "But he has a terrible mother. She left him, just left the pitiful thing all alone. He's better off without her."

"No, he isn't." Travis spoke firmly, but he was looking at her with...concern. It took her a moment to recognize concern on a man's face. For the past ten years, the only person who'd ever looked at her with concern had been Grace. Her sister was the only one who'd ever cared.

Nausea tried to get her attention, but Sophia pushed it away. She didn't want to acknowledge it or what it might mean.

"You've never had a cat before, have you?" Travis asked.

"Ages ago, but she was neutered. You should neuter your cats. You have to neuter this one's mother right away. She's a bad mother. She doesn't deserve to have any more babies." Sophia pressed the back of her hand against her mouth abruptly to conquer the nausea.

But it was too late. The thing she didn't want to think about was now at the forefront of her mind: the little plus sign on that stick. Motherhood. Babies.

The word *pregnant* might not seem real to her, but Grace and Alex had been so deadly serious about it. They'd sat her down at Alex's kitchen table to talk through the options.

Sophia had immediately pounced on giving the baby up for adoption. It sounded simple. There'd be this baby that she would never even have to see, really, and the adoption agency would find the perfect couple. The couple would be happy. The baby would be happy. No harm all around.

That pregnancy test had probably been wrong, anyway, but adoption was a simple solution for a simple equation: one unwanted baby plus one couple who wanted a baby equaled success. Sophia would be doing a good deed. End of family meeting.

"Sophia." There was a definite note of concern in Travis's voice now, to match the way he was looking at her. "She might not be a bad mother. Sometimes Mother Nature knows more than we do. But for what it's worth, I agree with you about having cats neutered. This kitten's mother found us a couple of weeks ago. She moved herself in and was already pregnant. Accidents happen."

*Oh god, oh god, oh god…*

Tonight, faced with a few ounces of fluff she'd almost stepped on, Sophia suddenly realized what she'd left out of the equation: herself. Doing a good deed? She was the failure in the equation, not the hero. She was giving the baby away because she knew, deep down, she would be a terrible mother. She'd tried so hard with Grace, but she'd failed. Grace didn't even want to live with her anymore.

Travis had said the cat might have decided she couldn't handle that baby. Sophia knew she couldn't handle a baby, either. So what did that make Sophia? A terrible, horrible, selfish cat.

Travis tucked his chin into his collar and spread his fingers out, trying to see the kitten. "He's moving around. That's a good sign."

Sophia backed away from him, scared of the little bit of brown fluff and all that it represented.

"I'm going to go now." Her voice sounded thin, too high. "Good luck with the kitten."

She turned tail and ran. And ran. As fast as she could in the stupid flip-flops, she ran so that she was out of breath when she got back to the house.

It helped. It was only a sprint, maybe the length of a football field, nothing like the miles she'd had to put in to prepare for battling monsters in *Space Maze*, but she felt a little more normal. She felt her lungs and ribs expanding, contracting, taking in extra air. Muscles she hadn't used in weeks were suddenly awake, alive. She smoothed her hand over her stomach. The nausea was gone, and she felt hungry.

What she didn't feel was pregnant. Not one bit.

The pregnancy test's instructions had cautioned over and over that the results were not always accurate. Really, all that had happened was that Sophia had skipped a period, which was an easy thing to do. She probably wasn't even pregnant.

She was here to hide from the paparazzi, that was all. Her sister and Alex had both told Travis that. Sophia would lie low here for a few more weeks and let the media turn its attention elsewhere. Once they began a feeding frenzy on some other celebrity couple, Sophia would fly back to LA and start hunting for a new agent.

*And you should make an appointment to get your tubes tied, because now you know you wouldn't be happy if you really were pregnant, and you'd be a lousy mother who couldn't take care of a baby, anyway.*

She glanced out the kitchen window toward the barn, where some knocked-up stray cat was apparently her spirit animal. If the kitten-killing cat had been sent to show Sophia how much she was lacking, she'd done her job tonight. It was a good thing Sophia was planning on letting someone adopt the baby, because she wouldn't be a good mother. It was a crushing revelation.

The only light on in the whole house was the little one over the stove. That was plenty. The boxes of nonperishable food were still lined up on the kitchen counter, and Sophia had spent the week working her way through them, left to right. She didn't need a lot of light to pour herself another bowl of organic raisins and bran flakes.

She sat at the table and poked at the dry cereal with her spoon for a while. The organic milk substitute had gotten warm that first day, so she'd dumped it down the drain. Without a housekeeper, a personal shopper, or a sister, it hadn't been replenished yet.

Sophia didn't care. She just wanted to sleep, even after the nap she hadn't meant to take outside today. That had been a stupid slip up. It would have blown her cover if anyone except Travis had come by.

She couldn't get her act together enough to do a simple thing like hide. She'd dared to go outside because the house felt too empty. The sun had felt good on her skin after four days indoors, so she'd stretched out and fallen asleep.

No surprise there. She'd been tired for years. She'd been looking for a break when she'd taken Grace for that vacation in Telluride, but five months of Deezee hadn't been very refreshing. She was more tired than ever now.

Except when she talked to Travis. She'd felt alive and awake when Travis had walked into that barn with no shirt on. Nothing like a half-naked, incredibly buff man to snap a girl out of a fog.

The expression in his eyes had taken her breath away.

Boy meets girl. Boy wants girl. Or rather, man wants woman. Woman had wanted him right back, with an intensity that she couldn't handle.

No surprise there, either. She couldn't handle anything in her life. But she'd felt like she was really alive for the first time in ages, so she'd been determined to see how far he would go.

Not very far. One touch with her finger, and he'd literally stepped back from her and put on a shirt. So much for her bankable box office sex appeal. She'd lost her career, her sister—and her ability to attract a man. She sucked. Her life sucked.

On that note, she left her bowl on the table, stumbled into the living room, and did a face plant on the sofa. She never wanted to wake up again.

# Chapter Seven

"Sophia, wake up."

She jerked awake, heart pounding.

"It's just me. Travis. Are you okay?"

She sat up on the couch and dropped her face in her hands, willing her heart to slow down. She hated to be startled awake, because her first instinct was to flail about in case Deezee and his crew were in the middle of pulling some prank, like drawing on her face with a Sharpie just before she was expected to make an appearance. *It's funny, baby, whatchu getting upset for?*

She'd had to cancel that appearance, disappointing fans and angering her manager.

"I'm not okay. You just scared me to death, shaking my arm like that."

"Sorry. Nothing else was waking you up."

She was waking up now, fully aware of where she

was and who was standing over her. "What are you doing here?"

"Checking on you."

"What are you doing in my house? Did you just open the door and walk in?"

"Yes."

"What are you, some kind of stalker?"

"No."

His implacable, even tone set her teeth on edge. "But you just walked into someone else's house. You don't see anything wrong with that, do you?"

"I knocked first." His cell phone was in his hand, but he slipped it into his back pocket.

She stood up, furious. "I deserve privacy. I rented this house. I get that you're all Mr. I-Run-This-Place, but the house is mine for the duration. You can't just walk in any time you please. Have you been spying on me while I was sleeping? Standing over my bed without me knowing it every night?"

"Of course not. Quit spooking yourself."

"Spooking myself? What does that mean? That's not even a thing."

"You're letting your imagination run away with you. I walked in just now because we don't tend to stand on ceremony out here in the country. We can't. If someone's in trouble, you have to help. You can call nine-one-one, but it can take a long time for help to arrive. We take care of each other."

The man sounded like he actually believed what he was saying. He was oblivious to the invasion of her privacy. Living in the country couldn't be that different than living in the city.

"You had no reason to think I was in trouble."

"I thought I'd come and tell you some good news, but it looked like nobody was home."

"So?"

"If you hadn't come back to the house, then where were you? You ran out of the barn like a bat out of hell, so I figured you'd made it back to your place in a couple of minutes, but it didn't look like you were here. You'd run somewhere else. It's full dark out there. You aren't wearing much, and a person can start to lose body heat pretty quick once the sun goes down. You only had on flip-flops. If you'd gotten hurt—"

"I was right here on my own couch, minding my own business."

"Good. Now I don't have to saddle up Arizona and go out to look for you."

*You would have done that for me?* But the calm way he was looking at her, the steadiness of his voice told the truth. Just the fact that it had even occurred to him to go looking for someone who might be missing was…

It made her feel kind of protected. A nice feeling.

Crap. It was hard to stay mad at a man who'd honestly been worried about her. Not just worried, either. He actually would have done something about it.

She crossed her arms over her chest, but she couldn't force any real sting into her voice. "Well, we need to have an understanding that you won't sneak into my house again. Where I'm from, that's called breaking and entering. It creeps me out. Even the paparazzi don't dare to walk in my door. Don't do it, okay?"

He took his time thinking about his answer. "All right."

"I mean it." She didn't need any man mounting horseback search parties for her sake. She didn't.

"This wasn't sneaking in," he said. "You have my word I never will. But if I think you're in trouble, I'm going to do whatever it takes to help you, whether you like it or not."

Sophia blinked. *Why, you bossy son of a—* But then she realized she was looking at his back because he'd left the living room to go into the kitchen. She hurried after him.

He had already turned on the lights in the kitchen. He picked up her dry bowl of cereal. "Is this all you ate today?"

She stopped cold. There was only one reason a man would ask about that. Only one reason. "The paparazzi got to you already, didn't they?"

His gaze narrowed again.

*I'm not the rattlesnake, dude. You are.*

"I want to see your cell phone." She was seething. "How long have you been in here, photographing Sophia Jackson's hideout? Documenting Sophia Jackson's Hollywood diet secrets? Did you take pictures of me sleeping? Did you?"

"You're spooking yourself again."

"How much did they pay you? The kid at the deli by my condo got two thousand dollars for writing down my sandwich orders for a week. He took a photo of my sister picking up a bag with subs in it. When I didn't order a sandwich the next day, he lied and took a photo of someone else's sandwich. He got the cash. You know what I got?"

Travis set the bowl down with a soft curse.

He didn't want to hear her story? Too bad. He needed to know exactly what he was doing by giving the paparazzi supposedly harmless details of her life.

"I got reamed by America for setting a bad example for the youth of today. The youth of today! Because one of those youths took a picture of some insanely greasy concoction and claimed it was mine. Then everyone said the only way I could eat like that and keep my figure would be if I abused laxatives or stuck my fingers down my throat after every meal. The fact that they photographed me going in and out of a gym every single frigging day was irrelevant when it came to how I might be keeping my figure, but that's beside the point. I was suddenly personally responsible for every poor teenager with an eating disorder. I know how this game works, Travis. You'll get cash, and I'll get punished."

She nearly choked on his name. Travis—the betrayal shouldn't have hurt this badly. She didn't really know him any better than the deli counter kid.

"I'm not talking to any damned paparazzi. I don't think I've ever said that word out loud in my life. Paparazzi."

"I'm not stupid," she said, feeling very stupid for having let down her guard for an instant. "Since when does a big, tough cowboy suddenly take an interest in what kind of cereal a woman eats?"

"Since the big, tough cowboy got scared. Bad." He started walking toward her, two steps that covered most of the big kitchen. "I didn't just knock. I called the phone, too. You didn't move when I turned on the lights. I had my phone in my hand because I was going to call nine-one-one if I couldn't wake you. My grandpa had diabetes. I've seen what happens when a person's blood sugar gets too low. You scared me. That's all."

He took another step closer. She didn't back up, but she crossed her arms defensively. He was a lot of man, looming over her. A lot of man with a lot of honesty in his voice, and concern in his expression, and really beautiful brown eyes.

He ran his rough-warm palm over her arm, from her shoulder to her elbow, and kept his hand there, firm. "I'm very sorry I scared you in return."

Sophia felt her world turning. Pieces of her mind tumbled and landed in a new order. A better order. If she lived her life a different way…if she didn't always assume the worst…if she could believe someone wanted to help her instead of use her…

She could have a friend.

It was what she'd hoped for with Deezee. Things with him had started out with this kind of instant attraction, this desire to trust a man she barely knew.

Hope hurt.

Sophia took a step back.

Travis bowed his head, a quick nod to himself. When he looked up, he was the remote, stern foreman once more. "Do you always sleep so hard?"

He meant, *Is there something I should know about, because I'm responsible for all the horses and pregnant cows and cats around here?* She could hear it in his voice.

The truth would guarantee that he'd think of her as some kind of crazy diva: *No, I'm just sad. When I'm really sad, I deal with it by checking out of the world and going into hibernation.*

She couldn't tell him that.

"I'm just making up for a lack of sleep. A few years' worth of sleep."

"And do you always eat such a spartan diet? You never went to the grocery store, did you?"

"Don't start with that." This was why she didn't have friends. No one walked a mile in her shoes. No one understood.

She imitated his unruffled, even tone. "'If you need groceries, then go to the grocery store.' Everything is so easy for you, isn't it? You get to come and go as you please on any horse that strikes your fancy. You know what to do if you find a half-dead kitten, so you don't freak out. Of course you can decide whether or not you'll head to the store for more groceries."

She was afraid she might cry, but only because she wanted him to understand.

"Do you know why I have to wait for my sister to bring me groceries? It's not because I'm a diva. It's because I'll get hurt if I go out by myself. It's happened before." She held out the arm he'd stroked. "See these little half moons? That's how much my fans love me. If I walk down a street, I'll let them take their selfies and then I'll try to say goodbye, and they'll dig their fingernails into me. 'No, wait. You have to wait until my friend shows up.'

"I have to smile. I can't pitch a fit or else I'm a bitch or a diva or a monster. I've been held hostage, forced to wait on a sidewalk for a stranger's friend while people start penning me in from every direction. The police will stop to see what the crowd is about and they'll smile and wave at me. So I just sign autographs until it's the policeman's turn, and then I have to smile while I ask them to keep people from hurting me. 'Gee, Officer, could you possibly escort me back to my hotel?'"

Oh, hell, her eyes were tearing up, but she didn't care. Deezee had gotten off on these stories. He'd wanted them to happen to him. But Travis was frowning, and she didn't know if it was because he believed her or if it was because he thought she was *spooking* herself again.

But she had more proof, a secret that only a few hairstylists knew about. She turned her back to him and started pawing through her hair, piling her hair up until her fingertips found it, that dime-sized bit of her scalp where no hair grew. "This is how much they love me. Right after *Space Maze* came out, I was spotted at a grocery store. Honest to God, I had no idea how much people loved that movie. They pulled the hair out of my head as a souvenir. That's love. Right there."

She jabbed at the spot, such a small scar left after so much blood and pain, but Travis's hand stopped hers. He smoothed his thumb over the scar. She closed her eyes, remembering his thumb on the sole of her foot, smoothing an adhesive bandage into place, making everything better.

"I'm sorry," he said.

She dropped her hands, and her hair fell back into place with a shake of her head, just like Jean Paul had designed it to do. It was such a great perk of fame, those great haircuts and free shampoo. What a lucky girl she was.

"I'm sorry," Travis repeated, gruff words that whispered over her hair.

She felt all the fight go out of her. She couldn't remember what was supposed to take its place. Before Deezee, before the breakthrough roles, before her parents' deaths…what had life been like when she hadn't fought for everything?

She opened the door so Travis could leave, facing him with what she hoped was a neutral expression and not a desolate one. "You don't have to worry if you don't see me around. I think any normal person in my position would stay out of sight. It's just that my future brother-in-law told me that the MacDowells said I could trust the foreman, so I... I showed myself to you. Everyone else will just have to think there's a vampire living in the house or something."

Travis nodded and picked his hat up from the table. He must have tossed it there instead of using the hook by the door. It was the sort of thing someone might do in a rush.

He walked out the door. Sophia realized he already had his boots on. He'd come in without stopping at the boot jack, breaking his own rule about boots in the house. He'd really been worried about her.

A little rush of gratitude filled some of the empty space inside her.

"Travis?"

He turned back to her, his expression serious, il-luminated by the light from the kitchen. Beyond him, the night was black, the night he would have ridden in, looking for her.

"I'm not a crazy recluse. I'm just a recluse, okay?"

"I get it."

She'd been holding her breath. Now she could breathe.

He tapped his hat against his thigh. "I never told you the reason I came looking for you in the first place. That kitten got more lively when he warmed up, so I found the mother cat's new hiding spot. She didn't object when I slipped him in with his brothers."

"Oh." She took a deeper breath. The night air felt fresh. "Oh, that's great news. She's not a terrible mother after all."

"I never said she was. She had her reasons. We just don't know what they were. I put out some extra food, in case she was worried about having enough to eat. The other barn cat will probably get to it first, but it's worth a try. When I left, she was pretty relaxed and letting all three kittens nurse."

Maybe Sophia was crazy after all, because it felt like Travis had just given her the best gift. "Thank you. Thank you so much."

"I wouldn't want you to get too hopeful. That kitten's had a rough time of it so far."

"But now he'll be okay."

"We've given him a chance, at least. I'll see you when I get back in a few days. Good night." He touched the brim of his hat, and walked into the dark.

A few days?

She shut herself in the house.

# *Chapter Eight*

She didn't wake up until noon.

What was the point? Everyone was gone again. Everyone meaning Travis and the horses.

Sophia was willing to bet that Travis had been saddling up those horses before dawn, true to the cowboy stereotype. She looked out the window toward the empty barn and tried not to feel resentful that the horses had been taken away. They had to work.

She wished she had to work. Resentment for her ex bubbled up, a toxic brew that made her stomach turn.

*Thanks, Deezee.*

Actually, Deezee was probably working, too. The more he partied, the more people wanted to pay him to appear at their parties. The more outrageous he got, the more bookings he got. Busting into that Texas Rescue ball and making a scene had been a smart thing for him to do. During their week in Saint Barth, his cell phone had blown up with offers.

Not hers.

A movie studio didn't make job offers to actors who skipped town without notice. A production couldn't build a PR campaign if their star said outrageous, unpredictable things. What helped Deezee's career killed hers.

Looking back, she doubted Deezee had realized how much he was hurting her. She doubted he would have cared if he had.

But she should have known better. She should have cared.

Deezee had lied to her. He'd cheated on her with other women. But he hadn't forced her to party like a rock star. That was her fault.

*Thanks, Sophia.*

She couldn't spend all day at the kitchen window, waiting to see which cowboy would come in at sundown. It wouldn't be Travis; that was all that mattered. She couldn't be seen by anyone else. She couldn't make another stupid mistake like she had yesterday, falling asleep on the picnic table. Alex and Grace wouldn't be able to pull another great hiding spot out of thin air. This was it. This was her only place to sleep, eat, hide and sleep some more.

But today, she didn't have the desire to go right back to sleep. She felt at least a little bit rested for a change. She'd slept in a real bed instead of crashing on the couch with the television on.

All week, she'd been avoiding the master bedroom. It was too spacious and too obviously someone else's room, with its family photos of little boys and a handsome father from decades past. She knew Mrs. Mac-

Dowell was a widow. She didn't like to look at photos of the dead father. She had her own.

But last night, after Travis had left, she'd wandered into one of the smaller bedrooms, one that looked like it was intended for guests. It had a queen-sized bed instead of a king. It had paintings of Texas bluebonnets on the walls instead of family photos. She'd been able to sleep there.

Great. So now she wasn't sleepy, but she still couldn't leave the house. Her one little foray to the picnic table yesterday had almost resulted in blowing her cover, because she'd lacked enough common sense to come back inside when sitting in the sun made her drowsy. She had no common sense. No self-discipline. She was in a prison of her own making, because she couldn't handle her own life.

Round and round her thoughts started to go. She hated them, because they always led to the same conclusion: she was a failure. She hated herself, and she was stuck.

But a new voice broke through the old soundtrack.

*If you want to go outside, then open the door and walk outside.*

Travis.

If he saw her standing here, if he could hear what she was saying to herself in her head, he would cut through all the nonsense with one of those infuriatingly simple solutions.

*You're a grown woman*, he'd say. A grown woman who was standing here, wishing she could go outside for a breath of fresh air but afraid that would be some catastrophic mistake. She'd fall asleep on a picnic table again, and let down Alex and Grace, and be laughed at in the press for being found on a cattle ranch, of all places. If she went outside, it would start a chain of disasters. It made sense to her.

Or it had, before last night. Before she'd spent some time with Travis and realized that all the puzzle pieces didn't have to go together in the complicated order she'd been putting them.

*If you don't want to be in here, then open the door and go out there.*

She opened the kitchen door, and stepped on a pile of zucchini.

She cursed as the zucchini scattered. She spewed every variation of the F-bomb that Deezee had ever shouted while playing a combat video game. She'd hated the way he'd lost control when he killed animated, imaginary enemies, yet she sounded just like him.

She shut up. It was zucchini, not the end of the world. Heck, her own *Space* character had managed to save an entire civilization without resorting to so much drama.

The zucchini rolled to a stop. A note was wedged into what remained of the pyramid by the door.

Sophia—

When I got to my house, I saw that Clay had left a bunch of zucchini in my sink. His mother had a bumper crop, and she stopped by the bunkhouse when no one was there and left a ton in their kitchen. I don't think it's breaking and entering if someone's mother does it. The real crime here is that nobody can eat as much zucchini as Clay's mother grew. I'm passing off some of it onto you. It might make a nice change from cereal.

—Travis

P.S. I left you some milk in case you don't actually

like your cereal dry. It's in the barn fridge. Please wear boots or shoes. You have enough scars. I don't want you to get any more.

Sophia stared at the letter. The man had been doing just fine, dropping little smart-aleck comments, but then he'd had to finish it up with that line about the scars. She must be crazy after all, because she felt all choked up by a hastily written P.S.

Sophia picked up the zucchini one by one, cradling them in her arm like a bouquet, and carried them into the kitchen. She put the zucchini in the sink. The letter she spread out on the counter. She read it again and smoothed out the crease. Read it again.

Then she went into the master bedroom, where Alex had left her suitcases. She hadn't unpacked them yet. Just reaching in and wearing the first thing she touched had taken all the energy she had, but now she lifted out the neat piles of clothes and carried them down the hall to the bluebonnet bedroom.

Trip after trip, she emptied the suitcases her sister had filled for her. As Sophia's personal assistant, Grace had been packing her bags ever since they'd moved to LA. Maybe Sophia hadn't wanted to unpack these final suitcases. Alex was going to be the person Grace took trips with from now on. These were the last shirts her sister would ever fold for her with care and love.

"This is depressing as hell." Sophia spoke the words loudly, but her voice didn't have to reach lofty rafters in here. The carpet and quilts of the guest bedroom absorbed the sound. The words weren't as scary out loud as they were when they echoed in her head.

Whether or not it was depressing, whether or not it

was some kind of symbolic final vestige of her life with her sister, the suitcases had to be unpacked now, because Sophia needed her shoes. The only boots she had were the thigh-highs with the killer heels, but she knew that Grace would have packed workout clothes and a selection of running shoes for Sophia to choose from, depending on her mood and her clothes' color scheme.

She found the sneakers. Sophia left the empty suitcase on the king-sized master bed. In her bedroom, she changed into a shirt that had sleeves and a pair of shorts that barely covered her rear but were made of denim. She laced up her most sturdy pair of cross-trainers and once more opened the kitchen door.

She wasn't going to fall asleep or get caught by a stranger or ruin her career. She was going to get some milk that Travis had left for her in the barn.

Nothing bad was going to happen.

The fresh air cleared the last bit of fog from Sophia's head as she walked the hundred yards or so to the barn.

The heat of the day was building. Her yoga instructor would say every molecule of hot air shimmered with energy that she could welcome into her lungs with intentional breaths. Sophia could practice here, doing yoga outside on the flagstone, holding poses that took all her concentration in the May heat. If she set an alarm clock tomorrow, she could get up a little earlier and go for a run before it got too hot.

If she really wanted more work in Hollywood, that would be the smart thing to do. Having a great body was an essential part of winning roles. If she let herself go too long without exercise, she'd pay a price. She really didn't want to keep paying for stupid decisions. *If you want to keep your fitness level, then work out.*

She'd have to be careful who saw her. But if only she and Travis were around, and he should happen to catch her in the middle of a workout in her painted-on exercise clothing…her muscles working, her skin glistening…

The possibilities sent a sizzle of sexual energy through her.

She slid open the barn door, using chest muscles that still felt strong despite weeks of laziness. Every LA personal trainer emphasized pectoral tone to keep the breasts high. Having good breasts was part of her job.

She'd only had to reveal them once in her career, during a love scene in a serious crime drama. Her male costar's bare buttocks had been in the frame as well. As makeup artists had dabbed foundation on his butt cheeks and brushed shadow into her cleavage, the two of them had attempted awkward jokes until the director had called for quiet on the set. For hours, her costar kept popping some kind of bubblegum-flavored mints that smelled grossly sweeter with each take. There had been nothing sexy about filming that scene, but the director had known what he was doing, and the final cut had looked scorching hot on the big screen.

The movie had only gotten modest box office distribution, but Travis might have seen it. Had he found it arousing? He must have. One couldn't be human and not find the finished scene arousing.

She shut the door behind herself. The interior of the barn was dim after the blinding sun. She took a moment to let her eyes adjust, leaning against the same post Travis had leaned against last night. He'd given her his time and attention, willing to talk. Only to talk.

Not willing to be seduced. Not even by a movie star.

That sizzle died. When she'd reached out to touch him, he'd pulled on a shirt and left her standing in his office. Unemployed or not, she still looked like a movie star. What had she done that had made it so easy for him to resist her?

She walked slowly down the aisle, evaluating her posture and carriage, working on it as an actor. If she saw herself on film now, what kind of character traits would she be relaying to the audience?

She hadn't been very convincing in the role of seductress last night. She didn't believe she was still a movie star, so she wasn't acting like a movie star. That had to be the problem. Deezee's infidelity had shaken her confidence. The publicity had been humiliating, so now Sophia must be giving off some kind of insecure ex-girlfriend vibe.

Guys hated that. If she could turn back time to the person she'd been before Deezee, she would have Travis eating out of the palm of her hand. He'd be grateful if she chased a water droplet over his skin with the tip of her finger, because the sexy and smart Sophia Jackson would be the one doing the chasing, not the depressed and lonely creature she'd turned into. Travis couldn't resist a movie star.

Could he?

He already had. When they'd met on the road, she'd seen the precise moment on his face when he'd first realized who she was, but he hadn't exactly fallen all over himself to get her autograph. He'd told her to get behind the wheel and drive herself off his ranch, actually.

*Don't call us; we'll call you.*

She paused at his office window. There was nothing in that functional space that implied he was enchanted by Hollywood or its stars. For the first time in her life, it occurred to her that being a celebrity could be a dis-advantage.

She'd just have to make him want her, anyway.

Men had wanted her long before she was famous. Really, that was why she'd become famous. People of both sexes had always noticed her. *Charisma*, Grace called it. An aura. Whatever it was, it was the reason Sophia had been put in films. The public might think movie stars were noticeable because they were already famous, but that wasn't how it worked. The charisma came first. They were noticed first. Stardom came second.

Where did Travis fit in?

The refrigerator was in the medical room. She headed for it while fretting over sex appeal and stardom, wondering if she could stand rejection from a cowboy any better than from a producer, and nearly stepped on the proof that everything she worried about, all of it, was insignificant.

At her feet, curled into a little ball in front of the fridge, was the kitten.

Sophia picked him up gingerly. It was humbling to hold a complete living being in her hand. He was still alive for now, but he couldn't survive on his own. The weight of his impending mortality should have been heavy. It seemed wrong that he was little more than a fluffy feather in her palm.

Travis had said the kitten was weak to start with, and Sophia knew next to nothing about kittens. She was going to lose this battle. It was a pattern she knew too well. Losing her sister, losing her lover, losing her career, failing auditions, failing to keep her scholarship…

Failing. She hated to fail.

She studied the newborn's face. "I'm not a very good mother, either, but I'm going to try, okay?"

Then she slipped the kitten inside her shirt.

## Chapter Nine

Travis was not obsessed with Sophia Jackson.

He just couldn't stop thinking about her.

He'd left the milk in the fridge this morning with no intention of returning for the rest of the week, but as the morning had turned into afternoon, he'd already started convincing himself that he should head back to his office this evening. There were too many things on his to-do list that he hadn't touched last night.

He'd touched Sophia's scars instead.

Why had she let him into her personal life like that? *I'm not a crazy recluse.*

She wanted to be understood, that much was clear to him. He just didn't know how much to read into the fact that she wanted *him* to understand her.

A pickup truck pulled up to the fencing they'd built for this year's roundup. Travis recognized the pickup as belonging to one of the MacDowell brothers who was coming to work these last few days of branding and doctoring. Travis was grateful for the distraction. He left the calf pen to greet Braden.

Braden MacDowell, like his brothers, was a physician in Austin. He'd taken over the reins at the hospital his father had founded, but he valued his family's ranching legacy as well, so it wasn't unusual to see him here. At least one MacDowell was sure to lend a hand during the busy months, if not all three brothers.

Travis respected the MacDowells. They visited their mama. They knew how to rope and ride. And they'd been wise enough to hire him.

Not to get too full of himself, but it said a lot that they'd asked him to keep the River Mack thriving as a cow-calf operation. They could've just rented the land out to a corporate operation that maintained its headquarters in another state. Travis wouldn't have stayed on the River Mack in that case. He preferred to work with a family that knew how to keep their saddles oiled and their guns greased, as the saying went.

"I just got away from the office," Braden said as Travis walked up to him and shook hands. "I trust there's still plenty of fun to be had?"

"Talk to me tomorrow about how fun it feels. You leave your necktie and briefcase at home?"

The ribbing was good-natured. Braden was in shape, but there was still a big difference between bench-pressing weights in a gym and hauling around a hundred-pound calf who didn't appreciate being picked up.

"I've got aspirin in the glove box." Braden dropped the tailgate and thumped an oversized cooler. "I brought supplies."

Travis helped him carry the cooler full of sports drinks closer to the working crew and then helped himself to one. He drank while Patch, one of the best cow dogs in Texas, greeted Braden.

They kept sports drinks in the barn fridge, too. When Sophia got the milk, she'd see them. Travis hoped she knew she was welcome to take whatever she needed. He should have told her that in the note, maybe, and damn it all to hell, he was thinking about her again. Would he go five minutes without thinking of her today?

"All right, back to work with you," Braden said to the dog, but to Travis's surprise, Braden didn't head for the work area himself. "How's Sophia Jackson treating my house?"

Travis forced himself to swallow his drink around the surprise of hearing her name spoken. She was a big secret he'd been keeping from everyone, but it made sense that Braden knew. Of course he knew; he must have signed the lease.

"The house looks the same as always. You can't tell there's anyone's living there."

"No sounds of breaking glass coming from inside? She hasn't set the couch on fire or gone rockstar and destroyed it yet?"

Travis frowned at the expectation that she might. The closest thing he'd seen to any wild behavior had been when Sophia had dropped the plastic wedges on the kitchen floor. No harm there. "I'm not one to spy on your houseguests, but there's been nothing like that."

*She cries a lot. She sleeps a lot.* Those insights were his. He didn't care to share them. It felt like it would be betraying Sophia. She didn't want to be stared at. She didn't want to be talked about. Fair enough.

"She's not my houseguest," Braden said, his tone tight. "She's my tenant."

Travis turned to look over the milling herd and the distant horizon, waiting.

Braden studied the horizon, too. "I was against renting the house to her, but one of the ER docs, Alex Gregory, is engaged to her sister. Alex seems to think she's salvageable. He offered to cosign the lease. If she destroys the place, he's good for it, but if my mother comes back from her year in Africa and finds her grandmother's antiques destroyed, money won't make it right."

Travis kept a sharp eye on the calm herd. There was no reason to believe they would suddenly stampede—but they could. "You got a reason for assuming she'd bust furniture?"

"You don't keep up with celebrity news," Braden said.

"I'm surprised you do." That was putting it mildly.

"Only when it affects me. Twice, Texas Rescue invited her to make an appearance to help raise awareness of their work. Twice, she blew their event. My wife and I were going to one of them. I was expecting this elegant actress. My wife was excited to meet her. Instead, this banshee ruined the ball before it even got started. I should have read the gossip earlier. She'd been trashing hotel rooms and blowing off events for months. Now she's living in my home. I don't like it."

It was incredible that MacDowell thought Sophia would destroy someone's family heirlooms, but Travis had known the MacDowells for the past six years. He'd known Sophia six days.

Travis killed the rest of his bottle in long, slow gulps. It took only twenty ounces for him to decide to trust his gut. Sophia didn't mean anyone any harm. He'd seen the physical evidence of the harm others had done to her, and he'd seen her crying her heart out when she thought she was alone. She was a woman who'd been pushed to the edge, but she wasn't going to destroy someone else's lifetime of memories. She just wouldn't.

"She's serious about hiding," Travis repeated. "She's not going to do anything to attract attention to herself. Your stuff is safe."

Braden was silent for a moment. "She's beautiful, isn't she?"

Travis turned his head slowly, very slowly, and met the man's stare. "We weren't discussing Sophia's looks. If you think my judgment is so easily clouded, we'd best come to an understanding on that."

He and Braden gauged one another for a long moment, until, inexplicably, Braden started to grin. "I trust you on horses and I trust you on cattle. I've known you to have a sixth sense about the weather. Maybe you don't find women any harder to read than that, but as a married man, I'm not going to put any money down on that bet. It puts my mind at ease a bit to hear that you don't think Miss Jackson is going to fly off the handle, but I'm still going to stop by and pick up a few breakables before I go."

Travis saw his opportunity and took it. "She won't answer the door if she doesn't know you. I'll go in with you. I've got work at my desk I can knock out while you're gathering up your breakables. If we take the truck, we can be done and back here inside two hours."

"I'm locked out of my own house, technically." Braden sounded disgusted. "Landlords can't just walk into the property once it's been rented out."

Travis paced away from the kitchen door and Braden's legalities. The zucchini was gone. Sophia had gotten up and gone out, then. He wasn't going to jump to any crazy conclusions. She wasn't dead or dying, languishing somewhere, needing his help.

Where was she?

There were no horses in the barn, or else that would have been the logical place to assume she was.

"Let's hit the barn," Braden suggested. "Maybe she'll show up while you're taking care of your paperwork."

Travis had barely slid open the barn door when he heard Sophia calling out.

"Hello? Is someone there? Can you help me?" The distress in her voice was obvious as she emerged from his office. He'd already started for her before her next words. "Travis! It's you. Thank God, it's you."

She started down the aisle toward him at a half run, clutching her heart with two hands.

They met halfway. He stopped her from crashing into him by catching her shoulders in his hands. At a glance, she didn't seem to be hurt. Her expression was panicked, but her color was normal and she seemed to be moving fine. "What's wrong?"

She peeled her hands away from her chest to show him. "It's the kitten. It's dying."

"It's the—" Her words sank in. Travis let go of her shoulders and turned away for a moment to control his reaction, a harsh mixture of relief and anger. He'd thought she was having a heart attack.

"Do you hear that?" she cried.

He turned to look, and yes, she was really crying. She dashed her cheek on her shoulder.

"His cries are just so pitiful. He's been pleading for help like that for six hours. I can't stand it. He cries until he's exhausted, and then he wakes up and cries again. I don't know what to do for him."

Her distress was real. She was just too softhearted for the hard reality that not every animal could be saved. Travis took off his hat and gestured with it toward the office. "Come on, I'll take a look. Did you say six hours?"

"I came in to get the milk from the fridge, and he was on the floor, just lying out there. I warmed him up like you did, but then I couldn't find the mother cat for the longest time. The kitten started crying while I went over every square inch of this place. It took me an hour to find her, but when I put the baby in with the others, the mother just up and left, like, 'Here, have three babies.'"

Travis pulled out his desk chair. "Have a seat."

"I've been in this chair all day. I couldn't look anything up on the internet about what to feed a kitten, because your computer is password protected."

"That it is."

She sat in the chair he offered, but she glared at him like he'd invented the concept of computer passwords just to annoy her. "You've got all these books on animals in here, but do you know what they contain? Info on how many calories are in a frigging *acre* of alfalfa to calculate how many calves it'll feed. Chart after chart on alfalfa and Bahia grass. What to feed a cow, how much to feed a cow, how much to *grow* to feed a cow. Who needs to know crap like that?"

"That would be me." Travis didn't dare smile when she was working through a mixture of tears and indignation. He let her vent.

"Do you know what those books don't contain? *What to feed a newborn kitten.* Not one word. I couldn't call you for help. You're out on a horse all day."

"I'll give you my cell phone number, but there's no reception out on the range. If you leave a message, it'll ping me if I happen to catch a signal."

Braden strolled into the office with a dish in his hand. "Looks like you tried to give it a saucer of milk. On my mother's fine china."

Sophia jerked back in the chair, clutching the kitten to her chest.

Travis had seen that skittish reaction too many times. This time, he put his hand on her shoulder, a little weight to keep her from jumping out of her own skin.

"It's okay. This is Braden MacDowell, one of the ranch owners. He already knew you were here. Your name's already on his lease."

She sniffed and looked at Braden resentfully. "I remember you from that stupid ball. You're the CEO of the hospital."

"Guilty."

"You shouldn't sneak up like that. I thought I was alone with Travis. Usually only one person comes in at sundown."

The implication hit Travis squarely. "What if it hadn't been me tonight? You would've blown your cover. I told you it wouldn't be me tonight. You came out of that office without knowing who was here."

"Trust me, I had hours to think about that while this kitten cried his heart out. I knew whoever came in was going to get a big surprise, and then he was going to get rich. I'd have to pay him hush money to keep my secret. It's like being blackmailed, only you go ahead and get it over with and offer to pay them up front." She rested her head back on the chair and sighed. "It's only money. That's the way it goes."

Travis was stunned.

She frowned at him. "What did you expect me to do? I couldn't just let a kitten die because the paparazzi might find me."

"No, of course not." But of course, she could have done exactly that. She could have left the kitten where a ranch hand might find it and then run away to hide in safety. But she'd stayed to comfort a struggling animal instead of leaving it to cry alone.

"Sorry I startled you," Braden said. "I'm surprised you remember me. We'd barely been introduced at the fund-raiser when you...left."

"I remember everything about that night."

With that cryptic statement, she resumed her tale of frustration, how the kitten hadn't known what to do with the milk, and how she'd tried warming it and holding the kitten's mouth near the surface. Her story was full of mistakes, but it wasn't comical; she'd tried hard to succeed at something foreign to her.

He noticed something else as well. Now that Braden was present, her manner was slightly different. She sat a little straighter and told her story in a more measured way. The contrast was clear to Travis. When she'd thought it was just the two of them, she'd been more emotional. Raw. Real.

Sophia didn't keep her guard up around him. There was a trust between them, an intimacy that she didn't extend to everyone. He wondered if she was aware of it.

"I tried leaving the three kittens together. I snuck away and stayed away for at least half an hour. I wanted to give the mother a chance to come back for them, in case she was just scared of me, you know? But when I came back, they were all crying. All of them. The mother cat didn't come back until I took this kitten away again." Her blue eyes filled with tears, and she quickly turned away from Braden. She spoke softly to Travis. "For a while there, I thought I'd doomed them all."

"You were doing your best. You were being as kind as a person could be." And if he turned his back to Braden to shut him out of their private conversation, well, there was no crime in that.

The kitten began another round of plaintive, hungry mewing.

"The road to hell is paved with good intentions," she murmured. "Listening to this kitten cry has been hell."

"I imagine it has."

She looked up at him, tired and trusting. "I'm so glad you're here."

The words stretched between them, an imaginary line connecting just the two of them for one moment. Then it snapped. Her sleepy-lidded eyes flew open as she realized what she'd said. "To help, I mean. I'm so glad you're here to help."

She was still scared, then. Still unsure of this power between them. It made her nervous enough that she put up her guard, which for a movie star meant shaking back some incredible blond hair and flipping her tired expression to one filled with a devil-may-care bravado. "Besides, you just saved me a fortune in hush money."

Braden chuckled, the expected response, but Travis saw through the act. This wasn't a one-sided attraction on his part, but she wasn't ready to admit it. Now was not the time or place to do anything with the knowledge. He was a patient man. It was enough to know that she wanted to see him as much as he wanted to see her.

She still held the kitten in two hands against her chest, so Travis gave her a boost out of the chair by placing his hand under her elbow. "Come on. Abandoned kittens need a specific kitten milk replacer. Let's see if I have any around here. If I don't, Braden will go to the feed store and get you some."

# Chapter Ten

The pickup rocked over the rolling terrain, sending the headlight beams bouncing off fence posts and mesquite trees. Although Braden drove with all the speed one could manage on rough roads, they were getting back to camp far later than Travis had expected. Travis was returning with a hell of a lot more baggage than he'd expected, too, and all of it was in his head.

Maybe in his heart.

Definitely in his body.

Damn it. Every time he thought checking on Sophia would set everything to rest, he got more than he bargained for.

They'd found some powdered milk replacer in the bunkhouse kitchen. There'd been just a few scoops leftover from some other cowboy's past attempt to help out another cat, so they'd taken it back to the barn. While

Braden had made the run to the feed store, Travis had taught Sophia how to mix the replacer, how to slip an eyedropper into the kitten's mouth, how to hold the kitten a little counterintuitively while feeding it.

There'd been physical contact between the two of them, and a lot of it. Shoulders and hips had brushed as they huddled over the kitten. Hands guided hands to find just the right angle or apply just the right amount of pressure. He'd cuffed up his sleeves, and the sensation of Sophia's soft skin on his exposed wrist or forearm ignited awareness everywhere. By the time the kitten had been settled into a small box with a bit of an old horse blanket, that incidental contact had become so addicting, neither of them had moved away.

Sophia had been nearly as relieved as the kitten when it fell asleep from a full belly instead of from exhaustion. It would have been the most natural move for Travis to drop a kiss on Sophia's lips. Not one of passion, but one of camaraderie, the kind between couples who'd been together through thick and thin.

He'd almost kissed her. *You did well.*

She'd almost kissed him. *Thank you.*

But in the end, Braden had returned with enough milk replacer for ten cats, and Sophia had drifted closer to the light over the barn sink in order to read the instructions on the can. They said a kitten this young was going to wake up and cry for a feeding every two hours.

Travis was used to long nights caring for young or sick animals. Braden was a doctor who thought nothing of overnight shifts, but Sophia...

It turned out that movie production schedules pushed actors to work without sleep as well. Sophia didn't flinch at the schedule.

With his head, his heart, his body, Travis felt himself falling for her too deep, too fast.

Too reckless.

The pickup truck bounced out of the rut in the dirt road, and Travis cracked his head against the side window.

He cursed at an unapologetic Braden. "Your breakables would've been safer in the house. They probably just flew out of the truck bed."

Braden kept his eyes on the road. "I didn't take anything out of the house."

"You're not worried she's going to break everything?" Travis knew the past few hours had shown Braden a different Sophia Jackson than he'd been expecting to see, but Travis wanted to hear him say it. Anyone who maligned Sophia should have to eat his words.

"I've been thinking about that."

Not good enough. Travis managed a noncommittal grunt to keep him talking.

"I did see some pretty incriminating photos, but she was never alone while she was flipping birds and screaming at those photographers."

"Paparazzi," Travis corrected him. But hell, were there photos out there of beautiful Sophia being so ugly?

"That jerk of a boyfriend of hers is behind her in every one, or sometimes in front. Looked like he was shoving her out of his way in one. After seeing the way he crashed that ball, he probably was."

It was the last thing Travis wanted to hear. Not after all that warmth, all that soft skin, all those tears for a kitten. He couldn't let go of that. He couldn't let go of the Sophia he knew. He couldn't accept that she had a boyfriend.

"You got any more details than that?"

"It was a black-tie event. Thousand-dollar donation per ticket. Red carpet to give the guests a thrill for their money. You know how it is."

"Not really." *Get to the boyfriend.*

"Everyone's all pretty and on their best behavior. Every camera in the house is pointed at Sophia. That's what she's there for, to give everyone a little taste of glamor. People pay an outrageous price to eat dinner in the same room as the celebrities."

Had Sophia once enjoyed that?

*Don't stare at me. Quit talking about me.*

"Next thing I know, some jackass in basketball shoes and a ball cap is jumping on the table. Walking on the silverware, kicking the centerpiece, making a lot of noise. Alex pulled Sophia behind his back. That was the first thing I noticed, Alex keeping Sophia behind himself, so I knew this jerk had come to cause trouble for her."

There was nothing Travis could do about it but listen. His hand was clenched in a fist on his knee.

"My brothers and I were ready to take him out. He was standing on my wife's salad, goddammit, but once every camera in the place was focused on him, he dropped to one knee and started apologizing to Sophia. As apologies went, it was crap. Maybe a sentence. Alex was pissed. Her sister was stunned."

"And Sophia?"

Braden hesitated for only a moment. "She ditched her commitment to Texas Rescue and left with him. She looked pretty happy about it, so no one tried to stop her."

Travis couldn't speak. A knife in the chest would do that to a man. The thought of Sophia choosing to be with an ass who'd destroy the happiness of everyone around him was like a knife in the chest.

"But you see how that turned out. She's here alone. After getting to know her a little bit today, it's obvious the two of them aren't as alike as the photos make it look. My guess is that she's hiding from him as much as the rest of the world."

They hit another pothole, which gave Travis the perfect excuse to curse again. "I should have been told. Alex said she was hiding from cameras."

"If the boyfriend turns up again, things will break. More than my grandma's antiques. That kind of hyped-up guy dances too close to the line."

"Got a name?"

"DJ something. Something inane."

"*Paparazzi* is an inane word, too. I'll let the men know we're keeping everyone off the River Mack ranch whose name we don't already know."


"We would've been here sooner, but the gate at the main road was closed," Grace said.

Sophia nodded at her sister as if that made sense.

"All the gates were closed this time. I had to get out three times to open them. I saw a guy on a horse at the last one, the foreman we met last time. We waved at each other and he rode away."

Grace was talking to her through the open window of Alex's pickup. She'd started talking the moment they'd pulled up, not waiting for Alex to shut off the engine.

"We didn't see any cows, though. Not this time." Grace hopped out of the truck and gave the door a pat after closing it. "But we brought the truck, just in case. We can drive off the road if we have to go around a cow again."

Sophia nodded some more, so full of emotion at seeing her sister that she wasn't really listening to what she was saying. It was just so good to see her face. She'd missed her so much.

Sophia hesitated at the edge of the flagstone. Her sister had been so adamant that Sophia should only call for an emergency, and Grace hadn't called her once, not one single time in the past week to ask how she was doing. Was this how their relationship was supposed to be now? Polite and friendly visits once a week?

Sophia wanted to run to her sister and give her a bear hug. Instead, she twisted her fingers together as she kept nodding and smiling.

Alex got out of his side of the truck and spoke to Grace. "Sophia looks like she missed you almost as much as you missed her. Is one of you going to hug the other, or what?"

"You missed me?" Sophia asked, but Grace couldn't answer because she'd already run up to the patio and thrown her arms around her.

"I've been so worried about you," Grace said, hugging her hard.

Sophia took a split second to think before blurting out something snarky. *Yeah, I could tell by the way you totally ignored me.*

She pulled back from the hug just far enough to smooth Grace's dark gold hair into place, a gesture that went back to their tween years, when they'd first started playing with curling irons and hair spray. "When you're worried about me, you could give me a call. I'd love to hear from you."

"But—but I have called you. A lot."

"The phone hasn't rung once. I just assumed you were busy with your new job and with…" She gestured toward Alex, who was standing beside the truck. Then Sophia realized she'd made it sound like Grace was busy getting busy with Alex, which wasn't a great thing to think about her sister, even if it was probably true.

Sophia almost blushed. "I mean, with your wedding planning. I thought you were busy planning your wedding." *Without me.*

"I called, but you never picked up, so I figured you didn't want to talk. Or maybe I was calling you too late at night."

"I'm up all night long. I'm taking care of a kitten. It needs fed every two hours. It's pretty exhausting, but I volunteered for it, so…"

"You did?" Grace's amazement was genuine. She wasn't an actor.

Sophia was. She pretended not to be hurt that her sister was amazed she would volunteer to sacrifice her sleep for something besides herself. For years, Sophia had cared for Grace, but the freshest memory was obviously of Sophia blowing off everyone and everything for wild parties.

"It's just for a few days," Sophia said, a brilliant performance of perfect cheerfulness. She didn't sound offended at all, not hurt one bit. "The vet is scheduled to come out then, and Travis is sure he'll know a mother cat somewhere that just had a litter and can take another kitten. This one is so young, its eyes aren't even open yet, so it really needs a cat mother, not me."

"Wow. I'm so impressed. I had no idea you knew so much about cats." Grace gave her arm an extra squeeze. "But I'm not surprised. You've always been able to do anything you set your mind to."

Sophia didn't know what to say to that. It sounded like her sister still admired her. Considering the front-row seat she'd had to Sophia's self-destructing spiral, that was something of a miracle.

Sophia didn't want to start bawling and ruin a perfectly lovely conversation. She blinked away the threatening tears and focused on the barn. "I got a crash course on cats from Travis. The foreman you waved at."

"He promised me he'd check on you. He has, hasn't he?"

Sophia nodded some more and wished he was here to check on her now. It would be nice for him to see that her sister didn't hate her. He'd only seen them together that first day, snapping at each other over a cow on the road.

Well, Sophia had been doing most of the snapping. Travis must think Sophia was the world's worst sister.

Alex was standing back, giving them some personal space. He really was a pretty decent guy. Handsome, too, in a doctor-like, Clark Kent kind of way.

He turned toward the barn. "Speaking of Travis, is he around? Where is everyone?"

"It's May." Sophia said it the way Travis would.

"What does that mean?"

She shrugged. "I have no earthly idea, but it's the answer to everything around here. Apparently, cowboys are scarce on a ranch in May."

"Or else they're out working on the range," Alex said.

"I think its calving season. We get a few injuries in the ER every year at this time from roundups."

"I'm dying to see this kitten." Grace sounded as carefree as Sophia could remember her sounding since the day their parents had died. Alex must be more than just a decent guy, because Sophia knew she hadn't taken any burdens from Grace's shoulders, not lately. Alex must have lightened that load.

He picked up some grocery bags from the bed of the pickup. "Let's get these inside and check the ringer on that phone. I don't want you two to miss any more calls."

Sophia reached for one of the bags, but Alex shook his head. "It's okay. I've got it."

"Thank you." She meant for more than the groceries. Could he tell?

He winked at her, his eyes blue like her own. Like a brother might have had, if she'd ever had a brother. "She's happier when you're part of her life. I want Grace to be happy, you know."

"I know."

"Let's go fix that dinosaur of a phone."

Grace opened her cab door and reached for a basket. "I almost forgot. Our neighbor grows vegetables, and you wouldn't believe how much zucchini he had. I brought you some. You don't see this in LA. Isn't it great?"

"Oh, zucchini. Yes. Great." .

If she could point at a mattress and smile for fifty bucks, she could certainly beam at a basket of zucchini that her sister thought would make her happy. Apparently, the gift of love in Texas during the month of May was zucchini, whether it was from a mother to a ranch hand, from Travis to her, from Grace to—

From Travis to her?

It would be crazy to think he loved her, just because he'd left her a batch of zucchini.

With a note that said he didn't want her to get any more scars.

As she held the door open for her family with one hand and balanced an overflowing basket of zucchini with the other, she couldn't help but look at the empty barn one more time.

A gift of love? She was being too dramatic again—but something felt different now. The zucchini had marked some kind of turning point. Before, Travis would have expected her to do something simple yet impossible: *if you need milk replacer, go to the feed store*. Instead, he'd sent Braden to get it.

It was almost June. May had been full of loneliness and failure and zucchini. But June might be different. A new month. A new vegetable? A new chance to spend time with Travis.

She could hardly wait for June.

# Chapter Eleven

Tomatoes.

June was only half over, but if Sophia saw another tomato, she might scream. Or barf.

It turned out the potted plants lining one side of the flagstone patio were Mrs. MacDowell's absurdly fertile tomatoes. There were so many, they ripened and fell off the vines, bounced out of their pots and split open on the patio, where they proceeded to cook on the hot stone in the June sun. Every deep yoga breath Sophia took brought in shimmering molecules of hot energy that smelled vaguely like lasagna.

The smell made her stomach turn.

She'd had such high hopes for June. She'd imagined basking in the sun, breathing deeply, feeling the health and strength of every muscle in her body as she went through all the yoga routines she could remember. Travis wouldn't be able to resist spying on her. Drooling over her silver-screen-worthy body, he would spend lots of time with her, and she wouldn't be lonely in the least.

Instead, she was the one who drooled over Travis, spying on him from the kitchen window. June had brought him back from wherever he'd been disappearing to, but although he spent part of every day in the barn, he was never alone. The ranch must be too big for just one person, because there were always other cowboys around. Usually, they left in pairs on horseback, off to do whatever the heck kept ranchers busy in the month of June.

Her eye was always drawn to Travis. She knew the way he sat a horse now, the set of his shoulders, the way a coil of rope always rested on the back of his saddle when he rode away, the way the rope was looped on the saddle horn and resting on top of his right thigh when he returned.

Not today. She heard what sounded like a motorcycle.

She ran to the window in time to catch Travis roaring away on an ATV. He was in jeans and a plaid shirt, as usual, but he wore no hat to keep the wind out of his hair. He drove the four-wheeler the way he galloped a horse, almost standing up, leaning over the handlebars into the wind. He looked so strong and young and free, something in her yearned to be with him.

"Wait for me." But saying the words out loud didn't make them seem any less pitiful than when they echoed in her head.

She put her hand on the glass, well and truly isolated. If only a director would yell *cut*. If only the prop team would help her out of a mock space capsule. If only Grace were waiting to bring her out of her self-induced sorrow, to remind her that it was only a movie, and the real Sophia could have a bowl of ice cream and paint her fingernails and never, ever have to wonder if she'd make it back to Earth.

Normalcy. It had always been such a relief to return to the normal world after experiencing a character's intense emotions. Now her real life was the unrealistic one, and her old, normal life was the fantasy.

As Travis rode away, Sophia kept her greedy eyes on him and indulged her favorite fantasy, the one where she wasn't famous yet and had no reason to hide. If she and Travis had met when she was nineteen instead of twenty-nine, she would have flirted outrageously with him. As a young cowboy, he wouldn't have been able to resist letting her hitch a ride to the barn on the running board of his ATV. She would've been the best part of his day, his pretty blond girlfriend holding on to him so she wouldn't fall off while he drove. He would've saved up his money to take her to the movies.

"Cut," she whispered to herself.

In real life, she was the one in the movies, a Hollywood star who couldn't hide forever. There was no stopping the fame now. She couldn't make people forget her face.

"No, really. Cut, before you drive yourself crazy."

She pushed hard with her hand, forcing herself away from the window. She was dressed for a morning yoga workout, but she hadn't kept track of where the ranch hands were. There were five different guys who showed up at least a few days each week. Who had shown up for work with Travis today? Was anyone still in the barn?

She couldn't go out to the patio if someone else might still be around. A few minutes of inattention while she'd wallowed in self-pity had cost her. Now she was stuck inside for the day. She'd already watched all of Mrs. MacDowell's DVDs and had browsed through some of her bookshelves. There were a lot of Hardy Boy volumes. The cover of a pregnancy handbook was so laughably 80s, Sophia had quickly shoved it back onto the shelf. There were a lot of cookbooks. She could give the air conditioner a workout by heating up the kitchen as she tried every single tomato recipe.

The sound of the ATV's engine surprised her. She glued her nose right back to the window. Travis was driving back at a more sedate pace, hauling a trailer full of square hay bales behind the four-wheeler, but there was nothing sedate about his appearance, nor its effect on her. His shirt was unbuttoned all the way, flaring out behind him like a plaid cape.

Sophia bet it was no big deal for him. The day was hot, the drive was easy, why not unbutton his shirt and let the air cool his chest? But for her, it was a very big deal. The sexual turn-on was instant, a primitive response to the visual stimulation of a man's strong body. Six-pack abs in low-slung jeans were a big *yes* in her mind. Weeks ago, when Travis had come into the barn dripping wet, she'd felt that same instant, heavy wanting.

It was heavier now, because now she knew Travis, the man with the hands that handled kittens and controlled horses. The man with the voice that never tried to shout her down. The man who'd listened when she poured her heart out, then gifted her with those three little words she hadn't known she'd needed to hear: *I get it.*

And yeah, the man with six-pack abs. Hot damn, he looked good. Really good.

He was looking right at her.

She jerked away and dropped the curtain, as if he'd pointed a telephoto zoom lens at her.

That was a mistake. Now he was going to think she was embarrassed, as if he'd caught her spying on him.

He had.

Okay, so she'd been spying on him, but she should have played it cool, like she'd just happened to be looking out the window, checking the weather. It was probably too little, too late, but she did that now, using the back of her hand to lift the curtain oh-so-casually. *Hot and sunny, not a cloud in the sky. Same as always.*

Travis turned the ATV and started driving it straight toward the house.

*Ohmigod, ohmigod, ohmigod.* He was coming to say hello. She tried to fix her hair with her fingers. She wasn't wearing makeup, which wasn't ideal, but on the plus side, she was in her yoga clothes. He wouldn't look at her face if she exposed enough skin. She started to take off the loose green cover-up she'd thrown on over her black bra top. But wait—he'd already seen her in the window in the green. She couldn't open the door in a black sports bra now. Too obvious.

The engine went silent. Sophia peeked out the window and saw six feet of rugged male beauty striding toward her, buttoning his shirt as he came. He started high on his chest, bringing the shirt together with a single button. Then the next one lower. One button after the other, he narrowed the amount of exposed flesh until only one triangle of tanned skin flashed above his belt buckle, and then that was gone, too.

She steadied herself with a hand on the doorknob.

If he took those clothes off with as much swagger as he put them on...

The knock on the door was firm. Suddenly, so was her resolve. She wasn't a giddy nineteen-year-old. She was twenty-nine, and she guessed Travis was around thirty. They were consenting adults, and after the sight she'd just witnessed, she couldn't think of a single reason why she shouldn't smile when she opened the door.

Her isolation had taken a turn for the better.

Travis was here. There was nowhere else she'd rather be.

"Howdy, stranger. Long time, no see."

Sophia Jackson purred the words as she opened the door.

Travis raised an eyebrow.

She draped herself against the door jamb as if she had all the time in the world. Her thin green top draped itself over her curves. She watched the effect that had on him with a knowing look in her eyes.

Yeah, she knew how good she looked. Travis put his hand on the door jamb above her head. He had no idea why the sex goddess was back, but it sure made ten in the morning on a Tuesday a lot more interesting.

"It's about time you came." She said it so suggestively, Travis knew she was teasing. Her eyes were crinkling in the corners with the smile she was holding back. "You told Grace and Alex you'd check on me. Are you here to hold up your part of the bargain?"

Her gaze roamed over him from head to toe, lingering somewhere around the vicinity of his belt before returning to his face. She'd done so before, after he'd hosed off at the barn. That time, she'd been serious and a little bit scared. This time, she was having fun, evaluating him as nothing more than a hunk of meat. Treating him as nothing more than eye candy.

He liked it.

But he didn't trust it. He waited for that moment of hesitation, her fear of this attraction they shared.

He didn't see it, so he played along, answering her question as seriously as she'd asked it. "A man's got to work sometimes. It's only been forty-eight hours since I talked to you."

She pouted prettily, picture-perfect. "But Grace and Alex were here for their little weekly visit at the same time. It doesn't count as checking on me when they're already checking on me."

"I'll keep that in mind." He shifted so that he leaned his forearm instead of his hand on the frame of the door. It brought him into her personal space. As they talked about nothing, he watched her the same way he'd watch a yearling when he approached her with bridle in hand for the first time.

Sophia didn't flinch from his nearness. "If you didn't come to check me out, then I have to warn you that this house is no longer accepting zucchini donations."

"I'm glad to hear it, because there aren't any left. Someone snuck into the barn and conspired with my horses to dispose of the rest."

She laughed and stood up straight, done with the exaggerated come-hither routine. She was still a sex goddess, whether she tried to be or not.

He stayed lounging against her door frame. "Samson incriminated you. I found zucchini in his stall. I'm surprised he ate any of it. Most horses aren't particularly fond of it, or else people around here would probably grow even more of it than they do now."

"I guess it all depends who's doing the feeding. Maybe some hands have just the right touch."

He didn't know why she was so lighthearted today, but she was irresistible in this mood.

It was a dangerous word, *irresistible*. He could imagine a future with an irresistible woman, but not with a celebrity. Sophia wouldn't be staying in his life, which was one reason he'd been staying away. He needed to enjoy this conversation for what it was and not think about what it might have led to in different circumstances.

"I'll see if Samson likes tomatoes tonight," she said. "They're going rotten because I can't cook them fast enough."

He got a little serious. "Don't do that. Tomato plants aren't good for horses."

She got a little serious, too. "Okay, I won't. I guess I would've figured it out when they spit them back out at me."

"They might have eaten them. Horses don't always have the sense to stay away from something that might hurt them."

And neither, he realized, did he.

"I didn't know," she said.

"Now you do."

"Déjà vu. Now I know fridges have casters and horses can't eat tomatoes."

He didn't have anything to say to that. If they were a couple, he would've dropped a sweet kiss on her lips and gone back to work. He would've anticipated having her alone tonight, a leisurely feast. Or hard and intense. Or emotional and gentle—any way they wanted it.

She bit the lip he was lusting after, but she looked concerned, not carnal. "So, if you didn't come under orders to check on me, why are you here? I hope the two kittens are okay. I looked when I went to the barn last night, but I couldn't find them at all."

Kittens. Right. He forced his thoughts to change gear.

"The mother moves them every day. She's a skittish one, but the two kittens are doing fine."

Sophia wrinkled her nose, instantly repulsed. "She's a terrible mother. I lost a lot of sleep because of her. I'm glad your vet found a new mother for the one she abandoned."

It was interesting, the way she hadn't forgiven that poor cat for isolating one of her kittens. "In my business, any time offspring are thriving without my help, then the mother's all right. Some cats make one nest and stick to it for a month, some move their kittens around twice a day. The bottom line is that there are two kittens in that barn I don't have to worry about, so she's good enough in my book. Don't be so hard on her."

Sophia put a bright smile on her face, a fake one, putting her guard up. "So, are there any other cheerful topics you'd like to discuss?"

A cat seemed a strange reason to put up walls. Travis stopped lounging against her door. He'd gotten entirely too comfortable when he had work to do. "I wanted to let you know we're burning off some cedar today. If you look off your front porch and see smoke, you don't have to come check it out."

Now she was the one to raise an eyebrow. "You thought I'd come see what's on fire?"

"You should. It's what you do on a ranch. You look out for each other, remember? You go see why someone's laying on their car horn. If something's burning, you'd better know what it is."

"I'm hiding. I couldn't check it out even if I wanted to, *remember*?"

The hiding was of her own choosing, as far as he could tell. She could decide not give a damn about the paparazzi knowing where she was, and she could decide not to care if they did take her picture. Travis had asked Alex and Grace about the ex during their last visit, and they'd assured him that the DJ was too busy partying in LA to give Sophia a second thought.

Yet Travis had seen Sophia's scars, so he didn't feel free to criticize her. Maybe he'd choose to become a hermit, too, if he walked a mile in her shoes.

He simply nodded to let her know he remembered that she had her reasons. "Now you know that if you see smoke today, it's intentional, for what it's worth. I've got to get back to work."

"Hey, Travis?" she called after him. "Are all your cowboys going to be at the fire? If it's safe for me to go outside, I'd like to go see the horses."

"Even if they can't help you get rid of your tomatoes?"

"I need someone to talk to."

He wished it was a joke.

"Yes, you're safe."

# Chapter Twelve

The horses were beautiful.

Sophia had only talked to them when they'd been standing patiently in their stalls at the end of the day. Of course, she'd seen them under saddle, working, but she hadn't seen them like this before.

She only came to the barn after sundown. She hadn't realized the horses spent their day in the pasture or the paddock or whatever this huge, fenced-in field was called. It ran from the barn at one end all the way to the stables at the other, a stretch of maybe a quarter mile. The horses were spread out the entire distance, swishing their tails and nibbling at grass. They looked happy and content, so much so that they paid her no attention as she stood on a fence rail in her sneakers and yoga clothes.

That was okay; she had Grace to talk to.

"This is so pretty. I'm glad I came out here on my day off."

Sophia was glad, too. The visit was a total surprise, which made it all the more special. Alex wasn't here, and Grace wasn't dutifully delivering groceries. This was just about them, two sisters who'd rarely been apart before this year.

Sophia jumped down from the fence and bent to scratch a black and gray dog behind the ears. When roundup had ended and all the horses and cowboys had come in, this dog had come, too, apparently part of the whole gang. Her name was Patch. Travis called her a cow dog, but she seemed keen to be with the horses.

"I brought you some of my neighbor's tomatoes," Grace said. "Don't let me forget to take them out of the trunk before I go. I probably shouldn't have left them in there. The whole car will smell like tomatoes in this heat."

The mere thought of the smell of tomatoes made Sophia want to gag.

Grace seemed extra talkative today, raving about her new job at the hospital where Alex worked. She was writing grant proposals and doing something with research studies, using all the organization skills she'd perfected as a personal assistant to a celebrity.

Sophia smiled and listened, but inside, she was hurting. Grace apparently had forgotten that her old job had been to work for Sophia. When she raved about how cool and great her new boss was, did she not realize that implied her old boss had been not so cool and not so great?

Sophia watched the horses and listened to how much better Grace's life was without her. She'd almost rather talk to the horses. She'd never done them wrong. They didn't care if she was famous or a loser or a famous loser.

"Do you know what I need?" Sophia asked.

Grace went quiet in the middle of her sentence. "What do you mean?"

"I need boots. Western ones, so I can learn how to ride. Get me four or five pair and bring them out next Sunday. I'll pick one. I need jeans, too. I've got those shredded Miami ones, but I need regular jeans, like Mom used to buy us. Something less than a thousand dollars. I'm not making any money right now."

"Sophie."

That was all Grace had to say. The warning note said the rest.

Sophia shut up, but Grace gave her the lecture, anyway. "I'm your sister, not your personal assistant. I'm not writing this down in a little notebook anymore, so you can stop dictating to me."

Grace seemed to know what kinds of thing sisters should do compared to what kinds of things personal assistants should do. Sophia didn't see this clear-cut distinction. Grace brought her groceries, for example, but when Sophia had handed her a pile of dirty laundry that first week, Grace had grown quite cool and informed Sophia that the house had a washer and dryer.

"I need a personal assistant. You promised to find me a replacement when you left me for Alex." Sophia didn't care that she sounded petulant. Sisters got petulant.

"I didn't leave you for Alex. I fell in love with Alex, and I still love you, too. I always will. Millions of people love their spouses and their siblings, both. I'm one of them."

She sounded so calm, so infuriatingly right. It reminded Sophia of the way Travis had talked to her, until she'd showed him her scars. "How do you suggest I do my own shopping for boots? You know I can't walk into a store. I could shop online, if I had any internet access. You're going to have to get me a laptop or a smartphone. Then I could be independent."

Grace bit her lower lip, a habit that Sophia knew she still did as well. She knew, because cameras caught everything.

"I don't think having internet access would be a good idea," Grace said.

"Why not?"

Grace couldn't quite look her in the eye. "Hackers will use it to find you."

"That's not the whole story, is it? What's on the internet that you don't want me to see?"

"It's just…things haven't really died down the way we'd hoped. Not yet. But they will. Um…when do you want to tell Deezee you're pregnant? Alex and I want to be—"

"I'm not pregnant." There. Those words felt much better out loud than rattling around in her head.

"What?" Grace's arm was suddenly around her shoulder. Her voice was all sympathy, shopping and laundry and every other offense forgotten. "Oh, Sophie. When did you miscarry? Why didn't you tell me?"

"I didn't. I was never pregnant in the first place. The tests can be wrong, you know. It says so in the instructions."

"So you got your period this month?"

That startled Sophia. She hadn't been paying attention, really, but she quickly counted the weeks up in her head. They couldn't be right.

She shrugged. "I don't feel pregnant. Look at me. Does this look like a pregnant woman's body?"

Grace looked at her, but not at her stomach. She smoothed Sophia's hair over her shoulder with an almost painful gentleness. The expression on Grace's face was unbearable. Concern, compassion, pity—just horrible.

Sophia turned back to the pasture and shaded her eyes with her hand. "Where's Samson? Do you see him? He's the big bay with black points." She forced a laugh. "Aren't you impressed with my cowgirl talk? That's just a horsey way to say brown with black trim. Travis left the ATV here. I bet he took Samson out for the day. Anyhow, Samson just loves Jean Paul's shampoo. When I get back to LA, I'm going to ship a gallon of it to the ranch."

"Sophia—"

"Just so he has it to remember me by."

"Sophia, you're pregnant."

She whirled to face her sister. "I am not. I wish I'd never done that test in the first place. It's just making everyone worry over nothing."

"You've missed two periods and had a positive pregnancy test."

Sophia kept her chin high. The fence rail was solid under her hands. She wasn't going to crack. She wasn't going to fall apart.

"I'm not, but it wouldn't matter if I was."

"It matters to me," Grace said.

"I had to get out of the spotlight for a little while, anyway, right? If I am pregnant, which I'm not, then

I already told you the plan. I'll just have the baby and give it up for adoption."

"Why would you do that?"

"Why wouldn't I? Some couple is out there just dying to have a baby. I'd be a surrogate mother. That's a really noble thing to do, you know."

"But you're not a surrogate mother. This is actually your baby."

"I don't want to talk about it." She started walking toward the barn, done with the whole conversation, angry at her sister for bringing it up.

Patch stayed with the horses, but Grace dogged her heels. "Well, I do want to talk about it. It's the whole reason I came out here today."

Sophia nearly tripped on those words. She'd been suckered into thinking that Grace had sought her out because she wanted to be her sister and her friend, but it was just a betrayal. She didn't want Sophia's company. It had all been a trap to force Sophia to talk about something she didn't even want to think about.

Sophia broke into a run, sneakers pounding relentlessly into the ground until she reached the barn. Until she reached the office. Until she threw herself into Travis's chair.

"Sophie! Where are you?" Grace stopped in the office doorway, breathless. "Don't do this."

"Do what? Not talk about something I don't want to talk about? If I'm pregnant, it has no bearing on you."

"Yes, it does. I'm trying to plan a wedding. My wedding. And I came here today because I wanted to ask you to be my maid of honor."

Sophia closed her eyes. She'd hated herself plenty of times before, but this one was the worst.

"But we need to talk about your pregnancy." Grace had tears in her voice. "I tried to be flexible. I chose a bunch of different locations, but the soonest I could book any of them was September. You'll be showing in September."

"And you don't want a pregnant cow in your wedding." Sophia murmured the words more to herself than to Grace.

"No. That isn't it at all. If you were keeping your baby, then it wouldn't matter at all that you were showing. You'd have nothing to hide."

Grace took a deep breath, and Sophia knew she was about to hear something she didn't want to hear.

"But if you want to keep everything a secret, then I have to respect that. I tried guesstimating when you were due and how long it would take for your body to recover so that people wouldn't suspect you'd ever had a baby. If you're due in January, I think you probably wouldn't be comfortable trying to pull it off until April, even with the way you work out. I don't want to wait until next April to marry Alex. I want my big sister in my wedding, but it's not just about having a white gown and a party and some photos. It's about actually being married to Alex. I want to make him those promises now. I want to start our lives together now, not next year."

Sophia knew she was supposed to say something, but she had nothing to contribute. Grace had thought everything through while Sophia had refused to think of it at all.

"If you don't want to be seen, I thought about asking someone else to stand up with me. I've made some friends, and...well, I really like Kendry MacDowell.

She's married to Alex's department chair, Jamie Mac-Dowell. When Alex was putting out feelers about finding a place off the beaten path, Jamie mentioned his mother's house was vacant, so that's how we found this place for you. His baby picture is on the wall in your house, isn't that funny? Anyway, his wife Kendry is my age, and—"

"I understand." Sophia didn't want to hear it. Neither she nor Grace had been able to make friends outside their two-sister world, not when deli clerks were bribed to expose them. She knew she should be happy for Grace, but she didn't want to hear how Kendry was going to hold Grace's bouquet while Alex put a gold band on Grace's finger and started a new life with her.

Her little Grace had lost the best mother. She'd gotten a skittish big sister as a poor substitute. But Grace wasn't letting anything get in her way now. She was doing so much better out of the nest on her own than she ever had when Sophia had dragged her around the world in pursuit of Hollywood dreams.

"I'm so sorry," Sophia said. She was. About everything.

"Don't be sorry. The wedding will be great. We're thinking about a ceremony earlier in the day. We found the cutest bridesmaid dresses, this lemon yellow that's short and swingy. It would be great for a daytime wedding. Kendry's expecting, too. She's further along than you are, so we were excited to find a dress that will work. Even though it's not a maternity dress, it will look cute on her."

*Stop. Please, stop.*

Sophia couldn't act her way out of this. *Kendry's expecting*, her sister said, like it was a good thing, something to look forward to. If it turned out that Sophia was really pregnant, there would be no excitement, only plans for damage control.

"It would look really cute on you, too. It's only June. You might change your mind by September. You could be in the wedding, too."

Sophia could only shake her head, a vehement denial, as her tears began falling.

She looked around the office, but there wasn't a tissue box in this male space. She already knew there were textbooks on crops and cows, a computer she couldn't access. There was a baseball on the shelf above the neat stack of T-shirts.

Sophia grabbed Travis's T-shirt and mopped up her face.

"Oh, don't cry, Sophie." Grace's voice was husky with her own tears, a sound Sophia remembered from those awful nights when they'd grieved together. "I just wanted… I wanted to talk to you in person. I've tried to ask you about it before, but you wouldn't…well, at some point, I just had to make the call, so we put the deposit down on this rooftop venue for September."

Sophia stood up, clutching Travis's shirt close in case she couldn't pull off the greatest acting job in her life. "September sounds like a good time of year for something outdoors on a rooftop. It won't be as hot as it is now."

Grace looked so concerned. Sophia was being as unselfish as she could. The least Grace could do was let herself be fooled by the act.

"This is just one day out of our whole lives," Grace said. "It doesn't change anything between us. We're sisters."

"Always." But Sophia felt a little frantic. She wanted to get out of the barn and go somewhere else. Be someone else.

Travis had a digital clock on the wall, the kind that gave barometric pressure and humidity and a lot of other stuff that wouldn't matter to Sophia once she gave up and went back to bed. "Look at the time. I have to go back to the house before anyone comes in from the range. Travis is the only one who knows I'm here. There are other guys working today, and one of them might come in any second."

It was a lie. Travis had told her she'd be safe, but she didn't feel safe. She needed to hide and lick her wounds.

Grace followed her out of the barn. "I've got a little bit of time before I have to go. I'm meeting Kendry at this florist that did her brother-in-law's wedding. Braden's. Do you remember Lana and Braden? They were at your table at the Texas Rescue ball...oh, never mind. Sorry."

"I met them. For about five seconds."

*Before Deezee showed up and I made the dumbest decision of my life.*

Grace did her best to keep talking as if that hadn't been an awkward reminder of a terrible event.

Sophia let Grace's voice wash over her as they walked side by side in the sunshine. The calm weather made a mockery of Sophia's inner turmoil. If she could just turn back time to the person she'd been before she met Deezee...

She'd thought the same thing after she'd tried to touch Travis's wet body and he'd turned her down cold. She'd been certain the pre-Deezee version of herself would've been more desirable. Yet this morning she'd flirted with Travis, and he'd dropped everything he was doing to stand a little too close to her under that kitchen door awning. He seemed to like the current version after all.

Grace had changed topics from her life to Sophia's. "I don't know how to keep you hidden at ob-gyn appointments, but there are midwives associated with the hospital who make house calls. That might work. They have patient confidentiality rules in place, but I'll look into a more comprehensive confidentiality contract, the kind we had for the housekeepers and staff back in LA."

Before meeting Deezee, Sophia had entrusted her day-to-day routine to her personal assistant, but she'd made all the big decisions herself. She'd set her long-term goals and planned out every strategic move to get there. Her reputation as a smart and savvy actor had been earned. Now, Grace was deciding Sophia's medical care for her.

"I'm worried about the press, though," Grace said. "If they wanted to know what you ate so badly, I can't imagine what lengths they'll go to for baby gossip."

Before Deezee, it had never been her assistant's job to decide what to do next. Sophia had never put that burden on her sister's shoulders.

"Hey, Gracie?"

They stopped by her sister's car.

"You've got enough on your plate without worrying about doctors and confidentiality and all the rest. I'm going to look into it."

"Are you sure? I was going to try making some anonymous calls to a few adoption agencies to see what's involved—"

"Stop, sweetie." Sophia took a deep breath. "You've

been an absolute rock for me, but I've got this, okay? I can make the calls, if and when I need to. You, meanwhile, are the bride, and you've got an appointment in town with a florist and some friends. Go."

"Are you sure?"

Sophia nodded. This didn't feel like acting. This felt like being herself. Not her old self, not her new self, just herself.

She used the T-shirt to gesture toward Grace's car as she smiled at her beautiful baby sister. "Go be the bride. Order your flowers. No one will look at them when they can look at a bride like you, but get the prettiest ones you can, anyway."

"Oh, Sophie." But Grace's voice wasn't sad. She was excited. "Thanks for being so understanding. I can't tell you how nervous I was about this. You're the best."

The T-shirt in Sophia's fist couldn't crack. She wouldn't crack, either.

"Oh, I almost forgot." Grace popped her trunk with a press of the button on her key fob. "Look, a whole basket of tomatoes for you."

# *Chapter Thirteen*

We got a visitor.

The text message hit his phone when Travis walked away from the burning pile of cedar saplings. Cell phones were unreliable like that out here. One part of an empty field could get a cell signal and another part couldn't.

The text was from Clay, who was working at the pond near the edge of the property that bordered the road to Austin. The time stamp indicated the text was two hours old, just now reaching his phone.

His cell phone pinged again, receiving another text.

Same car as Sunday.

Grace or Alex had come to see Sophia, then.
Travis put the cell phone back in his pocket. He felt

like more of a forester than a rancher today, since he'd been swinging an ax instead of throwing a lasso. It had to be done, though. The cedar could destroy a pasture in a matter of years, multiplying and spreading roots that would hog all the water and kill the grass his cattle needed for forage.

Another ping sounded, rapidly followed by more, all the texts that had been lined up, waiting for a satellite to find his phone.

Got another visitor.

The time was ten minutes ago. The text had been sent to all the men working the River Mack today.

Blue 4-door sedan? Anyone know it?

No.

No.

When Travis's voice mail played its alert sound, he was already halfway to the shade tree where he'd left Samson.

He listened to Clay's message as he walked. "We got a visitor, boss. I'm too far away to get a good look, but I don't know the car. It doesn't look like it belongs here. I'm knee-deep at the pond. Might be faster if you could meet 'em at the next gate."

There were three sets of gates on the road that led to the house. The main gate was the one Clay had seen. The second set of gates were about a mile and a half farther into the ranch itself, and the third set of gates were a mile closer to the house from there.

This year's new ranch hand, always called the greenhorn, was standing with a shovel near the fire, his phone in his hand. Clearly, he'd just gotten the texts, too, and was reading.

"You want me to come with you?" he called to Travis, with all the excitement of a first-year cowboy in his voice.

"You can't leave a fire unattended," Travis reminded him as he untied Samson's reins.

"I'm gonna miss all the fun."

"Greenhorns aren't supposed to have fun."

He swung himself into the saddle. His horse's idea of fun was to be given his head so he could run, so Travis pointed Samson toward the ranch road and let him go with a sharply spoken *gid-yap*. They covered the mile or so to the second set of gates in a handful of minutes. The blue car had gone through the gate, but it was still there, waiting for its passenger to close the gate and get back in.

Travis reined in Samson, then walked him to the middle of the road and stopped a little distance away from the car. He didn't recognize it. More than that, he didn't like the look of the man that was closing the gate—or rather, he didn't like the camera that the man held in one hand. It had a two-foot-long lens that looked like it was compensating for some shortcomings in some other department. That, or the man was a professional photographer.

"What's your business here, gentlemen?"

The cameraman looked absolutely dumbfounded to

see a cowboy on a horse in the middle of the road. City folk. What did they expect to see on a ranch?

The driver stuck his head out the window. "You're in the way. Move."

Travis didn't bother answering that.

The driver threw up a hand. "What do you want?"

"I just asked you that."

"We're going to see a friend of ours."

That lie didn't really deserve an answer, but Travis supposed he needed to spell things out for them. "You can turn your car around and head back the way you came."

"We're not leaving," the cameraman said. "We're not doing anything wrong."

"That's not for you to decide. You're on private property."

"What's your name?" the cameraman demanded, as if he had the right to know.

That definitely didn't deserve an answer.

The cameraman lifted the huge lens and took a few photos of Travis. "We'll identify you."

It would be humorous if they showed the photos to the local sheriff to file a complaint against him. Travis knew the sheriff and most of the deputies, of course, but it was more than that. This was Texas cattle country. The rules had been in place here for well more than a century. If a cattleman didn't want you on his property, then you got off his property. The sheriff would laugh these men out of his office for complaining about a foreman doing his job.

The driver pulled his head back into his car. Stuck it out the window again. "C'mon, Peter. Get in the car."

Once the cameraman was in, the driver revved the

engine. He inched the vehicle forward, then revved the engine some more.

*Pushy little bastards.*

So these were paparazzi. Had to be. Travis imagined it would be a nuisance to have them following him and taking pictures while he walked down a public street. Coming onto someone else's land and sticking a camera in their face took nuisance to a different level. Trespassing was illegal. Trespassing and then taking photographs took a lot of gall.

Years of this would wear on a person. Travis had a better idea now of just how much it had worn on Sophia.

The car lurched forward a full car length, rushing his horse before slamming on its brakes. Samson threw his head up and gave it the side-eye, but he stayed under control. Travis gave him a solid pat on the neck, turned in his saddle, and pulled his hunting rifle out of its carrying case. He pulled a single bullet out of the cardboard box he kept in his saddlebag.

Carrying a rifle was part of Travis's job. Predators had to be dealt with; they'd found the remains of a calf that had been lost to a predator just yesterday. Travis would never kill a man over photographs, but he'd never let a car kill a horse, either. If he were to fire this weapon, every cowboy in hearing distance would come to check it out. If Travis happened to fire that signal shot in the direction of one of the car's tires, well, things like that happened.

One thing that wasn't going to happen? These men weren't getting any closer to Sophia.

Travis opened the rifle's chamber. Empty, as it should be unless he was about to use it. He slipped the bullet into place and locked the bolt into position. It made a satisfying metallic sound for the benefit of the trespassers. Travis set the rifle across his thighs and waited.

The driver and the cameramen started making incredulous hand gestures. Then the driver laid on the horn, nice and loud. Nice and long.

Travis smiled. Wouldn't be long now.

Clay had already been on his way, so he arrived first. A few minutes later, Buck, a young hand working his second year on the River Mack, rode up. Buck was as good-natured and laid-back as they came, but between the text messages and the car horn, he arrived looking serious. The men stayed on their horses, flanking Travis.

"This road's getting mighty crowded," Travis said.

The driver laid on the horn again, longer and louder.

"Seems rude," Clay said.

"Doesn't he?"

The driver got out of the car. "This is very interesting. What are you guys hiding? Why don't you want us to visit our friend?"

"We may be here awhile," Travis said to his men. "He doesn't understand the concept of private property."

The driver addressed Travis's men, too. "Either of you fellas know Sophia Jackson?"

Well, hell. Now it was like playing poker. Travis had to act like he didn't know the cards he held in his own hand.

"Her sister lives here in Austin. We spotted the sister coming out of a bridal shop, then she drove out here to this ranch." The driver squinted at Clay. "Isn't that interesting?"

"Not particularly."

Travis would have to call Alex this evening and let him know Grace was being followed.

"Rumor has it that Sophia Jackson's sister is planning a wedding on this ranch." He made a show of taking his wallet out of his back pocket. "We're just looking for a little confirmation."

"The movie star?" Buck was genuinely incredulous. "What in the hell is this man talkin' about?"

"I believe he thinks we run a catering service," Travis deadpanned. "You cater any weddings lately?"

Buck laughed, although Travis doubted he'd been that funny. Buck just liked to laugh.

The cameraman gestured to his grandiose lens. "Look, I'm just trying to do my job. To capture all the beauty of a wedding, I need to scope out the venue first. Is there a gazebo? Will there be a reception tent? Is Sophia Jackson going to be the maid of honor?"

Buck leaned around Travis to speak to Clay. "I thought you were digging an irrigation ditch today. Didn't know you built weddin' gazebos for movie stars." He cracked himself up with his own joke.

The driver, however, got impatient or insulted. It didn't matter which. What mattered was that he shoved his wallet back in his pants and got behind the wheel again. With his hand on the horn, he put his car in gear. It rolled toward the horses slowly but relentlessly.

Buck stopped laughing.

"Is he playing chicken with us?" Clay asked no one in particular.

Travis didn't believe in playing chicken. He didn't like trespassers, and he didn't like horses being threatened with a car that could kill them. He picked up the rifle, sighted down the barrel, and fired.

The front left tire deflated instantly.

"Never did like games," Travis said, using thigh and knee to keep Samson calm after the gunfire.

"It's about to get real," Clay murmured.

"Yep."

The driver started shouting, jumping out of his car and waving his arms like a caricature of a New York taxi driver. The cameraman got out and started photographing his flat tire.

"Make sure you get my gate in the background, so you can explain to the sheriff how far onto private property you were when your tire blew up." Travis turned to flip his saddlebag open and get another bullet out of the cardboard box. "I'll say this one more time: turn your car around and get off my ranch."

"But you shot out my tire. You *shot* it." The driver was more incredulous about that than Buck had been about movie stars.

"You got a spare, don't you?" Travis pulled back the bolt on the rifle and chambered another round. "How many spares you got?"

Clay nodded toward the west. "Company's coming."

Travis glanced at the two riders coming toward them with their horses at an easy trot. "Good. Haven't seen Waterson in a while." He looked back at the driver. "You get to changing that tire. We have some visiting to do."

It took the driver and cameraman longer to figure out how to get their spare out of the trunk and set up the jack than it did for Luke Waterson and one of his hands to reach the road. Luke was one of the owner-operators of the James Hill ranch, which bordered the River Mack.

He rode up to Travis and shook hands. "Happened

to be in the neighborhood when I heard someone's car horn get stuck. Then the gunshot made it interesting."

"Nice of you to stop by."

"What do we have here?"

Travis leaned his forearm on the pommel of his saddle, keeping the rifle in his other hand pointed away from men and horses. "I believe this here is what you'd call the paparazzi."

"Paparazzi? Which one of you is famous?"

As the men laughed, Travis spoke under his breath to Luke. "Mrs. MacDowell has a houseguest."

"I see." Luke *tched* to his horse and turned him in a circle, until he stood beside Travis. "Looks like we'll be staying until these paparazzi can get their tire changed and get on their way. How long do you think that'll take?"

"They're a little slow on the uptake," Travis said. "I'm gonna say twenty minutes."

"I'll take fifteen."

Clay was skeptical. "Ten bucks says thirty."

In the end, it took them the full thirty minutes, so Clay collected enough beer money to last him a month. Buck was sent to follow the car out to the county road. Waterson and his man headed back to the James Hill. Clay went back to clearing out pond weeds.

Travis turned his horse toward the house.

He had that impatient feeling again, that need to lay eyes on Sophia. *Need* was perhaps the wrong term. The photographers hadn't made it very far onto the ranch, so there was no need to think she was in any kind of distress. She was probably talking to the horses or taking a nap or even holding those yoga poses that had turned him into a voyeur. Travis *wanted* to see Sophia again.

Want and need were all twisted up inside him when it came to Sophia. If he just checked on her, then he'd be able to put his mind at ease and go back to his routine.

Travis told himself that lie for a mile, until the white pillars of Mrs. MacDowell's front porch came into view, and he saw Sophia standing there, hurling tomatoes at the sky.

# *Chapter Fourteen*

He might as well have been invisible.

He'd turned Samson out to the pasture and put on a fresh shirt. His hair still probably smelled like smoke, but Sophia noticed none of it when Travis walked up the front porch steps and joined her by the white pillars. She didn't acknowledge him at all.

It didn't matter. He leaned against a pillar and felt the tension inside him ease, anyway. She was here. He was here. It felt good.

She continued her little ritual as if she were in the middle of a meditation. She chose a tomato from a basket, examined it carefully, and then threw it with considerable skill.

"Had a bad day?" he asked.

"You could say that."

"I'm about to make it worse."

She paused, tomato cupped in her hand.

"I just met my first paparazzi."

"Oh." Her knuckles turned white on the tomato, but as he watched her, she loosened her grip. "I could crush this, but then I'd have to clean up the stupid mess myself."

"You could throw it."

She did.

"Nice arm," he said.

"My daddy taught me."

Right there, just like that, Travis felt something change. The hard squeeze on his heart was painful.

Standing on the porch less than an arm's length from Sophia, he saw her as a child, one who loved her daddy, a young girl determined to learn how to throw a baseball. She might have had pigtails, or she might have been a tomboy in a ball cap, but she'd been somebody's little girl.

Now she was a too-beautiful woman but a very real person, doing the best she could in the world, same as everyone else. She was mostly kind; she had her flaws.

She was irresistible. And the reason she was irresistible was because he was falling in love with her.

Strangers with cameras came to photograph her because that was a crazy side effect of her job. It had nothing to do with Travis and Sophia, two people standing on a porch, throwing tomatoes.His arm was already warmed up from a day spent chopping trees and handling horses and sighting down a hunting rifle for one easy tire shot. He picked up a tomato and threw it for distance, centerfield to home plate.

"Wow," she said.

"My dad taught me."

"Do you see your dad very often?"

Rather than answer, he picked up another tomato. Although he'd played shortstop, he took his time like a pitcher on the mound. Wound up. Threw.

"Now you're just showing off."

He winked at her, as if he were still a young college jock. "I can throw a baseball farther than a tomato."

She picked up another one. Studied it. Threw.

"Why are you killing tomatoes?" he asked.

"I'm sick of them." Her little hiss of anger ended in an embarrassed duck of her chin. "It's wasteful, though, isn't it? But I'm not a bad person. They were just rotting in place, anyway."

His heart hurt for her again, for the way she didn't want to be thought of as a bad person. The little girl had grown up to be defensive for a reason. She was judged all the time, not just for whom she dated, but for how her face looked, what she wore, what kind of sandwich she ate.

"I'll tell you a rancher's point of view. The tomatoes came from the land, and you're putting them back into the land. That's not wasteful. Birds are going to come out of nowhere tonight and have a feast, and I bet you'll see a few tomato plants popping up here next spring. In the catalog of possible sins a person could commit, I'd say throwing a tomato is pretty damn minor. You're not a bad person."

"I won't be here next spring." She sounded wistful. It was a gentle warning as well, whether for herself or for him, to not get too attached.

"I know." He threw another tomato, a sidearm hard to first base to beat the runner.

"So, do you see your dad or not?" she asked.

"Dad and I are on speaking terms again."

"What happened?"

"He slept with a married woman. It wasn't with my mother."

"I'm so sorry." Her voice, her posture, all of it softened toward him. For him. "That must have been awful."

"Tore up two families with one affair. But it's been fifteen years. We talk. Take in a game together when I'm in Dallas. Do you see your dad?"

"My dad passed away. The same instant as my mom, actually. Car crash."

He couldn't pick up another tomato.

"It's been ten years. I was nineteen. I became Grace's legal guardian. She was all I had left. She *is* all I have left. Now she's getting m-married."

The tiny stutter said it all.

"In September." She took a breath, and a little of the actress appeared. "Grace came out here today to tell me she'd set the date. She's planning everything without my help, since I'm kind of a liability in public, with the mob scenes and stuff. She's running her own life. She doesn't need me anymore, and I'm so proud of her for that. I really am. And she's happy and excited and everything a bride should be, and I'm so happy about that, too."

Travis waited.

Sophia traced the edge of the tomato basket with her fingertip. "But deep down, I wish she still needed me, and that, for certain, makes me a bad person."

"No, it doesn't."

It was shockingly easy to pull her into his arms. It was shockingly perfect, the way she fit against his chest. She burrowed into him, her cheek on his collarbone. She brought her arms around his back, as if they'd always hugged away the hurt like this, as if they'd always fit together.

"Who is watching?" she asked. Not *Is anyone watching?* Just *who.*

"No one. It's only three o'clock. The men are working."

He set his cheek against her hair, the scent of her shampoo less dominant than the smell of sunshine. She'd spent the day outdoors, then, not in the dark and the air conditioning.

He savored the smell of her skin as he held her, but the embrace was not entirely about comfort. Hunger demanded attention. Travis felt her breasts soft against his chest, felt the heat of her palm on his shoulder blade, and told himself it was enough.

"The paparazzi aren't watching?"

"They won't be back unless they can afford a lot of new tires. They got a flat. It will happen again. Every time."

Tension spiked in her every muscle. "But they'll be back. They'll keep coming back."

He hushed her with a *shh* and another, the same way he soothed a filly being approached by a rider for the first time. "They think Grace might be scouting out the ranch as a place to have her wedding. When she gets married somewhere else in September, they'll stop wondering if her famous sister will show up out here."

"Oh. That's possible. You might be right."

"Don't sound so surprised."

She lifted her cheek. "Don't be so nice to me."

"It's very easy to be nice to you."

She set her hand on the side of his face, and he closed his eyes at the sweet shock of a feminine touch.

It had been a while since he'd been touched by a woman, but it was more than that. It mattered that it was Sophia's fingertips that smoothed their way over his cheek, Sophia's palm that cupped his jaw. Sophia, Sophia—he couldn't get her out of his head, not since the moment he'd first laid eyes on her.

When her thumb traced his lower lip, he opened his eyes just to see her again.

She looked sad. "This has no future."

"What doesn't?" He knew, but he wanted all the cards spread on the table.

"This thing between us. It has nowhere to go."

"I know." He bent his head, and he kissed her. Like the hug, it was as natural as if they'd always kissed. Of course he would press his lips to hers. Of course.

"I don't know where I'll be a year from now. I don't know where I'll be a month from now."

"I know where you are this moment." He placed a kiss carefully on her upper lip, to stop the tears that were threatening to start. "We have this moment."

She kissed him. Her mouth was soft but her kiss was strong. No hesitation. When he thought he'd like to taste her, she opened her mouth and tasted him. In contrast to her words of warning, she kissed him without any doubts.

He had no doubts, either. If this kiss on the porch was all they could ever have, he still wanted it. He needed one moment, just one moment, to stop denying this power between them. Want and need were the same thing: he needed to kiss her more than he wanted to breathe. He wanted to kiss her more than he needed to breathe.

The slide of her tongue was firm and perfect. It satisfied him deep inside, a moment of relief because that hunger had been answered. *Ah, finally, a kiss.* But then the hunger demanded more.

He wanted to know the shape of her, so he let his hands slide and explore. Her body was softer than it looked when she saluted the sun in those God-blessed yoga clothes. Her muscles were relaxed, languid. He shifted their embrace from one of comfort to one of desire. Her hips pressed against his hardness, a moment of bliss—but then he needed more.

Her hands tugged his hair harder than he'd expected. It was just what he wanted, just what he needed—for a moment. Then greed built like a fire, consuming them both. She rose up on her toes to get closer to him, so he cupped her backside and held her tightly in place.

Not tightly enough. She could still move, and she did, sliding up another inch along his hard body, straining for more as they stood on the porch, reaching for something clothing made impossible.

"I'm gonna lose my mind if you do that again." He was warning her, or he was begging her.

"I know. I know." Her words were panted out, raw with need, no purr, no seduction, nothing deliberate.

Still a sex goddess. *More* of a sex goddess.

She couldn't go higher on her toes, but she tried, hands in his hair, flexing her arms, seeking him. If they were only horizontal, she could slide up his body, and it would all work perfectly. They'd fit together, they'd find the release that was desperately needed now, right now, if only they were horizontal—

"Please." She panted the word against his mouth, and he knew exactly what the rest of the desperate plea was. *Please fix this. Please finish this. Please give me what I need.*

He kept one hand buried in her hair, cupping the back of her head, and watched her intently as he opened the door, waiting to see if that was what she really wanted.

It was; she told him what he needed to hear. "Yes."

She knew what she wanted, and she took the first step, bringing him with her, like a dancer leading with an arm around his waist. Two steps brought them inside, and he slammed the door.

Clothes were coming off. His hands slid under the loose green top to the black spandex underneath, the kind of sports bra that never came off easily, damn it, until he felt the hooks in back, thank God. She made short work of his belt with her sure hands while he unfastened her hooks. Her soft breasts spilled free. He filled his hand with one breast, a moment entirely of touch because he could not see her beneath the green top. Not yet.

He kissed her breast through the shirt. In response, she gasped and her hands on his fly shivered to a stop. She was his. She was perfect. This was all he wanted. Then the hunger roared again, and it wasn't enough.

He scooped her top up and over her head. She was so beautifully cooperative, raising her arms so he could draw the shirt completely off, shaking her wrist for him when the bra stuck there.

Together, they tossed away the barriers. She kicked off her sneakers and went to work on the button of his jeans. He dragged his shirt over his head while trying not to lose sight of her bare breasts, as beautiful as the rest of her, with one tiny, dark freckle on the curve of her left breast, just off center of her cleavage, a sexy imperfection he wanted to savor.

She unzipped his fly and slid her hands beneath the waistband to push his jeans to the floor.

Now she hesitated, but the look on her face was one of desire, not fear. After a pause to enjoy the anticipation, she closed the space between them and pressed her nude body against his.

*Yes.* Yes and absolutely yes, it felt absolutely right when she wrapped her arms around his shoulders and wrapped her legs around his waist. He lifted her higher, holding her thighs in his hands as she cried an inarticulate sound that meant *yes*, this was what she'd begged him for. They needed to get horizontal soon, needed to find a bed or a couch or hell, the floor would work—

But all Sophia did was take a breath, and it was enough to align their bodies at just the right angle, with just the right amount of pressure, and he was sheathed inside her.

He rocked backward, leaning against whatever piece of furniture was behind him, completely undone at the sensation. Nothing had ever felt so good, nothing in his life. He couldn't move, couldn't breathe. Sophia was hot and wet and all around him. All his.

Hot and wet, so wet…

He wasn't wearing any protection.

Her breath was in his ear. He rained kisses down her neck. "The pill," he managed to say. "Tell me you're on the pill."

"No. Don't you have a condom?"

He shook his head sharply. It wasn't something a

man needed to carry to work on the open range, damn it all to hell.

"Just—wait—don't—" He steeled himself—the coming sensation was going to be climax-worthy, but he couldn't, not without protection—then he cupped her bottom and slid her up and off his body. He was sweating from the effort to keep control, a desperate man. "Do you have a condom? In your suitcase? Anywhere?"

"No. I swore off men. Forever." She unwrapped her legs from his waist but stood on her toes before him, arms still around his neck, their bodies still pressed tightly together. "I didn't know there would be you. I never thought there could be you."

She kissed him again, loving his mouth the way their bodies wanted to be loving. He kissed her the way he couldn't have her, although God knew they were both willing.

Still, knowing she wanted him eased something in his chest, and her skin felt glorious against his skin, so when she ended the kiss, Travis found that he could smile, even tease her. "So when you said this wasn't going anywhere…"

She gasped-laughed and smacked his chest, but she was quick with the comeback. "You said we had one moment. It sounded kind of romantic at the time, but…" She made a little *shoo* motion with her hand. "There it was. Hope you enjoyed it."

"Oh, hell no. We're having another moment." There were a hundred ways to please a woman, and he was more than willing to try them all with Sophia.

He pushed her just a foot away, so he could finish stepping out of boots and jeans. She watched, then she touched, one finger trailing down his arm, then one finger trailing up the hard length of him.

He cursed softly, and she laughed, because she knew exactly what he meant by that curse.

She bit her lower lip. "The MacDowells lived here, right? Three guys. Don't you think they might have left something behind in a nightstand from their college days?"

Travis kicked the jeans out of his way and they held hands, jogging naked together through the house to the bedroom hallway. From one room to the next, he took the nightstand on the left side of each bed, she the right, but their search turned up nothing.

"They would've probably been expired, anyway," she said, hands on her hips, wrinkling her nose in disappointment while she talked to him, as if it were perfectly natural to chat with him in the nude. "Aren't you guys the same age?"

"Give or take a few years. I'm thirty-one, so yeah, we're looking for ten-year-old condoms."

They laughed at themselves, but the sound of an ATV brought them both to the window to steal a peek, side by side.

"The greenhorn's back from the cedar burn."

"Now what?" she asked.

"Now I hope he doesn't notice Samson's out in the paddock, so I won't have to explain where I've been later." Travis ran his hand lightly down her back, marveling again at the dip of her lower back and the curve of her thigh. "Much later, because I'm not leaving now. We've got some creative moments in the immediate future."

She kissed his cheek, such an absurdly innocent move. "You still smell like smoke."

"Had I known the best moment of my life was going to happen today, I would have showered before stopping by to throw tomatoes. And I would have brought a damned condom. Spontaneity isn't my strong suit."

She touched him, fingertips smoothing their way from his smoky hair down his chest. "You could take a shower here, and I could try to figure out just what your strong suit is."

"Is that shower big enough for two?"

"Let's find out."

Shampoo and slippery soap led to more laughter. Hands made discoveries, laughter faded into something more intense. Bodies were finally, shatteringly satisfied. As far as spontaneous moments went, although they'd been caught unprepared for basic necessities, Travis could have no complaints.

When he was dressed once more and walking the familiar path to his house, it wasn't the sex that occupied his thoughts; it was the moment that had come afterward. Under the steady, soothing stream of the shower, he'd cradled her against his body for a long, long time. Neither one of them had wanted to move. The water had run down their skin, and the silence between them had been as powerful as everything that had come before.

He was in love with her.

It could go nowhere. It was a fluke they'd found themselves on the same ranch. She was leaving, had been destined to leave since before she'd arrived.

They'd had their moment.

As he walked into his empty house, he already knew it would never be enough.

## Chapter Fifteen

"I'm getting married!"

Sophia smiled at her sister's excitement as she pulled groceries out of a brown paper bag. Eggs, flour, real sugar. Sophia had so much time on her hands and such a plethora of Mrs. MacDowell's old cookbooks, she'd decided to try her hand at baking a few things to supplement her frozen dinners. Besides, she could sneak the results of her successful attempts into the barn after dark. Not for the horses, but for Travis, her secret lover for the past two nights.

And tonight. She would definitely find him again tonight after sunset.

With a little thrill inside that she hoped wasn't obvious, she scooped up the five-pound bags of flour and sugar and headed for the pantry, laughing at her excited bride of a sister. "Yes, I know you're getting married.

September twenty-fourth. It will be here before you know it."

"No, I'm getting married in five days, and you're going to be my maid of honor."

Sophia stopped in the middle of the kitchen. "What?"

"Somebody had a big party planned at the place we booked for September, and they canceled it. It's Fourth of July weekend, which might not sound so romantic, but I think it will be special. The rooftop patio overlooks Sixth Street. You can see the Capitol all lit up for the night, and the city will have fireworks going off all around us."

"But that's less than a week away. A wedding in a week?" Sophia held the ten pounds of flour and sugar steadily as she stared at Grace. "Is that even possible?"

"The florist said she could do it. The corporation that canceled their party had already booked a bartender and music, so we're just scooping up the people they had reserved. Kendry and Jamie weren't going out of town for the holiday, anyway, so I have my bridesmaid and Alex has his best man. If you're in the wedding, then Alex wants to ask his friend Kent to be a grooms-man, so we'll have two girls, two guys. Please say yes. It's perfect."

Alex came in the kitchen door. "I found Travis."

And then Travis was right there, hanging his hat on the hook, and Sophia wasn't sure how to act.

Travis had left her bed at dawn in order to get to the barn before his men, or so he hoped. She wondered if he'd made it there first. If he hadn't, then she wondered how he'd explained arriving from the direction of the MacDowells' house and not from his own. Had anyone arrived early from the bunkhouse?

She couldn't tell from Travis's face whether that had happened or not. He stood near the door with his usual impassive cowboy demeanor, but Sophia knew what he looked like when he laughed. She also knew what he looked like when he was at his most primitive, head thrown back, muscles straining, powerless to stop the climax she'd brought him to.

The flour slipped from her arm. She hitched it back up.

Alex looked like a very pleased Clark Kent. "So Grace told you the big news?"

"Just a second ago. I hardly know what to think."

Alex explained to Travis. "We're getting married this weekend."

"Congratulations." Travis stole a look at Sophia. He knew about September. She'd been throwing tomatoes, wishing her sister needed her in September. She hadn't wanted her sister to need her this badly, though. Not badly enough to ruin her own wedding.

"Are you sure this is what you want?" Sophia asked Grace. "There was nothing wrong with September. I'm afraid you're not going to have the wedding you want if you try to cram this in on short notice. What about your cake? What about your dress?"

"There was something definitely wrong with September. You weren't going to be there. You were so nice about it, but when I drove away, I didn't even make it halfway to Austin before I started crying."

"You seemed so happy when you left."

"Well, a hard conversation was over. You'd been so generous about it all, but I realized that I was settling for something I didn't want. I want you in my wedding. I started feeling kind of sorry for myself, that because of the paparazzi and all the pressure you're always under, I wouldn't get my wedding the way I want it. The bride is supposed to get what she wants, right? Well, this bride wants her sister. I sat down and called all the venues on our list one more time. It was my bridezilla moment."

Sophia couldn't help but laugh at Grace's pride in her supposed diva fit. "That's the sweetest bridezilla moment I've ever heard of."

"Seriously, Sophie, it's going to be one of the biggest days of my life, and I need you there. I just can't imagine getting married without my sister as my maid of honor."

"Oh, Grace." The tears were instant, blurring her vision. The sugar slipped from her arm, but somehow Travis caught it before it made a spectacular five-pound splatter on the tile. She smiled up at him through her tears. "Thank you."

"You're welcome." He took the flour from her.

Sophia wasn't sure why Alex had invited Travis in for this little family moment, but she was glad he was here. He'd been there for her when she was upset that her sister didn't seem to need her, so it seemed right that he got to share this happy moment, too.

Now that Travis had freed Sophia's arms, she could hug Grace, precious Grace, the sister who still needed her. "I can't believe you're doing all of this just so I can be in your wedding. Thank you." She turned to Alex. "And thank you. You're okay with this?"

The way his expression softened when he looked at her sister made Sophia feel mushy inside.

"I wanted to marry her yesterday," he said. "I wanted to marry her the day before that, and the day before that.

I'm very okay with this weekend instead of waiting for September. Very."

Sophia squeezed Grace's hands. "So you're doing this. What can I do? What about your dress? Do you want me to call in some favors? You look so good in Vuitton. I could ask them to overnight me some samples in white. I'll tell them it's for a big event. That's the truth, too. I'm sure we'll be photographed enough to make it worth their while."

Grace squeezed Sophia's hands in return. "I already had Mom's wedding gown taken out of storage and shipped here last month. It just needs cleaned and fluffed. The dress shop is going to detach the old crinoline and I'm going to wear a new one underneath, but they have that kind of thing in stock. It's not a problem at all."

"You're wearing Mom's wedding dress?"

Grace bit her lip. "I should have asked you. The crinoline is a minor alteration, I promise."

"You don't need my permission. I'm not your boss. It's as much your dress as mine."

"Yes, but is it okay with you?"

"You're going to be such a beautiful bride, you're going to make me cry, anyway, but this is really going to be unfair. I'm going to look like a blubbering mess in all your photos."

Because being with her sister felt like her old life, Sophia started brainstorming their usual plans. "We'll have to fly Tameka in to give me bulletproof makeup. If my nose turns red, I'll be in all the gossip rags as a coke addict or something. That's just what we need when I'm trying to let the controversy die down. We can fly in Jolin with Tameka. She does such great hair."

"No." Because this was not their old life, Grace interrupted. "I've already got a hairstylist here. Austin isn't exactly a backwater. My stylist is really good. The only person we're flying in from LA is you."

"Me?"

"It will look that way. We're going to sneak you off this ranch and fly you to the Dallas airport. You'll get a nice first-class seat from Dallas back to Austin. Everyone will text their friends that you're on their plane, and when you land here, the paparazzi will assume you flew in for the wedding. You, me and Kendry are going to set up base in a hotel suite, so that Alex doesn't see us before the big day."

Alex turned to Travis. "Which brings us to why I asked you to stop in. Texas Rescue, completely by coincidence, has decided to conduct a training exercise tomorrow. It involves extracting a practice patient by helicopter and transporting her to the Dallas airport's medevac facilities. We were wondering if we might be able to use this ranch as the starting point. It looks like you've got plenty of room for a helicopter to land around here somewhere."

As Travis and Alex worked out locations and timing for her escape, Sophia stood at the counter with Grace, pretending to be absorbed by their conversation. She really just wanted to look at Travis.

She reached into the brown paper grocery bag, and pulled out a random box. Instant oatmeal. That was fine.

But Travis, ah, Travis, he was more than fine, and he would be hers tonight.

Another box. Toothpaste. Fine.

She would have to make the memories of the coming night last for the next five days, though. The thought of not seeing Travis for nearly a week was hard. She'd just found him. Once she left for Austin—

"Sophia." Grace jerked Sophia out of her fantasy. She was shaking her head *no* as she pushed Sophia's hand back into the grocery bag.

"What is it?" Sophia looked into the bag. In her hand, she held the neat, rectangular box of a pregnancy test. She stared at it in horror; she'd almost taken it right out and set it on the counter.

"Why?" she whispered. "Why would you do this?"

Grace pulled her out of the kitchen with an artificial smile for Alex. "Girl stuff to talk about. Shoes for the dresses. Be back in a second."

Sophia yanked her arm free in the living room, the same room in which she'd stripped Travis just two short days ago, the room in which he'd stripped her. She wanted to stay that way, bared to him, unafraid to be her true self. He'd seen her tears and tantrums, her scars, her fears. When she'd thought she was being terrible, he'd stood beside her and thrown tomatoes at the world. Dear God, he'd said it was easy to be nice to her. He'd kissed every inch of her body.

Now Grace had brought a pregnancy test into her kitchen.

"Why?" Sophia pleaded.

"You need to know, Sophie. You can't keep telling yourself maybe it was a bad test, maybe you'll get your period. Once you know for certain, you can decide what you want to do."

*No!* The word was stuck in her head. She didn't dare say it out loud; it would come out as a scream that echoed off the rafters of this great big lonely house.

Grace had it so wrong. Sophia would *not* get to decide what she wanted to do. Once she knew for certain, then she would have no choice but to deal with adoption agencies and obstetricians. She'd have to deal with Deezee in the worst possible way.

What she wanted to do was spend more time with Travis. That would no longer be an option, because what she would have to do was tell him she was pregnant by another man, and her time with him would be over.

She'd always known her time with him would be short. This wasn't her house. This wasn't her career. She could not hide here forever and go broke. But dear God, when she'd stripped herself bare in this room, she'd thought she'd have more than two days. She needed more than two days.

"Sophie?"

"July seventh." The words sounded polite, if stiff. They should have sounded like they'd been ripped from her soul. "I should get my period on the sixth or seventh. If I don't, I'll do the test."

Sophia forced herself to relax her shoulders, and tilt her head just so, and let the tiniest bit of an encouraging smile reach her eyes. "So in the meantime, let's set that aside and focus on your wedding. I wouldn't want to have to tangle with Bridezilla Gracie. She sounds pretty fearsome."

Judging from the relieved hug Grace gave her, Sophia Jackson had just delivered another Oscar-worthy performance.

## Chapter Sixteen

Sunset finally came.

The men left for the day—the young bachelors to crash in the bunkhouse, Clay to his own place off the ranch—and Travis experienced the piercing anticipation of having Sophia all to himself.

At the first sound of the barn door sliding open, he left his office and headed for her, his boots loud on the concrete, and he knew he had the arrogant smile of a man who knew he was minutes away from getting exactly what he wanted with the only woman he wanted it from.

"Sophia."

Her sneakers were silent and so was she, tackling him so that he caught her and they turned 180 degrees, his arms around her body, her hands in his hair, their mouths meeting. It was like this every night now, this first moment of pent-up desire that had to be released in a crashing kiss.

He set her back on her feet, but she began kissing her way from just under his jaw down his neck.

He loved it, but he had to ask. "Are we celebrating a good day or blowing off steam after a frustrating day?"

She shook her hair back. "So many emotions."

"The scene with your sister? That had to be a good emotion." He didn't know why she couldn't have made the wedding in September, but clearly, the coming weekend had worked out for everyone.

Sophia locked her hands together behind his waist, as he did to her. Hips pressed together, focused on one another, they talked among the disinterested horses. Travis enjoyed the prelude; Sophia wasn't the only one who looked forward to having someone to talk to every day.

"I thought my role in Grace's life was kind of over. I can't believe she wants me in her wedding that badly. Just as badly as I wanted to be there."

"I can. If you were my sister, you'd be my hero, too."

"Hero." She wrinkled her nose.

"You stepped in when your parents died. You saved the day when her life could've easily fallen apart. You achieved your own success at the same time, and pretty damned spectacularly. I started downloading the line-up of movies that you star in. I didn't realize there were so many."

"I wouldn't say I starred in them all, if any. Except for *Pioneer Woman*, most were just small parts. Supporting actress or ensemble work, at best."

He gave her a tug, pressing her more tightly against the hardness that was inevitable when she was in his arms. "It's impressive. You're a hero, but I thank the heavens every day that you are not my sister."

She deflected his praise. "I hope I didn't show how surprised I was when Alex came in the kitchen door with you. It was kind of fun to have to pretend we're just neighbors, or whatever we are. You were a very good actor, by the way."

"Poker face. I could hardly look at that blue tile countertop now that I know it is exactly the right height for—"

She stood on her toes and twined one leg around his. "For a midnight snack?"

He dropped that casual kiss on her lips, the one that a man could give a woman when he knew he had time with her. He took her hand to lead her to his office. "We need to talk about who knows you're here, though."

He sat in the desk chair, knowing she'd sit in his lap and drape an arm over his shoulder. She did, but she was frowning. "Who knows I'm here?"

"Just the MacDowells who signed the lease, and Grace and Alex. But someone else who is physically on the property should be aware, for days I'm not here. I want to let… I want…what are you doing?"

"I'm leaving tomorrow for five days. I want to stock up on my moments." She turned to straddle him.

He laughed a little until he realized she was serious. Her hand slipped in his back pocket for the protection he was now never without. She stood to wriggle out of her shorts. When she started to undo his jeans, he didn't object, not in the least, but there was an edginess about her tonight that wasn't familiar.

"There's a perfectly good bed about a hundred yards away from here," he said.

"I want you to think of me while I'm gone. Every time you sit in this chair, I want you to remember a special moment."

That didn't need an answer. It was obvious he'd never look at this chair the same way again. But there was that underlying edginess again, so he answered her anyway. "I'm never going to forget you, Sophia. Not one moment."

She looked at him, blue eyes filled with what he could only call longing, and he wondered for the millionth time if this thing between them was really destined to end.

She closed her eyes and kissed him as she tore open the foil wrapper. With her hands, she sheathed him. With her body, she sheathed him again, and he was lost to any kind of further analysis except *yes* and *more*.

He unbuttoned her cotton shirt, exposing the inner curves of breasts shaped by pink lace. He kissed the precious freckle first, then tasted as much softness as he could through the lace. She rode him, making him shudder almost immediately with the need to maintain some semblance of control. With his hands, he tilted her hips to make sure she was making the contact she needed for her own satisfaction.

She put two fingertips on his forehead and pushed his head back against the chair, then grabbed his wrist and moved his hand to the arm of the chair. Leaning forward, pink lace so close to his face, she spoke into his ear. "Hey, Travis? Sit back and relax. I've got this."

She did. She definitely did.

He tried to take in the moment, tried to comprehend that this dream was real, so unbelievably, incredibly real. When they reached their completion, Sophia collapsed against him, her head on his shoulder. As her soft breath warmed his neck, he wrapped her tightly in his arms and savored this moment, too.

The tenderness stayed with him, every time. Sophia seemed to want it as much as she needed the physical release. She was a sex goddess who cuddled afterward. He was the man who appreciated just how irresistible that combination was.

It might be impossible to live without it.

She wriggled closer yet, keeping him inside her. His body felt thick and full, but sated—for now. It was clear to him that the hunger for her would never be satisfied for long.

"I can't believe I have to leave you for five days," she said. "I don't want to. Not when we've just discovered each other."

He kissed the top of her head. Twirled a strand of silver and gold around his index finger.

She pouted. "It's kind of like the honeymoon phase, you know? That's a rotten time to be apart. It's not like we're some old married couple and we've been together ten years or whatever. Then five days wouldn't be such a big deal."

Was she trying to convince herself that the power between them was just a novelty, a new toy they'd lose interest in someday? Surely an old boyfriend hadn't lost interest in her and looked for greener pastures somewhere else.

"Sophia Jackson, if you push me into a desk chair and straddle my lap ten years from now, you will get exactly the same response from me. Ten years from now, twenty years from now, I will never have had enough of you."

The moment was suddenly charged with tension instead of tenderness. He'd crossed a line. He'd said something he shouldn't have, not when she'd told him from the first that this thing between them was going nowhere. It certainly wasn't going ten years into the future.

He wouldn't take it back. It was true: he would want her forever. He brushed the lock of her hair across his lips, and let it go.

She picked up her head and sat up a little straighter, then smiled as if she didn't have a care in the world. "I'm looking forward to making more moments. We've got to stock up five days in one night. I hope you ate a big lunch."

It was cute. She was overlooking his serious statement, offering to get them back on track. It was her olive branch.

He accepted it. "We may have to build in a dinner break. It will be more than five days. I spend a week with my family every Fourth of July."

Abruptly, the conversation was serious again. "You won't be here when I get back from the wedding?"

"Not for the rest of the week."

"No, you can't leave," she pleaded, startling him with her intensity.

He slid his hands up her ribs and gave her a reassuring squeeze. "I can't leave the ranch in May, but I do take time off. July is the slowest month for ranching. The calving's done, the weaning hasn't started. The cattle have plenty of natural grass to graze on. If I'm going to leave, this is the time to do it."

"You won't be here when I get back from the wedding? You'll be gone the rest of the week?"

"Right." He tried to soothe her with a smile. He offered his own olive branch, an easy way to keep things light. "But I'll make it up to you when I get back."

"Can you change your plans?"

The edginess was unmistakable, as if it were critical that he be available this week just so they could sneak into bed together after sunset. As if time were short, and this week in particular was all they had.

Something was so obviously wrong, dangerously wrong.

He held her more tightly. Her ribs expanded with each panicky breath between his palms.

"My family's expecting me. My mom, my grandparents, brothers, sisters. Most of us are in ranching one way or the other, so this is our big holiday get-together. Kind of like Christmas for the Chalmers family."

He shouldn't be able to speak so calmly. How could he explain the mundane routine of his life when the best thing to ever happen to him was literally about to slip from his grasp?

She put her hands on his shoulders, prepared to use him for leverage as she stood, but he stopped her, a reflexive grip to keep her from leaving.

Her fingers dug into his shoulders, as if she didn't want to leave, either. "When will you be back?"

"Sunday." He tried to make it sound as normal as it was.

"What date is that? July tenth? Eleventh? It's past the seventh, for sure."

"Something like that. I'd have to look at a calendar."

She said nothing, but misery was written all over her face.

"For God's sake, Sophia. Be up front with me. Is this your last week in Texas or something?"

"No, it's nothing. I hope. I don't know. I don't know what I'll be dealing with next week. This thing between us…"

She kept stopping, running out of words. He couldn't tell if she was angry or frustrated, nor if it was directed at him or at herself.

"What about this thing between us?"

"I knew it couldn't last long," she said defensively. "I told you there was no future in it."

"This thing." He was disgusted with the term. "You mean this connection. We are connected in every way we can be at this moment. So at this moment, you owe me, Sophia. What are your plans? What's happening after this week? You can't just disappear without a word."

She looked away. "I don't think I will."

"You 'don't think'? What kind of answer is that?"

He deserved more. They deserved more.

"I don't even know how long your lease is for." He was angry that he should have to fight for basic information from her. He released her abruptly, but she clutched him as if he was her lifesaver.

What was going on?

She set her forehead against his, pinning him in place with such an intimate motion. Their noses touched as she whispered. "I have the house until January, the whole time Mrs. MacDowell's on her mission trip."

"But? Talk to me, Sophia."

"I swear I don't know what's next, Travis. The future is really up in the air, but believe me that I'm not ready for this to end. I want to be here when you come back. I do."

He wanted to take all these intense, bewildering emotions and push them into passion, make love to her until they were reduced to what they understood, communication of the most basic needs. His body was growing hard inside her. He couldn't talk like this, and hunger be damned, they needed to talk.

He set her aside, stood and turned his back to her. Got rid of the condom. Tucked his shirt in. Prayed for... God knew what. Just a prayer: *please.*

*Please, let me keep her a little longer.* She was everything to him.

What was he to her? Someone she might leave, someone she might not?

He turned around. She stood in his ranch office in her sneakers and short-shorts, with her million-dollar hair and lovely features. She didn't look like anything else in his world. She had no connection to his life.

And yet this *thing*, this power, this connection between them existed whether it should or not.

He'd known from the beginning she wasn't going to stay. Knowing it and facilitating a helicopter to take her away were two different things.

He forced himself to ask the question. "Are you going back to LA? Since the wedding forced you out of hiding, are you done here?"

"We'll make it look like I'm flying back to LA, just like we're making it look like I'm living there now. Grace is basically inviting the paparazzi to find her wedding by making sure I'm seen flying in. All I can do in return is try to appease the paparazzi so they don't get too aggressive and ruin her big day. I've got to stop and answer when they shout questions at me, smile while they take photos. They'll tell me to 'look this way' or 'twirl around and show us your outfit,' and I'll have to do it so they'll go away."

She trailed her fingers over the computer keyboard on his desk. "It will help. They love a cooperative star. But it won't be enough to bury all the negative publicity I already generated, so I'll come back here after the wedding. I need to continue staying off their radar."

She flicked a glance his way. He was sure his relief showed. He felt like he could breathe again.

She pushed the space bar on his keyboard, but nothing happened. He'd powered the machine down for the day.

"Have you never typed 'Sophia Jackson' in your search bar, just to see what horrible things I did?"

He shook his head.

"You weren't tempted, even a little bit?"

"Braden told me enough."

"Oh. The ball. I don't think all those Texas Rescue people are going to be too thrilled to see me at the wedding. Alex is one of their doctors, you know. Half of the guest list volunteers for them. Maybe they'll give me a second chance to make a first impression." Her gaze drifted from the keyboard to the floor as she shrugged one shoulder. "Just kidding—I know it doesn't work that way."

Perhaps Sophia had brought it on herself, but Travis feared she was going to be very uncomfortable for her sister's sake. She was going to appease the paparazzi. She was going to spend a night with people who had reason to think badly of her.

There wasn't a thing he could do to erase Sophia's

past. Not one thing, but he tried to offer her some encouragement. "Braden had less to say about you than about the guy that jumped on your table."

She looked up quickly at that. "You know about Deezee?"

"Braden said he stepped on his wife's dinner and gave you a crappy apology."

"That's as good a summary as any, I suppose." She gave a halfhearted chuckle.

"Do you think he'll show up again?" Travis had that restless feeling again, that need to keep an eye on her—but Texas was a big state, and he'd be almost three hundred miles away with his family on the wedding day.

"That was all orchestrated by his publicist. Deezee is too lazy to set anything up himself, so I doubt it."

Travis couldn't leave without making sure she had some kind of plan in place. "If he does, don't try to appease him. Don't try to calm him down or take him aside. If he wants attention, you won't be able to save your sister's wedding from his type."

"The only reason he'd be there would be because of me. I think I'd owe it to everyone to try to stop him."

"Let Alex handle it. It's his wedding, not yours. Jamie MacDowell's the best man, right? You're the maid of honor, so you should be near Jamie. And you know Braden."

"He kind of hates me."

"He doesn't. You'll be safe with the MacDowells. Quinn will probably be there, too."

"I take it Quinn is the third one in all the family portraits at the house. I'll only recognize him if he still has braces and a bad middle school haircut."

"I'm serious, Sophia. I don't want you trying to deal with this Deezee jerk."

For once, he wished the paparazzi had been right. He wished Grace had been setting up a wedding tent here on the ranch. He'd be here in September. He'd be here if Sophia got harassed. Hell, she wouldn't get harassed on his ranch in the first place. That was the point of her hiding here.

But now she was going to fly away, without him.

She acted like she didn't care, scoffing like she was some kind of tough street kid. "Deezee's got no game. It would just be a lot of noise. Same old, same old. While you're gone, you can log on to your favorite celebrity site and see if anything exciting happened. If it's really juicy, it might make TV. That would be a fun topic around your family dinner table. 'Look what this crazy chick who's staying on my ranch did.'"

He recognized the voice: she sounded like the woman in the thigh-high black boots, the one who said she didn't care when she cared so desperately. He knew her, and he loved her. It made him sick to think that he might have come home to find her gone to LA forever.

It would happen, sooner or later. In the meantime, he wanted to cherish her while he could, yet they were standing on opposite sides of a desk chair.

"I'm sorry, Sophia."

"For what? I'm the one who hooked up with a loser. But hey, I've helped countless people make a living off entertainment gossip as a result. It's all good."

That scoff. It was such an act. She couldn't hide her pain from him.

He sent the chair rolling and hugged her. She held herself stiffly, as if she didn't need affection. He held her as if they'd just finished another round of amazing sex instead of a round of bad feelings and painful subjects, because she needed to skip right to the tenderness. So did he.

"I'm sorry you can't go anywhere without a camera in your face. I'm sorry you need a place to hide in the first place."

She made a small sound, a yip of pain like a hurt animal, and then she was hugging him back, burrowing into him in that way she had.

He realized she was physically hiding. He wrapped his arms around her more tightly, cupping the back of her head with his hand, letting her hide her face behind his forearm. He was grateful his life's work had given him the muscle she could literally hide behind.

"You've got a safe place here. Go do your wedding and get the paparazzi eating out of your hand. When you're done, come back here, and be safe."

She took a shivery breath. "But you won't be here."

It wasn't just the sex, then. It wasn't even the friendship and the camaraderie. She felt safer around him.

"I'll be back Sunday. Until then, Clay will know you're here. You won't be alone."

She shook her head against the idea. "Don't tell Clay. The more people who know about me, the less safe I am. Grace and I learned that the hard way. It's been just me and Grace for years."

"But now it's you and Grace and Alex and me, and you're still safe. You could depend on Clay, too." He stopped cupping her head and moved to lift her chin instead, wanting her to see that she had options. "You know Jamie and his wife, Kendry. Count on them. Braden MacDowell and his wife. She's a doctor. She

knows how to keep someone's confidentiality. Quinn
and his wife are trustworthy."

"I've never trusted that many people. Ever."

"But you could. The ranch that owns the Appaloosa
is just a few miles away, and the Waterson family is
as solid as they come. When the paparazzi came calling, all I had to tell Luke was that the MacDowells had
a houseguest, and he was there for me, no questions
asked. You don't have to be so very alone, Sophia."

He let go of her chin to caress her face, not surprised
his hand wasn't quite steady. He had too much emotion
coursing through him. He loved her so damned much,
and he wanted to give her this gift. "I'll build you a
whole safety net here, baby. You can come here to stay."

She wanted it. He could see it in her expression as
clear as day, but she didn't say yes. It hurt her not to say
yes, but she didn't say it.

She raised her own unsteady hand to touch his face.
"I love… I love that you care."

"I care."

"Did I ever tell you my secret fantasy about you?"

She was done with this moment of tenderness, then.
It wasn't enough for Travis, but he was a patient man.
He couldn't force Sophia to trust him any more than
he could force a horse to trust him. Things took time.
Things had to be earned.

For her, he would meet her on her terms. She wanted
to talk fantasies.

"Does this fantasy have to do with more office furniture?" he asked.

But her smile was fleeting.

"In my fantasy, you take me on a date. We have a
drink together at a place with a nice dance floor, and

we talk while we have our first dance. By the second dance, maybe we stop talking, because it's so special to be moving in sync, and thinking this is a person you'd like to know better. You drive me home and say good-night, and you tell me you'd like to see me again. There are no cameras. No one calls me names on social media. No one runs a background check on you. No one cares at all, except the two of us, because we're the ones falling in love."

His heart squeezed so hard, he could only whisper her name.

"But it's a fantasy, you see, because that will never happen. This thing between us, it has no future, no matter how much I wish it did."

They had a future. He just didn't know what it looked like yet. But Sophia was afraid now, skittish and spooked, and he needed to be patient.

"We have this moment," she said.

He tried not to be spooked himself at the way she said the words, as if this could be their last moment.

"How would you like to spend it?" he asked.

"I want to make love to you all night and pretend that I don't have to leave for a wedding tomorrow."

"Then that's what we'll do."

He scooped her up as if she were the bride and carried her out of the barn.

# *Chapter Seventeen*

Sophia was the weird one.

She stuck out like a sore thumb at the reception, and nobody wanted to talk to her. She'd thought she was lonely at the ranch during that first month, but she'd forgotten how lonely she could be when surrounded by people. She just didn't fit in.

It had started at the airport. The flight attendants had been so deferential, but she'd told herself they treated all the first-class passengers that way. Then the passengers had started holding their cell phones at slightly odd angles, and she'd known she was being photographed. *OMG. Look who is on my plane!*

She couldn't even go to the bathroom like a normal person. She had to practically clean the bathroom before she left, careful to make sure she left no drops of liquid soap or a crumpled paper towel that would mark her as a slob. *OMG. Sophia Jackson left the lid down on the toilet. Does that mean she went number two?*

The only time she'd been able to forget she was different than everyone else had been in the hotel, when it had been only her, Grace and Kendry MacDowell. Kendry had overcome that invisible distance between celebrity and fan pretty quickly, and they'd had such fun as co-conspirators, trying to make Grace laugh through her bridal jitters. If only there were more Kendry Mac-Dowells in the world...

*I'll build you a whole safety net here, baby.*

Travis. That man was something special. That man deserved a good life with a good woman, not with an outcast like her.

*OMG. Sophia Jackson is at this wedding reception. She eats only shrimp and strawberries. What a freak.*

Sophia stood in no-man's land, somewhere between the bar and the band. It was too embarrassing to sit at the head table, because Grace and Alex were on the dance floor, as were Kendry and Jamie. The other groomsman, Kent, was a bachelor who'd been pulled onto the dance floor by a group of single women who weren't letting him go any time soon. Sophia couldn't sit at the table alone.

*OMG. Sophia Jackson is like a total bitch. She won't speak to anyone.*

She kept a pleasant, neutral smile on her face and watched her sister glow with happiness.

The wedding ceremony had been gorgeous, a traditional service in a white church. At one point it struck her that Kendry was standing next to her with a tiny life growing in her belly. What if she, Sophia, were doing the same? In the hush of the church, surrounded by flowers and lace, pregnant had seemed like an ultra-feminine, almost divine thing to be. Even if Sophia wasn't going to raise the baby herself, it was a miracle.

Would Travis see it that way?

It wasn't July seventh. She didn't have to worry about that yet. With luck, she'd never have to worry about that.

She glanced at the roof of an adjacent building. She'd been holding still too long. The cameraman had a clear angle to her. She moved to the other side of the bandstand.

"May I have this dance?"

Travis. The man behind her sounded just like Travis, and when she turned around, she saw that the handsome man in the suit and tie was Travis.

"It's you. Oh, it's so good to see you. I'm dying to hug you, but there are at least four telephoto lenses on us right this second from a roof and two balconies."

"I missed you, too. Would you care to dance?"

"That would be lovely, thank you."

The band was playing a slower song, the kind where the man and woman could hold each other in a civilized ballroom pose and sway together, even if it was their first dance. She really almost felt like crying, it was so perfect.

"I didn't know you were here," she said. "I didn't see you at the ceremony."

"I saw you. You looked radiant up there. Whatever you were thinking, it looked good on your face."

This was their first dance, but they weren't strangers. Sophia lowered her voice. "I may have been thinking about you and a certain desk chair?"

"I don't think so."

"You and a kitchen counter?"

"Wrong again."

Oh, this was wonderful, to dance and flirt and feel like she belonged at the party. "How do you know what I was thinking?"

"Because I know the look on your face when you think of countertops and chairs, and that wasn't it. Probably a good thing when you're standing in a church."

It was wonderful to be with Travis, who knew her and didn't ask about filming *Space Maze* or whether she'd done her own stunts in *Pioneer Woman*.

"So what do you think I was thinking?"

"You were probably thinking about the child you helped raise, and how she's turned into a lovely woman. Grace is a beautiful bride. You must be very proud of her. I'm very proud of you."

Sophia felt her happiness dim. She had been thinking about a child, but it was one that, if it existed, would end this fantasy with Travis sooner rather than later.

"Grace was a teenager when I took over, not a child."

"You need to learn how to take a compliment. For example, you look very beautiful all dressed up. I've only ever seen you in yoga clothes and shorts. And one pair of thigh-high black boots. What did you do with those boots, by the way?"

She smiled. "I didn't know you owned a suit. It's kind of surreal to see you away from the ranch."

"Now that is exactly how not to return a compliment. I think you're very intriguing, though. Can I get you a drink?"

That's when it hit her. "Travis Chalmers. You're giving me my fantasy, aren't you?"

But he'd already turned to introduce her to a man he knew. Then a woman. He got the conversation onto a topic that everyone found interesting, and then he melted into the crowd. She hated to see him go, but she knew it would save anyone from guessing they were a couple.

She danced with some of the men she talked to. Then Travis returned for a second dance, as she'd known he would. A drink, two dances, an invitation to go out again: the fantasy she had said would never come true.

They swayed in silence this time, not just because that had been her fantasy, but because her heart was too full to speak for at least two verses and a chorus.

"This isn't just about my fantasy, is it? You came to make sure that the Texas Rescue people gave me a second chance."

"I think they like you. God knows the men are happy enough to dance with you. They just needed to see me do it first, so they'd know you were a mortal even though you look like a goddess. Beauty can intimidate people."

Tears stung her eyes. That hadn't felt like a compliment as much as a benediction. Travis believed in her. She didn't want to be the weird one, even if it meant she was the beautiful weird one, and he understood that.

"Clay is going to call you to tell you if I make it home safely, isn't he?"

"Yes, he knows you're living in the house now. I told you that I would do anything to help you whether you liked it or not. Telling Clay was one of those things. I couldn't leave you isolated in hiding. Anything could happen, even a house fire, and no one would have known you were there. It wasn't safe. Clay knows, and only Clay knows."

Subdued, humbled, she asked, "Where's Deezee?"

"He's working at a club in Las Vegas tonight. You won't be embarrassed by him, and your sister has already forgotten he exists."

*I love you.*

She wanted to say it, she was dying to say it, but Deezee did exist, and her sister wouldn't be the only one reminded of it if July seventh turned out the way Sophia feared.

"I'd like to see you again, Sophia. I'll be out of town for the rest of the week, but could I take you to dinner on Sunday? There's a place just outside of Austin that I think you'd enjoy."

She tried to play her role. "Really? Where?"

"My house. Genuine Texas cuisine."

She wrinkled her nose. "Zucchini and tomatoes?"

"Steak and a baked potato. Dress is casual. I'll pick you up at eight."

Her voice was thick with tears as the song and her fantasy ended. "I'll see you on Sunday. Have a nice visit with your family."

By Sunday, she would know one way or the other. Either she'd tell Travis she loved him, or she'd tell him she was pregnant with another man's child.

They had to part without a kiss.

Sophia wondered if she'd ever get a chance to kiss him again.


July sixth came and went without any hoopla. Sophia talked to Clay a bit and to Samson a lot.

The seventh came and went as well. Sophia tried throwing a few tomatoes, but it was too lonely without Travis leaning on a pillar, evaluating her technique. Instead, she breathed in the shimmering hot air as she poked around the front yard until she found the goose salt shaker, dirty but unbroken. She took it into the house and scrubbed it until there was no trace of evidence that Sophia had once pitched it into the night sky.

On the eighth, she had to do the pregnancy test. She'd promised. She intended to, but she felt that need to hibernate. She slept most of the day, and by the time evening fell, she thought it would be best to wait until morning. She'd gone back to Mrs. MacDowell's 1980s pregnancy handbook and flipped through the opening pages gingerly, with one finger. There seemed to be something magical about the first urine of the day. So really, she might as well go to bed and do the test first thing in the morning.

On the morning of the ninth, she took the test. She could no longer fool herself: she was pregnant.

She cried the entire day.

The movies had gotten it all wrong. The end of the world was not an isolated, brown landscape.

Sophia woke to summer sunshine pouring in her bedroom window, mixing with the bluebonnet paintings on the walls. It was beautiful.

But it was Sunday.

Travis was coming back, and at eight in the evening, he'd pick her up to take her back to his house for dinner. There, she was going to tell him that she was pregnant with another man's child, that she'd been pregnant all along but too stubborn and willful to admit it to herself, and because of that, she'd sucked him into a hopeless situation.

It was the end of the world.

Black seemed like the appropriate color. Sophia

dressed in black yoga clothes, tied on her sneakers, and went to visit the horses.

As always, Samson liked her best. She leaned on his great, warm neck and wished someone would yell *cut*.

The barn door slid open. After five days back in the public eye in Austin, that old reflex to keep her appearance together had returned. She stood properly, shoulders back and down, ankles together, hand on hip—but with her other hand, she tickled Samson under his chin. She hoped it was only Clay coming back for something he'd forgotten. No matter what Travis said, she didn't want more people knowing she was hiding on the ranch.

"Now, this is a fantasy."

"Travis." She drank in the sight of him as he stood just inside the barn door. He looked so achingly good, as if she hadn't seen him for a year instead of a week. Less than that, since he'd surprised her at her sister's wedding.

"To see a woman as beautiful as you are hanging out in cute shorts, talking to my horses, well, you just know that's some rancher's fantasy. Luckily, I'm a rancher."

She wanted to run and throw herself in his arms the way she always did, spinning him halfway around with the impact.

But she was pregnant. She held still.

Travis had no hesitation. He strode toward her, single-minded, confident. He scooped her up and spun her around, bringing enough momentum for the two of them.

His arms felt so strong. He smelled so good. Somehow, she'd been so focused on how they were going to be apart, it was startling to have him here—and still so happy with her.

Because he didn't know. Not yet.

"I didn't think I'd see you until dinner." How could her voice sound so normal when she was dying inside?

"I missed you," he said.

"I missed you, too." It was true. Surely she was allowed to say that.

He linked his arms around her waist, the way they did when they settled in to catch up on how their days had gone. Had he missed just talking to her? She thought her heart might burst.

"I watched a couple of your movies because I missed you so much."

She was grateful to talk about anything except what she needed to talk about. "Which ones?"

He named the crime drama, the one with the smoking-hot sex scene.

"Oh. That one." She felt her cheeks warm as she looked toward the tack room. She couldn't hold his gaze.

"I want credit for keeping my eyes on yours and not letting them drop lower, but if you don't look at me, how will you know how good I am at pretending I'm not thinking about your body?"

He sounded amused.

She looked at him then. "That scene doesn't bother you? I mean, knowing anyone could watch it?" She knew so many fellow actors whose significant others were bothered greatly by those kinds of scenes, even when carefully arranged bedsheets protected privacy. Her costar's girlfriend had been standing by as they filmed that one, anxious and jealous and making the role ten times harder to play. She'd been far more of a diva than any actress Sophia had worked with.

Travis kept his arms locked around her waist. "I've

seen rated R movies my entire adult life without thinking twice about it, but it is strange when you know one of the actors. It took a few scenes for me to adjust to hearing you speak with a Boston accent. If you're worried about the sex scene, don't be. I could tell it wasn't real."

"Oh, it's not. It's really not. There are a dozen people working, and you have to hold yourself in the most unnatural way, and there was this awful bubblegum smell, and I remember being thirsty and worried about how to deliver this line that I didn't think my character would really say, and they put makeup on everything. I mean everything."

"I know."

"You do?"

In the moment of silence that followed, she forgot they had no future. She could only think how lucky she'd be to have such an even-tempered man as her partner in life.

"How?" she asked, holding her breath.

"It didn't look real to me. Not the look on your face, which was sexy as hell, don't get me wrong, but it wasn't what you really look like with me."

"Oh."

He kissed her lightly. "You look sexier with me."

"Oh."

"I could guess about the makeup because your freckle was missing. The one that's right here." Without taking his eyes from hers, he placed his finger precisely on a spot just above the edge of her bra, on her left breast, exactly where she knew she had a little black dot.

"Oh. They hide that all the time, even if I'm just wearing a low cut gown or a bathing suit."

His grin slowly grew into a smile. "Good. I love it. I'll keep it to myself. The audience doesn't get the same you that I get."

She wanted to smile back, but she was dying inside. *We have no future. We have no future.*

"The movie I'll never watch again was the pioneer one," he said.

"That was my best. Everyone says so." The words came out by rote despite her frantic thoughts.

"You died. I don't ever want to know if that looked realistic. I can't watch that one again."

He kissed her as if he couldn't bear to lose her, and she kissed him back the same way. *No future, no future.*

She would lose him, soon, but she wasn't ready to say the words. She was supposed to have had until eight o'clock to prepare herself to say the words.

"Why are you here? I mean, why did you leave your family so early for me?"

"That was why—for you. I couldn't wait until tonight to see you. I just gave Clay the rest of the day off. I realize your fantasy includes a very traditional dinner that might end in a peck on the cheek, but I was going to try to persuade you to try a different fantasy now."

Her body was her traitor in every way. She knew she couldn't sleep with Travis again, but her body didn't care, pregnant or not. Just being near him was enough to make her come awake and alive once more.

Patch saved the day. With outstanding timing, she ran into the barn to greet Travis as if he'd been gone ten years.

Sophia stepped back to give the dog room. She pretended she didn't see the quizzical look Travis threw her.

"How're you doing, Patch?" He bent down to pet her with both hands. There was something odd about the way he did it, almost like he was checking something, deliberately feeling his way from the dog's shoulders to her tail. "Still feeling good, girl?"

Sophia grasped at the distraction. "Is there something wrong with her?"

Travis stood again. "I wouldn't say it's wrong. She's going to have puppies. Judging from the amount of time she's been spending in Samson's stall, she's planning on having them there. I'll have to move Samson when she gets a little closer. They're best friends, but I wouldn't want him to step on a puppy."

Sophia felt her stomach tying itself into knots. "I can't take another abandoned animal crying from starvation. Is there replacer milk for puppies? Do you have any? We should get some right away. Right away."

She must have overreacted. Travis's quizzical look deepened into concern. "Patch is a good mother. This is her second litter, so I don't anticipate any problems, but sure, we'll keep some replacer milk here. I won't leave you with a starving newborn again, I promise."

He kissed her again, not on the lips, but on the forehead.

She told herself that was for the best. It was already starting, this transition from lovers to friends that she was going to rely on. She'd had time, too much time, to think about her options, and no matter what Grace had said, there weren't many.

Sophia had nowhere else to hide. She was going to have to stay on this ranch for the duration of her pregnancy, and that meant she was going to see Travis. Staying on good terms with him was essential, because frankly, she was scared to death to be without him.

She had a good speech she needed to be ready to deliver tonight that talked about how they'd be able to coexist quite nicely together despite their history. It left out the part about being scared.

Until tonight's dinner, she needed to not freak out. She smiled brightly at Travis. "First the cat, now the dog. Is everything on this ranch pregnant?"

Travis kept looking at her, but she told herself he was smiling indulgently. "We try to keep it that way."

She tossed her hair, praying for normalcy. "You know that sounds terrible, right?"

"That's the ranching business. We had a ninety-seven-percent pregnancy rate in the cattle last year. That's a very good year. But I don't breed cats. She did that on her own. And I suspect Patch here found herself a boyfriend over at the James Hill."

"If she'd been neutered, then you wouldn't have this problem." She couldn't quite keep her tone light. She'd said the same thing after the cat. She'd thought the same thing about herself.

"I wouldn't say Patch having puppies is a problem. She's the fourth or fifth generation of River Mack cow dogs. She's got real good instincts, passed down through her line. People in these parts are glad to have one of her puppies. This will be her second litter, though, so we'll have her fixed. I don't want her to get worn out. I need her working the herd this fall."

"What happens this fall?"

He was silent for a long time. Then he walked up close to her and, as if she were some kind of precious treasure, held her head gently in his hands and rested his forehead on hers.

"The last time we were together before the wedding we talked just like this. You weren't sure if you'd still be on the ranch this week. You said you'd have a better idea of what the future holds when I came back. I'm back. Do you know? Are you going to be here this fall?"

It was hard, so hard, not to dive into the safety of his arms. He'd hold her close and she'd feel safe and everything would be all right.

Those days were over. Those days never should have been, so she stayed on her own two feet and answered him honestly. "Yes, I'll be here all the way until January."

As close as they were, she could feel the relief pass through his body, but she could see his frown of worry as well. She wasn't a good enough actor to fool him. He knew she was holding something back, but being Travis, he didn't push.

"Well, then," he said. "Would you like to see what the ranch looks like beyond the house and barn? It's a Sunday in July. There won't be a soul for miles around. I'll drive you around and tell you what you can expect from now until Christmas."

*And tonight, I'll tell you what to expect.*

But she was being offered a reprieve, a stay of execution, and she loved him too much to deny herself his company, just one more time.

# Chapter Eighteen

"I didn't realize there were so many flowers."

Sophia looked out the window of the white pickup truck. She was all buckled in, huddled by the door, and sad. The ranch had so much beauty, and she'd missed it all when she'd first arrived.

"What did you think it was if it wasn't flowers?"

"Brown. I just thought I was coming to live in exile on some ugly brown planet. But it's flowers. Yellow, purple and orange." She felt a little defensive. The old Sophia was just so pitiful. "You put those colors together, and you get brown."

"Until you take a closer look. Which you are."

She closed her eyes against his kindness. Of course she was in love with this man. How could she not be in love with this man? And he was going to hate her so very soon.

"Stop being so nice to me."

He drove in silence for another little while. "Why are you finding it so hard to be nice to yourself?"

She didn't answer him. Out the window, there were babies everywhere. Quite literally, every single cow had a calf suckling or sleeping underfoot. She could see the satisfaction and pride in Travis's expression—or she had seen it, before her misery had spilled into the pickup.

Travis slowed down the truck and squinted at a distant tree. "There she is. It's about time."

He parked the truck a little distance from the tree and got out. There was a cow under the tree, sleeping peacefully on her side. "You can come out if you want. Just be quiet about slamming the door."

Travis walked a little closer to the cow, not too close, and then crouched down. He checked his watch. And he waited.

And waited.

The minutes ticked by, until Sophia couldn't stand it anymore. She got out of the truck and practically tiptoed up to Travis before dropping down beside him.

"What's going on?"

"She's the last heifer of the season, and by season, I mean she's so far out of season, she's in a class by herself."

"I don't understand."

Travis checked his watch again as the cow huffed and made a halfhearted attempt to get up. The cow fell still again.

"We have our calving season in April and early May on the River Mack. That's when we want the herd giving birth."

"All at the same time?"

"More or less. You have to ride the herd several times a day, looking for new babies to doctor, making sure the mamas are on their feet and nursing, and sometimes—" he stood up with a sigh "—you have to pull a calf."

He walked back to the truck, dug around the back, and returned with some blue nylon straps and a pair of long, skinny plastic bags. "This little lady tricked us pretty well. We thought she was pregnant during breeding, but turns out she wasn't. Then a bull jumped a fence, and here she is, totally out of sync with the rest of the herd. Accidents happen, though."

The cow moaned again. Travis shook his head.

"What's wrong?" Sophia stayed crouched on the ground, her fingertips on the grass for balance.

"She's a first-time mother. She isn't doing too well. She must have been at this awhile. See how tired she is?"

And then Travis walked right up to the laboring cow. Sophia stood to see better. There were two front legs poking out of the mother's...body. Legs with hooves and everything. Sophia cringed.

The mother seemed to get agitated as Travis stood there, but then the hooves poked out a little farther and the nose of a cow came out, too. Travis came back and crouched beside Sophia.

Nothing else happened for an eternity. He checked his watch and picked up the blue straps again, but then the cow made a pitiful sound of pain and the whole head of a tiny cow came out with its front legs.

"There you go," Travis said under his breath.

Sophia sat on her butt. "I'm gonna be sick."

He turned his head to look at her. "You've never seen anything being born?"

"No." She couldn't look. "What are the blue straps for?"

He seemed amused, which, given that he was in full cowboy mode, meant one corner of his mouth lifted in barely-a-grin. "You can wrap 'em around the calf's legs and help the mama out. It's called pulling a calf."

"You're kidding me. This is what you do all day? I thought you rode around on a horse and shot rattlesnakes or something."

He turned back to the laboring cow. "I do that, too. These mamas go to a lot of trouble to have their babies. It's the least I can do to make sure the babies don't get bit by something poisonous."

*He would be the best father in the world.*

The thought hit her hard, followed equally hard by sorrow at the memory of Deezee. She'd been so unwise, so very unwise.

But then the cow moaned and the entire calf came out in a rush of blood and liquid. It just lay there, covered with gunk, and Sophia's heart started to pound. The world got a little tilted. She grabbed Travis's arm, digging her fingers into his muscle to keep herself vertical.

"Come on, Mama," he said quietly.

The mother wasn't moving. The baby wasn't moving.

Then Travis was moving, on his feet and heading toward them as he pulled the plastic bags over his hands and arms—they were gloves. He grabbed the baby's nose, its lifeless head bobbing as he jerked some kind of membrane from around it. Then he grabbed the hooves in his hands and simply dragged the calf out of the puddle of grossness and across the grass to plop it right in front of the mother's face.

This was birth. This horrible, frightening death and

membranes and pain—*oh, my God*. Sophia rolled to her hands and knees and tried desperately not to vomit.

What had she been thinking? That she'd do yoga and eat well and sport a small baby bump? Maybe toward the end, around Christmas, she'd be a little bit roly-poly for a few weeks, but then the baby would be born and go off to some wonderful adoptive family and everything would be clean and neat and tidy. She'd move on with her life.

That wasn't how it was. She had to give birth, she had to *labor*, there was just no way out of it. There would be gushing yuck and pain and exhaustion. And if, at the end of it all, the poor little baby didn't move...

What if the poor little baby didn't move?

She dug her fingers into the dirt and panted.

"Sophia."

She was dimly aware that Travis had come back. She heard him cursing, saw bloody plastic gloves being dumped on the grass. His clean arm was strong around her waist as he picked her up and set her on her feet, but he kept her back to his chest, which was smart because she was about to throw up.

"Baby, it's okay. Look, the mama's taking care of her calf now. She was just too tired to get up and go do it, so I helped her out. It's okay."

"No, it is *not*!" She wrenched free from him and ran a few steps toward the truck, but there was really nowhere to go. "I don't want to do it. I don't want to."

"Do what?"

"You're a man." Her words were getting high-pitched, rushing together. "Would you want to go through that? It's awful. She could've died. That baby could've died. I don't want to do it."

"It's okay. You don't have to do anything." He captured her in his arms again and tried to soothe her, making little shushing noises like she was the baby.

She started to cry. "Yes, I do. I'm the woman."

She could feel him behind her, shaking his head like he was dumbfounded, but how could he be? He was the one who'd just gotten out straps and gloves. "Okay, you're a woman, but you're just spooking yourself. You're not going to give birth anytime soon."

She was crying so hard now, she was doubled over at the waist. She would have fallen if Travis didn't have his arm around her. "Yes, I am. I have to. I'm pregnant."

Travis was an ass for the next seven weeks.

For the first few minutes, he'd held Sophia as she'd choked and cried, although it was frankly a toss-up which one of them was more staggered.

Pregnant. They'd been careful, except for that very first time. He'd only been inside her for a minute, and he hadn't climaxed—but it was possible. That could be all it took, as they'd been warned in sex ed pamphlets given to them a hundred years ago at school. He'd assumed he was the father.

It would be nice to be able to claim that he'd felt some noble calling or had a divine moment of parenthood fall upon his shoulders at the news that Sophia was pregnant, but in fact he'd been trying to hold a woman who was about to vomit, and he'd been doing math. June plus nine months.

"March?" That had been his first brilliant contribution to her distress.

"January," Sophia had gasped, and his world had gone to hell.

His horse tossed his head. Travis was holding onto the reins too tightly. Again. He tried to relax in the saddle, but it was damned hard when he was getting closer to the house. He hadn't caught a glimpse of Sophia in seven weeks, but that didn't stop him from looking.

The rest of July had been a haze of hurt feelings. One of the reasons she'd come to the ranch in the first place was to hide her pregnancy once she got bigger. *She should have told me. Her sister should have told me. Her brother-in-law should have told me.*

He hadn't questioned that assumption in July, but it was the first week of September now, and he did. Why should they have told him? He was a stranger to them. How did he think that first day should have gone? Grace and Alex, standing by their open car doors, should have said what, exactly? *Are you the foreman? This is our sister, Sophia. She's pregnant.*

August had been hot and slow on the ranch. Travis had only ridden half days as he watched the cow-calf pairs thrive on summer grass. The indignation had changed to something else. *If only she'd told me at the beginning. If only her sister had told me. If only I'd known...*

But it was September now, and he realized he'd never finished the thought.

If only she'd told him at the beginning, *then what?*

DJ Deezee Kalm would still be the father. The week of the wedding, Travis had verified Deezee's schedule to make sure he'd keep away from Sophia and her sister. *If only I'd known...*

He still would have kept Deezee away from Sophia. The man was still a jerk. He'd still made life hard for Sophia in more ways than leaving her pregnant and alone. He'd hurt her career, her income, her self-confidence.

Sophia was planning on giving the baby up for adoption. Travis had been incredulous when she'd told him so on that awful day. His whole life was spent watching mothers rear their young. He couldn't imagine Sophia not wanting to rear hers, but now he wondered what kind of influence Deezee might have been on that decision.

Travis had that impatient feeling again. He needed to lay eyes on Sophia. Seven weeks was far too long.

He let his horse walk faster. The house wasn't far away now. He knew the terrain like the back of his hand. Down this slope, up the next rise, and he'd see the white pillars.

The old lie came to him as easily as it had so many times before. If he could just check on Sophia, then he'd be able to put his mind at rest and move on.

A gunshot rang out.

In an instant, Travis's thoughts crystallized: the only thing in his world that mattered was Sophia.

She was in danger.

# Chapter Nineteen

"Damn, girl. You look like a pregnant cow."

Sophia didn't bother to answer Deezee. She was twenty-one weeks along, halfway through her pregnancy, so of course she had a baby bump. She still wasn't wearing maternity clothes. Her stretchy yoga top covered her fine. Obviously, Deezee had never seen a pregnant cow if he thought she resembled one.

Deezee shut the door to his car, a black luxury sedan. He wasn't driving it, though. That privilege belonged to one of his ever-present buddies. Sophia didn't recognize this particular buddy. The back doors opened and two more men came out.

*Afraid to be alone with your own thoughts, Deezee? Still?*

But she wouldn't say anything out loud. She'd been expecting her lawyer, the one who was supposed to arrive first with the adoption papers for Deezee to sign with her. She'd texted Clay that a black sedan would be coming onto the property today, so it had come through all three gates unchallenged, she was sure. She'd never expected Deezee to arrive in such a traditional car.

Her little burner phone could only text and call, but it couldn't do either of those things right now, because it was in the house, and she was on the patio. If she made a run for the door, she had no doubt someone from Deezee's crew would get there before she had the door closed and locked behind herself. She didn't want to be locked in the house with these guys.

None of Travis's men would be coming to check on her. And Travis himself? He wasn't speaking to her. She'd never seen a man as shocked as he'd been when she'd told him the baby wasn't his.

Clay was her only point of contact at the ranch now, and she'd told him she wanted the black sedan to come to the house. Round and round, back to the beginning: Sophia was stuck for the next ninety minutes with Deezee and his posse.

A little shiver of fear went down her back.

"You're early," she said, then immediately wished she hadn't. They were almost three hours early. The lawyer had arranged it so that he'd be here long before they were, and Deezee was never early to anything, until today.

"No prob, girl. Let's check out the new place. What do you have to drink?"

She was an actor. She needed to pull this role off. "I don't have anything you like. I'm pregnant, so…no alcohol." She held up her hands and shrugged. "I think if you go back to the main road and head west, the very next road takes you to a local bar. That might be fun.

The lawyer won't be here with the paperwork for another hour, anyway. Might as well go do some shots."

One of the backseat buddies liked the idea. *Please, please, please talk your gang into going.* Of course, the next road to the west didn't lead to a bar. It led to the Watersons' ranch, but Deezee would probably drive a good half mile in before he realized it. Maybe the Watersons would detain them.

Travis trusted the Watersons. They would've been part of her safety net, if she'd been smart enough to accept it. She hoped the Watersons would forgive her for sending Deezee onto their property, but if they were friends of Travis, it was her best bet for safety.

"Let's go," the backseat buddy said, enthusiastic to find the bar.

Hope swelled in Sophia's chest.

"Nah-nah-no-no-no." Deezee waved off his buddy with a shake of his blinged-out fingers.

Hope burst like a bubble.

"I gotta check this place out. We are in the *sticks*. Damn, girl, whatchu do out here all alone?"

*I cry.*

She smiled. "Well, like you said, you've now checked the place out. This is all there is." She snapped her fingers. "You know where there might be some beer? In the bunkhouse. Just go past this barn and follow that fence. You can't miss it."

She knew exactly how the hands who had the day off would react to these four storming into the bunkhouse. *Please, Deezee, go get some beer from the bunkhouse.*

"Why are you so anxious to get rid of me?"

Sophia had not done her best acting. She was nervous. She'd never felt so vulnerable, and Deezee could see it.

"Don't you want to party anymore?" he asked. "Oh, yeah. You got a bun in the oven." He turned to his friends. "How about that, boys? I'm not shooting blanks. Who knocked up Sophia Jackson? This guy."

The gunshot took her completely by surprise. She jumped a mile. Even Deezee dropped the f-bomb on his friend for the deafening sound.

The man had pulled out a handgun and was aiming it at the barn. "Just testing out the 'you can't hit the broad side of a barn' thing." He fired again. "My father used to say that. I hated my father."

"Stop!" Sophia ran from the patio toward him. "There are horses in there. Dogs. Cats. You'll hurt something."

She grabbed his arm, but he shook her off and fired again.

"Please," she begged. "It's a real barn. You'll kill something."

"Give me that." Deezee held out his hand for the gun. He took more careful aim than his friend. "Calling the shot. Eight ball in the corner pocket."

*"Stop!"* Sophia yelled, lunging for his arm before the sound of pounding horse's hooves could register in her head.

Travis was there, off his horse while it was still galloping. He shoved Deezee's arm down. The gun fired into the dirt, then he twisted it from Deezee's grip. Travis ejected the magazine, cleared the chambered round, and then threw the empty gun as far as an outfielder to first base.

"Sophia, get in the house."

Deezee adopted all the arrogant posture he was capable of, but he backed up a step. "Who do you think you are, ordering my wife around?" He turned to the driver. "Show him the marriage license."

Sophia blinked as Travis decked her alleged husband.

Deezee was out.

"What the eff, man?" the driver said to Travis. "You planning on taking on all three of us now?"

"Yes."

None of the three made a move against him.

"Sophia, get in the house." Travis repeated the order through gritted teeth.

She wanted to stay by Travis's side, but she felt the baby kick. This wasn't just about her safety, so she ran for the kitchen door as more men from the River Mack came thundering up the road.

"I want to go check on the puppies."

"Sophia, please, try to relax. Buck said the animals are all fine. Are you uncomfortable?"

She was lying on the couch with her upper body in Travis's lap and his arm supporting her neck and shoulders. His other hand hadn't stopped smoothing over her hair, her shoulder…her belly. She hadn't been this comfortable since the last time they'd made love.

"I'm fine. How are you? You're the one who had the fistfight."

"You're the one who's pregnant. My God, Sophia…" He cradled her closer for a moment, then put his head back and sighed.

"I'm okay, really." Her heart felt more and more okay each time he did that. "I never threw a punch."

"You didn't have to throw a punch to have all your muscles pumped full of adrenaline. I can feel that my muscles are worn-out from the tension, and yours are way more important than mine right now." His hand smoothed its way over her belly again.

"Thank you."

He was silent.

"Thank you for treating me right, and for coming to my rescue, and for being an all-around decent man."

"I've been an ass. You should be kicking mine instead of apologizing to me. I love you, Sophia. I have from the very first, and I could kick myself for wasting the entire month of August feeling sorry for myself."

"Well, it's kind of a big deal to find out your lover is carrying another man's child. Don't say it isn't."

His hand drifted over her hair again, petting her, soothing her. Loving her. "Okay, let's get this settled. It's a big deal, I agree. But I could have talked to you about it. I could have asked you my questions, instead of asking myself questions over and over that I couldn't possibly know the answer to."

"I know I should—"

"There's more."

He looked so fierce, Sophia's heart tripped a little.

"I apologize for taking so long to realize the obvious. I kept saying to myself, 'if only I'd known,' until I finally realized it wouldn't have mattered. What if I'd known you were pregnant when you first arrived here? I would have found you fascinating, anyway. What if you'd had this cute baby bump when you were throwing those tomatoes? We still would've ripped off our clothes in the living room."

"Travis—"

"What if you'd arrived here with a newborn baby? I still would have fallen in love with you. The key is you, Sophia. I will always love you."

"I'm—I'm—" She gave up and snuggled into his chest, because he was big and strong and she could. "I'm going to live on that forever. That fills my heart up."

He kissed her, which was exactly what she wanted.

"Aren't you angry with me at all?" he whispered over her lips.

"No. I watch you through the window every day. You've looked so grim, and I've known it was because of me. I'm so sorry."

She didn't want him to think the worst of her. "I know this sounds hard to believe, but I really was in denial. I read that the pregnancy test could be false positive, and my brain just seized on that as the right explanation, because it was the only explanation I could handle. My career wouldn't be impacted. I wouldn't be tied to Deezee in any way. You came later, but once I met you, that was all the more reason to just ignore the possibility. I sound like an idiot, don't I?"

"There's nothing about you that sounds like an idiot." He kissed her sweetly, casually, like he had hours to kiss her whenever he pleased. "I'm sleeping here tonight. It's going to be a while before I can let you out of my sight. That's not too rational, either."

"I like that, though. You know you won't be sleeping with a married woman, right? I really want you to know I'm not in denial about that. Deezee is just trying to stir up gossip with that paperwork."

"I know. I'm glad the lawyer is releasing a statement for you."

The lawyer had shown up punctually, only to find himself being asked to clarify all kinds of points of law beyond adoption. A quick internet search had cleared up the alleged St. Barth's marriage certificate. Thirty days' notice was a minimum requirement to marry on that island, and they'd only flown in for the weekend.

More importantly in Sophia's mind, she'd never said *I do*. Deezee's antics at the altar had been her last straw. She'd thrown her bouquet at him when she was only half-way down the aisle, something that had made her look terrible in photos, but it had been her one justifiable tantrum.

She pulled far enough away from Travis to look at him directly. "I'm not married, and I've never been married."

He studied her for a moment. "Are you thinking of my dad?"

"Maybe. Yes. I know you don't admire what he did. I think you would never sleep with a married woman."

He brushed her hair back from her eyes. "If I had to wait for your divorce to be final, I would. After meeting Deezee, there's no way I would want you to stay married to him. Am I grateful that we don't need to wait for a divorce?" He laughed to lighten the moment. "That's like asking me if the sky's blue."

Sophia wished she could smile back. "You must question my judgment for even thinking about marrying him. I do. Grace hated him from the first, but he wasn't always quite so bad. He started using the drugs they sold at his raves. Then he started using even when there wasn't a party on. It got pretty out of control before I left him. It's magnified every flaw a hundred times."

"Sophia?"

"Yes?"

"I don't care about Deezee. You are an amazing woman no matter who you used to date."

Sophia placed her hand on her belly.

She cared. And she was scared.

# Chapter Twenty

"I've got an early Christmas gift for you."

"Seriously?" Sophia asked. Travis thought she sounded equal parts excited and skeptical as she dumped the last scoop of oats into the trough in the mare's stall. "Wasn't a house enough?"

She'd fallen in love with the century-old foreman's house. She loved that it had a little parlor and a library and a dining room instead of one expansive space—so Travis had bought it for her. The MacDowells sold it to him along with a dozen acres or so, just enough land to make a nice little residential property along the edge of the River Mack. The renovations, including the baby's room, would be finished by the end of January, when Sophia's lease was up.

Until then, he would continue to live with her in the main house. Never again would he go seven weeks without seeing her. Sophia's next movie would begin shooting in July, and her new manager had added contract riders to keep the future Chalmers family together. Sophia's housing on location would accommodate the baby and a nanny, and Travis would arrive via the studio's private jet midway through the shooting schedule. Private jets and cowboys might seem an odd combination, but Travis figured he could handle the luxury. He'd go through hell to be with Sophia. If he had to adapt to luxury instead, well, there was no law that said life always had to be hard.

He walked up behind Sophia and slipped his arms around her, above her round belly, below her breasts, which had become even more lovely with her pregnancy. "I had a different kind of gift in mind."

"Here in the barn?" she asked, sounding like a sex goddess.

"Like that would be the first time."

Sophia pretended to droop her shoulders in disappointment. "I'm going to have to take a raincheck on that gift. I feel as big as a house this morning."

It was cool in the barn in December, so she wore a fluffy green sweater. Travis noticed that she rubbed her last-trimester belly in a different way today than usual, although the baby wasn't due for three weeks. Maybe the sweater was just extra soft and touchable to her.

Maybe not.

Sophia was adamant that a home birth was the only way to keep her birthing experience private. Her midwife could reach the ranch in a little less than an hour, but Travis didn't find that as comforting as Sophia did. He'd witnessed hundreds of animal births in his life, but Sophia was no animal, and he hoped when the contractions began, she'd change her mind and let him drive her to the hospital. She was no longer placing the baby up for adoption, so secrecy was no longer paramount. Her well-being was.

That was a discussion for next week's appointment with the midwife. Today was Christmas Eve, and he wanted to put a smile on Sophia's beautiful face.

"Close your eyes," he murmured. "Don't move."

He went into Samson's stall and scooped up the black-and-gray puppy he'd hidden there. The pup was four months old and probably fifteen pounds, but it was still a puppy with oversized paws and soft fur.

He placed the soft fur against Sophia's soft sweater. "Happy Christmas Eve."

"Oh! A puppy." Her smile was exactly what he'd hoped for.

For about five seconds.

Then it faded in confusion. "Wait. Is this one of Patch's puppies?"

"Yes. She was returned. I thought you might want to keep her."

"The poor thing. Poor, poor puppy." She buried her face in its fur and burst into tears.

Travis scratched the dog behind the ears. "Baby, the dog is happy. Why aren't you?"

"She was returned because she wasn't good enough, was she?"

"No, Roger just got a job offer in another state, and since he'd only had the pup for a few—"

"You don't have to keep pretending for me." Her tears fell as she kissed the puppy.

Having a fiancée in her final trimester had taught Travis that tears were possible over just about any topic.

He wouldn't dismiss every tear as hormones, however, not when he knew the unique challenges Sophia faced.

"Come into the office and sit. You and the puppy." He held the desk chair for Sophia, gave her a tissue from the box he'd learned to keep on his desk now that it wasn't just him in the barn, and then he waited to see if she would tell him what was really bothering her.

She did. "You said that everyone wanted Patch's puppies because she's a great cow dog, but for this litter, the father was a mystery. Now the dogs are being returned. It's the father, isn't it? Even with a great mother like Patch, people assume the puppies just aren't good enough. It's so unfair. The puppies didn't do anything wrong."

He crouched down in front of her. "This is the only puppy that's come back to the ranch, and it's because Roger got a job offer in another state. He'll be in an office building all day. That's it. I wouldn't lie to you, Sophia. That puppy is desirable, I guarantee it, whether we know who the father is or not."

"Maybe I should've stuck with my plan to place the baby up for adoption. No one would have known who the biological parents were. The baby would have started life with a clean slate."

That wasn't coming from as far out of left field as it seemed. "You saw the news today that Deezee was convicted of drug trafficking."

She placed one hand on her belly. "That's this poor baby's father. Everyone knows it. Deezee made sure of that, and now he's a felon. How can I make up for that? I'm not that great when it comes to motherhood material. Here's Patch, this legendary cow dog, and even she can't make up for the father. People think her sweet puppies aren't good enough because the f-father—"

"Sophia, listen to me."

Travis hated the son of a bitch who had just been convicted. He wasn't just a drug dealer who'd come to this ranch waving around a gun that could have injured Sophia, but he was the man who'd messed with Sophia's head, too. The fact that she'd once considered herself in love with Deezee still undermined her confidence in herself.

"You are going to be a great mother. I know this from the bottom of my soul. The fact that you are worried whether or not you'll be good enough for this baby proves that the baby is getting a mom who cares."

He'd tell her that as many times as it took. Deezee had told her crap for five months. Travis was going to tell her truths for the rest of her life. Travis was going to win.

She let go of the puppy with one hand and placed her palm on her belly in that same low place.

Travis covered her hand with his. "No one is ever going to look at this child and think he or she isn't good enough. Deezee chose to sell drugs for money. That's not DNA. That was a choice. Anyone from any parent could make the same choice, or not. Deezee's not going to be around to teach this baby about bad choices. I'm going to be."

He had to stop and clear his throat. Then he thought better of it. Let Sophia see how much he cared.

He looked up at her, and he knew she saw the unshed tears, because she looked a little bit blurry. "I cannot wait to hold this baby. This is the most exciting thing in my world. I may not have contributed any DNA, but I'm going to be part of this child, too. I'm going to teach 'em when to say 'gid-yap' and 'whoa' and not to let their horse step on their reins and to eat their zucchini and to love their mama. That's you."

Sophia's tears subsided. Her breathing was steady and the puppy in her arm was calm. Travis knew their future was bright. Just when Travis had relaxed, Sophia slayed him. "There are a million reasons I'm going to love this baby, Travis, but here's one of the biggest. If it hadn't been for this baby, I would never have come to your ranch. I would never have met you. For that, I will always owe the baby one."

Travis had to bow his head and clear his throat.

"Me, too, Sophia. Me, too."

Under their hands, he felt her stomach draw tight. She wasn't livestock, not at all, but Travis had felt that same kind of contraction in horses and cows. It could pass and not start again for another three weeks. It could be nothing.

"I don't like the look of the weather out there," he said. "Let's put this puppy back in her hay and head back to the house."

Sophia was suddenly keenly interested in rearranging all the ornaments on the Christmas tree.

Travis ran a ranch. He was a big believer that Mother Nature knew what she was doing, but as far as nesting instincts went, this one wasn't particularly useful.

"I'm gonna call the midwife," he said.

Sophia stopped in the middle of switching the locations of a sequined ball and a glass ball. "Why? I feel fine."

Travis nodded. "That's good, baby. Glad to hear it." He dialed the phone.

Outside, the rain turned to sleet.

The radio announced the highways were closed. Travis imagined that children all around Austin were afraid that Santa wasn't going to be able to get his sled through the bad weather tonight. He was afraid the midwife wouldn't.

He was right, damn it all to hell.

In the end, for all the times he'd insisted to Sophia that she wasn't a beast, he was grateful that there were similarities. It made the whole process a little less bewildering. They'd decided ahead of time which bed to use and had plastic coverings and extra sheets prepared. But as Sophia walked around the house rearranging Christmas decorations, he noticed she kept going into the master bathroom, a room he hadn't seen her use once in the four months since he'd begun living with her. It reminded him of a cow who'd kept returning to stand under a particular tree, or a mother cat who'd decided to leave her nice box for a treacherous rafter at the last minute.

He picked up the supplies the midwife had left last week and carried them into the master bathroom.

"I think I'll take a bath," Sophia said. "Then maybe we can watch a Christmas movie on TV."

She got undressed and sat in the tub, but she never turned the water on. She wasn't having any painful contractions for him to time, and the midwife kept telling him on the phone that a first labor could take twelve hours, easily, if Sophia really was in labor. By then, the roads would surely be open.

So Sophia sat in the dry bathtub and Travis pretended that was normal. Then the first painful contraction hit, and poor Sophia went from nothing to full-out labor in no time.

"I don't think this is right," she said, panting to catch her breath.

"Everything is working just like it should."

The pain was scaring her. "But it doesn't always work out. You lose calves every year. We almost lost that kitten—"

But another contraction hit her before the last one ended, and she started trying to do her *hee hee hee* breaths like the online course had taught them.

Another contraction. God, they were coming hard. Fast. His poor Sophia.

Travis kissed her temple, wet as it was from pain and the effort to handle the pain. He knelt next to the tub and kept his arm around her shoulders. He felt so utterly useless.

The contractions left her limp. He could only support her with his arm.

"That calf," she panted. "Mother Nature would have taken that calf and the mother with it if you hadn't been there to help."

"No, baby. You're remembering that wrong."

"You had those straps."

"I didn't have to use them, remember? I just watched and waited, and that baby was born just fine. Your baby is going to be born just fine. It hurts like hell—" and God, he wished he could do something about that "—but it's going just fine."

The contraction started building again, the pain rolling over her as she gripped his hand and tried to breathe.

"That heifer almost died. She couldn't move. She was so tired." Panic was in her voice. She was losing it, the pain was winning, and Travis thought his own heart was going to break a rib, it was beating so hard.

She looked too much like her pioneer movie character, the one that had died onscreen.

Help wasn't coming, not until the sleet stopped. Travis couldn't control the weather. He couldn't control Sophia's labor. This was the most important event of his life, the one thing in his life he absolutely had to get right, and he was powerless.

Sophia lifted her head and started panting. *Hee hee hee.*

God bless her. She was still at it. She didn't have a choice. She couldn't quit.

He couldn't, either.

He shoved the fear and the images from that damned movie out of his head as he shifted his position a bit, leaning over the edge of the tub and adjusting his arm to hold Sophia even closer. Her fingers loosened on his as the wave receded.

She plopped her head back onto his arm. "I can't do it. This can't be Mother Nature."

"Listen to me. You are doing everything right."

But she wasted her precious energy to roll her head on his arm, *no, no, no.* "That calf would have died. You had to drag her over to that heifer."

Travis hadn't realized how heavily that still weighed on Sophia. They'd never talked about it before now. This was a heck of a time to talk about anything, but he didn't want her worrying about what could go wrong.

He kissed her temple again. "Everything is going to be okay. When you saw me drag that newborn calf over to the mama, I was just being helpful. She was tired, so I just brought that baby up close to her so she could take care of it. And you know what? When your little baby is born, if you're too tired to move, that'll be okay, too. I'm gonna scoop up that little baby and hold her right here for you." He brought his other arm across her breasts and completed a circle around her, keeping the woman he loved in his arms. "And it's gonna be you and me and that brand new baby, and the three of us are gonna be just fine."

"I'm sorry. This is…just…" She still looked a little unfocused, but not so panicky.

He could feel her body going under the contraction. "You're doing great."

"…just not how we planned it."

"I wouldn't miss this for the world."

"I love you."

He thought he'd never heard the words uttered in a better way. They pierced his soul. "I love you, too."

She let go of his hand and gripped the edge of the tub. The last of that dazed and confused expression lifted as she frowned fiercely. "I think—I feel like I should push. It hasn't been long enough, has it? What time is it? Ohmigod, I'm not kidding. I need to push. Am I supposed to push?"

Travis nodded. "If you think it's time to push, then you should push. I know you're right."

"Okay. Then I'm going to have a baby now."

He dropped one more kiss on her head. "You do that, Sophia. You do that."

And she did.

In record time, in a bathtub on the River Mack ranch on Christmas Eve, Noelle Jackson Chalmers was born, healthy and loved.

Travis wept. No one had ever been given a better Christmas gift.

\* \* \* \* \*

We hope you enjoyed reading

## *A Stone Creek Christmas*

by *New York Times* bestselling author

# LINDA LAEL MILLER

and

## *A Cowboy's Wish Upon a Star*

by *USA TODAY* bestselling author

# CARO CARSON

Originally HQN Books and
Harlequin® Special Edition stories!

From passionate, suspenseful and dramatic
love stories to inspirational or historical,
Harlequin offers different lines to
satisfy every romance reader.

New books in each line
are available every month.

www.Harlequin.com

BACHALO1118

SPECIAL EXCERPT FROM

**H** HARLEQUIN®

™

# SPECIAL EDITION

*Major India Woods thought house-sitting in Texas
would be just another globe-trotting adventure—until
her friend's neighbor, Major Aidan Nord, shows up. But
their hot holiday fling is interrupted by his two little
girls, and India thinks she might have just found her
most exciting adventure yet!*

*Read on for a sneak preview of the next
American Heroes book,*
The Majors' Holiday Hideaway,
*by USA TODAY bestselling author Caro Carson.*

The dog bounded between them, back and forth, until the
man stopped just an arm's distance from her, leaving the
dog turning in the tightest of circles.

"Good morning." He nudged the dog out of the way
with a gentle knee.

"Yes. You must be the neighbor." Her thoughts were
making her blush, but her cheeks were probably red from
the chilly air anyway, and the red coat was probably
bringing out the color, too, so she hoped she looked
more bold than bashful. "I thought you were the general
contractor."

"No, I'm not."

"No. The real contractor showed up this morning and
he definitely wasn't…" She let her eyes take a quick
dive down the placket of his button-down shirt to the
lean waist revealed by the opened bomber jacket. More

slowly, she lifted her gaze back up to his tanned throat, his face. "He wasn't you."

He hesitated at that, then tilted his head a bit as he studied her, his eyebrows lifted a little in surprise, his mouth suppressing a smile. "And you were disappointed?"

"Maybe a little." She stuffed her hands into the coat's pockets, feeling the heat in her cheeks, but he wasn't mocking her. There was nothing about him that was arrogant. Confident, comfortable—but not arrogant. Unlike her, he wasn't flustered in the least.

India pictured Helen's note in her mind, with its hastily scribbled addendum at the bottom: "Fabio at Nords' first night." That sounded like there were multiple Nords. Had Helen meant to write *Nords'* or *Nord's*? Was there a wife?

*Oh, what the heck. You only have a week. Just ask.*

"So…" She nodded in the general direction of the golden-bricked house. "Is there anyone else at your house? Maybe a wife?"

His reaction was a little surprise again, a negative shake of his head with a bit of a smile, but his eyes were watching her with an expression that was a little…sad?

"No," he said. "Just me."

*Don't miss*
The Majors' Holiday Hideaway by Caro Carson,
*available November 2018 wherever*
Harlequin® Special Edition books and ebooks are sold.

www.Harlequin.com

Copyright © 2018 by Caroline Phipps

HSEEXP15072

# HARLEQUIN®

# SPECIAL EDITION

**Life, Love and Family**

Save **$1.00**

on the purchase of ANY

Harlequin® Special Edition book.

Available whever books are sold,
including most bookstores, supermarkets,
drugstores and discount stores.

---

# Save $1.00

## on the purchase of any Harlequin Special Edition book.

Coupon valid until December 31, 2018.
Redeemable at participating outlets in the U.S. and Canada only.
Not redeemable at Barnes & Noble stores. Limit one coupon per customer.

**52616134**

**Canadian Retailers:** Harlequin Enterprises Limited will pay the face value of this coupon plus 10.25¢ if submitted by customer for this product only. Any other use constitutes fraud. Coupon is nonassignable. Void if taxed, prohibited or restricted by law. Consumer must pay any government taxes. Void if copied. Inmar Promotional Services ("IPS") customers submit coupons and proof of sales to Harlequin Enterprises Limited, P.O. Box 31000, Scarborough, ON M1R 0E7, Canada. Non-IPS retailer—for reimbursement submit coupons and proof of sales directly to Harlequin Enterprises Limited, Retail Marketing Department, Bay Adelaide Centre, East Tower, 22 Adelaide Street West, 40th Floor, Toronto, Ontario M5H 4E3, Canada.

**U.S. Retailers:** Harlequin Enterprises Limited will pay the face value of this coupon plus 8¢ if submitted by customer for this product only. Any other use constitutes fraud. Coupon is nonassignable. Void if taxed, prohibited or restricted by law. Consumer must pay any government taxes. Void if copied. For reimbursement submit coupons and proof of sales directly to Harlequin Enterprises, Ltd 482, NCH Marketing Services, P.O. Box 880001, El Paso, TX 88588-0001, U.S.A. Cash value 1/100 cents.

5  65373 00076  2  (8100)0  12400

® and ™ are trademarks owned and used by the trademark owner and/or its licensee.

© 2018 Harlequin Enterprises Limited

BACCOUP15072

#1 *New York Times* bestselling author

# LINDA LAEL MILLER

## presents:

The next great holiday read from
Harlequin Special Edition author Stella Bagwell!
A touching story about finding love, family and a
happily-ever-after in the most unexpected place.

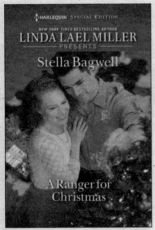

*No romance on the job—*

Until she meets her new
partner!

Arizona park ranger
Vivian Hollister is not
having a holiday fling with
Sawyer Whitehorse—no
matter how attracted she
is to her irresistible new
partner. Not only is a
workplace romance taboo,
but she has a daughter to
raise. So why is she starting
to feel that the Apache ranger is the one to help carry on
her family legacy? A man to have and to hold forever…

### Available November 20,
### wherever books are sold.

www.Harlequin.com

HSE46613

# Get 4 FREE REWARDS!

## We'll send you 2 FREE Books plus 2 FREE Mystery Gifts.

FREE
Value Over
$20

Both the **Romance** and **Suspense** collections feature compelling novels written by many of today's best-selling authors.

---

**YES!** Please send me 2 FREE novels from the Essential Romance or Essential Suspense Collection and my 2 FREE gifts (gifts are worth about $10 retail). After receiving them, if I don't wish to receive any more books, I can return the shipping statement marked "cancel." If I don't cancel, I will receive 4 brand-new novels every month and be billed just $6.74 each in the U.S. or $7.24 each in Canada. That's a savings of at least 16% off the cover price. It's quite a bargain! Shipping and handling is just 50¢ per book in the U.S. and 75¢ per book in Canada*. I understand that accepting the 2 free books and gifts places me under no obligation to buy anything. I can always return a shipment and cancel at any time. The free books and gifts are mine to keep no matter what I decide.

Choose one: ☐ **Essential Romance**
(194/394 MDN GMY7)

☐ **Essential Suspense**
(191/391 MDN GMY7)

Name (please print)

Address                                                                 Apt. #

City                               State/Province                    Zip/Postal Code

Mail to the **Reader Service:**
**IN U.S.A.:** P.O. Box 1341, Buffalo, NY 14240-8531
**IN CANADA:** P.O. Box 603, Fort Erie, Ontario L2A 5X3

Want to try two free books from another series? Call 1-800-873-8635 or visit www.ReaderService.com.

---

*Terms and prices subject to change without notice. Prices do not include applicable taxes. Sales tax applicable in NY. Canadian residents will be charged applicable taxes. Offer not valid in Quebec. This offer is limited to one order per household. Books received may not be as shown. Not valid for current subscribers to the Essential Romance or Essential Suspense Collection. All orders subject to approval. Credit or debit balances in a customer's account(s) may be offset by any other outstanding balance owed by or to the customer. Please allow 4 to 6 weeks for delivery. Offer available while quantities last.

**Your Privacy**—The Reader Service is committed to protecting your privacy. Our Privacy Policy is available online at www.ReaderService.com or upon request from the Reader Service. We make a portion of our mailing list available to reputable third parties that offer products we believe may interest you. If you prefer that we not exchange your name with third parties, or if you wish to clarify or modify your communication preferences, please visit us at www.ReaderService.com/consumerschoice or write to us at Reader Service Preference Service, P.O. Box 9062, Buffalo, NY 14240-9062. Include your complete name and address.

STRS18

Looking for more satisfying love stories
with community and family at their core?

Check out **Harlequin® Special Edition**
and **Love Inspired®** books!

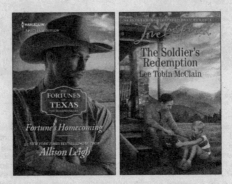

**New books available every month!**

---

**CONNECT WITH US AT:**

Facebook.com/groups/HarlequinConnection

 Facebook.com/HarlequinBooks

Twitter.com/HarlequinBooks

 Instagram.com/HarlequinBooks

Pinterest.com/HarlequinBooks

ReaderService.com

 **HARLEQUIN®**

**ROMANCE WHEN
YOU NEED IT**